MATTHEW P. GILBERT

SINS OF THE FATHERS BOOK 2

ALSO IN THE SERIES

You've already read: Dead God's Due

You're reading: Mad God's Muse

Up next: War God's Will

ACKNOWLEDGMENTS

Many helped along the way. As before, some I have forgotten, and for that I apologize. Some have forgotten me, and for most of those, I make no apology.

- My wife, Jessica, for listening, suggesting, correcting, musing, and sharing the dream with me.
- Everyone who helped go over this until their eyes bled, or listened to me talk way too much about how cool it was and chose to continue our relationship despite knowing the risks.
- Paul Hetzer, whose timely encouragement made all the difference.

Ilaweh teaches patience through frustration.

PROLOGUE
ONE MILLENNIUM PAST

AM *I a god?* It was a strange question to ask oneself, and yet it was not the first time Alexander had done so. Each time he took the Eye in hand and crossed from the mundane world to the green, ethereal realm within, the questions came. *Is this the true world? Have I lived my life in some sort of shadow up to now?*

That was one way to see it. The same people inhabited both realms. The terrain was unchanged. It was so very like his own world in shape and composition, and yet as different as a living, breathing man was from a skeleton. The world inside the Eye held so much *more*.

Or perhaps it is simply me that is different. I can see *so much more.* That felt closer to the truth. To take up the Eye, to walk through the green, swirling mists, was to slip into the mind of an immense being, one completely unbound by earthly chains of gravity or the frailty of flesh. Gone were the limitations of space and time. He could go anywhere, even into the heads of others, with a simple thought. He could see everyone in the world, hear them speak, even speak back to them. Like his vision, his mind expanded as well. It was nothing to converse with hundreds as if each were his sole focus.

I have put on a god's cloak, and now I have his vision and his burdens.

For the moment, he had chosen a position miles above the ground, overlooking the many battles being fought at his direction. There had been no travel time, no journey. He had simply willed it, and arrived. Where his own eyes would have failed him at such distance, the Eye's vision was flawless: the simple desire to focus on a location showed him the most minute of details, even things he could only guess at as a mortal man.

He could see *intent,* both in men and beasts, colored auras he had come to understand as a code: red was an enemy, green an ally, pink announced wounded, and black was for the dead. There were so many more, some colors Alexander could not even perceive with his own eyes, and each had its subtle meaning, but his goal was simple: everything should be green. *That is my imperative.*

Satisfied with his understanding of the war, he began to issue orders, calling out through the ether to the hundreds receiving his instructions. *Supplies will be needed here. Reinforcements are required on these fronts. Wounded need evacuation.* Men everywhere needed to hear his voice to shore up their resolve. He could not lie to them, nor they him when he spoke through the Eye.

And now I live as they do. I share their pain. It is the least I can do.

He flitted from body to body, seeing the battle from each pair of eyes in turn. When his men triumphed, he felt their joy. When they fell, he lived their pain. How many blades had ripped through his guts this day? How many of his bones had shattered? How many cries of agony and fear had coursed through his mind?

How many times have I died?

It was becoming more and more difficult to know where he

himself ended, and his men began. Within the embrace of the Eye, it felt more as if he, his soldiers, even his enemies were no more distinct than drops of water in the sea. *We all spring from the same well. Our individuality is illusion, just like the distance between us.*

Still, each had different tasks. Some missions were more important than others. Alexander strained to isolate the one voice. *There.*

"Forgive me, Alexander!" cried the soldier. *"I have failed you."*

Alexander was with him in an instant, blood jetting from their neck in a crimson stream from a vicious javelin wound. *"Take heart. We are not finished yet."* Pink, fading to black. He fell, and that part of his vision went dark.

"Who will stand for him?" Alexander cried out through the twisting nether. *"Our need is great! He* must *not fall!"*

More voices called back, *"I will."*

Alexander felt the sickness in his gut as strongly as he had just felt the weapon in his throat. *Choose one to die.* Such decisions were for gods, not men. *I have my duty, too. I will not shirk it.*

One pair of eyes closed. Another reopened. Alexander hauled the javelin from his neck, then withdrew. This one would complete his task on his own.

From the dim, tiny perspective of his own eyes, he saw his Imperator, Xanthius, enter the command tent, crested helmet tucked under his arm. The old soldier's gray eyebrows arched downward toward his square, chiseled jaw in disapproval. *He does not understand.*

Xanthius looked on his Emperor with a despair he tried desperately not to show, but it was a pointless endeavor. Alexander knew everything. That was the horror of it all.

Half boy, half man, Alexander sat atop a cot, haggard and slumped against the tent's central pole, his face lit by an eerie, green glow Xanthius knew all too well. Alexander's long, brown hair hung partly over his face, unkempt and lifeless. His skin was pale and sickly, though at least it bore no sores. *Yet. They will come, though, if he continues to neglect proper hygiene.*

Alexander stirred slightly. His gaze shifted slowly toward Xanthius, unfocused and distant, as if he were drugged and unaware, though Xanthius understood enough now to know that was illusion. The boy clutched at the Eye of the Lion with skeletal hands, the skin covering them thin as parchment. The bright metal of the small lion's head glowed a soft green, reflecting the light from its normally amber eyes. Alexander gazed into the distance, his own eyes glowing the same soft green as the accursed thing he held.

Can you not see it is killing you, child?

Xanthius had watched this slow death, this degeneration of Alexander's body and soul for months. When they had begun this venture, the Emperor had been healthy and whole, trained well by Ilawehan fighting men. His goal had been noble: avenge his father, retake the crown, and drive the Meite rebels and their wretched 'free men' from the halls of power.

Freedom. A mad illusion. I have my master, as do all men. Even Alexander, it is plain to see.

Alexander turned toward Xanthius, and the glow faded both from his eyes and the lion's, but dark clouds hung behind his vision, still. "We are at war. Sacrifices must be made." He offered a thin smile. "You, too, looked better when we set out."

Xanthius felt the sudden urge to abandon a lifetime of duty, to simply leap forward and seize the poisonous thing from Alexander's hands. The boy was far too weak to resist.

"Would you take it for yourself?" Alexander mused.

"Damn you! Can I have no thought to myself these days?"

Alexander shook his head, his face drawn and weary. "Nor can I. I am not thin because of any poison. I feel their hunger. Our men, their men. If I am sick, it is at the thought of eating when they cannot. I take only what I must, what I need to continue our mission."

He's deflecting me. If he knows my thoughts, he's chosen not to answer the most important question. Xanthius set his jaw and stood erect, hands clasped behind his back. "Since you speak of it, Emperor, what *is* that mission? What *are* our victory parameters?"

If Alexander noted the use of his title over his own name, he gave no sign. He took up the Eye again and turned away. "I see further, now," he sighed.

Decorum be damned. I can endure no more of this. "What will satisfy you, Alexander?" Xanthius shouted. "Must every man in the *world* bend a knee or die?"

Alexander was silent, gazing into the distance for so long that Xanthius turned to leave. "*That will not be enough,*" Alexander called in a voice not his own, but that of an unearthly choir, beautiful and chilling like an approaching blizzard.

Xanthius spun in surprise to see that Alexander had risen and stood facing him, arms raised high and wide as if to encircle the world, the Eye dangling from a chain gripped in his frail hand. The Lion seemed to wink and leer at Xanthius in the eldritch glow.

Alexander's eyes blazed with green fire, and his face shone with a powerful emotion Xanthius could not quite recognize.

The choir spoke again, setting Xanthius's teeth on edge.

"*They must join us.*"

We were conquerors here.

Tasinal knew he should be more focused on the conversation between Amrath and Noril. A strategic discussion ought to have the nominal leader of the Meite order actually participating, but in truth he understood little about complex details of large scale battle. Personal combat he knew well enough, but that was not the topic at hand. Besides, it wasn't as if he would actually make the decisions on the matter. Amrath would do that, as he had always done. *I am a figurehead, a face to present to the public, nothing more. I'll fight when he tells me to. If that call ever comes.*

Which was, of course, the central problem: Amrath, as yet, had not chosen to fight at all since the initial uprising, preferring to leave the actual war to the newly liberated masses. It was not a popular decision, neither with the weaker folk who resented the lack of sorcerous aid, nor with the Meites themselves, who, now that they had had a taste of blood, found they liked it well enough.

Ah, that first taste had been sweet, indeed.

Tasinal sneered at the offensively opulent structure that housed them, the Great Hall of Aristodemos and his pack of jackals, lawyers, and whores. *But I repeat myself.* It was a mighty edifice, certainly, brick and stone and marble; high, strong walls to hide behind and count the treasure extracted from the people and not have to hear them wail under the burden. It had done just fine against the oppressed and the weak.

The Council of Twelve had walked through those walls as if they were paper, and left a trail of blood and retribution the likes of which Laurea had never seen. *Sic semper tyrannis.*

Few had escaped their wrath, and that went for the furniture and building as well. Talus, the artist of the Twelve, had demanded they leave the scene as it was, declaring that the destruction itself was a monument to what had occurred here. "Let it serve as a reminder to the next would-be tyrant." He had wanted them to leave the corpses as well, but Amrath had drawn the line at that, Mei be thanked. The reek it would have sent up in high summer would have been enough to test the will even of Meites.

With a shudder at the thought, Tasinal returned to the present. Amrath, weary and haggard, sat in the ruins of Aristodemos's throne, his normally animated face creased with worry, his green eyes dull and lifeless as Noril, standing at a table before the throne, continued his stoic report of their growing losses. Amrath's blonde hair hung partially over his eyes, unkempt and listless like its owner. Tasinal struggled not to turn his eyes to the stained and cracked marble floor. *It is too painful a sight, to see him defeated like this.*

Defeated he was, though, and Noril was flagging as well. Noril's clean-shaven jaw bulged, and his short-cropped, graying hair bristled. *He looks quite like Xanthius. I wonder if they are related somewhere along the lines?* "How many more lives will we sacrifice in a lost cause?" Noril demanded. "It is time for us to take to the field ourselves."

Amrath heaved a deep sigh, part frustration, part despair. "If the people do not win their own victory, what have we bought them?" He swept a hand about him indicating the ruined halls of power they had made their headquarters. "Did we begin this rebellion to be their masters, or to help them throw the yoke from their own shoulders?"

"We did not plan to contend with gods, Amrath!"

"No," Amrath said, casting Tasinal a pointed look. "We did not."

Tasinal could feel his cheeks burning, but said nothing. *I think I'll just shut up and let them do this. No need to make a target of myself, after all.*

Noril offered him a wry smile. "I would have kept the weapon, too, Tasinal."

Amrath shrugged, as if words were not needed, then seemed

to decide otherwise. "We all would have. But he made the decision, so he feels the pain. It's a burden of leadership."

I said I was going to shut up, but apparently that will not be possible at this time. "*You* argued to go to Torium! And *you* named me leader. No one is confused about who really runs things!"

Amrath raised an eyebrow in appreciation of such insolence. His face brightened a shade. "Are you my puppet?"

Bastard! But it was a fair point. "Nay. You speak truth. The decision was mine."

"Then own it."

"I *do* own it! How was I to know he would give it to our enemies if we chose not to let him take it away? I may have to accept the consequences, but I'll accept no blame from anyone for it, not even you!"

"Well said," Amrath replied. "It's as I told you, you've made a fine leader."

Noril folded his arms over his chest and stood straight, as if issuing a command from on high. "We need to act, Amrath."

Amrath pursed his lips. "If we cannot win, we must submit."

Noril looked as if his head might explode at this. "*Submit?*" he roared, his voice echoing off the shattered tiles. "It would be better we all die than leave him with that thing!"

Amrath leapt to his feet, fury burning in his eyes. *The lion was never asleep, just resting.* "Don't you think I know that?" he shouted, pounding a fist against the arm of the throne. The arm split from the seat with the force of his blow and hit the floor with a report like a whipcrack. The marble beneath Amrath's feet split in a lengthening spiderweb shape that grew directly at Noril. "Have you talked to Yorn? Do you understand what that damned thing *is*?"

Noril slowly lowered his gaze to the crack in the floor at his feet and scoffed. He looked back at Armath in defiance. "I understand well enough. Torian black sorcery, mind control!"

Amrath's energy seemed to drain as quickly as it had come. He sank slowly back into the throne, once again defeated and miserable. "So your answer is 'no', then. Because it is much, much worse than that."

"How can it be worse?"

"It's not mind control," Amrath spat. "It's a collective. They are volunteers. They *want* what is happening to them."

Noril's rage fled him in an instant, and his face began to tremble as he tried and failed to conceal his horror at such a concept. "You can't know that," he muttered.

"I *do* know it."

"How?"

Amrath waved the question aside with a listless hand. "It doesn't matter. What is important is that we seize the Eye from him at all costs."

"A moment ago, you were talking surrender. One does not make demands from his knees."

Amrath nodded slowly, and rose to his feet. The misery on his face was gone, replaced by grim purpose. "I don't intend to make any demands. I intend to surrender. I also intend to kill a man and take from him something that should never have existed. They will both happen at the same time."

Despite knowing silence was a better choice, Tasinal could not contain his shock or his words. "Are you suggesting what I think? Treachery? Under a flag of truce?"

Amrath gave Tasinal an icy stare. "I am not confused about what I propose."

Noril shouted, "It's a confession of pure weakness!" He pointed an accusing finger at Amrath. "To *yourself*!"

Amrath turned gaze to Noril, frowning. "So it is, and not something I do easily. But lying to myself is worse. In the face of this abomination, we are all weak. Will we compound weakness with cowardice and flinch from what we know must be done?"

For long moments, none of them spoke. At last, Tasinal asked in a soft voice, "It could trigger a collapse, yes?"

Amrath nodded, the weariness once again creeping into the corners of his eyes. "It's hazardous terrain, but not insurmountable. We must all keep our reasons for this well in mind, remember our priorities. As for me, I am convinced that it is not weakness to use whatever means I must. It is not death we face. It's being robbed of all we are."

Noril shuddered visibly. "Absorbed into the collective."

Tasinal shook his head in vehement denial. "Better to suffer a collapse!"

Amrath nodded back at them. "Just so. One would still at least have the ability to disagree, to deny, even if he lacked the power to resist."

Noril slammed both fists against the table, hard enough to rattle it. "I cannot believe it is possible! This thing *cannot* rob us of our very souls! Surely that is only for weaker minds?"

Amrath grunted at this. "Yorn isn't certain, and neither am I. The Eye speaks to those dark, bestial parts in men, the pieces that long to be led, to belong, to follow the herd."

"I am not so certain I would call such people men," Noril said with a scowl.

"Oh, please," Amrath sneered. "How many nights have you gone to bed, alone with your thoughts, feeling beset and misunderstood by the world, by the people who ought have faith in you? It's the human condition. Would you not, perhaps, in a moment of weakness, fall victim to a calm, soothing voice promising you community and purpose?"

"I make my own purpose, and I need no 'community'."

"Suppose we *are* immune!" Amrath shot back, growing more exasperated by the moment. "What of the rest of the people we liberated? How many have died to preserve that freedom? Do we leave them to their fate and abandon the ideals that motivated us? I see that as an even greater risk of collapse, a larger confession of weakness!"

Noril ran a hand through his bristly hair as he absorbed Amrath's argument. "What do you propose? *Exactly.*"

"A summit under truce, to offer our surrender. We will slay Alexander and take the Eye. Once Yorn has destroyed it, we will all surrender ourselves to Xanthius in truth."

Tasinal felt something in him twist at this notion. "If we are rid of the Eye, we no longer need to surrender. Why would you do such a thing?"

"It's hard enough to justify what I plan. Going the whole distance, I think, would be too much on my part. Hypocrisy is, for me, the deadliest poison I can imagine."

"It's not hypocrisy to change one's mind."

Amrath began to chuckle at this, then broke into full, honest laughter. He flashed Tasinal a wicked grin, his green eyes once again filled with merriment and confidence as if nothing had ever been amiss. "No. We can always fight another day."

Noril, still dour, nodded at this. "They will never agree to such a thing unless we press them. We *must* fight, Amrath. *All* of us. No more proxy wars, no more half measures. We unleash our wrath in full, until they beg us to come to the table."

Amrath rose from the throne, nodding. "Yes, brother, I know. It is time once more to slay tyrants and their minions. Let us begin."

Xanthius is angry with me again. He will be angrier when he knows why I summoned him.

Alexander saw through the hazy lens of his normal eyes his

Imperator enter the command tent and stand to attention. Xanthius's face was creased even deeper than usual with worry. Alexander held up a hand for patience. "A moment, Imperator. I would speak to you with my full attention."

Amrath and the rest of the Meites had taken the field after all, and what had once been certain victory was now in doubt. Alexander's people were pinpricks of green in his vision, tiny and vulnerable. The Meites were great, crimson searchlights cutting swathes through the green, leaving only black in their wake.

He was still convinced his side would emerge victorious, but at what cost? Thousands of lives, perhaps hundreds of thousands. The Meites were no mere soldiers. They were demigods! Even now, he felt a thousand of his people shriek in terror as the ground shattered beneath their feet, quaking and heaving. Alexander fell with them into the darkness, over and over. He burned alive, felt his head collapse under driving hailstones, watched the very stones in the earth rise up and crush him like a bug, or shoot through him like arrows. Each of the enemy had his own flavor to his killing, his own personal style, but all ended the same: black across his vision.

In less than a week, they have decimated my forces.

Alexander called out through the mists to the enemy leader, "It is not right that you are here!"

He could not see inside the man's head, only hear the response. "Speak not to me of propriety, Boy King! I might crush their bodies, but you crush their souls!"

"I bring order to your chaos."

"You bring misery and evil, just as your father did!"

"You and your kind murdered my father."

"We executed a tyrant."

"My father was a good man!"

"Is that what they told you?"

Alexander withdrew a moment, feeling suddenly overwhelmed. The butchery of his people, this poison whispered in his ear, it was too much.

"If you would stop this slaughter, do as I demand," the enemy called to him. "Accept our surrender in person." He shut himself off then, and would hear no more.

Alexander, too, had heard enough for the moment.

With a sigh, Alexander shifted his vision more fully back to his own body, to fight an entirely different battle. His Imperator understood less and less of what was happening, and Alexander had no ability to explain. It was not possible to communicate the vision to someone whose viewpoint was still so narrow.

"You can't do this," Xanthius declared.

"It is done. I have made my decision."

"It's a trap!"

Alexander focused his attention on Xanthius, despite the welling cries of his people. "I must accept their surrender in person."

"Elgar take such foolish notions!" Xanthius shouted. "I will go."

"No," Alexander commanded. "It must be me."

"They will kill you!"

Alexander said nothing for a moment, his attention focused on the cries of his men as the Meites cut through them like wildfire in a dry wood. "One way or another, this ends. You will be needed here in the event I fall."

Xanthius stared at him. "What are you saying?"

Alexander gripped the Eye in his hand, feeling strength and purpose flow into him as he spoke to *everyone*. "I am saying, Xanthius, that if I fall, then there can be no surrender. Not of anyone."

Xanthius's eyes grew so wide it seemed they would burst from their sockets. "Mei! Stop it!" he cried out in horror. "Do you not realize what you're doing?"

Curious, that you should call upon the god of our enemies at such a time as this. "Civilization is at a precipice. On Cofletere, there is still hope. If I fall, you will leave no one alive on Prima to threaten it."

"Alexander! By all that is holy, recant! Slay an entire continent? It's *madness!*"

Perhaps. The whole world has gone mad, it seems.

"You have your orders, Imperator."

CHAPTER 1
THE CHANGELING

NARELKI eyed the stern, pock-marked face of the orderly barring her entrance to the spotless tiled hallway, making no secret of her disdain. The man was a commoner with no concept of his station, or what she could do to make it considerably worse. "You will stand aside at once."

Craterface clenched his jaw and folded his arms across his chest. "I have my orders. Doc said he's too violent."

Narelki felt a twitch beneath her left eye, and wrinkled her nose at the antiseptic smell that permeated the entire building. The indignity of this place, the *reek* of sickness both physical and mental was unbearable. "What sane person wouldn't be?" How her son Aiul had ever tolerated running the hospital was beyond her. Was it any wonder he was half-mad, now that he had been confined here?

Maranath, dressed in his usual drab, brown robe, pulled at his white, tangled beard and glared down at the orderly with equal measures of shock and annoyance. "Do you have any idea who you are addressing, boy?" he asked, his voice gravelly and sure, without a tremor despite his age.

Craterface shot him a sneer. "Doesn't matter. I have orders."

Narelki could barely contain her fury. That this pathetic *creature* dared speak to them in such tones was *intolerable*. She cast a quick look toward Maranath, seeing her thoughts reflected in his ancient, blazing eyes, before turning back to the orderly. *If we had just a bit less self-restraint, your own mother wouldn't recognize what we left of you.* When at last she spoke, her voice was little more than a whisper. "Do you know what happens if I pull my support from this institution?"

Maranath stepped closer to Craterface, invading his personal space. "Or what could happen to your head, say, if I were slightly more annoyed than I am now?" The old sorcerer clenched his right hand and smacked it into his left. A gaping, fist-sized hole suddenly appeared in the marble wall near Craterface's head, spraying a rain of tiny shrapnel in all directions. One small missile cracked the glass reservoir of a wall lantern with a sharp ping, sending a streamer of oil down the ceramic tiles beneath. The orderly stared at Maranath in horror, blood welling from multiple new pinholes on his cheek as he silently mouthed, "*Meites!*"

From down the hall, an anxious male voice called out, "Matriarch Narelki! Allow me to assist you!" The tapping of his rapid footsteps echoed from the walls as he approached, a small writing pad clutched against his chest, his face concerned, save for his eyes. They were bright, electric blue, cold fires above the marble cliffs of his high cheekbones and narrow, long face. Those eyes seemed calm as death.

Narelki regarded the newcomer with her own, cold stare. He wore the white robe of a physician, but she couldn't place him. *He seems familiar at that, though.* "And you are...?"

"Healer Rithard, Mistress."

He was young, this one, and nervous. *As he should be.* She waited a moment for him to continue, then raised an eyebrow in annoyance. *Why are youths not taught proper manners these days?* "Surely you are no commoner?"

The healer's eyes widened in surprise. "No, Mistress." He hesitated a moment, as if searching for the right words. "I am Rithard... of House Amrath."

Maranath snickered, and Narelki, for all of her concern, found herself slightly amused as well, though she could not allow it to show. "Ah. My apologies to you," she offered with a curt nod. *Of course he seemed familiar. He might be mistaken for my own son, except for the black hair. I can't be expected to remember every-one, after all.* She inclined her head toward the trembling orderly. "You will explain this, I presume?"

"I accept full responsibility, Mistress. I gave the order that no one was to see Master Aiul. I hadn't meant to apply it to you, of course, but I should have been more specific."

Narelki cast an imperious glare at the orderly for a long moment, then muttered, "You may go."

Craterface stepped gingerly to the side, away from the hole in the wall, gave a deep bow, then fairly bolted down the hallway. Maranath smiled and waved at the fleeing orderly. "Excellent judgment. Bravo."

Rithard pulled at his robe as Narelki turned toward the door again. "Ah, Matriarch, I would very much like to speak with you about the current situation before you enter. You should be prepared for what you will see."

Mei, what's happened? "You will speak to me here and now."

Rithard glanced toward a door farther down the hallway. "Mistress, I think it best if we discuss things in a more private location."

Narelki found herself bristling at this, even though it was a perfectly reasonable, prudent thing for Rithard to suggest. These were Aiul's underlings, after all. It simply wouldn't do to have his failings exposed to them. *I'm spending far too much time with Maranath these last few days. I fall back into old ways, but I lack the old strength. That is a good way to end up opening my wrists.* She offered Rithard a smile she hoped seemed genuine, and nodded. "Of course."

Rithard escorted them past a small reception area and into his office, offering a courteous nod to an attractive blond receptionist as they passed her desk.

His office, in contrast to the rest of the hospital, was warm and inviting, filled with the smell of sandalwood. Framed testaments from various elders lined the paneled walls. Rithard closed the door and gestured toward two leather-bound chairs that stood in front of a large desk. "Please, have a seat."

"We'll stand," Narelki told him. "We don't intend to be long, do we?"

Rithard shook his head vigorously, clearly indicating that he understood she was giving him a command, not asking a question. "Of course not, mistress. I'll get right to the point." He cleared his throat and clasped his hands behind his back. His eyes seemed to wander away from a direct confrontation, preferring the floor or the walls. "Master Aiul received severe head trauma while incarcerated. When he arrived here this morning, he was confused and violent. It took five orderlies to subdue him, and even then he managed to injure his best assistant. The poor woman needed stitches."

Narelki took a moment to absorb the unexpected news. "And how does he explain this?"

Rithard's expression was a mixture of pity and misery. "He doesn't speak at all, Mistress. If he comprehends either spoken or written word, he shows no sign of it. He is catatonic, or he is savagely violent."

Narelki gasped at this. "Will it pass?"

"It may."

"Days? Weeks?"

"Or months. Or never. The brain is a foreign land we view from afar. Its workings are known only little."

Narelki could barely contain a wail of grief. She felt Maranath's hand on her shoulder, steadying her, and for once she was grateful to have him at her side.

"What caused this?" Maranath growled. "There will be grave consequences if I find this was from some abuse."

Rithard turned up his palms. "I can't say for certain, but it doesn't seem so. Caelwen says Master Aiul knocked himself unconscious trying to escape his cell. He was unresponsive when they found him. The injuries I see are consistent with that story."

Maranath grunted. "Well, Caelwen is not apt to lie. I'll trust his word on it, then."

Narelki turned to Maranath, once again so full of rage she could barely contain it, though this time it was directed at a much more substantial target. "House Noril had a duty to protect him from this. I will hold them accountable!"

Maranath bristled and shot back, "Their man is *dead*. I'd say he paid for his mistake well enough."

"Davron should never have put a fool in such an important position. He is liable."

Maranath fixed her with a stern glare, his blue eyes dancing, vibrant, full of life and lightning. "This is not the time or the place to discuss such matters," he told her, saying each word slowly. "Compose yourself."

Fortunately for the both of us, I've had some experience with composing myself, unlike you. Narelki held his gaze a moment, long enough to remind him she was stronger than he might think, then turned back to Rithard. "That was not for your ears."

The healer seemed to be focusing on a document on his desk. He looked at Narelki innocently. "My apologies, Mistress. I'm afraid I was distracted. What was not for my ears?"

"Very good. I shall remember you for that."

Rithard offered her a knowing smile. "It is good to be remembered."

"Now I would see my son."

"Of course," Rithard said, then paused, again looking squeamish. He rubbed at the stubble on his chin a moment, then continued. "There is one more thing."

Narelki said nothing, waiting for him to continue.

Rithard opened his mouth slightly to speak, but two full seconds passed before any words came out. At last, he stammered, "There has been some damage to his face."

Aiul awoke with a start, head cloudy with the last vestiges of sleep, and breathed a sigh of relief. "A dream," he whispered. "Only a dream."

The pain fell upon him like a meteor. There was no single source, though each of the hundred or so violations of his flesh wailed with a slightly different pitch. Their song, in turn, pulled him from half consciousness into full awareness, to be crushed anew with an agony of spirit made all the more excruciating by his brief moment of hope.

He closed his eyes and lay on the floor in silence for what seemed an eternity. The cold, damp stone of the cell against his cheek; the blinding agony in his head; the sharp tang of blood; the utter emptiness he felt inside at his loss; all could be dismissed as illusion, if only he refused to open his eyes and concede his situation. He would will it untrue, believe it into unbeing, and things would return to how they had once been.

It was futile, he knew. He had never been the sort of man who could deceive himself, and even here, with the greatest of incentives, he had no choice but to face reality in all its jagged, bloodstreaked glory, to confront the fact that Lara was gone, and he was responsible. His arrogance, his pride, his sense of duty, all had brought agony and death to the one person who mattered to him. He felt his guts twist as he remembered more. *"Two* people," he whispered.

Even as he sobbed quietly, drowning in guilt and shame, that piece inside him, his own jagged edge, pricked at his heart and mind, unwilling to accept the full blame. It was his failure, yes, but not his fault. Kariana's hand held the blade that rent Lara's flesh. Yet even that was not the whole of it. Kariana was a weakling, a hedonist. She had no real power but what she was permitted by the elders. It was Nihlos itself, in all its spiteful apathy, all its adherence to precedent and ritual, that had allowed a monster like Kariana to thrive, had made it necessary for him to act, and in the end, had killed his family.

Between gasps of pain and grief, his lips, still wet with blood, left a trail on the damp stone beneath him, a strange kiss of agony. "You will be avenged, my loves," he whispered A bright, jagged thing flashed in his mind, hot and sharp, tearing at the deep parts of his soul. "All Nihlos will pay."

Narelki moved quickly as she exited the small, padded room. *I need air!* The vision of her son, broken, a doll tossed against a wall and left shattered on the floor, still burned at her mind as the reek of excrement and sweat still burned in her nose.

She felt tears welling in her eyes. *His face! What have they done to his beautiful face?* In truth, she had no idea. His entire head was swathed in bloody bandages, and that made it all the worse, somehow. To see him battered would have been one thing, but to not see him at all? *How bad must it be that they would need to bandage everything?*

Again, Maranath's hand was on her shoulder, firm and steady, seeming to pour strength into her. "He's alive, Narelki. And he'll heal."

"Into what?" she gasped. She covered her face with her hands to hide the shame of her weakness, but surely anyone nearby would hear her sobbing. "A monster? And what of his mind? Rithard—"

Maranath waved the question aside. "Pay no attention to that charlatan. Aiul is strong like his father. He always has been. He'll make a full recovery, mark my words."

The grief and fear in her mind seemed physically hurled to the side as the shock of Maranath's comment forced its way in. *How could you bring him up at a time like this?*

For a moment, she simply stared at him, speechless. Maranath's face remained concerned and fatherly, showing no sign of guilt or malice. *Grandfather. He meant to say grandfather. Slip of the tongue, slip of the mind. He's getting old, Meite or no. His mind is failing him.*

She swallowed hard and tried to put the horror of that thought out of her head, along with all the others vying for dominance. With some effort, she managed to offer him a tearful smile, hoping he saw nothing in her expression to give away her realization. *If he knows, if he feels himself slipping....*

"Of course," she said with a nod.

Rithard closed the door to his office behind him and leaned against it, taking a deep, shuddering breath. *That went well, all things considered.* He stood several seconds, waiting for his breathing to calm, then crossed to his desk, sat heavily in his chair, and jerked open the largest drawer. He drank straight from the bottle of brandy he kept there, taking no real pleasure in it. It was medicinal, not for entertainment.

He noticed with detachment that his hand was trembling. *How odd. I don't feel this fear very deeply, but my body, it seems, does.* He took another mouthful of liquor, swallowed it with a grimace, and closed his eyes to wait for the effect.

After a while, Rithard raised his treacherous hand in front of his face, pleased to see the shaking had passed. *Now, to finish this.* He opened the top desk drawer and removed the sealed envelope he had placed there. He had been uncertain as to whether he would actually carry out this plan, and it would not have done to send his missive until he was committed, but now that he was, the letter was imperative.

Rithard rose and opened the door. He waved the letter at the receptionist outside. "Have this taken to my mother at once. It's vital."

The girl looked up at him from her desk, confusion in her crystal blue eyes. "I'm sorry, sir, but I don't know your mother," she said hesitantly, as if afraid she would be punished for her failure.

Rithard put a palm to his face and shook his head with a wry smile he didn't actually feel. "I'm sorry. I was thinking of the other girl." *The one Aiul put in hospital this morning with ten stitches and a concussion. I hadn't fully decided until then.*

He handed her the letter with a flourish. *Better she think I'm deliriously happy than contemplating the likelihood I won't survive the week.*

"My mother is Teretha Prosin."

CHAPTER 2
VOYAGE INTERRUPTUS

AHMED stood once again at the ship's railing, gripping it lightly to steady himself against the gentle rolling of the deck. He looked down at his hands, pleased to see his skin color had returned to a healthy, chocolate brown. The winter had been hard, and at the height of it, Ahmed had been shocked to find himself ashen, pale like a dead man. Now, the sun had returned, and he felt human again.

He stared out over the waves, pondering the strangeness of the sea, the small miracle of the ship floating upon it, marveling at the brilliant orange glow of the sun slowly setting. It was less alien as time passed, more familiar. He was still fairly certain he would never choose the life of a sailor, but he could endure it, if need be. He had grown stronger in Yazid's absence, less in spite of it than because of it. Such was Ilaweh's way, to harden a man by taking away the things that propped him up, the things he leaned upon.

"Grow stronger or die," Ahmed said softly. "I miss you, Father."

It had been a long and often stressful trip since Yazid had fallen. Brutus had begun preparations to launch for Xanthia the moment he returned from Nihlos. Had Sandilianus been a single day later to return, Brutus would have left him in this accursed barbarian land. Sandilianus's tale of sorcerers and strife amongst the leadership of the savages simply made the return to Xanthia even more pressing to the captain.

Ahmed had stood on the bridge with the two of them, listening to the tale. "It is a mistake," he had told them. "Ilaweh has work for us here, yet."

Brutus's nearly black face seemed to grow even darker, his broad nostrils flaring as he turned to Ahmed. The captain was clearly in no mood for such talk. "What do *you* know, boy?" he shouted.

Sandilianus said nothing, simply stared at Ahmed, almost unrecognizable through the swelling, bruises, and wounds still in need of stitching. Even so, the expression on his olive-skinned face spoke loudly, his sharp features growing even sharper.

So he does not hear me, either.

Ahmed had no fear of a beating. Had it been merely that, it would have been so much easier to stand his ground. But beneath the withering glare of the two veterans, men of the world, men who knew reality and death like their own bodies, he felt his conviction shrivel. What he *knew* without doubt from his visions shriveled into a mere belief, and then simply, "It's just a feeling I have."

Brutus nodded in triumph. "Just so. And I will not endanger my mission for a 'feeling'."

Ahmed felt rising anger. "I am Yazid's second. His place falls to *me*. It should be *my* decision."

Brutus regarded him with shocked, wide eyes, then burst out laughing. "*You*? An unblooded boy in charge of me and my men? Preposterous!"

"The prince said—"

Brutus raised a fist, more statement than threat. "Do *not* speak of what you do not know, boy! The Prince said I was to serve *Yazid*."

Ahmed could not contain himself at this. "And Yazid is dead, while you are not!" he shouted. "How did you serve him, dog?"

Brutus moved far more quickly than Ahmed expected, though he did not hit nearly so hard as Yazid. Ahmed barely felt woozy from the blow, and retaliated with his own. The two men grappled, then fell to the floor, hammering at each other. Sandilianus banged his fist against his chest with little enthusiasm.

Ahmed was hardly surprised to find himself pummeled fairly quickly into submission. Nevertheless, he had managed to score several telling blows on the captain, and was damned proud of it. He lay against the bulkhead and laughed, spraying blood from his lips.

Brutus crouched on a knee beside him. "You laugh? Truly, I am impressed, boy. You will not call me a dog again, eh?"

"Don't call me boy."

Brutus chuckled and wiped at his bloody nose. "Fair enough." He stood and called out, "Tahir, set a course for Xanthia, best speed."

Tahir poked his head out from the door of the chart house, his wiry, orange beard trembling with annoyance. "Aye, captain, but there's an interesting wrinkle there."

Ahmed wiped blood from his face with the back of his arm, unable to fully suppress his loathing for the orange-skinned, half-breed blasphemer. It was best to keep his mouth shut about it and settle for a contemptuous sneer. Likely, Brutus and Sandilianus shared his thoughts, but he might still receive a second beating for speaking out of turn. *One is enough for the evening.*

Sandilianus ground his teeth. "Then come the fuck out with it instead of dangling it like a damned prize for us to admire, eh?"

Tahir scowled at him, but he was nodding, too. "Aye. The thing is, I reckon we're about two-thirds around the continent.

The best course is to continue forward and finish our map, assuming we don't run into anything crazy."

Sandilianus, still annoyed, pursed his swollen lips and grimaced in pain. "We have the old map. Continents don't grow arms or legs."

Tahir looked at Sandilianus in wide-eyed shock. "They damned well grow reefs, fool!" he shouted.

Sandilianus raised his eyebrows and blinked a moment, then grinned sheepishly. "Hmm, well, I *have* been hit in the head a lot lately."

Brutus held up a hand for silence. "What kind of time difference are we talking?"

Tahir squinted and scratched at the red, wiry hair on his chin,. "Hard to say, figuring in distance and winds. Best guess is near two months difference." He shrugged. "If the wind stays the same."

"Will it?"

Tahir shrugged again, this time adding an exasperated sigh. "It *should*, but it's the damned bottom of the world. I never been there. Can you beat a man you just met? There's lots of variables."

Brutus nodded in appreciation of the problem. "Very well. We move forward, then. Can we save time if we skip the mapping?"

Tahir shook his head. "Not much. A week at most, if we cut around the last corner and head straight for home." His face grew very serious. "I reckon the map is worth a week, Brutus. It's hard military intelligence, and it'll cost a lot more if we have to come back for it later."

"I know. Finish it, then, and take us home. If we see any natives who seem weak, we can try consulting with them. I don't want to risk any encounters we won't definitely win, should it come to blows."

He pointed to Ahmed. "Give me your hand." Ahmed reached

upward, and Brutus hauled him to his feet. "I like you better after fighting you. Let's have a drink."

Things had gone well with them after that, both finding new respect for one another. Brutus invited Ahmed to take Yazid's quarters in the officers' berthing, a small cabin adjoining Brutus's own. Ahmed had expected Brutus to make some advance toward him, and was prepared to fight, even if he would lose, but the captain had apparently been serious about his convictions. Ahmed was "polluted by women's weakness," and Brutus would not taint himself with such, not even second hand. For his part, Ahmed was greatly relieved to hear this. He would have given what was due had it been won fairly, but he had no taste for men. He would not have enjoyed it, merely endured it, and likely earned another beating for being sullen.

None of the pursuers Brutus feared had ever materialized, but their journey had been far from easy. The weather had been their fiercest enemy. The southern edge of the continent was bitterly cold, despite the fact that it was high summer. They had been battered by freezing rain as they struggled past treacherous ice. Snow had been so thick at times that they had no choice but to anchor and wait for the blinding white to pass. Ahmed found it all terribly annoying and inconvenient that the world worked this way. It was confusing enough that the seasons should be reversed in the Southern Hemisphere, and too much that North and South be reversed as well, science be damned. North should be cold, not South. The gods seemed mad at times.

Now, as he stood at the rails remembering Yazid, it was at last warm again. They were much farther north, their map almost complete. Soon, they would turn the ship for home, and then what would he do? *We are not supposed to leave!*

Yazid would have had the answers. Had it not always been so? Ahmed could not remember a time without him, a rock to cling to in any storm, and the loss cut him deeply. He knew, because Yazid had told him, that his mother had died shortly after his birth, that Yazid's order had taken him in, trained him, but he did not remember another father. *Few children remember even one, though.*

Ahmed tightened his grip on the railing and ground his teeth in frustration. *I am failing you. They will not listen.*

For a thousand years, the prelates had kept Xanthius's writings, preserved his warning, passed it down from generation to generation: Elgar will return. Stand vigilant.

Ahmed heaved a deep sigh, feeling tears well in his eyes. *I never imagined it would be me.*

He was unworthy, barely more than a boy, and tasked with swaying men of substance that they should abandon their every instinct and follow him, to risk their lives for a prophesy Ahmed himself barely believed.

And there was the rub. He knew the words, but he had never truly believed. He had never placed faith in writing and prophesy beyond that which would get him past his next lesson. He heard the voice of Ilaweh directly, sometimes soft, sometimes crashing in his ears, but it was that, not the prophesy, that had always driven him.

Now they are the same. Ahmed felt as if his guts would sink through him and the ship, knowing now that what he had always imagined a fairy tale was true: the world would become as ash if strong warriors did not stand and give all they had.

It falls to me, and I am not ready. How could a man cope with such a burden? And how could he possibly convince a man like Brutus? That was the most damnable part: in a purely logical world, Brutus was *right*. But Ahmed knew with grim certainty that there was more at play here than cold logic. Ilaweh called them to war.

I don't know what to do!

It was a lie he told himself, for truly, Yazid's voice still rang in his ears, even though Yazid was gone: *"You will do what is right, Ahmed. You will follow your head and your heart."*

Ahmed laughed softly to himself, and couldn't help but speak back to the ghost. "And when they disagree?"

He was startled from his musing by Brutus's voice. "When who disagree?"

Ahmed turned from the rail to face the captain approaching. Brutus wore no shirt, only a pair of dark breeches, and his eyes seemed to float, disembodied, in the failing light, his skin blending seamlessly into the growing shadows. "Head and heart," Ahmed answered. "Which to trust?"

Brutus looked at Ahmed with suspicion, as if he thought the question some sort of military ruse. "You are the prelate. Do you truly not know the answer, or is this your way of preaching?"

Ahmed shrugged and picked at his tunic. It had once been white, but it was now gray and threadbare. *Like me.* "Yazid was a prelate. I am confused. You know that. It is why you do not listen to me."

"Why should I listen to you, when you do not listen to Ilaweh?" Ahmed frowned at this, but Brutus did not retreat. "You know it is so. How else would a man reconcile such a disagreement?"

Ahmed turned back to the waves, feeling his heart shrink within his breast. "We are not supposed to leave, Brutus. Not yet."

"Ah, this again?" Brutus heaved a great sigh and joined him at the rail. "I will not change my mind."

Ahmed could feel the soldier's harsh gaze like the sun on his back, and turned to face him, returning Brutus's scowl. "Ilaweh is mighty and his vision long. We are small to him, and our lives very short."

Brutus snorted. "You think this is some great enlightenment to me? I've seen enough blood to know Ilaweh is hard and ofttimes cruel."

Ahmed struggled to contain himself, to explain rather than grow angry at Brutus's willful ignorance. "Most of us are like plants in Ilaweh's garden. Sometimes, it is necessary to destroy some of the crops for the good of the garden. Does the farmer weep for this? Why should he? The crop would be plowed under at the end of the season anyway. There is a reason he planted many seeds, and he will do so again in the spring."

Brutus looked at him with a thoughtful expression. "Most of us. But not me, I think. My brothers and I, we will bear no fruit. What are we in your allegory?"

Ahmed chuckled. "Perhaps you are herbs, Brutus, desirable in your own right."

Brutus's sudden laughter echoed out over the waves. Tahir poked his head from the chart house, glared at both of them, then slammed the door closed again. Brutus clapped Ahmed on the shoulder and smiled broadly. "You preach strangely."

Ahmed felt his heart sink like the ship in a trough. "You do not hear me."

"I stand here before you, do I not? I am not deaf."

"But you do not take to heart what I am saying. You still intend to defy Ilaweh."

Brutus shot him an irritated look. "So *you* claim." After a moment his expression softened. "And what if you are right? If it is truly Ilaweh's will, then he will have his way despite me."

Ahmed grimaced at this, feeling sick. *It is not the sea this time, though.* "Such thoughts have consequences." He paused a moment, looking at Brutus's resolute expression, struggling to find a way to reach him. "When a farmer tends his garden, he destroys much, even as he preserves. He pulls weeds from the ground, treads upon insects, shreds spider webs. From the perspective of an ant, it is a cataclysmic thing. If we leave it to him, our works are but gossamer shimmering in the wind, to be torn aside in his passing."

Brutus shook his head, unmoved. "Ahmed, I have killed hundreds, and watched many of my brothers fall. Do you not think I have made peace with this notion long ago? I live and die by Ilaweh's will, as do all my men. I am no plant in a garden, and neither are you."

"Then what are we?"

"Swords. Weapons in Ilaweh's hands, instruments of his will. We may individually dull and break from the power of his blows, but we are many."

Ahmed strained to appreciate the thought. "Then who is our enemy?"

"Villains. Liars. Thieves. Anyone who tries to take more than his fair share, or strikes at the innocent."

"Nebulous," Ahmed replied "Anyone could be our enemy, then."

"Aye, it is so. Any fool."

Ahmed waved the discussion aside. None of it truly matched reality. Allegories rarely did. "Will you not at long last hear me? I tell you, I know this in my heart. Ilaweh wills that we stay. He has work for us. The prophesy—"

"I have heard you. You have not heard me. I do what I think is best, just as you. I accept the consequences."

Ahmed fumed at this, and Brutus stiffened, tensing for a fight, but Ahmed knew now that this battle could not be won by physical blows. "And the rest of your men?" he asked, his voice quiet and grim. "Your decision is for them as well."

"They are not my men if they do not feel the same." Brutus glowered at him. "And you? Do you quiver in fear, perhaps, that Ilaweh's will might end your life?"

Ahmed shook his head, thinking of Yazid again. "No. Only that I might fail him." *As I am now.* He closed his eyes, trying to find some other words, but there were none. For good or ill, the decision had already been made.

Brutus clapped a heavy hand on Ahmed's. "Then let us rest. Ilaweh's will be done."

Ahmed looked back out over the waves, feeling helpless, as the disc of the sun dipped below the horizon. "It surely will."

Ahmed woke to the sound of crashing timbers and shouting men. There was no doubt in his mind as to why. The only real question was who would survive.

It was pitch black in the captain's cabin. There should have been lanterns burning! He leapt from his hammock and staggered, almost falling as the deck ambushed him from an unexpected direction. It was not flat beneath him as it should be. Ahmed was no seaman, but even he knew this was a bad thing. How could the ship stay afloat if it tilted and filled with water?

"Ahmed!" Brutus shouted from his cabin. There was an odd edge to his voice, enough to set Ahmed's intuition singing. *This will not be good.*

"Here! I'm coming!" Ahmed felt his way along in the dark, trying to overcome the disorienting sensation that he was climbing downhill, at last finding the opening between their cabins. There was no privacy aboard a ship, so there was no door to battle, only a makeshift curtain they had hung. Ahmed struggled through the opening, blind.

Light flared as he entered, and he raised an arm to shield his eyes. Brutus, sitting against the bulkhead, adjusted the wick of a lantern he had somehow salvaged. He hung the lantern on a wall hook that was no longer in quite the correct position for the task. The lantern settled at an awkward angle, tilted almost to spilling its oil on the floor, its flickering light casting shadows skittering over a skewed, slanted world.

Ahmed almost wished it were still dark. The ceiling above

Brutus's hammock was splintered, and a huge spar of wood had fallen on the captain, pinning him. Brutus grimaced and beckoned Ahmed forward. "To me! Quickly, before it is too late!"

Cold water swirled about Ahmed's ankles as he moved quickly across the tilted deck and seized the massive weight pressing Brutus to the floor. He hauled at it with all his might. Brutus shook his head a moment, then pushed against it as well, leaning forward, the cords in his neck popping out from exertion. The spar moved, but only inches.

Ahmed grimaced as he saw the grim depth of Brutus's predicament: the huge timber was more than just a weight. It had not broken cleanly. A sharp spindle had sunk deep into Brutus's belly, passing right through him and into the bulkhead behind.

Brutus's hands slipped first, and then Ahmed's. Brutus cried out in agony as the spar slammed back into place. The ship itself seemed to scream with him in empathy, straining wood and creaking lumber wailing in their own version of pain. Their vessel, like her captain, was dying.

Brutus leaned his head back and looked up at what should be the sky above him, gasping in misery. "It is no use! Do not behave like a woman!"

Ahmed shook his head, trying to stay focused. From elsewhere on the ship, he could hear screams and shouts, but here and now were what mattered most. "We try again!"

"Even if we get it off, I am still dead! There is no time!" Brutus's eyes rolled in his head as he struggled against the pain. "You must bring my papers to the prince! Swear it to me, prelate, in the name of Ilaweh!"

Ahmed ground his teeth. The water had grown higher now. It was approaching his knees, and Brutus's chest.

Brutus grabbed Ahmed's shirt and pulled him close. The captain's face was a mask of pain, but his eyes burned bright with purpose. "Swear it!"

"By Ilaweh, I *swear*."

"Quickly then. In my footlocker. There is an oilcloth bag."

Ahmed opened the locker, and found the bag at the very top. "This?"

"Yes. It must reach Prince Philip. Go quickly. If you don't clear the wreck, it will drag you down with it!" Brutus gasped and fell silent, eyes closed. For a moment, Ahmed thought the captain was dead, but at last he opened his eyes and said, "There is but one thing more. I ask a favor of you, not for duty, but for friendship."

Ahmed felt his guts churn, certain what Brutus would have him do, and sick with the knowledge, but he accepted the burden nonetheless. "Name it," he said as he tucked the oilcloth bag into his shirt.

"Do not let me drown, brother."

Ahmed clenched his jaw and nodded.

Brutus pointed. "My sword. There. It is a fine weapon, Ahmed. It has slain many. It's yours now. Use it well."

Ahmed took the scabbard and drew the blade from it. The metal sang as it quivered in the air. Brutus smiled at him. "You were right, brother. Go. Save the world."

Ahmed raised the blade. "I will try, brother. Ilaweh is great."

"You will *succeed*. That is not a hope, it is an *order*!" He chuckled softly, then grew somber. "Ilaweh is great. I am ready." Brutus leaned his head to the side to offer as easy a target as possible.

Ahmed struck Brutus's head from his shoulders with a single, swift blow and silently gave thanks to Ilaweh for guiding his hand. He shook the blood from the sword, sheathed it, and stood a moment, knowing it was unwise, but feeling compelled. A comrade had fallen, one Ahmed had come to call friend. Brutus's passing should be marked. No words were needed. Brutus was not that sort of man. But a few seconds of silent respect were appropriate, and worth risking.

Ahmed managed half a minute before the ship gave another violent lurch. He heard more splintering, and new screams from the main deck. *I know! Hurry up.* He waded toward the cabin door, tried the latch, and felt his belly fill with ice. The door wouldn't budge.

Calm yourself. If it is Ilaweh's will, you will live. It was easy enough to accept in theory, but unlike Brutus, he had no one to spare him from drowning.

He tried the latch again, making certain he had actually released it. No good. Something heavy was blocking the door. Ahmed took a deep breath. The water was rising quickly, almost to his hips. He was running out of time.

He hurled a shoulder against the exit, and felt the weight on the other side shift. The door yielded slightly, perhaps an inch, but no more. He tried again, and a third time, but it was the same.

Ahmed could feel the panic in his heart, yowling and searching for an exit like a cat in a shower. He crushed it down, knowing that it would do him little good. Still, he felt its claws tearing at him from within. He drew Brutus's sword and began hacking at the door. Perhaps the top was clear, and he could crawl over the obstruction.

The ship lurched again, more violent this time, with a groan that sent shudders throughout the frame. The floor tilted beneath Ahmed's feet, water churned, and he lost his footing.

When he surfaced again, it was to blackness. The lantern was out, and he had no idea where the door was. The panic in him drew strength from this and surged at the chains of faith with which he had bound it, a frenzied beast intent on freedom.

The water was at his chest now, and freezing cold. He could taste the sea on his lips, or was it blood? His, Brutus's, who could say? It was quiet now, just the sloshing of the rising water and the sound of his own labored, shuddering breath. He struggled to reorient himself, to find the door again. Surely, if this was the end, it would not be because he had not tried. But the door was simply *gone*. He pounded his fists against unyielding wood in frustration.

The ship groaned again, and he heard wood creaking under pressure. A board, perhaps right next to him, gave way with a sharp report, and water rushed in. Something hit his chest, something small but hard. He reached for it, but found nothing. Another groan came from overhead, and then a great splintering, shredding sound. Ahmed simply stood. How could he know if he were avoiding a blow, or leaping into one? It was in Ilaweh's hands.

The water was rising faster now. It was up to his neck. This was his end, then. He shook his head at the irony, that a man from the desert should suffer such a death. He felt the fear in his heart subside, replaced with acceptance. He was ready, as difficult as the path was. *Ilaweh's will be done.*

As the water closed over his head, Ahmed Justinius looked up one last time before he closed his eyes, and saw, in the pitch darkness, a twinkling of light. The door was over his head, and through the hole he had hacked in it he could see the moon.

Energy surged into him as he seized the edge of the wood. He could not strike a blow against it, not under water, but he could pull. He did so with all his might.

Ilaweh, if it is your will that I die, let me die well. And if it is not, then give me strength!

Ahmed felt as if his arms would tear themselves from his body. Five seconds. Ten. Fifteen. His muscles tightened even more, and his breath burst from him in a cry of exertion. This would be his last chance. Twenty seconds. Twenty five.

The door gave way with a splintering crack that Ahmed heard even through the water in his ears. The moon above wavered with the water covering him. He clambered through the opening and burst to the surface, sucking in air in great gasps.

He was on the main deck, what was left above the water at any rate. He saw men leaping from the railings, and remembered Brutus's warning to escape the ship before it went down, or he would be dragged down with it.

Ahmed struggled to climb the tilted deck, to reach a high point and jump as the others were doing. He couldn't help but smile at the irony. He had no idea how to swim.

I will learn, he promised himself. *I will learn right now.*

He leapt over the rail and into the dark, rolling waves. He watched the others, and tried to do as they did, digging and crawling through the water like sand. In the distance, he saw lights, and what looked like land, and his heart sank.

Too far. Far too far, and I am exhausted and freezing, and out of my element. Ilaweh, I have failed you. Yet he swam on.

Ilaweh's will would be done.

CHAPTER 3
THE DEAD GOD

Aiul had realized fairly quickly that, while he was in a prison, it was not *the* prison. His cell was far from luxurious, but there was at least enough space in the small, brick room to stand and pace. It even included a toilet. The door was clad in iron. Aiul tested it, and found it locked just as he had expected.

He spied a small view port at eye level in the door. His captors had been either negligent or kind enough to leave it open. It restricted his view to a narrow section of the chamber outside his cell, but he could see working lanterns on the walls, proof that he was most definitely not in the pit.

It was the next morning before he saw anyone. The newcomer was dressed in black mail, a guardsman of Nihlos, though his armor bore no markings of house or rank, and he wore his helmet with the visor down.

"You, there!" Aiul shouted. "What is the meaning of this? Where am I?"

The guard ignored Aiul and went about his business. He refilled and relit lanterns, then turned briefly toward Aiul's cell, as if verifying all was in order. "The traitor lives," he called out in a loud voice, as if he were informing others.

Then he turned and disappeared up the stairs.

Shirini stirred at the steaming pot of soup again. It was sooner than necessary, but she had her rituals. When troubled by events beyond her control, she gave extra attention to the details she could actually influence.

She had no real need to even be here. As a principal of House Noril's slaves, she had many underlings she could task. She might have spent her time gossiping, even napping, though of course she would be held responsible if her people made a mess of things. That, she supposed, was part of why she was here, but the greater part was simpler, and something she would never admit to the others: she loved the work. Cooking was a joy, an art, a solace. She needed it now.

Across House Noril's enormous kitchen, Parala and Cyndi, both young trollops who spent far too much time sowing dissent amongst the male slaves, tittered as they cut and laid out biscuits on a pan. Shirini scowled at them in disapproval, but said nothing. She had been young, once, too, and had done her share of gossiping. *But I kept my skirt down more than the two of them, that's certain.*

Cyndi pressed a cup into the flattened dough and giggled at the farting sound it made. "What do you reckon he did? The man in the prison?"

"I heard he stole from the house," Parala said as she slid a tray of biscuits into one of the many brick ovens.

Shirini stirred her soup again vigorously, not deigning to look up as she spoke. "You two cluck like hens, and with about the same result. There's no man in the prison."

Cyndi gaped at her. "Yes there is! Everybody knows it. My boyfriend saw them bring him in."

Shirini gave her a hard look. "Which one would that be, missy? The liar, the tale-spinner, or the one too stupid to mind his own business?"

Cyndi, chagrined, stared at the floor and said nothing. Shirini waved her spoon at the two of them. "There ain't no man in the prison, you hear me? If you know what's good for you, that's the tale you'll tell. Don't test me."

The two girls grew somber, but Parala brightened quickly. "How about the woman in with Master Davron?" she asked, a leer on her face. "Can we talk about her?"

Shirini sighed and turned back to her pot. "If you keep your voice down. And you better keep up on them biscuits, too. It wouldn't do for us to lay a poor serving for her, would it?"

Cyndi snickered at this, and made a show of slowly peeling a biscuit and gently, painstakingly moving it to a baking tray. "If we make a good impression, maybe the Master will get himself an heir."

Shirini slapped her spoon on the counter. "First off, it's not your business to be meddling in such things." She allowed herself a wry smile as she continued, "And how in Mei's name can we hear what they're saying if you two keep nattering on?" She folded her arms across her chest, smiling with satisfaction as the girls' eyes widened, and they nodded in conspiratorial agreement. Cyndi gestured sewing her lips shut, and the kitchen fell silent save for the gentle farting of dough and scraping of pans.

Shirini looked out the serving window into the dining room where Master Davron and his guest sat at a low coffee table, talking quietly. *Not quietly enough, now that these chickens have the idea.*

The woman was a real looker, with long, raven hair, deep green eyes, and full, red lips. She had noble written all over her, but her build was anything but. Noblewomen tended to be way too thin in Shirini's opinion, but this one bucked that trend. She had bosoms to rival Shirini's own well-cultivated pair, and her red, silk dress was cut to display them well. More, her hips were wide and fine in contrast to her narrow waistline. Shirini winced at her own broadened waist, then shrugged with good nature. She'd had enough babies, and was enjoying being done with that part of life. She felt no guilt at enjoying eating at least as much as cooking, and there was plenty of interest from the men despite it. *Not so much from the younger ones, but then I prefer men to boys anyway.*

Davron's guest crossed her legs and leaned in seductively, but her eyes gave lie to the pose. "How long do you intend to go on with this foolishness? It threatens my only son, and for what?"

Davron offered her a patronizing smile. He was a damned fine specimen of a man, Shirini mused. He dressed well, but without pretense, and had bulges in all the right places, quite a feat for a man of his age. "It will go on as long as it amuses me," he told the woman. "I'll decide if he lives or dies in my own good time." The woman opened her mouth to speak, but Davron help up a hand. "I have no sons, but I had a nephew, until recently. He was a useless thing, really, partial to debauchery, but his mother loved him. He was a regular at Tasinalta's disgusting orgies. For once in his life, the fool found a use for his balls beyond fucking, and the South-landers cut him down like a dog."

The woman smirked at this. "No sons, you say? Imagine that. Don't care for girls do you?"

Davron laughed in appreciation of the gibe. "I like 'women' not girls. The problem lies with my wife, if you must know."

"So set her aside."

Davron sneered at this. "Perhaps that's how you handle such things in the lesser houses," he said. "In house Noril, we value loyalty, history, duty."

The woman answered with a seductive smile. "That's good to know."

Shirini growled to herself, and clutched her spoon in anger. *Who are you, bitch, to mock him so?*

Narelki stared at her trembling hands, willing them to be still, but the best she could manage was to quiet their shaking, not eliminate it. Her gut churned in helpless, blind objection to reality. *Once, that would have been enough to move worlds.* She felt her eyes burning as tears welled, uncertain if they were for Aiul or for her own lost self.

I will not do this! She clamped her eyes closed and gritted her teeth. *There must be* something *left! Some tiny shred, at least! People change all of the time, but they don't simply turn in on themselves and vanish. A snake can't simply swallow its tail until it pops out of existence!*

And yet that was just what it felt like. Whole pieces of her were gone as if they never were, and now the one piece she had left, her son, was being torn from her as well.

How many times had she come lately? Ten, Twenty? She had lost count. There were no handholds for memory because nothing changed. Aiul said nothing. He gave no indication that he even knew she was there, much less that he recognized her. Of course, the damned bandages made it impossible to read anything in his eyes or his face.

Someone behind her politely cleared his throat, and Narelki dashed the tears from her eyes before she turned. Rithard, hands clasped in front of him, offered a single, solemn nod of greeting.

It was far too late to pretend she was anything but shattered, but she stood straight and regarded him imperiously nonetheless. He would not be fooled, but he would at least know she had her dignity, and that she intended to preserve it as best she could.

Rithard tried to strike a pose of his own, that of the concerned doctor who only wanted to ease the pain of others, but it was clearly not his best skill.

He was certainly brilliant, Aiul's equal in intellect, perhaps even his superior. She had worked that out very shortly after meeting him. That had prompted her to ask some questions, and the answers had all painted a picture that matched her personal assessment almost perfectly.

He was ruthlessly efficient, as the financial statements showed since he had taken charge of the hospital. He did not ordinarily see patients. He worked with the dead, determining causes, and liaised with the city guard on homicide investigations. Rumor had it that he was solely responsible for solving several grisly murders.

So he was to be respected, both for his skills and his willingness to serve the House outside of his comfort zone. But there was a reason he chose to work with the dead. Try as he might, he was detached, analytic, and cool. His sympathetic smile didn't quite reach his icy eyes. *So like my own. How did I not know he was of Amrath when I met him?*

As a physician, Aiul always had the right words, would have made physical contact, a hand on the shoulder, some sort of human touch, and not merely for decorum, but sincerely. Rithard did his best, but for him, this was process, and one still not fully perfected at that. He hesitated, uncertain of his place, or if he would cause harm. Perhaps it had as much to do with her station as his own lack of expertise in such matters.

"You may speak," she told him as she daubed her eyes with a kerchief.

"To be frank, I was considering what to say," he admitted,

though he was not at all shy about it. "I know it is not my place, but it's obvious these visits take their toll."

"And what would you have me do?" she shot back. "He is my son."

Rithard frowned as he nodded, clearly less than pleased at her response. "And he is my charge. That makes you my responsibility as well, to the degree you will permit it."

"You would dispense advice? Then be quick about it." She immediately felt guilty at her shortness. *We are quite alike, I think.* She gave him a sad smile. "It's not you. I am simply overwhelmed, as you just pointed out."

"Matriarch, far be it from me to tell you how to live your life, but I can tell you the facts, if you will hear." He paused, and Narelki acceded with a curt nod. "There has been no change in his condition. I have not given up hope that he may recover, but I believe it is time for us to at least consider the fact that his condition may be permanent. Surely, whatever happens, it will happen in its own due time." Rithard fell silent a moment, as if gauging her reaction. "It is my professional opinion that you are causing yourself unnecessary harm by neglecting your own wellbeing of late. It is my duty to see to his care, and I assure you, I do all that I can. But any change that may occur will be gradual. There will be plenty of time for me to alert you. You need not be here every day."

Narelki regarded him in stony silence. His words were hard, bordering on insubordinate, but she had invited them, and more to the point, they were *true*. She held his gaze a moment longer, searching for some crack in his facade, some hint that he was shirking rather than offering honest counsel, but she saw nothing of the sort.

With a sigh, she lowered her gaze. "And what is your prescription, doctor?"

Rithard nodded, more comfortable with her submission. "Why

not weekly, or even bi-weekly visits? I give you my word, Matriarch, I will inform you personally if he changes."

Narelki stared at the marble floor in silence. "Very well," she said at last. "I'll expect regular reports, of course, and immediate notice if his situation changes, for better *or* worse."

"Of course."

Narelki dabbed at her eyes again. "Then you will excuse me. I have neglected my own duties of late. See that you keep to yours. You're proving yourself a most valuable asset to the House, and I will not forget it."

Rithard bowed deeply. "It is good to be remembered."

Alone in his office, Rithard sat at his desk, his head buried in his hands. *I am a villain, a monster, a traitor!* Yet, what choice had he been given? *Oh, let's not strike the martyr pose. It may have started that way, but you're a co-conspirator now, lying, betraying family, and for what?*

Surely the greatest benefit he was gaining from this whole fiasco was that he was not spitted on Davron Noril's sword. *Not yet, at any rate.* Davron had simply shown up at Rithard's office in the wee hours of the morning after the incident and made an offer Rithard found difficult to refuse. But Davron had not been present today, nor any other since. Rithard had become ever more a willing participant as his treacheries mounted.

"I will be taking charge of your patient," Davron had told him. Just that. The Patriarch of House Noril had been dressed for battle, in full armor, leaving no doubt that he had come prepared to fight if need be.

"I think not!" Rithard had answered.

Davron shook his head in amusement and lowered his hand to

his blade. "I think *so*. You have two choices. I take your patient, or I hurt you and *then* take your patient."

"You wouldn't dare."

Davron's face grew dark. He grabbed Rithard's collar in a swift strike, twisting it as he lifted Rithard off the ground with a single arm. "You misunderstand your situation and my resolve."

Rithard clawed at Davron's arm, struggling to breath. *How can he be that strong? It's impossible!*

Davron, a grim smile on his lips, held Rithard for a moment to drive home the point , then hurled him to the ground. "Your patient conspired with foreigners," Davron said as he began pacing back and forth, examining the various framed testaments on the walls of Rithard's office. He cast a disgusted look toward Rithard, then continued, "His reckless behavior has led to several deaths, including those of your cousin, Marissa, and his *own wife.*"

He spun back to Rithard, eyes blazing, his right fist clenching and unclenching in barely contained fury. "And the council punishes him with what? A slap on the wrist, and even that will be called back after this mess! I won't have it!"

Rithard rubbed at his neck, still gasping from the impact with the floor. "This is *madness*! Narelki will have you in chains!"

Davron spat on the floor and sneered. "For what? Assault and kidnapping? Versus treason, malfeasance and criminal abuse of power? I doubt I have much to fear." He hovered over Rithard, his fist still working as if he was only just restraining himself from violence. "Of course, I have no intention of yielding like a whipped dog, either. If they want a war, then I will give them one, and it will be more glorious than anything Nihlos has witnessed in eons." Davron paused, looking at Rithard as a hunter might watch a deer. "So you see, physician, in the grand scheme of things, you are merely a bit player. Killing you to get what I want is the least of what I am prepared to do."

"Yes," Rithard stammered. "I see that quite clearly, now."

Davron reached a hand down to Rithard. "I'm glad we understand one another."

Rithard, still woozy, had to admit to himself that he welcomed the assistance, even if it was from the same person who had just manhandled him. He took Davron's hand and rose to unsteady feet. "So am I."

"Good. Now bring me my prisoner, and make certain he is pliable. I'm sure you have the right drugs."

Rithard continued to rub at his throat as he tried to form a response. This was all moving too quickly. He preferred to contemplate things before acting, but Davron was not the contemplative sort. "And what will I tell his mother? She'll be here as soon as she hears the news about the prison. She might even be on her way here as we speak!"

"Then you should hurry," Davron told him, his voice cold and uncompromising. "What you tell them is of no concern to me, as long as it's far from the truth. I've no doubt that in due time I'll have to confront the weaklings and make a stand, but I would have all the time I can to prepare." Davron jabbed a hard, armored finger into Rithard's chest to drive his point home. "Convince them, healer. I'll be back for you if you don't. It may be difficult, but it's not complicated."

Rithard drew in a shuddering breath and ran his hand through his hair. As usual, his body reacted to fear of its own accord, but he did not feel it as much as he might have shown. Already, his mind was racing, generating strategies, rejecting some, cultivating others.

There might be a way through. It's audacious, and treacherous, but there is a path. "I'll need some time," Rithard told him. As Davron opened his mouth to object, Rithard held up a cautioning hand. "Not long. A half hour. If you want this to remain secret, that's the price. I can do no better."

Davron ground his teeth. "A half hour, then. No more. Get on with it."

The plan was devilishly simple. He would tell Aiul that he intended to sedate him because he was behaving erratically and might be a danger to himself or others. That would surely provoke him into precisely the sort of frame of mind to justify the sedation, and Rithard would have witnesses to it. From there, it would be a fairly simple matter to switch him with a catatonic patient. Everyone knew Aiul had suffered trauma to his head. His face had been covered in blood when he had been brought in. It would be a simple matter to exaggerate things, and convince others that it was worse than it had seemed once he had cleared the gore away. Bandages would hide the face.

It was a gamble, to be certain, but one he had to take. Perhaps, despite his best efforts, he would be caught. It was likely, even. At least Davron would be exposed at that point, and perhaps think twice about carrying out his threats, provided he believed Rithard had made a genuine effort.

As for that, there was no predicting what Davron would believe or do. Rithard was only certain of what would happen if he refused to comply.

It had gone spectacularly well. Aiul had erupted like a volcano, shouting at the top of his lungs, trashing the room, and fighting like a caged beast as Rithard and five orderlies struggled to hold him in place for the nurse to inject him. It was unfortunate that, at the last moment, Aiul had gotten an arm free and shoved the nurse hard enough to send her crashing to the floor. On the way down, she cracked her head on a table, sending a spray of blood across the tile. That had played to Rithard's advantage, to be certain. She was a fine witness to Aiul's irrational, violent behavior, but she hadn't deserved it. As Aiul succumbed to the drug, Rithard had rushed to her aid, and the rest of the staff came just in time to see him begin stitching her wound.

Once Aiul was safely locked away, the rest had been easy. Rithard had shuttled some of the staff out of the immediate area with claims that it was for their safety, others with the simple argument that it was improper for them to see the heir to House Amrath in such a state. They had all heard the fight, seen the blood, and the rumors were spreading like plague. No one suspected a thing.

Davron offered a cool nod of appreciation as he took charge of his prisoner. One of Davron's men, a slave named Salastin, had arrived while Rithard had been busy arranging the affair, and the two men from Noril dressed Aiul in armor and dragged him out between them, just two soldiers bringing their drunk friend home.

It never ceased to amaze Rithard how easy crime was, if one had a head for it and a desire to break the law. No one ever watched too closely, and everyone saw what they wanted to see. *I would have made a most excellent murderer.*

This crime, of course, was a bit more difficult. Davron and perhaps others knew the truth, which was always dangerous. It might come back at him some time, and Narelki would surely want his head, but Rithard had leverage there: he knew with certainty that she had been behind the first attack on Lara, the one that had set everything else into motion, and he would use that knowledge to save his skin, should it come to that.

Narelki had covered her tracks well. Even Rithard might never have worked things out without a crucial data point. Her only real mistake was overestimating her thugs' intelligence. The fools had been stupid enough to seek charity care for the wounds Aiul had given them in the very hospital he ran! Fortunately for them, Aiul had been busy elsewhere. Unfortunately for Narelki, Rithard had been the one to treat them, and was able to connect the pieces as the rest of the information came to light.

Everyone talks, not intentionally, but they volunteer data for gossip, or to cover a lie. A group of slaves chattered quietly about the Matriarch sending Slat on an errand the night before, certain it was to arrange a rendezvous with a lover, though none had seen such a suitor arrive. Rithard's patients were tight lipped about the source of their injuries, saying only that there had been a fight. The wounds were obviously blunt force trauma, and Aiul's favored weapon was a mace. Caelwen recounted over a drink how dreadfully tired he was, having tailed Kariana the whole evening. Aiul himself had ever been willing to volunteer his thoughts on his mother's meddling in his relationship.

Means. Motive. Opportunity. And the only other possible suspect, Kariana, was accounted for by a trustworthy source. Therefore, Narelki had sent them.

He'd had no proof, nor had he felt the need to find any. But he had shared the knowledge with his mother. Until recently, he had harbored some small guilt about that. It had seemed prudent to mention to *someone*, in case things got out of hand, and he could hardly bring it to anyone in Amrath, much less to Caelwen. They were long time friends, but Caelwen would have demanded action, and Rithard had wanted nothing of the sort. No, it was best to keep it in the family.

And if half his family happened to be spies and traders of information? His mother would benefit if she could find proof, and Prosin would keep the knowledge quiet until it was important enough to share.

Events of late, however, put things in an entirely different light. One might even call his sharing of that secret prescient. As it turned out, his mother *had* found proof, and according to her, the only person she had told was the Matriarch of her House.

Rithard poured himself a drink and grimaced at the thought. Maralena Prosin was a wicked harridan, and had brought considerable shame to the House with her aggressive power plays. *It will be a fine day when she finally comes across my table. Then we'll see if she actually has a heart at all.*

He raised the glass to his lips and paused, suddenly feeling as if he had been struck in the head with a hammer. His hand went numb as realization coursed like lightning through his nerves, and the tumbler of liquor slipped through his treacherous fingers to dash against the floor.

Rithard stared at the amber liquid and the myriad glass fragments, as if they might, given time, form legible words that could help. "Mei," he gasped, his voice hoarse with emotion.

She engineered the whole thing, and now I'm holding the bag.

A season in the abyss is a timeless expanse. Without the sun or moon, days bleed together into weeks and months with no clear demarcation. Time becomes fluid, pooling in eddies, even seeming to loop back on itself on occasion.

Aiul marked the passing of the days by the pronouncement of the guard: "The Traitor lives." Or he imagined so, at any rate. Who knew if the first meal came in the morning or at midnight? There was no reason to believe the schedule was consistent, and many to believe the reverse, if his suspicions of late were true.

He had decided after a while that it was his captors' intent to drive him to suicide, a convenient means of circumventing the Elder's orders that he not be killed. It was, he conceded, a cunning plan, one that might actually succeed if he allowed it. Resisting at least gave some sense of purpose, and so he counted the days as best he could.

At first, he had assumed he would be found soon enough. Surely his mother was looking for him, or Maranath? But as the time passed, by his reckoning stretching to months, his doubts had grown. Perhaps he wasn't even in Nihlos anymore. Rithard might have even told them he was dead.

Rage swept through him at the thought of his treacherous

second. *My own cousin! How could we have ever trusted his tainted Prosin blood?* The rage passed as quickly as it came. *Who knows if he had anything to do with it? He might be dead, or imprisoned as I am.*

Aiul felt as if his head were swelling toward explosion. A brief, bizarre symbol flashed in his vision, brilliant red. He had seen it many times before, and knew what it meant, but by the time it came, there was no changing things.

He leapt from his cot and hurled the mattress to the floor, his voice a meaningless roar. It was frustrating to have nothing to smash but bedclothes. He spied the heavy metal tray from his previous meal, seized it up, and began battering it against the cell door.

"Who are you?" he screamed. "What do you want from me?"

It was not the first time he had resorted to a tantrum to attract attention. The guards, while not visible, were indeed nearby, within earshot at least, because they responded quickly to his outbursts, and this time was no exception.

The guards did not speak. He could see little of them behind their armor, but they were clearly different men at different times. There were discrepancies in size, posture, and movement. Some seemed apathetic, others amused, and one actively hostile. It was Hostile who came down the stairs, his face hidden, but the rage in his deep blue eyes gave him away.

Aiul pressed his head against the metal door and glared at the guard through the eye slit. "Release me, dog!" he shouted.

Hostile slammed a mailed palm into the door. Aiul jerked backward, teeth ajar from the impact. The guard chuckled darkly, which was more reaction than Aiul had seen from any of them before.

Wary, Aiul looked through the slit again, careful not to actually place his head on the metal. "Mei as my witness, I'll kill you for that some day!"

The guard laughed at this, but there was no humor in his eyes. "Why stop with Mei? Why not make a deal with the Dead God, eh?" He kicked the door, setting it ringing again. "You're going to need more than one god to get out of here, Traitor."

"I will!" Aiul roared, slamming his fists against the door from his own side. "I'll bargain with Elgar if it means I taste your blood!"

"The name's Salastin," the guard sneered. "For when you and your Dead God are ready." He turned and walked away, calling over his shoulder, "The Traitor lives!"

Aiul watched him go in blind fury. He pulled at the edges of the eye slit as if he might peel the metal back with his bare hands, howling his hatred through clenched teeth, the muscles in his arms standing out like cords. For long moments, he was transfixed, a demonic statue, teeth bared and a-grind. Then he heard a sharp report from his left jaw, and it was enough to bring him to his senses. The strange, familiar symbol flashed in his vision again, then faded.

Mei, I've cracked a tooth! This could get very bad for me indeed.

I would make a most excellent murderer. Rithard smiled at the irony of the thought, now that he had set his mind to just that. *But it is true. And I will get away with this.*

Planning was everything. So many fools killed on the spur of the moment, passionately, understandably. Rithard was rarely consulted on such cases, due to the ease of solving them. On the few occasions he had been, it was child's play to work out motives, means, opportunity, and point the authorities in the right direction.

Murder, in the end, was just another human behavior, albeit a forbidden one. Men killed because they were angry, because they were greedy, because they hated. Catching a murderer consisted largely of working out which of the three applied, and finding who fit the bill. Once one narrowed the list of possibles, the evidence was usually all too easy to find.

Not so, in this case. There were damned few who could even fathom Rithard's motivation. They would have to be clever enough to work out a masterful deception that had confounded even him for quite some time. How could anyone know he wanted her dead, when they have no idea what she had done?

Nothing much. She just engineered death and ruin on both sides of my family, with me likely included on the list of victims.

Rithard paused in the bedroom outside Maralena's bath. She was surely within, indulging her decadent tastes. He shook his head at the expense of the silk sheets, the polished, intricately carved headboard. Such vanity. It's a wonder she didn't just have it all made of gold and be done with it.

He removed a vial from his pocket and checked the contents. It held a rarely used drug, one that only he or Aiul would possibly recognize: a powerful sedative used for surgeries. In carefully measured doses, it brought temporary oblivion and paralysis of most muscles, a godsend for both patient and surgeon. A massive overdose, administered through the carafe of drinking water she kept by her bed, would lead to unconsciousness and heart failure in just a few minutes. It had no smell, no color, and no odd side effects beyond those he desired.

Were there risks? Certainly. He had come here unobserved, but he might be seen leaving, still. He had a clever lie, one that would pass even his own mother's keen sense of truth: Maralena had summoned him here, wanting information about Aiul's condition. There might be some suspicion, but without motive, it would pass. Maralena had plenty of enemies, some of them Meites.

Bookish, dispassionate Rithard would be forgotten in the storm of accusations.

And worst case, if he were caught, and she lived? The ultimate play would be to tell her exactly what he had intended, and why. Of course, he would also lay out in exacting detail what he had worked out about her machinations, and that he had written all of it down. Were he to suffer an 'accident', the document in question would end up in the hands of his good friend Caelwen, as well as his Matriarch Narelki and their family friend, Maranath Aswan.

He had every base covered. He opened the vial and was about to pour its contents into the carafe, then froze at the sound of the bath door opening.

Rithard almost dropped the vial in his shock. He quickly spun to face the newcomer, seeing only a vague figure within the cloud of steam that came rushing from the bath. *I'll strangle her. I've no choice, now. I can recover, if I have the will.*

"Oh, my," the newcomer tittered, the voice decidedly male. "What have we here?" The steam dissipated slowly to reveal a tall, sharp-featured man, draped in red and black robes. He flashed Rithard a razor smile and cocked his head in amusement.

Rithard's heart sank as he scrambled to find a believable lie. *Well, it would seem I am less competent at murder than I imagined. Still, it's damnably bad luck.* "We have similar, bad taste in women, I suppose."

The man snorted laughter. "You're standing there, pouring something into her water, and I'm supposed to believe you're her bed mate?" He shook his head, still laughing, and touched a finger to his lip in mirth. "A jilted lover, here for revenge, is that about the shape of it? Ridiculous." He laughed again, this time with a darker, malevolent undertone. "This is terribly embarrassing, friend, but it seems I may have eaten your lunch."

"What have you done?"

"The same thing you intended, I'd wager, only with panache. Really, poison? Longing for a part in a penny dreadful, are we?"

Rithard felt his jaw clench, but he offered the man only a placid, blank regard. "I'm afraid I don't know your name."

The man's demeanor shifted from humorous to threatening in an instant. Rithard felt himself begin to sweat, and knew full well it was not from nerves. The room was hot like a furnace now, in the space of moments. "Count that as a blessing. We could end this with neither of us knowing names, and both walking away alive, eh?"

"A Meite assassin," Rithard muttered, more to himself than as a reply. "Who could have predicted that?"

"Maralena, had she the sense to think things through." The Meite glared at Rithard. "Do you intend to be difficult about this?"

Rithard paused a moment, then slipped the vial back into his pocket. *I have what I wanted, it seems.* "I never saw you."

The Meite's smile beamed, and the room cooled in an instant. "Nor I you." With a wink and an impish grin, he turned to depart, then seemed to reconsider. He turned back, his nose wrinkled as if he smelled something foul. "Mei! I can't do it that way! Not when you've looked me in the eye. It would be pure cowardice." He locked eyes with Rithard and announced imperiously, "My name is Sadrik Tasinal."

Rithard maintained eye contact as he considered. "I am Healer Rithard of House Amrath," he answered after a moment.

Sadrik nodded in appreciation. "I know that name. You have courage, Rithard. Will you keep my secret, if I keep yours?"

"I will. I've no quarrel with you."

"Nor I, you. And now that I know what sort of man you are, we might even be friends someday."

Rithard nodded and said, "It is good to have friends."

Shirini stirred her soup again, smiling at the perfect silence in her kitchen. Young hens did indeed learn, it seemed. Not that it mattered much, in that the master and his lady 'friend' were making no effort at all to be discreet. They sat at Davron's table, cold fury so chilling the air between them that Shirini almost expected snow.

Davron glared across at the mystery woman, hands clenched into fists, his face dark with anger. "I will not ask again, witch! Where is it?"

Parala cringed as she mixed dough. Cyndi laid a heavy beef roast on the counter and hissed, "What's he talking about? I missed it in the larder!"

"Shh!" Shirini waved her spoon for silence.

Parala answered softly, "He thinks she's stolen his father's sword."

Cyndi's eyes widened in appreciation. "Did she?"

Shirini stirred her soup furiously and muttered, "If you'd shut up we might find out!"

Cyndi mimed a sewing motion on her lips, then reached for a tenderizing mallet. Shirini gave her a look that must have communicated exactly how stupid a thing that would be, because Cyndi changed course and reached for the salt and pepper instead.

Some young hens learn slower than others, I guess.

Other than rolling her eyes, the dark-haired woman (whom Shirini had named "The Bitch") did not respond, and Davron grew even more incensed. "Answer me!"

The Bitch fluttered her eyelashes in feigned shock. "How dare you accuse me of theft!"

"Oh, I doubt you're the thief," Davron replied. "You had someone else do your dirty work for you, no doubt. Isn't that how you Prosin weasels do things? Dead drops, cut-out agents, plausible deniability?"

Shirini and her two underlings stared back and forth at one another in shock. *The Bitch is House Prosin!*

The Prosin Bitch threw back her shoulders and inclined her head. "I work in information. I do favors for people, they tell me things. Other people do me favors and I tell them things. That doesn't make me a thief."

"You think me a fool, that I can't make the connection in timing? Really, Teretha, I expected a better lie than this."

In the kitchen, the two younger girls were bobbing and swaying in silent victory dances. Shirini tasted the soup, feeling very satisfied indeed. *Teretha Prosin. Now we know your name.*

Teretha looked genuinely offended at this. "*Really*, Davron," she sneered, mocking his tone. "Is there anyone you *haven't* pissed off these last few months?"

Davron dismissed her charge with a wave. "Do you have it or not?"

"I could acquire it, for a price. Provided *you* meet *my* price."

Davron's nostrils flared and his jaw bulged as he mulled this over. At last, he asked, "What are your terms, snake?"

"What do you think?" she shouted. "I want you to protect my son from this madness you've instigated!"

Davron darkened at this, but nodded, less an agreement than an acknowledgment. "There are no guarantees in such matters. I can only promise to do my best. And such things have a way of coming back if politics shift. It's the work of a lifetime. At what point have I done a good enough job to close the deal?"

"Fair enough. Then you will promise to do your best as long as you live. And you will give me another son, to insure against the possible loss of the one you have risked."

Davron burst into sincere laughter at this. "Shall I pull one from my pocket?"

Teretha rolled her eyes again, then pointed at Davron's crotch. "From your trousers, fool, or do you still not know how babies are made? You risked my son in Amrath. You will give me the heir to Noril. When he is born, I will return your father's blade. It will be his by rights anyway."

In the kitchen, Parala had both hands clamped over her mouth, eyes bulging, and Cyndi held up a fist in triumph. Shirini gave her an approving nod.

Davron, mortified, leapt to his feet, his face red with fury. "And what of my *wife*, witch?" His fist rose into the air as if it were not entirely under his control.

Teretha glanced at his threatening gesture and smiled, showing no sign of being intimidated. "Please. How will beating me help your position? It could only help mine."

"I should enjoy it, though!"

"You might enjoy my counteroffer as well, if you weren't so stubborn. You said you liked women." She grabbed his fist and brought it to her breast, Davron seeming helpless to resist her. His hand relaxed, then tightened again, kneading her flesh with relish. Teretha's voice was almost a purr as she said, "Here is a fine specimen, a comely one at that. Don't pretend it wouldn't please you."

Davron took a deep, shuddering breath and pulled his hand back, grabbing it with his other as if to restrain an unruly child. "What do you prove with this? That I'm a man? I'd be a liar to say I have no appetite for what you propose, but I will never betray my wife."

"Betray? You are an elder of Nihlos without issue. I doubt even your wife would count it as treachery if you were up front with her about your intentions. You needn't marry me. Just claim the child."

Davron looked her up and down, still restraining his offending hand as he considered. "A fine specimen, to be certain. But I am not fond of the taste of defeat."

"Then choose not to taste it as defeat. Choose to see it as a mutually beneficial and *pleasant* alliance." She reached again for his hand, drawing it toward her crotch, but Davron jerked it back as if he had been burned.

"Not here, not now. I must speak with my wife, first. I will not betray her."

Teretha smiled coyly and sipped her wine. "Of course."

In the kitchen, Shirini raised her eyebrows suggestively over a tin cup of port, and the other two sipped at theirs, barely stifling giggles. "This, young'uns, is how we cook."

In the end, it was neither the solitude nor the nightmares that broke Aiul's will. It was the shattered tooth. Such terrible nightmares plagued him, visions of Lara's body being stabbed over and over, his unborn child knowing the kiss of steel before it knew the sweet taste of air in its lungs, blood running from Kariana's blade. Sleep itself had become an enemy, one that stole upon him at his weakest moments and tormented him beyond the limits imposed by the reality of the waking world.

Ironically, he had found the tooth something of a comfort for a while. As the infection entered, he could taste the rot, and then came the throbbing. The pain drove the memories from his mind and held back sleep. But then it grew worse, and he could not sleep at all. At best, he dozed for a few minutes at a time before awaking to sheer misery again. His captors offered him no relief. Salastin took great joy in his agony, and told him to pray harder.

If he had only had the most basic of tools, just a simple knife or an awl, he could have extracted it, perhaps, but since his last outburst, they no longer even gave him eating utensils, just a metal bowl.

In a state akin to a living nightmare, Aiul lost track first of time, and then reality. He had moments of lucidity, but they came less frequently as the days and nights passed. It seemed to him that at times, he was back in the cell where he had watched Lara die, and at others he was here again, with Salastin pounding the door, asking if he had died and spared them both any more misery.

Aiul had gone beyond caring. As strong as his will had been, the passing months of deprivation and misery ate at him like acid, burned away his resolve until there was little left of him but a shell. He no longer prayed for salvation, merely death. It was not in him to take his own life, not with the pride and the lust for vengeance that raged within him, but he would have welcomed that burden be lifted from him by some merciful accident of injury or disease.

It will come soon enough. The infection will spread. I'm doomed. It will be a hard death, but the pain will eventually stop. That's all that matters, now. The realization was comforting.

It was then, as Aiul lay waiting for the end, drowning in despair and disorientation, that the voice first spoke to him.

It was no mortal sound that assaulted his ears. The words were horror shaped into words, meaning imposed upon a thousand screams, the dripping of blood, the scurry of hungry insects over corpses. His nightmares paled to insignificance compared to the fear that gripped him at its sound.

"How long will you suffer here, child?" it asked, only that. Then silence.

Aiul curled into a fetal position, gripped with a terror he could not explain. For long hours he lay, motionless, afraid even to move, scanning the dim corners of his cell, looking for the source of the voice. He tried to tell himself that it was simply a delusion brought on by a brain infection, but he could not quite convince himself that his rational explanation was the truth. At last, he fell into an exhausted sleep. The nightmares still played in his head, but they were weak things now. The images were the same, but whatever had chilled his soul with those few words had, it seemed, numbed his capacity for horror. The visions of Lara were just images now, meaningless against the backdrop of raw, primal fear he had experienced. Even the agony of his rotting tooth seemed dulled, grayed out, insignificant compared to the voice.

When he awoke, confused, trying to decide if he were truly awake or in a fever dream, the voice struck again, this time playing on all of his senses. The prickly, burning snap of the hangman's noose going taught, the reek of rotting flesh, the taste of ash and bitter poison, the stomach-twisting betrayal of a brother, all poured over and into him, a tide of corruption and depravity that threatened to drag his mind into its depths with its undertow.

"Blood calls for blood," said the voice.

Aiul screamed. He screamed again, and again, and again. He did not stop until at last Salastin burst in and beat him into uncon-sciousness.

There was no escaping into dreams, this time.

Aiul found himself on a barren plain that extended in all directions as far as he could see. Cold, gray light, its source invis-ible, filtered through dark clouds overhead, illuminating a scorched wasteland. There were no plants or animals, only dirt and rock, dust and wind, and all about, blackened areas where fire had scoured the surface of color. It was gray and lifeless, a world of ash.

He scanned the horizon, searching for something, anything

that might serve as a sign of life, but saw nothing but more of the same rubble.

He heard a laugh and felt his heart quicken as the fear filled him. It was the voice! He was certain of it! It was weaker, but it still chilled him to the depths of his soul. "Who are you?" he shouted to the gray sky, looking about frantically. "What do you want of me?"

"*You called to me,*" the voice answered. The words had the same strength as before, and he felt the terror rising in him again, the urge to scream and bury himself in the earth as the sensations of horror, grief, and madness bored into his soul.

"I can't bear it!" he cried out. "Leave me alone!"

"You called to me," the voice repeated, "And I am come."

Aiul covered his ears struggled to anchor himself against the storm. "Who are you?" he cried out again.

"*I have many names,*" the voice answered. "*Destroyer. Violator. Monster. Hater.* Elgar. *You called out to me, and I am come.*"

"No," he whispered, both a denial and a plea. "I didn't mean it. Please—"

"*Liar!*" The sensory assault was changed now. It was the sight of a trusted lover caught in bed with a best friend, the sound their sighs together, the burning of flame in the heart and mind. But it was the taste that made it bearable, the sweetness of standing with a boot on that former friend's neck as he grovels and begs for mercy that he knows can never come.

Aiul staggered and collapsed, overwhelmed, face down in the dirt, raising his arms above his head like a shield, desperate to block out the cacophony. He waited, cringing against more words, but the next sound he heard was the crunch of metal on gravel, right beside his head.

Slowly, trembling, he opened his eyes to see a steel boot standing inches from his face.

From Aiul's vantage point, the newcomer seemed ten feet tall.

Tiny death's heads, some graven into the armor's plates, others embossed and adorned with black gems for eye sockets, leered downward at him, mocking him with their mindless grins and empty stares. The mail he wore was blackened and scored, as if he had just walked from a battlefield. Fresh blood and gore streaked the surface of his armor, splattered from slain enemies. Dark, viscous liquid oozed from breaches in the mail, running into the eye sockets and between the grinning teeth of the skulls. He wore no helm, however, and that, in particular, tore at Aiul's mind.

The face looming above him was his own.

Aiul blinked rapidly, in shock, his mind reaching for denials, and finding purchase on minor details, at least. The eyes were not his own green, but instead pools of pure black, windows into a cold abyss, full of hate and malice that made his muscles tremble with weakness. The hair, too, was changed, not his dirty blonde, but a sickly, gray-white, the color of sun bleached bone. The wind whipped it about the doppelganger's head, strands of it striking toward the sunken, unblinking eyes and caressing high, ashen cheekbones like the hands of a lover.

"I am come," the figure said, this time in Aiul's own voice, rather than *the* voice. It, too, was subtly different, more sinister, cold, but again, close enough that it could not be construed as mere happenstance.

"What do you want of me?" Aiul whispered.

The figure cocked its head quizzically. "A meaningless question. What could one such as I seek from the likes of a wretch like you?"

"Then leave me," Aiul replied. Even the fear was gone now. His entire being had gone numb, overloaded, his mind unable to find a handhold to brace itself against the onslaught of madness. He rose to his feet and looked Elgar squarely in the eye. "Begone, Dead God."

Elgar laughed. "You would dismiss the Destroyer with a wave your hand? Truly, your arrogance is a marvel to behold! I have not seen its like in…eons."

"It's not arrogance. It's not even bravery."

"Yes," Elgar said. "The calm that comes when one understands that he is truly defeated." He spoke now in his own voice again, and Aiul was powerless to stop the sensations. He heard Lara's screams with a clarity that his own ears could never have matched. He tasted her blood on his own lips, felt the blade rend her flesh. And could he hear a small, high pitched cry, deep inside?

"*In such a moment, one might find true freedom, had he the will,*" Elgar continued. The images of Lara burned from Aiul's mind, washed away by new screams, cries that no longer tore at his soul but thrilled him like a powerful symphony. Nihlos was in flames, its people rushing about in random panic. He was drunk with the euphoria of unfettered, untiring, merciless hatred. His arms, swinging a huge, misshapen club, rose and fell, again and again, caving in the skulls of everyone about him, men, women, even children. A thousand faces shattered under his assault. Blood and gore flew at each strike, and it tasted sweet on his lips. The visions shot through him in brief flashes, an orgy of rage, a climax of vengeance, spiraling higher and higher until it seemed he would explode with joy.

He came to his senses to find himself on his knees, sobbing. Elgar's hand caressed his shoulders, like a parent might soothe an anguished child.

"Do you offer this to me?" Aiul choked.

"I do."

"And what is the price?" Aiul asked, certain that he knew the answer. "My soul?"

Elgar took Aiul's hands in his own and pulled him to his feet, but gave no answer. Instead, the Destroyer raised his hands to his own neck and removed his gorget. Elgar's throat had been ripped open, his head half severed from his body. Black, oily blood oozed and bubbled at the wound, as it might from a man who had bled out and was breathing his last.

"Such a victory, such a liberation as I would give you, is its own price," said the Destroyer.

"I don't understand," Aiul whispered.

Elgar raised a gauntleted hand to Aiul's throat. Spikes erupted along the fingers with a sharp, metallic sound. Elgar held them lightly against Aiul's throat, waiting, his black eyes gazing deeply into Aiul's own, the points of the spikes pricking Aiul's flesh. "Your mind is too small," Elgar whispered. "But your soul understands."

"Yes," Aiul answered.

Elgar tore out Aiul's throat.

House Noril had several prisons, some more secure than others. Given his choice of duty, Salastin would definitely have preferred the minimum security, in that it was just easier work, but for The Traitor, he was willing to suffer a little.

Aiul's rebellion had been a bitch of a night for both Noril and Luvox. They had all bled and choked and fought. When it was done, Salastin had been surprised and more than a little nervous to be summoned by Master Davron himself. He had done nothing heroic to merit a commendation, but he couldn't think of anything that would get him punished, either. *Unless I killed someone I ought not have in the chaos.* All sorts of mistakes happened in actual combat, often enough fatal. Quelling a riot was hardly precision work. Someone important could have managed to get mixed in with the rock-throwing commoners and gotten his head cracked in the confusion. That thought had eaten at Salastin's guts as he made his way to meet with his Patriarch.

In the end, it was nothing like he had feared. It was an altogether different sort of disaster. Davron had no reward or punishment for him, only grim news. Salastin's cousin was dead, cut down at the palace gates. Two friends he'd known since childhood had also perished in the fires and chaos of the undercity. They had all been good men doing their duty. The Traitor had killed them, as surely as if he had stuck a dagger in their chests.

When Davron approached him later with the chance of evening the score, Salastin leapt at the opportunity. That the Patriarch would invite a slave to do battle at his side, especially on a secure, black operation, was a tremendous honor. That alone would have swayed him, but the thought of avenging his cousin and friends was even stronger motivation.

Salastin had been volunteering for this gig since he and Davron had dragged The Traitor's stinking carcass into this cell, and he intended to be here for the duration.

That being said, guard duty was usually a crashing bore, and left a lot of time to fill. Salastin and five others, armed and armored, sat at a small, wooden table, cards in hand, tossing coins into the pot and daring one another to meet their challenges.

"Bastard," one growled at Salastin. "You're bluffing."

Salastin said nothing, inscrutable, giving no sign of his unbeatable hand. After a moment of tension, he raised an eyebrow, taunting his opponent. It was sweet, gulling him like this. There was more than a week's pay to take from his victim, and Salastin savored the kill. They stared at one another, tension mounting, when their stare down was broken by a mad cackle from one of the cells.

It was a small thing, but enough to end the brief duel. Salastin's mark broke eye contact and turned his cards face down.

Salastin could barely contain his fury as he raked in his winnings. The fool would have played on, but for the laughter.

He rose and strode down the stairs to Aiul's cell. On his way, he grabbed a truncheon from its place on the wall. He would make the Traitor pay for costing him coin. *That's the excuse, anyway. He's paying for everything else, too.*

Salastin inserted his key and turned it, then cursed. The lock wouldn't budge! He slammed the eye slit open and peered into the cell. Aiul stood gazing at floor, body shaking in silent laughter, his hands clutching at his ragged garment.

"I don't know what you've done to the lock," Salastin growled. "But it will be the worse for you when I get it open!" He slammed a boot into the steel door.

Aiul's laughter grew, deep and malevolent as he raised eyes of pure ebon toward his tormentor. "Your name is Salastin," he said, and stepped toward the door.

"Whatever game you're playing, you're going to suffer for it," Salastin spat.

"Suffer and die," Aiul agreed, bringing his own eyes to the slit.

From a distant corner of his mind, Aiul watched the horror unfold, not with his own eyes, but from a perspective outside himself entirely, as if he were a disembodied spirit. *Perhaps that is just what I am. I should be afraid, but I am not.*

He saw his right hand rise and slam against the cell door, the impact like a meteor falling from the heavens. The sounds of tortured metal, rending stone, and Salastin's cry of shock rang out through the cell block as the door exploded from its jamb, propelling the guard across the room and dashing him against the far wall in an explosion of blood and gore.

The other guards charged down the stairs, weapons in hand and ready for anything except what they actually found. The cell door slowly peeled itself from the wall with a wet, sickening squelch and crashed to the floor, revealing all that remained of Salastin: a shattered, bloody wreck, barely recognizable as human, slowly oozing down the wall. *He's just another bug crushed underfoot, now. As the rest of you are about to be, I think.*

They turned from the gruesome mess to gape at Aiul, or rather, Elgar wearing Aiul's flesh, as he emerged from the cell. He was gaunt and haggard from deprivation, his skin flushed a bright pink, his hair bone white. Steam rose from him as if he had just stepped from a hot bath. His grin seemed to nearly split his head, so wide was his expression of pure joy, a baring of fangs in abject hatred. Blood ran freely from his ears, eyes, and nose, staining his teeth.

Elgar spoke to them in The Dead God's voice, "*I am Monster,*" he said, the sound and emotion ripping through the building in a shock wave.

"*Ravager...*"

The guards trembled in their armor as he approached them, but they were frozen in place.

"*Destroyer!*" His voice thundered from the bowels of the prison, shook loose mortar from the stones, and rattled the streets of Nihlos above. Elgar reached out, seized two guards by their necks, and dashed their heads together, smashing their skulls in a shower of blood and gray matter. He punched a fist into the chest of a third, tore out his still-beating heart, and crushed it in his grip, spraying the walls and ceiling with even more blood.

The remaining two guards, still unable to even raise a hand in their own defense, stood trembling and silent as Elgar laughed, his voice tearing at their souls like a scourge.

Even in his disembodied state, Aiul found he had no stomach to watch further. He had hated Salastin and reveled in his just end, but Aiul did not even know these men. He had no eyes to close, but he could at least shift his focus away from what was to come.

He heard the sounds well enough, though, the snapping of bones and rending of flesh, a soft, wet sound like cloth being torn. *The true horror is their silence. They know what is happening to them. They can feel it, I'm certain. But they can't move, can't even scream. Mei, what have I done?*

More blood splattered against the wall, seemingly at random, but somehow accreting into an obscene pattern, a sigil of destruction and death. The gore bubbled and smoked like acid as it ate its way into the surface, burning into the stone an indelible mark of Elgar's passing — a crow picking at the eye socket of a grinning skull.

The Destroyer raised his hands above his head and closed his eyes, breathing in the scent of terror and death, then spoke a single word: "Rise."

The broken flesh of the guards answered his call, reassembling itself as best it could. Elgar's warriors rose to their feet, steady and fearless, dead hands taking up weapons once again, to follow him from the prison.

Aiul felt himself falling into blackness. *Perhaps this is the end.*

Then he knew nothing.

Kariana moaned with pleasure, her body writhing on silk sheets as her lover ground against her, her mind clouded by the drugs she had taken to heighten the experience. What was his name again? Oh, it hardly mattered, some lesser noble from House Veril. The drugs made it seem lovely, though it was still clearly artificial. A lover with skill was much preferable, but they were few and far between. Mr. Right-Now worked fine with certain enhancements.

Thoughts licked at the edges of her consciousness like annoying insects, gnats of reality intruding on her reverie. With effort, she managed to focus her attention and open her eyes slightly.

The door to her quarters was open, and a man stood at the foot of her bed, gesticulating, shouting…what? She eyed him momentarily, considered inviting him to join them, if only to shut him up, but something seemed odd about that notion.

Her lover rose and rolled off the side of the bed with surprising speed. Her senses returned suddenly, like the lifting of a veil, and with them, outrage at being interrupted. "Caelwen!"

Her bodyguard pointed a mailed finger at her lover, the expression on his face lethal. "You're done. Get out."

The lover glared back at him with as much dignity as a naked man with a raging erection could muster. "You don't order me, Caelwen Luvox!" Kariana couldn't help but titter at how he looked. When all of the passion was stripped away, men looked a bit silly, aroused and bouncing around like that.

Caelwen was not feeling merciful, it seemed. He swung his fist and sent the man crashing to the marble floor. Kariana had a moment of genuine empathy for him. She could certainly appreciate why he would be upset. Men always were when they didn't get to finish their business. And it was too bad, really it was, that he hadn't fallen on a pillow. There were so many scattered about. But when Caelwen followed up his blow by drawing his sword, things grew decidedly more serious in her mind. "Caelwen, what are you doing? Stop it!"

Caelwen ignored her and glared at the other man. He gestured toward the door with his blade. "Get your things and get out. *Now*! You can dress in the hallway if you like, but I'd advise you to just keep running!"

Nobility often came with a certain pride, a false, pretentious air. Kariana couldn't help but approve of Caelwen's graceful demonstration of true nobility and power. Her lover (what *was* his name?) hesitated a moment, as if testing his scrotum and finding it withdrawn into his body. He suddenly bent and began gathering his clothes quickly, like a chicken pecking at seeds. Well, at least that solved the problem of his not having finished, she supposed. Cold steel, cold shower, they were probably quite interchangeable.

As her lover scurried out, clothes clutched to his crotch, Kariana raised an eyebrow at her bodyguard. "Why, Caelwen, are you *jealous*? Did you come bursting in here to have me for yourself, perhaps?"

Caelwen was not amused. "Don't be ridiculous. Get dressed at once. We must flee!"

Kariana fetched her robe from the bed and shrugged into it. "Flee? Oh, no, the blood of Tasinal does not *flee*. You flee if you like. What will you be fleeing from, I wonder?"

Caelwen was losing his cool self-control, she could see. It happened so rarely. How lovely that she could be a part of it, even the cause of it! Everyone needed to feel human once in a while. He would ultimately thank her. She couldn't quite suppress a giggle, even though she knew there was something very wrong. Caelwen's expression, his eyes, both fairly sang of something terrible, but it was difficult to react as she ought. The drugs made everything seem less important.

"Aiul has escaped Davron's prison," Caelwen explained. "He's rounded up a small army and he's headed this way now."

In the space of a second, Kariana went from feeling fairly in control back to drowning in syrup. "What?" she stammered. It made no sense. Aiul was in the hospital.

"He's headed *here*!" Caelwen shouted. "We have to get you clear *now*!"

Kariana shook her head in a desperate attempt to clear the effects of the drugs. It helped a bit, but it still felt as if her brain were made of cotton. "Why doesn't someone stop him?" she mumbled. "Where are the guards?"

Caelwen's face grew dark with anger, his mask of self-control slipping and falling all the way to the ground. Kariana was fairly certain she could hear it clattering against the marble. He slammed a fist against the wall in frustration. "You mean *after* we account for several hundred dead on your account? We have fewer with every passing moment! Swords break on his skin! He kills men with a single blow, and the corpses rise up and follow him!" He seized her by the arm and jerked her toward the door. "Now, Empress, we'll be going, whether it's under your own power or under mine. I'll let you decide, if you do it quickly."

Kariana was, for once, speechless. She allowed herself to be pulled toward the door, confusion and fright vying for supremacy in her. What was Caelwen even saying? Aiul was *invulnerable*, and had an army of dead guards? It was madness. If it were anyone but Caelwen, she would think it was a joke. "I don't understand!"

"Survive now, understand later!"

Even as Caelwen spoke, a chill wind rushed in through the open doors. The dozens of candles guttered, and most failed, plunging the room into near darkness. An agonized scream of anguish and horror echoed from the corridor outside Kariana's quarters, followed by sudden and grim silence. *Well, I suppose he won't be telling me his name anytime soon, now.*

Caelwen stiffened and released her arm, moving to interpose himself between her and the doorway. "Stand behind me, Empress. Keep me always between you and him, and run the moment there is a path!"

Kariana had no idea what was going on, but she had her doubts as to whether Caelwen's plan to sacrifice himself would make any real difference. "I can talk to him. Make him see reason, maybe."

Caelwen laughed, a harsh, cruel sound. "That worked so well the last time, eh?"

Aiul entered the room alone, striding purposefully, ignoring Kariana and Caelwen as if he were unaware of them. The mere sight of him was enough to convince Kariana that Caelwen was absolutely right, there was no chance of reasoning with him, though not for the reasons Caelwen imagined.

That is not Aiul.

He was covered in blood, steam rising off him, and thin, starved practically. *Mei, look at his hair!* She felt her guts twist to see him like this, but it lasted only a moment. It *looked* like him, in a shallow way, but the movement, the bearing, everything that made a man who he was besides the flesh he wore, all of that was terribly, impossibly wrong.

He went directly to the wall behind Kariana's bed. Without any indication of effort or strain, he took hold of the brass bed's foot board, lifted it into the air with a single hand, and hurled the entire frame aside to expose the wall. The bed landed against the far wall with a tremendous crash. Somewhere, beneath the fear and buzz in her head, Kariana winced to see it crumple. That bed had a lot of memories for her.

Aiul moved to the center of the wall, made a fist, and punched a hole in the plaster. His arm sank in up to his elbow.

It took several moments before Kariana understood what he was doing, but when it at last penetrated, she found herself so choked she could barely strangle out words. "Stop!" *Oh, no. Mei, no not that!*

Caelwen gave her a quick, curious glance, his attention still focused on Aiul, but said nothing. It irked her, even through the numbness of the drugs. *Of course. I know nothing. Pay no attention to me.* Suddenly furious, she punched him hard in the back.

Her knuckles wailed on contact with his armor, but at least it got his attention. "We can't let him take the Eye!"

Caelwen looked at her as if she were mad. "I have *one* priority, here. It's time for you to run!"

Kariana's heart was pounding so hard she felt as if she might collapse. The drugs were gone. Even fear for her own skin was a dim thing. All she could remember were her father's words: "Inside this vault is the end of the world. It must stay there."

How can this happen on my watch? I don't want this job! I never did! "You're not supposed to know about it! *Nobody* is! We have to stop him! It's *my* duty, Caelwen! I need you to trust me!"

Caelwen turned and looked at her briefly, trying to keep Aiul in his sight as well. Her bodyguard seemed moved by whatever he saw on her face. *Yes, Caelwen, I really am scared now. And I don't understand it either. I just know what they told me.*

Caelwen's anger seemed to soften as he turned back toward Aiul. "Very well, Empress. I doubt we survive this, though."

"If we don't stop him, *nobody* survives!"

Caelwen flashed her a look of shocked admiration before focusing on his enemy once again. "Then may we both die well today."

"I don't know how to die well," Kariana muttered. "But I'll fake it, like I do everything else."

Aiul turned at the sound of her voice and smiled at her. Blood covered his face and soaked the rags he wore. "The blood of Tasinal, the city of nothing, as promised," he observed. He turned back to the wall, his arm still sunk in the wall nearly to his shoulder, and pulled. The plaster bulged, cracked, then exploded outward. Half of the wall collapsed and fell to the floor in a rain of debris as he hauled a strong box, the size of a small oven, through the hole. His fist had penetrated the metal box as well, and it hung like a hammer from his arm. Aiul peeled back the metal with casual ease, the squealing, rending sounds of tortured metal filling the room as he exposed and withdrew the contents: a thick silver chain, from which depended a single stone, a simple sphere of amber.

Why my watch? The question felt rhetorical, now. *Because mine is the weak one.* The pounding in her temples was a familiar thing now, the natural response to impotent rage and being stupid enough to act anyway. *I'm already dead, just like the South-landers. I wish I could remember the name of their god. He would be good to call on, now. I'll just have to hope he hears me anyway.*

"My brothers cannot help you, now," Aiul said absently as he held the necklace up, as if verifying it was genuine. Kariana saw Caelwen's attention on her waver, and took her chance. She lunged forward, a near-bestial cry on her lips. *Then I'll help myself, you fuck!*

Caelwen tried, but she had timed it well. She easily avoided his attempt to restrain her and charged Aiul like a bull, crashing her shoulder into his back at full speed, fully intending to knock him flat. To her shock, the impact felt more like she had run at a statue or a mighty oak, rather than a man made of flesh. Her charge ended with a sudden, painful, bone-jarring stop that rattled her teeth in her head and set her reeling. Kariana swayed briefly, then staggered backward, arms pinwheeling. Aiul took no notice of her as she fell to the floor in a heap, cracking her head soundly on the floor for good measure.

Kariana saw the rest of it through a red haze: Caelwen rushing forward; Aiul seizing him by the throat and holding him up like a rag doll. Caelwen kicked and swung his blade, but it was useless. Aiul plucked the weapon from his hand and tossed it aside.

I'd miss you, Caelwen, you stuffy old soldier, if we had any hope of surviving. Don't feel bad. We never had a chance. At least we tried.

But what was this? Aiul was talking to him. *Well, as victor, one sometimes needs to pontificate before killing, I suppose. It's only proper.* But that didn't seem to be what was going on. She could almost make out the words, but there was an annoying humming in her ears, the perfect match for her blurred vision and splitting headache.

Suddenly, she understood what was being said, though not so much through sound as from impact, as if she were being beaten with the words. She felt rats gnawing at her bones, and the scritch-scritch sounds of their teeth forming words in her mind: "And so the Eye of the Lion entered the world of men once more, to wake the Sleeper. This is how the world ends."

The assault of words tore into her mind, too much to withstand. As she watched Caelwen tossed aside like a child's toy, her vision faded from red to black.

CHAPTER 4
COMMANDOS

AHMED'S vision returned slowly, a gradual brightening from black to bloodshot orange. He opened his eyes, found himself staring directly into the sun, and quickly closed them again. He was warm now, and for a moment, it seemed all would be well. Then he tried to draw a breath.

His body seemed to move of its own accord. He hurled himself onto his stomach, the claws of a hundred cats scraping at his lungs and his belly. He heaved and vomited seawater onto the sand beneath him. It seemed as though he were filled with it.

Shouts erupted around him.

"Ahmed lives!"

"Liar! He is dead as stone, I saw him!"

"Dog! Come and see!"

A moment later, someone knelt beside him. Ahmed looked up briefly to see the sharp features of Brutus's second in command, Sandilianus. The soldier stared at him, eyes wide and searching. He placed a hand on Ahmed's back, then, apparently satisfied, said, "So he is. I am glad to be wrong."

Ahmed, fairly busy trying to breathe, simply nodded a response.

Another shout. "Ho! Tahir is dead!"

Ahmed, still unable to speak, managed to struggle to his feet as Sandilianus leapt up and called out in an incredulous shout, "What? How is he dead?"

Sandilianus charged toward where Tahir lay on the sand, surrounded by four of the crew. Ahmed lumbered after him, almost stumbling in the sand. One of the men was trying to explain what had happened. "He called to Ilaweh, and then he dropped dead."

Sandilianus looked doubtful. "*Tahir* called to *Ilaweh*? You are certain?"

The crewman nodded, and Sandilianus shook his head in wonder. "Then we can guess why he is dead. He must have hit his head, and hard. It's the only way Tahir would be talking to Ilaweh!"

The others murmured agreement, and Ahmed nodded too. It was easier than speaking his true thoughts. In his heart, Ahmed felt Sandilianus had the right of things the first time. *I was dead, and Tahir alive.* Somehow, Tahir had taken his place. *That is madness!*

Yet it felt true.

Perhaps I hit my head, too. He decided that it would be best to take stock of himself before doing much else, especially contemplating insane notions. Save for the water left in his lungs, which was still forcing itself from him every few moments in fits of ragged coughing, he was reasonably whole. His shoulder ached from where he had bashed it against the cabin door, and he had plenty of bruises and scrapes, but these were nothing. No broken bones, no gashes or anything requiring treatment, certainly.

With a start, he remembered Brutus's papers and the charge the man had lain on his shoulders. Ahmed reached inside his shirt and sighed his relief to find the oilcloth bag just where he had placed it. As he pulled it out to examine the contents, something hard and heavy fell from his shirt.

He bent to retrieve it and wiped sand from its surface. It was metal, and just large enough to fill his palm, covered in years of calcified accretions, but clearly artificial. It was difficult to see what it had once been, though it seemed it might have been a depiction of a face. There was a hint of a nose, a mouth, perhaps an eye. But it was strangely proportioned, if so.

The sword Brutus had given him had also, miraculously, made the journey to shore. Ahmed had stuck it in his belt, and Ilaweh had been kind. Ahmed used the point to carve at the deposits on the lump of metal, gradually clearing the surface as best he could with such a tool. He was pleased to see that his guess had been correct. It was a face, or at least half of one, the right side of a tiny lion's head, mouth open in a roar, empty eye socket staring at him in blind fury. Likely there had been a gem there, once. The other side was smooth and flat, with no sign that there had ever been a left side at all. *But why make half a lion head?*

Ahmed shrugged. *Might as well ask why it ended up in my shirt, for all the good it will do.* He held it in the sunlight, examining it, trying to work out what sort of metal it was. It shone like gold, but it was far too hard. Even steel did not scratch it.

He tucked the piece into a pocket. It would make a nice souvenir, a memoir he could show to his children someday, and tell them of the time he had sailed the ocean, been shipwrecked, and almost drowned. For now, he had other matters to attend. He checked the integrity of the papers in the oilskin pouch, then called out, "Everyone, assemble. I have orders given to me from Brutus before he perished."

Sandilianus shot him a curious look. "So you are in charge now, boy?"

Ahmed held up Brutus's sword. "If you wish to question it, I will show you who is a boy."

Sandilianus raised an eyebrow in surprise. "You would go steel with me over it?"

Ahmed considered a moment, then lowered the sword. "Fists."

Sandilianus nodded. "Wisdom is good in a leader. Swords or fists, I *would* destroy you like a child, but I would be wrong to do it. You are Yazid's second, and if what you say is true, Brutus's now as well."

"*If?* You accuse me of lying? I nearly died with him!"

Sandilianus waved a hand dismissively. "I accuse you of nothing, but you protest much. That makes me wonder." He cocked his head to one side and smiled, balling his hands into fists again, as if considering accepting the challenge after all. "What mission did Brutus give you?"

By now, most of the others had gathered around and were listening. Ahmed looked about, but saw little faith on their faces. Sandilianus was the key, then. He alone would determine how things went.

Ahmed raised the sword again, overhead, on display. "Brutus gave me his papers and this blade. The papers, he charged me to return to Prince Philip. The blade, he gave to me as my own."

"Why would he do that? Abandon his duty and turn it over to you?"

"He was trapped. The water was rising, and he did not want to drown. He told me to stop behaving like a woman and do what I had to do."

Sandilianus slapped his knees and laughed out loud. "You speak truth, then. Those are surely Brutus's words. "He raised his open hands for all to see, and the battle was over, the tension between them evaporating into nothing. "So that is why he gave you the sword, eh?"

"Aye."

Sandilianus nodded respectfully at this. "And how does it sit with you? Have you ever killed a man before?"

Ahmed found he could not quite meet Sandilianus's gaze, and his throat felt swollen and thick. "Bandits and such, yes. But never a man I knew. I did not like it. I did what I had to do."

Sandilianus rose to his feet. "Then Brutus chose well." He turned to the rest of the men and looked them over, daring them to defy him as he called out, "What are your orders, sir?"

Ahmed felt the mantle of leadership settle upon his shoulders as if it were a physical weight. It was heavier than he had expected, no longer theory, second guessing and 'if I were in charge' swaggering.

First, I must take stock of what I have. He counted the faces. Nineteen men, plus himself, an army of twenty. How many were Brutus's men, and how many were sailors? *It doesn't matter. They are all Xanthians.* "Our goals are simple. We must survive, and we must find a way home. We have neither supplies nor a ship. We have no money, and so we cannot pay. We have no friends, and so we cannot borrow. How many are armed?" Ahmed was pleased to see all but one arm raised high.

Sandilianus laughed out loud. "Bashir, you fool! How many times have I told you, better to lose your dick than your blade!"

Bashir grinned sheepishly. "Better to lose my blade than drown, eh? I had to hack through a wall to get out, and the blade stuck."

Ahmed laughed at this, remembering his own narrow escape. "Then you will use a club for now. There are plenty on this beach to be had." Laughter rippled through the men at this, and some of the men kicked at wreckage from the ship to accent the point. Sandilianus nodded in approval.

Ahmed waited for the chatter to die down before continuing. "We go to war of necessity, not enmity. We will harm no one unless we must, and we will take nothing we do not need. As soon as it is dark, I, Sandilianus, and three men of his choosing will scout. I saw lights from the sea last night. There is a town nearby. For now, we salvage everything we can from the wreckage. If we are to go to war, we will need shields. One for every man is the least I expect by nightfall. Ilaweh willing, we'll find some armor and javelins, too."

The men were eager to be led, once they had accepted a leader. They fell to the task of scavenging with gusto. By the time the sun hit the horizon, they not only had arms and armor for one and all, but had rounded up food for dinner and even recovered Bashir's lost sword. The most pleasant surprise, by far, was the discovery of a spyglass. Tahir had managed to salvage one, and they discovered it when they buried him in the sand.

Ahmed, Sandilianus, and their men set out shortly after dark. Ahmed was grateful indeed for Sandilianus's help. The man had a knack for direction. He found the small fishing town in an hour, whereas Ahmed might have taken the whole night. *This is another lesson of leading: you are not smarter than your men.*

Sandilianus pointed toward a small, sheltered beach a few miles in the distance. "There, I think. According to the natives a hundred leagues back, it is called Brust, though I wouldn't even trust that much. We paid them good coin, and the dogs led us onto a reef."

Ahmed raised an eyebrow at this. "Did they tell us to go north or south to avoid it?" he asked, though even as he spoke the question, he knew the answer.

"South," Sandilianus groused. "And that is what we did..." He trailed off a moment, started to speak, then paused with his mouth open, eyes wide with sudden understanding. "The old map...and the Nihlosians called us Southlanders! They reckon north and south opposite of the way we do, don't they?"

"Aye. I think it is so."

Sandilianus's face grew suddenly haggard and pained as the

realization sank in. "And we might have saved our brothers had we realized it."

Ahmed shook his head vehemently. "I think not. If you must blame someone, then blame Brutus."

Sandilianus scowled. "So we'll blame the dead man? Convenient."

"I told Brutus for months that Ilaweh wanted us to stay, but he would not hear of it. I warned him just last night that it was dangerous to defy Ilaweh's will, that it could turn ill for us if we forced him to intervene. Now we see the truth of it."

Sandilianus rubbed his eyes a moment and heaved a great sigh. "Do you speak truth, Ahmed, or do you say this just to make me feel less guilty?"

Ahmed laid a hand on his shoulder and squeezed. "I swear to you in the name of Ilaweh, it is true."

"Then let us do his will."

The moon shone bright in the night sky as Ahmed observed the town through the spyglass, he and his party lying low in the grass of a nearby hill. It was a village of a few hundred, perhaps a thousand, mostly primitive buildings of straw and mud, with some larger places built from rough-hewn logs, nothing terribly unusual. But the people! They were the same small, brown men he had seen in Aviar! "This should be easier than we thought. These people are cowards by nature."

Sandilianus looked at him with suspicion. "How could you know such a thing from looking?"

Ahmed considered letting the elder soldier think him possessed of uncanny power, but it would be disrespectful. "I have seen them before. The barbarians in Aviar capture them and sell them as slaves."

"Truly? And they do not fight?"

Ahmed shrugged, still scanning the town. "Some do. Most don't, though. We should be able to intimidate them well enough, which is good. I want no killing unless we must. Now, as to whether they have anything worth taking…"

He panned over the town, which was situated at a small harbor. Boats dotted the shore, most small, but Ahmed saw one larger vessel that might meet their needs. Ahmed passed the spyglass to Sandilianus to get his opinion.

Sandilianus grunted in surprise. "That is a Gruppenwalder ship!"

"The Gruppenwalder dogs are trading in slaves?"

Sandilianus continued looking through the spyglass. "The Gruppenwalders trade in everything, including ships. There is nothing to say the people who own it are *from* Gruppenwald." He continued watching for a bit, then sighed, his face grim. "There is no one fighting, and the men on deck are the same as the men in the streets."

"Perhaps they bought the ship."

"You are good of heart, Ahmed, but you are young and foolish."

Ahmed flinched, wounded to be spoken to in such a way. "I thought we were friends."

Sandilianus lowered the spyglass and, grinning, handed it back to Ahmed. "We are, which is why I call you a fool, as opposed to allowing you to remain one, eh?"

Ahmed scowled, but the logic was good. "What am I missing?"

"Maybe nothing. We'll know soon enough."

Ahmed grinned and waved a fist at Sandilianus. "Damn old men, always talking in riddles! Why will you not just tell me?"

Sandilianus offered him a sly smile. "I will tell you *why*. It is because it makes me seem very clever. That makes my men confident and loyal." He clapped a hand on Ahmed's shoulder and squeezed. "If I predict and I am wrong, I look a fool. But if there is anything amiss, even though it may be other than what I thought, then I will simply smile and let others draw their own conclusions."

Ahmed chuckled in amazement. "A fine lesson in leadership! Let us get the men and have this ship, then."

It was so easy, it was improper to call it an 'attack'. Under cover of darkness, they entered the sleeping town and made their way to the wharves. They met all of three men, single foot patrols, guards looking for thieves, not soldiers. Not a one offered resistance. One even volunteered his own rope so he could be tied instead of knocked out or killed. They obliged him, once they finally understood his words. The accent here was different than in Nihlos, the words even harder to follow until the ear grew accustomed to them.

Ahmed looked down the pier at their target, then cast Sandilianus a questioning glance. Sandilianus nodded. "It will do."

Ahmed was about to give the order to take the ship when he felt his focus shift to his left, as if an invisible hand were literally turning his head toward something it wanted him to see.

Sandilianus noticed the change. "What's wrong?" he whispered.

Ahmed peered into the dark to his left, trying to answer that very question. "I don't know. Something…" He trailed off, letting the hand in his mind guide him. He felt connection as a clicking sound in his mind. What was pitch black moments before took shape, black on black, dark, hooded figures skulking just beyond the wharf. He pointed at them. After a moment of squinting, Sandilianus nodded. He could see them as well. They were carrying something that looked for all the world like a corpse, but it was too dark to be certain. He spoke what he felt as a command in his soul: "I must go."

Sandilianus shot him a withering glare. "*Now*?"

Ahmed shrugged. "Ilaweh calls. Can you take the ship without me?"

Sandilianus rolled his eyes and answered in a sarcastic tone, "We'll manage somehow."

"Then do it. I will investigate. If I am not back in ten minutes, leave without me."

"That's time enough to kill a man, I suppose."

"Or three. Or be killed myself."

Sandilianus clapped him on the back. "Good luck."

"And you." Ahmed laid his right hand on his sword pommel and set off in the direction of the hooded figures as Sandilianus issued hand signals for the men to advance on the ship. The men raised shields, formed a phalanx, and began to advance down the pier.

Ahmed ran quickly down the wharf, his eyes tracking the nearly invisible group. There were three of them, and they were without doubt evil men. He could taste the wrongness of them on his tongue like spoiled milk. The thugs turned down an alley and faded into deeper darkness.

Ahmed moved quickly, but low and close to the wall, listening. It was always better to surprise the enemy than be surprised by him. He smiled as his prudence was rewarded by the sound of voices.

"We do it here," a deep, gravelly voice said. A moan, distinctly female, followed this pronouncement. *Not a corpse, then. A captive!* Ahmed seethed, but stayed his hand. *Successful warfare requires intelligence.*

He stepped forward as silently as possible. At the corner of the wall, he stopped and peered around. Three hooded figures, one large and with a great belly, two smaller, stood facing each other. On the ground between them lay a bound and gagged woman. The larger man was shoving a torch at the bound woman's face, taunting and laughing at her as she cringed away.

"Fool!" one of the smaller men said, his voice high-pitched and nervous. "What will you do if a guard comes?"

The third man slurred, "Then he will meet the same fate!" as if he were drunk or injured.

"It's madness!" Cautious complained. "We risk exposing the whole murder!"

The fat man slammed a meaty fist into Cautious's face, and the smaller man fell to the ground with a cry.

Slur gave a nasty chuckle. "Elgar does not reward cowards!"

Ahmed felt as if he had been struck by lightning at the sound of that name. The Dead God was the very definition of unspeakable evil, and his followers depraved madmen. If these men served him, they must surely die, and quickly, before they could carry out whatever vile plan they had hatched.

Ahmed heard someone cry out in the distance, "'Ware boarders!" Sandilianus had engaged the ship, then. Time was short.

With his left hand, Ahmed reached to his back and hooked his fingers into his shield grip. His right gripped Brutus's sword. *My sword now,* he reminded himself. He took a deep breath. *Ilaweh be with me.*

He sprang from behind the corner, sword and shield locking into battle positions as easily as a man might point his fingers. With a loud war cry, he charged them.

Fatso, wielding the torch, turned to meet him and got a sword through the throat for his stupidity. The torch fell to the ground and spun, sending shadows scurrying over the alley walls like a flock of crows. Slur jerked a dagger from his belt and came as well. Ahmed boggled at such stupidity, but went along with it. He slashed Slur's hand off at the wrist. It spiraled off into the darkness, still clutching the dagger, as Slur's face contorted in agony. Ahmed smashed the edge of his shield into Slur's ugly face for good measure. Blood and teeth flew as Slur slumped to the ground, unconscious.

Cautious stood blinking at Ahmed, his face a mask of confusion and shock. Ahmed cocked his head and stared at him in sheer amazement. "Shall I kill you too, fool?"

Cautious turned and bolted. Ahmed watched him until he was out of sight, wary of treachery, but the man seemed well and truly fled. Who could blame him?

Ahmed bent to the gagged and bound woman. She was frenzied, struggling against her bonds, her eyes fixed upon him and filled with raw terror. "You are safe now," he said softly, and took her hand to untie it.

Rather than calming, the woman redoubled her efforts to escape. She tore her hand free and began trying to snake away, at last settling for rolling.

"Fool! Hold still!" Ahmed grabbed her and forced her flat against the ground as he cut the rope binding her wrist. He immediately regretted it. The woman lashed out at him as he reached to remove her gag, raking his face with her nails.

He gave her a sharp slap to the face, trying to break her from her panic. "You are safe now!"

The woman stared at him in silence for a moment, then screamed, loud and long. "Demons! Black skinned demons!"

Ahmed struck her with a furious backhand and leapt to his feet, shame and fury boiling within him, "Barbarian bitch!" She fell over backward, blood flying from her lips, sobbing. Ahmed immediately felt guilty, even as he felt justified, but it mattered little. Sandilianus would even now be boarding the ship. Between the sounds of battle and this idiot's screams, the guards would surely descend en masse any moment.

"Demons!" the woman moaned as he rifled the corpses. One

had a few coins, but they were otherwise paupers. Ahmed considered the woman. Ilaweh wanted her saved. Fine, she was saved. There was nothing in the bargain about gratitude. Still, just a bit would have been nice.

"You can find your own way home. I'd hurry before Cautious finds his balls and comes back to finish his business!" He spat on the ground beside her, put away sword and shield, then turned and sprinted down the alley for the ship.

When he reached the foot of the pier, he was heartened to see that his men were indeed in command of the vessel, and it appeared there had been precious little bloodshed. A number of crewmen were being persuaded at sword-point to get on with the business of casting off. Ahmed saw only two bodies, and for all he knew, they may have simply been unconscious. All was good after all.

Shouts from behind him quickly shattered this illusion. He cast a look over his shoulder to see a large group of men heading toward him, at least fifty. Sandilianus ran to the bow and shouted "'Ware archers!"

As if queued, arrows zipped past Ahmed from behind, whizzing like bees, one coming close enough to graze his already injured cheek. Aboard the ship, his men brought their shields up and formed a wall, reserving their blades for the seamen. Ropes flew from bollards and sails billowed from their resting spots as curses and threats rang through the night.

Ahmed zig-zagged as he sprinted down the rickety pier toward the gangplank. It would do little against massed fire, but it might spoil any shots aimed specifically at him. He was more of an 'extra points' target for most of his run, but getting up the gangplank would take him into real danger. At that point, it would be in Ilaweh's hands.

He was ten yards from safety! The ship was moving now, the gap between the hull and the pier widening with every passing second. Ahmed cursed silently as the gangplank fell away into the water. It was too far. He would never make it. Another arrow whizzed past him and creased his left shoulder. He had to try.

There was no time even for a small prayer. He would just have to hope it was part of Ilaweh's plan. He reached the edge of the pier and leapt, but it was as he had known all along: too far to jump. His boot missed the deck by two feet, and he plummeted toward the dark water. He would surely die this time, either drowned or punctured by arrows. Ah, well. The mission would continue without him. He had done his part.

Sandilianus moved quickly. He hurled a weighted rope toward Ahmed with the precision of a marksman. It caught Ahmed in his chest, a hammer blow that knocked the breath from him, but he managed to hold on.

Arrows plunked into the wooden hull as Sandilianus hauled him up. Another thudded into the shield on his back. He was a tempting target now, indeed, helpless and hanging from a line, swinging just enough to add sport to shooting him in the head like a dog. As Sandilianus pulled him up toward the rail, several of his men lowered their shields over him as well. Ahmed breathed a sigh of relief as he heard the arrows thunk against the shield frames. His death had once again been forestalled by the grace of Ilaweh.

Sandilianus took his hand and hauled him over the railing. Ahmed sank to his knees, gasping with exhaustion. He waited there, just breathing, until they were beyond arrow range, then clambered to his feet and called out, "We are victorious!"

The men raised a great cheer and pounded their swords against their shields in celebration, all the while keeping a wary eye on their captive crew.

Ahmed nodded and smiled. It was enough for now.

CHAPTER 5
REPERCUSSIONS

IN the great hall of House Noril, Narelki was slowly losing the battle to retain her sanity. She might have surrendered to the strong urge to clamp her hands to her head and scream, save that every noble of consequence in Nihlos would see her doing it. *They're all here, all of the elders, packed into Davron's bloody arena.*

It was a hard place, full of echoes from the many conversations going on in tones ranging from banal humor to abject panic. The tiles on the floor were hard, dull slate. The chairs were hard wood, without cushions. The walls were hard granite, and where they had any decoration at all, they were adorned with weapons. *No one is intended to be comfortable here. That's the point, obviously.*

A small, raised speaking platform stood at the end of the room. Davron, flanked by Polus and Maklin, was explaining the details of "the recent crisis." Both Polus and Davron were armed, armored, and streaked with gore from black-booted feet to gray temples.

The details were nearly as crazy as the rumors. The dead rising and killing, and some invulnerable creature assaulting the empress? *Madness!* She looked toward Maranath, who stood with Ariano. Both seemed to be taking things very seriously, their faces grave and angry. She looked about for Prandil, at last spying him leaning against a wall, alone, his expression blank. She knew him well enough to understand what that meant: he was disturbed and brooding, and wanted no conversation.

Prandil looked up suddenly, making eye contact, sorrow in his gaze. He shook his head as if in sympathy, but for what she had no idea.

Enlightenment came quickly, however, from Davron. "According to Caelwen, the man who attacked them was Aiul Amrath."

Narelki whipped her head around to face the podium. "Impossible!"

Davron scowled at her. "Possible. And worse, the trail of gore leads directly back to my own prison, here."

"It's *impossible!*" Narelki nearly shrieked. "He's in the hospital right now! He hasn't left since he was a guest in your prison the last time! He hasn't been *able* to!"

The hall grew silent. Davron ground his teeth, searching for his next words, while Polus fidgeted with a buckle on his armor.

It was Maklin who spoke first. "It was Aiul, Narelki. Dozen's of witnesses saw him."

Narelki opened her mouth to argue more, when she felt a gentle hand on her shoulder. "We've been deceived," Maranath said softly. "Let's talk."

Narelki glared at Davron a moment longer, the truth slowly seeping into her consciousness, as Lucreta called out, "What about the ghouls? I hear they might be contagious!"

Maklin coughed, waving a hand while he caught his breath. "Ridiculous. They were no such thing. Reanimated flesh, yes, but automatons not ghouls. Nothing to fear there."

Lucreta stamped a foot on the floor. "Don't dismiss me like that, you old windbag! How do you know?"

"Because they were stabbing people with swords, not biting them! Who's the sorcerer here, you or me, hmm?"

Maranath guided Narelki to the rear of the crowd and into a quiet corner. "Wait a bit. Let them chatter until they get bored with the flashy parts. Then we'll see justice done."

Narelki nodded, struggling to control the rage burning within her. Across the room, she saw Ariano glaring back at her, a sufficiently chilling thing to cool her anger a bit. She nodded toward the old sorceress. "Will it ever pass?"

Maranath pursed his lips, then shook his head. "I think not. She calls you a traitor."

Narelki suppressed a shudder. "I thought as much. She's already dealt with Sadrina and Maralena. I suppose I'm next on the list."

"You're under my protection, and I've made that clear to her. And you're only half right, you know. She went after Sadrina." He pulled at his beard, as if considering his words very carefully. "Maralena was an entirely different matter."

Narelki didn't bother to hide her contempt for an obvious lie. "Please! I may no longer be a Meite, but I recognize the work!"

Maranath raised his hands in mock defense. "Now, now, I'm not *lying*, just leaving out some details that don't concern you."

Narelki gasped as she made the connection. "*You?*"

Maranath's face lit with genuine mirth at this. "Me? Oh, my dear, I'd not have left nearly so much intact as that, had I committed the deed."

"Who, then? You could at least tell me that much! Prandil?"

Maranath held up his hands again, this time in surrender. "It was Sadrik. That's all you'll hear from me on the matter, and that's only to convince you Ariano isn't running through the council looking for revenge."

Narelki gaped in amazement, for the moment forgetting even the problem that had brought her here. "Sadrik? Mei, I would never have thought—"

"Nor I." Maranath folded his arms across his chest and fixed her with a stern look. "That's all you get."

"Fair enough. It's some comfort, at least." She looked down at the floor, ashamed of what she was about to ask, but seeing no choice. "So Ariano calls me a traitor now. And you?"

Maranath's expression grew pained, then contemplative. "I will admit, I had similar thoughts when it happened. Thoughts I came to reconsider once we left the courtroom."

"Of course," Narelki said with a sneer. "How could you hold a grudge against such a pitiable creature?"

Maranath looked at her reproachfully for a moment, then shook his head in sadness "Your words, not mine." He gestured toward Ariano. "I'll want to speak with her about this mess with the hospital before we get started carving up Davron. If it comes to a fight, we'll all need our reasons at the forefront of our minds."

"I can't see why she would care. For all the show she's made over the years, she couldn't even be bothered to visit Aiul."

"Well, in all fairness, as it turns out, he wasn't there." He waved the issue aside. "She'll care because Davron's gone against us."

"Because he's gone against *you*," she corrected. There was more Narelki wanted to say, cutting remarks about Ariano's lack of concern, but in point of fact, Davron was her enemy, and she would prefer Ariano to be on her side of the fight. "What of Prandil and Maklin?"

"They are aware of the situation, and I'm sure they will stand with us if it comes to that."

"He must not get away with this, Maranath! Neither he nor Rithard!"

Maranath looked at her squarely, the light dancing in his

ancient eyes reminding her as always that he was nothing like the old man he seemed. "They won't. That you can count on."

Consciousness returned for Kariana with the grace and subtlety of an elephant stomping her skull, only backwards. There was blackness, then incredible pain in her head, and at last a sudden, blinding light. Her whole body ached like she'd been beaten, and not in a good way. In the distance, someone was shouting.

Her vision slowly focused, halos and blurs resolving into sharp images. Caelwen knelt beside her, gently shaking her shoulder. She noted with alarm that his armor was bloodied, as if he had been in combat recently. "Empress, you must wake!"

His tone. He's worried. This is very serious. Kariana shook her head as if to physically clear the cobwebs. "Where are we? What happened?"

Caelwen stood, towering over the small cot where she lay. "House Noril. We lived."

Kariana winced. "Are you sure? About me, I mean?" She moaned softly as she started to rise, then thought the better of it. "Hurts lots. I guess you're right."

Caelwen shook his head in disapproval. "This is no time for jokes. They'll come to blows soon. Nihlos needs its empress." He paused there, seeming to consider a moment, then added, "I need you, too."

Kariana pushed herself up to a sitting position and slung her legs over the edge of the cot. " What's going on, that you would say something like that? "

"It's bad. Aiul left a clear trail to follow, and it doesn't lead back to the hospital. It leads back to House Noril. The place has been redecorated with body parts, so it's hard to miss."

Kariana felt cold fear filling her innards. "Mei! *Noril*? Where *we* are right now?"

Caelwen nodded, his face grave. "The Meites are accusing Davron of being behind the plot. Everyone's blood is up. It's explosive."

Kariana considered this a moment. "I don't suppose leaving them to kill one another is an option? We've already fled once today. I'm warming to the idea of fleeing, really. I could get used to it."

Caelwen gave her a wry smile at this. "I think this is an enemy we ought engage."

For a moment, Kariana simply looked at him, for once in her life seeing the man, not the stone. His close cropped, blond hair; his chiseled, square features, haloed by the stubble of a long day; his troubled, gray eyes; he was not just handsome. He was...noble.

What struck her most though, was that he was *afraid*, and not for himself. "This isn't just duty, is it? It's personal."

Shame bloomed on Caelwen's face as he reluctantly nodded. "Healer Rithard of House Amrath is implicated, too. He's been lying to Narelki for months about Aiul. Both sides would like to see Rithard dead, if I read things correctly."

"Davron is behind this?"

Caelwen hesitated. "I think so. Not in the attack, but it looks to me as if he spirited Aiul away the night..." He paused again, then muttered, "The night you and Lara had your encounter."

"But *why*?"

Caelwen chuckled sadly. "For all of your worldliness in the bedroom, you are very sheltered about some things in life, aren't you?"

Kariana scowled, but let the comment stand. It was, after all, essentially true. "So educate me."

"For revenge, Empress. My old master has a long memory, and balls of steel. He's not like my father. He doesn't bend. The

Council's decision did not sit well with him. He made his own justice."

Kariana sighed, absorbing this. "And what is it you want from me?"

"I beg you, save Rithard. It is not just that he is my friend. He is a man of very special talents."

Kariana could not entirely suppress a smirk at this. "I never thought you of that persuasion."

Caelwen's face hardened into a scowl, but the corners of his mouth twitched in a hidden smile. "I should think if I were, I'd choose a lover of sturdier stock than Rithard. He's a slip of a man."

"Opposites attract."

"These are different talents," Caelwen answered in an acid tone, then grew more somber. "I've worked with him on some difficult cases. He knows how villains and madmen think. I have seen him reconstruct crime scenes in such detail that if I hadn't known better, I would have arrested him as the guilty party."

Kariana feigned a pout. "And here I thought I'd found out something interesting about you."

"I'm sorry to disappoint, but I'm of ordinary stock in such matters." His eyes pleaded to her. "Rithard is my friend. One of very few. I *know* him. If he's guilty, he must have reasons, and we ought to hear them. If you don't intervene, I think he won't survive the night."

You've saved me over and over. What's one more enemy compared to that? She held out a hand weakly, her arm feeling much heavier than usual. "Help me up. I'm still a little woozy, but I've done this kind of thing drunk before. It will be pretty much the same."

Holding Caelwen's arm for support, Kariana made her way to the great hall, occasionally stopping to rest. Only when she was within sight of the others did she muster her reserves and walk alone. *I can do this. It's only for a little while.*

Narelki and Davron stood near the speaking platform. Narelki, her face a mask of fury, was invading Davron Noril's personal space. She was lithe, but tall, and looked him in the eye without having to crane her neck overmuch. Kariana noted the gore on Polus and Davron's armor with a mixture of awe and disgust. *Hopefully, that was the zombies.* She looked slowly about the room, taking a headcount.

The Meites were gathered together, isolating themselves from the others, their faces grim. Even Maklin was focused and angry.

The rest of the elders milled about, clearly nervous, including the new Prosin leader, Balthar, a tall, lanky man with a face like a weasel. *I bet you'll think twice about crossing me, won't you?* They all looked at her expectantly as she entered the room, their expressions those of lost, frightened children searching for a parent. *Seriously? Suddenly I'm the savior instead of the stupid whore?*

Narelki waved a fist at Davron, who was shaking his head and laughing at her. "Laugh now, bastard! You won't get away with this!"

Davron dismissed her with a wave. "I told you before, I will handle the situation."

"Do you actually think I am that stupid, or are you fool enough to think you'll intimidate me?"

Davron's demeanor changed from amused to threatening in an instant. He hunched his shoulders as he leaned in toward Narelki, shouting, "It's not your place! You are neither authorized nor qualified to arrest *anyone*!"

"I am authorized to do what I damned well please with members of my own house! I have no intention of letting you send a band of thugs to silence him!"

Davron slowly but forcefully extended his hand and pushed

Narelki away, eliciting a screech of outrage from the Matriarch of House Amrath. The Meites watched in stony silence, and the rest of the elders again looked at Kariana with expectation and horror.

"I say you protest too much," Davron growled, withdrawing his hand and lowering it to his sword. "Rithard is indeed *your* creature. And does anyone here actually believe you didn't know your own son, even if his face *was* bandaged? I say you set this up yourself to shame my house." He turned to the crowd and swept a hand through the air. "Surely it doesn't escape anyone's notice that sorcery was the prime driver in this mess, and here we are, all of the sorcerers and has-beens united." He looked pointedly at the Meites before locking eyes with Narelki again. "If you think killing me will be as easy as it was with Maralena and Sadrina, think again."

Narelki's voice cracked as she shouted, "Are you *threatening* me?"

Davron's voice was cold like steel as he answered, "I am telling you point blank that I can clear this scabbard and take off your head before any of you can stop me. Make of that what you will, cunt."

Maranath bristled at this, and stepped forward. "You go too far, Davron! Shall you and I dance?"

Davron looked at Maranath with cold, calculating eyes. "You may frighten the rest of them, but I am no weak-willed fool. Steel has always been effective against your kind, if the man wielding it has the will."

"And you think you have it, eh, boy?"

Davron sneered at this, not backing down. "I *know* I do, *old man.*"

Polus, standing behind Davron and out of his field of vision, gave Kariana a sharp look and mouthed, "Do something, fool!" Kariana could almost feel the impact of his boot against her backside. *So, I have at least some temporary allies. Better than nothing.*

She gathered herself and shouted at the top of her lungs, "What is the meaning of this?"

The hall fell silent, as all eyes turned toward her. Davron regarded her with a look of utter contempt. "You forget yourself, Kariana. My home, my rules."

"If you'd prefer, I could call an emergency session. I'll see you all in the courtroom in, say, ten minutes? You can make it if you run."

Davron looked for a moment as if he would challenge her, then gave Maranath a final glare and stepped back, his hand still near his blade, but no longer clutching it. "Some other time, old man."

Maranath nodded to him and, with some effort to master himself, took a step back, too. "Any time you like, *child*."

Kariana looked at Davron, then Maranth, making certain they knew she was addressing them. "If you want to fight, you're welcome to petition me for formal permission to duel. You'll have it, as soon as this crisis is done. For now, I'm taking official charge of this mess."

Davron and Maranath both raised their right hands in surrender, gesturing they would keep their peace. But Narelki shook her head vehemently. "No! I will not have it!" She stepped forward and raised a fist to strike Davron, who regarded her with a cool, condescending glare.

Polus's voice thundered over the chatter that immediately erupted. "Meites! Will you restrain your people, or must I intervene?"

Prandil stepped forward and gently tugged at Narelki's arm. "Not now, my love. Come. This is not the hill to die on."

To Kariana it seemed that it was less Prandil's words that reached Narelki, than an almost imperceptible shake of the head from Ariano. At this, Narelki relaxed almost to the point of collapsing, and allowed herself to be towed aside at Prandil's gentle insistence.

Kariana felt a chill. Narelki was intimidating, to be certain, but Ariano was the only person in the room that Kariana genuinely feared. She breathed a sigh of relief to know she would not be facing off against the wicked crone. She had no illusions of the outcome. Narelki's submission made that all the more clear.

Kariana looked about at the elders, probing, trying to measure things. It seemed they were content to let her call the shots. "Caelwen, go and collect Healer Rithard."

Polus nodded his approval. "Bring him to the prison," he told his son. "I'll meet you there."

"No," Kariana said. "Bring him to me."

Rithard sat at his desk, studying two glass decanters. One, his medicinal liquor, stood open, nearly empty. The other contained the sedative that he had, ironically, intended for Maralena. *Perhaps we will put it to use, yet.*

He had consumed enough of the liquor to feel a strong buzzing in his head. Most of his muscles had stopped their annoying spasms sometime after the second drink, and after the third, his jaw and chest relaxed enough that he could breathe properly and think without distraction. The fourth and fifth had been nothing more than insurance against the return of his symptoms. As usual, he didn't feel his fear so much as emotion. It was physical, and temporarily alleviated.

What to do? Doubtless, his life was about to end, one way or another. If Davron didn't arrive shortly and skewer him, Narelki would surely have her thoughts on vengeance.

Rather than viewing his final moments as pointless, Rithard

believed they were crucial. There were decisions to be made, consequences to choose, and a confession that, depending on how he slanted it, might buy one or both of his problems a ticket on the same coach to Elgar that they had booked for him.

Death via the sedative would be painless and easy, and spare him considerable embarrassment. Taking his own life would be seen by many as absolution for his crimes. His name might not be quite so tarnished. But it hardly mattered. He had no children, and his only legacy was the one he had made catching villains. That would be hard to salvage, even with his suicide. They would call him a villain, even if they conceded he had found honor in the end. His own villainy would taint his accomplishments still, perhaps beyond salvage.

Likely, Davron would make his work quick. Narelki might draw things out. In any event, the information he had entrusted to his mother would certainly come out, and prove devastating to both houses. Taking his own life would remove any control he might exert on the process. And despite knowing her vengeance on him would be terrible, Rithard could not quite bring himself to hate Narelki. He *had* wronged her. It was to save his own life, but he had betrayed her, still. Did he perhaps have a duty to spare her the worst of it, if not to her, then to his own House?

Rithard was jarred from his musings by a loud banging on his door. He poured the last of his liquor into his glass and called out, "Come in. I've been expecting you."

The door opened quickly, filled by... someone. It took a moment for Rithard's vision to focus, but when it did, he very nearly poured his drink down the front of his shirt.

Caelwen stood before him, looking both furious and terribly sad. "I doubt that very much."

Rithard nodded and took a gulp from his glass. "As a matter of fact, I expected someone else." He ran a hand over his face in misery. "I seem to be slipping, lately. Missing things, getting blindsided."

Caelwen slowly shook his head in resignation. "You didn't miss anything. You just got lucky, and things fell another way. There was no predicting this." He closed the door and faced Rithard again, his hands clasped together in front of him as if he didn't trust them to keep their peace. "Tell me. Why?"

Rithard set his glass on the table, avoiding Caelwen's judgmental gaze. "It's nothing convoluted. I wanted to live. And I've done terrible things in that pursuit, now likely pointless." He buried his face in his hands and began to sob quietly. "I might have come to the same end with my integrity intact, if I'd had *your* courage."

Caelwen slammed a mailed fist on the desk, toppling the decanter of anesthetic. "Stop mewling! I need that wonderful mind of yours intact if we're to find a way out of this for you!"

Rithard lowered his hands and watched the decanter roll off the edge of the desk and shatter on the floor, scattering its contents in a rain of shards and droplets. "It seems you've helped me resolve a difficult decision," he muttered.

"Know this, Rithard. I begged a favor from the empress, and it was she who intervened and sent me here. I don't know what arrangement you may have made with House Noril, but if I know my old master at all, he has every intention of coming here to kill you, and the empress's orders be damned."

"Who do you think I was waiting for?"

"We need to go. *Now.* Use that damned brain of yours and find us a way to elude them!"

"Then we are doomed." He gestured toward the empty bottle of liquor. "I've turned it off for the evening. I didn't see having the opportunity to make use of it again, really."

Caelwen snatched up the bottle and hurled it against the wall.

Rithard felt a shard of glass prick his cheek, but made no complaint, nor move to rise.

"Damn you, I'm doing this with or without your cooperation!" Too quickly for Rithard to follow, Caelwen moved in to grab him. Rithard felt himself hurled into the air, and came down hard enough on Caelwen's mailed shoulder to knock the wind from his lungs. He wheezed in protest, but it was useless. He was in no shape to aid or resist.

"Keep quiet! I'm saving your life, damn you!"

Caelwen had set Rithard on his own two feet once they'd navigated the stairs. The drunken fool was weaving badly, but at least he was quick enough about it. Caelwen slammed open the front door of the hospital and froze. "Mei." *Thirty seconds more. That's all I needed, but it's not to be.*

Fifteen cobblestone stairs below, Davron and his contingent of men were just arriving. Caelwen counted six armed men in addition to his old master. They quickly spread into a wedge, Davron at the point, but drew no weapons.

"Stay here," Caelwen told Rithard. "You're like as not to fall down the stairs and break your neck, and I'm no fan of irony."

Rithard nodded his compliance, though Caelwen had his doubts how long Rithard's promise would last, with no one here to mind him. *Best to get this done quickly, then.*

As Caelwen jogged down the stairs to meet his harriers, Davron snapped a salute, and Caelwen returned it out of reflex.

"Caelwen, be a good lad and surrender your prisoner. Let's not make this difficult."

This was no good. Everything Caelwen knew about fighting, he had learned from the man who now stood against him. "That wasn't the agreement."

"I made no agreement. Tasinalta can issue all the commands she wants, but without our support, they're farts in the wind." Davron lowered his hand to his sword hilt, still not taking hold of it, but communicating his clear intent. "Surrender my prisoner."

Caelwen answered him through clenched teeth, "You know I can't do that."

Davron had the look of having eaten something unpleasant. "Honor, eh?"

Caelwen nodded. "You're the one who taught me that silly notion."

"If I'd known I might have to kill you over it, I might not have." Davron heaved a great sigh. "Don't be stupid. This will kill your father."

"This isn't about my father. It's about my duty. And yours."

Davron pointed an accusing finger at Caelwen, his face showing real anger. "I say this *is* my duty, boy, and yours is to stand aside! Who are you to say otherwise?"

Caelwen squared his shoulders and put his hand on his sword's grip. "A man with conviction and a blade."

Davron stood silent, taking the measure of the situation. At last, he drew his own blade in a fluid motion. "You learned well, Caelwen. You were my best student."

As Davron advanced, his men drew their own weapons and advanced with him.

Caelwen grimaced. "There's no honor in this."

Davron turned a chilling gaze toward his men, and they hurriedly sheathed their weapons. "It seems some of my own blood could learn a lesson from you," he said darkly. "If I die here, Caelwen is to proceed unmolested. Am I understood?"

As a group, and with considerable embarrassment, Davron's men nodded and stepped back.

Rithard cleared his throat and stepped forward. "This will not be necessary," he said in only slightly slurred speech. "I'll go with Davron."

Caelwen glared at him. "I told you to stay put! You're lucky you didn't kill yourself on the stairs!"

Davron laughed at this. "That would have been unfortunate all around."

Caelwen found Davron's tone odd. It should have been mocking, but he seemed sincere, even angry that Rithard might be injured. He put the thought aside. This was no time for second guessing. "You're too drunk to make that decision, Rithard, and in any event, it's not your choice. My orders are to deliver you to the empress. I mean to fulfill those orders."

Davron pointed to the ground with his sword. "Sit, coward. Men are speaking."

Rithard seemed to have found some courage in his drink however. He stood on wobbly legs and declared, "A man is speaking now. I've enough on my conscience. I won't have this as well."

Davron barked laughter. "Found your balls in a bottle, eh? Well, then, I will address you on those terms. Clearly, you are ignorant, even if you have learned to be brave. A challenge has been issued and accepted. It is not your place to interfere."

"I'm making it my place! I have conviction, too! This is senseless! I surrender to you!"

Davron sighed and shook his head. "You have no say. I am willing to settle this with personal combat, if that is Caelwen's choice, but if you interfere, I will rescind my offer. You know Caelwen well. That will likely end in his death. Now show some respect and be silent."

Rithard looked at Caelwen, his clouded, guilty eyes asking if this was truly Caelwen's will. Caelwen gave Rithard a quick nod. "Thank you. You are a true friend, but as he says, this is not your choice."

Looking miserable, Rithard bowed his head and stepped back, folding his arms against his chest and staring at the ground, clearly unconvinced, but at least accepting that the game between Davron and Caelwen had to be played out now.

Davron eyed Rithard a moment longer, then nodded his approval. "Well done. Drunk you may be, but I charge you as our referee. Let no dishonorable move go uncalled." He turned back to Caelwen and nodded. "So many times I've said this, but I never expected to do so in such circumstances. Let us begin." He slipped into a fighting stance, and Caelwen did likewise.

Their swords arced and clashed against one another. There was strength behind Davron's blows that Caelwen had never felt in training. His former master was almost superhuman in his speed and power. Every blow Caelwen blocked rattled his bones.

"Yes!" Davron cried, and slashed at Caelwen with such speed and fury that Caelwen could barely interpose his own blade in time. The force of the blow left his arm numb and battered his own sword aside. Davron's followup opened a gaping hole in Caelwen's chestpiece. "Do you feel it, boy? *Real power!*"

Caelwen staggered briefly, then pressed back with a battle cry, raining blow after blow at Davron, but his master was blindingly fast, his stamina terrifying. Even as Davron stepped back, stoically weathering Caelwen's flurry, giving ground, Caelwen knew Davron was still fully in control of the fight.

Davron smashed Caelwen's blade aside again and lunged forward with his elbow, sending Calwen sprawling. "Now you see!" Davron cried. "Now you understand why I have no fear of Maranath and his ilk, eh!" He paused, waiting for Caelwen to regain his feet. "But there is one thing you do not see yet, boy."

Caelwen struggled to stand as quickly a possible to get his blade up, panting, finding it difficult to force his legs to obey. Davron waited, sword extended, giving him time. Caelwen brought his own weapon to bear again. "And what is that?"

"You shouldn't either." Davron held his blade out, but made no move to strike. "You should fear *me*. Will you not yield? I beg you, for your father's sake."

Caelwen had never been the sort who could lie to himself. He was tired, dreadfully so, and Davron seemed to have a limitless reserve of stamina. Older or not, Davron was still far and away his better. But to give in now would betray everything Caelwen had ever stood for, most of it taught to him by the very man who was about to take his life. *I would rather die as I lived than throw that away.* "You're going to have to kill me, Master."

Davron's face twisted with rage. "Fool!" he roared. "Why will you make me do this? *Why?*"

Caelwen offered a sad smile. "I am the man you made me. How would you or my father remember me if I crumbled now?" He held his blade up in a salute, and Davron returned it.

"It was an honor to train such as you." Davron slashed the air with his blade and struck a fighting stance again. "One last game, then."

Caelwen nodded and brought his own blade to bear. "Tell my father I died well."

Davron nodded and came on like a hurricane, an irresistible force of nature. Sparks flew from their blades as they slashed and parried, but each blow felt to Caelwen like a bolt from the heavens. He gave up any hope of offense, and focused on blocking, but he had nothing left. His hands and arms were numb, his breath ragged and bursting from his chest as he struggled against the inevitable.

"Fight!" Davron bellowed. *"Fight,* damn you, if you would have me say you died well!" The blows kept coming, perhaps not so hard or fast as before, but relative to Caelwen's ability to stop them, they were crushing. Davron was simply too strong, too fast, too skilled. Caelwen cursed himself as he blocked a blow and felt his sword ripped from his hand by the force of the impact.

Something hit his head hard, and his vision burst into a million stars, a brilliant flash of light filling his mind, driving everything else out, even pain. As he sank into darkness, the light fading to black, his last thought echoed his last words.

Tell my father I died well.

CHAPTER 6
KNIGHT OF FEAR

LOGRUS tugged at the reins of his horse, directing the creature seemingly at random as he scanned the rolling hills searching for anything that seemed familiar, that matched the vision he had been given the night before. The task seemed hopeless. Skeletal trees and a blanket of snow conspired to hide landmarks, to smooth over differences of terrain that might otherwise make for contrast. A less skilled man might have ended up wandering in circles, but Logrus was an accomplished tracker. It was one skill among many that he had acquired by sheer need, rather than tutoring. Surviving twenty years or more as a fugitive required a man to learn much, or perish, and Logrus was not the sort of man to lie down and die.

He pulled at his beard as he searched for signs of passage or recognizable landmarks. Steam poured from his nose in wisps, and from his horse's flaring nostrils in great gouts. Tracker or no, this might well be an impossible task for him alone.

In the distance, crouched on the horizon, lurked Nihlos, the city of the 'demon men', an ancient, cunning wolf poised to strike at its prey. The walls of the city were an arrogant sneer; its tall, looming towers were covetous, grasping talons that would pull down the moon and stars had they the reach. The city's ever present cloud cover huddled over its shoulders like a gray cloak, modulating the weather and warding against the snow, even as it shrouded the machinations of the city from the eyes of outsiders.

Logrus was aware that he was in some danger by coming so close to the city. Certainly, the Nihlosians were hostile to anyone not of their blood, regarding all others as either enemies or cattle. Still, he had little choice, and at any rate, he was not as afraid as some might have been. He had killed a few Nihlosians in the past, out of necessity, and had been no more impressed by them than by any other man he had fought. They were tall, and had good reach, but they were flimsy. Nevertheless, he took a moment to check the short, curved blades he carried, one on each hip. He had secured them well, but repetition and double checking were habit with him, as natural as breathing.

From Nihlos, he knew, his quarry would have traveled due west, toward the setting sun. But from what gate, and how far? Logrus had no way of knowing, and time was of the essence!

It was, he realized, the wrong way of thinking. He was forgetting, as he often did, his faith, and reverting to his old ways. It was indeed a time of need, and clearly one in which his skills were not sufficient. Still, success was necessary, and providence would come. When opportunity presented itself, he would be prepared, and he would act, knowing that he could not fail, would not be *permitted* to fail.

He would have to get closer to the city, and the horse would be a hindrance. He tethered the creature in a small copse of trees, where it would have at least some shelter from the cold. As for himself, the cold was irrelevant, and had been since the change. It was as unpleasant as ever to be half frozen, but it did him no real harm. He set off on foot, pushing through the knee-high snow.

Parasin hated the snow almost as much as he hated dealing with prisoners. To be saddled with both at the same time was nigh intolerable, and worse, it was a fool's errand. How were he and a handful of drunks and thieves ever supposed to locate The Traitor's corpse in the midst of this miserable, icy sea? It was worse than a needle in a haystack. At least a haystack was *warm*. And for that matter, who was to say The Traitor was here at all? Rumor had it that swords had shattered against his skin. Why would this horrid wet slush be the end of him where steel had failed?

Parasin noticed one of the prisoners had stopped beating the snow and was crouched down, shivering. The guard smiled, pleased to have opportunity to inflict a little misery on someone else for a change. He had no idea what the prisoner's name might be, nor did he care. Names were for humans, not animals.

"You there!" he shouted as he slogged through the snowdrifts, but the prisoner gave no indication that he heard. Parasin booted him in the small of his back, expecting a cry of pain, but the prisoner made no sound. He simply rolled over into the snow, still shivering, and fell on his side. Parasin gasped as he saw the man's face.

The eyes were open so wide as to be almost comical, and his mouth gaped in an unvoiced scream. It was as if, at the absolute height of his terror, he had been paralyzed, frozen somehow.

Parasin felt the hair on the back of his neck begin to rise, and he drew his sword as he surveyed the scene. The prisoner had been crouched in front of a snow covered stump, but nothing else seemed out of place. He prodded gently at the stump with his blade, and gasped as he saw what appeared to be cloth beneath the snow. It must be the Traitor! At last! And none too soon, he thought. Whatever had frightened the prisoner, Parasin wanted no part of it, anymore than he wanted the snow or the prisoners. Now he could be done with all three!

As he bent to brush snow from his prize, a hand, its flesh putrid and rotting, its nails sharp like talons, struck at him from the depths of the heap and buried itself in his throat. He saw his own blood spraying upon the snow like a fountain as the thing emerged from the snow. It was man shaped, and even wore a cloak, but it was skinless, rotting, and skeletal, its dead eyes shining with hateful purpose as it regarded him. The other hand struck him, this one penetrating his heart. Within moments, darkness overwhelmed even the pain and fear, and then there was nothing for Parasin.

Logrus paid no attention to the prisoners as they fled, screaming in terror. He needed to move quickly, before more guards came. It was true, he could not fail, but still, it was best not to test that theory. Faith required honest effort, as well as conviction.

Logrus regarded the prisoner on the ground with an almost amused curiosity. It was a rare reaction, but one that he had seen before. What had the poor wretch seen, he wondered? Some minds, when touched by his gift, could conjure horrors so profound that their creators could not endure them. He considered a moment, unwilling to kill for no reason, but decided it would be merciful. With a single, practiced motion, Logrus ran the curved blade across the prisoner's throat and opened it to the air. Warm blood erupted over his hands and jetted into the snow, steaming, but still the man gave no indication that he was even aware of his fate.

Logrus cleaned his blades and his hands in the snow, replaced his weapons at his belt, then turned to the guard's corpse. He extended his hand, palm down fingers splayed, over the body, and held them there as he gathered his thoughts and his will.

It was difficult to use, this gift, and Logrus found it distasteful, but it was also the most direct means of getting the information he needed. He turned his mind toward the events in his life that engendered the appropriate emotion, the occurrences that connected him to the source. There were many, but one stood out amongst all the rest, the sight of his mother's cold, dead eyes staring up from her pillow, the pain and fear clouded but still visible, the dark, finger-shaped bruises on her neck fairly shouting of her murder. He ground his teeth at the memory, now twenty years old if a day, yet still as fresh in his mind. It cut him like glass, and his soul seared with hatred at the injustice.

"Rise, flesh, and remember," he commanded, keeping the image of his dead mother in his mind's eye. He jerked his fingers upward, as if controlling a marionette. The corpse played along, jerking as if it were attached to strings, then slowly rose to its feet, fresh blood running from its wounds.

"What have you done to me?" it croaked.

"Be silent, flesh!" Logrus commanded. "You must obey me. You will only speak when spoken to."

The zombie moaned softly, trying to cry out, struggling against the dark power that compelled it, to no avail.

"You sought the prisoner who fled this city, yes?" Logrus asked

The zombie nodded.

"Do you know the route he took from the city? By which gate he fled?"

Again, the zombie nodded.

"Speak now and tell me."

"The third gate on the south side," the zombie rasped.

"And due west from there, yes?"

"Yes."

"Then I am done with you. Speak no more. Return to the city and attack your brethren until you are destroyed."

The zombie moaned in protest, but lurched off toward the city nonetheless. Logrus watched it go with some level of sympathy. It was one thing to command dead flesh into service, but quite another to have it retain its memories. Still, it had been necessary, and there was no kinder thing to do for the creature than see it destroyed. Now, its second death could serve as a distraction to draw attention from him, as well. Logrus nodded in satisfaction at the economy of the situation as he returned to his horse.

With the correct origin and orientation, Logrus had little trouble locating landmarks that matched those from his vision. There was the group of bushes that reminded him of a group of old women doing laundry, a ditch like a bowl, and a bend in the creek where it looped back on itself, creating a small peninsula some fifty yards long. There, in the center, beneath a canopy of evergreens, he would find his target.

Logrus pushed through the low hanging branches, noting with satisfaction the scuff marks on the ground and the telltale breakage of needles. It was indeed warmer here, warm enough for a man to survive the weather, for a while at least. Ahead, he saw a darker shape on the straw-covered ground.

The stranger was tall and lanky, and lay splayed, face down, his limbs at odd angles, another marionette whose strings had been cut. In truth, Logrus mused, that was probably a very apt comparison. Logrus knelt and brushed aside the man's long, bone-white hair, and pressed a finger to the stranger's neck. There was a pulse, but it was weak and reedy. He had arrived none too soon.

Logrus rolled the man over on his back, and suppressed a gasp of surprise, settling for raising his eyebrows. It was a more quiet gesture, and thus safer. There was a great deal of blood on the man's face, but it did not hide the pallor of his skin, the gentle slope of his eyes, the high cheekbones, the thin lips that seemed to curl into a sneer even while the man slept. He was Nihlosian!

"You are fortunate that I am sent to help you," Logrus said.

He poured water from his flask onto a cloth, and set to cleaning the blood from the man's face. "Otherwise, I think I would kill you on general principles." Logrus examined the man further, assuring himself that there were no surprises, no wounds that would prevent moving him, then scoffed at the notion. Of course there would be no wounds. It was fever, exhaustion, dehydration, and shock, just as it had been with every other knight who had survived the transformation.

With a grunt, he hefted the man over his shoulder and struggled to his feet.

"A Nihlosian," he chuckled to himself, shaking his head in amusement.

For Aiul, life ended briefly, in a downward spiral of dizziness and confusion. It resumed with a jarring impact. The red, jagged thing flashed in his mind, brilliant, then faded.

Bloodshot eyes snapped open to blackness. Someone moaned softly in the darkness, a cracked, damned sort of half whisper, half wail. It continued, intermittently, for several minutes as his head swam with confusion and dizziness, until at last he realized that it was coming from *him*. Annoyed by the sound, he struggled to end it, and force meaning upon the random workings of his vocal chords.

Time passed, how much, Aiul could not say. From time to time, a slave came and administered medicine or ran a cool, wet cloth over his fevered body. Confused as he was, Aiul was certain he hated the slave. He was a cruel-faced man, with a dark, pointed beard and hard, smoldering eyes, and he had about him a fearful air of purpose. Worse, he was ghostly, appearing from nowhere in the darkness to loom above Aiul like some hungry spirit, an angel of death who, for the nonce, chose to spare Aiul from the abyss.

There would be a high price later for such mercy, Aiul was certain.

"Leave me," he whispered at the spirit slave, and struggled vainly to push the cool cloth away, but the creature was strong, irresistible. "Let me burn, damn you."

"Rest," the slave admonished, as it ministered to him.

"Too much pain," Aiul moaned. "Let me go to her. Please, let me go."

"It is not my decision," the spirit told him. "It was yours, and you have made it. Now rest."

Aiul sank into the darkness again, defeated, and dreamed a pleasant dream of Nihlos burning.

"Slave!" Aiul shouted. "Come at once!"

He had no idea where he was, nor how he had come there. But there had been a slave, he was certain of it, and he would have an explanation soon enough.

He had wakened only moments before to bright sunlight streaming in from the room's single window. For that small moment, in the confusing semi-amnesia of half sleep, he had drawn a few, precious breaths of pure joy, untainted by the bitter taste of failure, loss, and pain. How long had it been since he had seen the sun, or tasted air not steaming with the scent of filth and decay? How long since the damnable *agony* of his tooth had been silent?

But as he had come to accept, happiness was, for him, something to be stolen, never owned. All too soon, the memories returned, and he was once more what he had become over the last months, a damned thing kept alive merely as a source of amusement.

As he waited for the slave, he struggled to make sense of

things, desperate to find a sense of continuity, to fill the missing time. And yet, it wasn't *missing*, not precisely. There were hazy, indistinct memories of blood and screaming, warm and pleasant rather than fearful. They were not quite his own, he knew, but somehow, he had been there, was allowed to share them. And there was a brief glimpse of a concept beyond his ability to grasp, a hatred so intense that his mind could not appreciate its full expanse. Like a cube drawn on a sheet of paper, it was reduced in his mind to a mere projection of its true nature, and even that was enough to overwhelm him if he focused on it. With some difficulty, he pushed the image aside and tried to concentrate on his location. He needed concrete facts, not the conjurations of a fevered brain.

"Slave!" he shouted again, annoyed now. "Damn you, answer!"

His sick bed was a sturdy, roughhewn construct that filled most of the small room it occupied. The room was part of a larger building that was, apparently, made from whole logs. The technique was unusual to him, but certainly it seemed to hold the heat well enough. Assuming, he considered, that the seasons had not changed during his madness.

He was naked, save for a pendant on a silver chain that hung about his neck. It was unremarkable, a simple marble of amber, and meant nothing to him. Likely, he thought, it was some primitive charm meant to help the healing process. Or, just perhaps, it was a true charm. His recent experiences had been bizarre enough that he could believe he was in the hands of a sorcerer, and difficult enough that he decided not to risk removing it just yet.

He had just begun to look about for something to clothe himself, when the slave at last bothered to answer his call.

"So you've come through it," the man observed, a wry smile on his lips. As the newcomer leaned casually against the door frame, a bundle of cloth in his arms, his eyes seeming simultaneously cold and amused, Aiul suppressed a shudder at the sight of him, memories of nightmares still fresh enough to surround the slave with an air of malevolence. He was, in waking sight, an ordinary enough man. Aiul guessed they were about the same height, six feet three inches, but the slave was bulkier, hairier, and a shade darker than Aiul considered normal.

"How long must I call before you attend me?" Aiul growled, glaring at the slave.

The man stared blankly at him a moment. "No slaves here."

Aiul was annoyed by the man's disrespectful tone, and embarrassed to think he might have taken a high tone with his actual benefactor. "I meant no offense," he said, nodding. "I assumed..." He trailed off and stared at the hardwood floor.

"Logrus," the newcomer told him.

Aiul looked at him again, confused. "What is a 'logrus'?"

"Me."

"Ah." It seemed to be a day for humiliation and poor assumption. "I am Aiul."

Logrus tossed him the bundle. "Clothes. Food's in the kitchen. You'll need it." He turned to leave.

"Talkative," Aiul observed, but Logrus kept walking without response. With a sigh, Aiul examined the bundle of clothes, finding a woolen, hooded robe, along with leather pants, shirt, and boots. All of the garments were well made, better than Aiul would have expected, and all were black, hardly Aiul's favorite color, but it was preferable to being naked.

Once he had managed to stand and walk without losing his balance or consciousness, the difficult part of the journey to the kitchen was over. From there, it was a simple matter of hobbling toward the sounds of cooking and the heavenly aroma of frying meat. He had thought himself slightly sick to his stomach, but the smell awoke within him a ravenous hunger.

The kitchen, like the bedroom, was small but warm. Logrus

was here, eying him with the same curious stare, and tending a feast of bacon and eggs on an iron stove that seemed to fill the tiny room. He tossed a plate toward Aiul as he staggered in. Aiul's reaction, slow and half hearted, was not sufficient. The plate sailed past him and shattered against the wall.

"Reflexes a bit slow still," Logrus noted with a shrug.

Aiul was not amused. Silently, he took a seat at the small table, and lay his head on his arms. Between the vertigo, the weakness, and the hunger, it was difficult not to moan, but he had been embarrassed enough this morning, and, through sheer will, managed to remain quiet.

"It's like a hangover," Logrus explained, as he turned the eggs. "Assuming you survive to this point, anyway. Many don't."

"What are you nattering about?" Aiul mumbled into his arms.

"Later," Logrus told him. "After you eat." Aiul waited, unmoving, feeling as if he might vomit, until at last he heard the thud of a heavy plate being laid before him. The smell of the food, as close as it was, drove back the vertigo and nausea, and within moments, he was gobbling the meal with his bare hands.

Logrus belatedly tossed a fork to him, and Aiul was clear headed enough to catch it this time.

Logrus slid a pitcher of water across the table. "Drink," he said. "It will help the weakness."

Aiul nodded, and drank deeply from the pitcher. "Where did you learn your knowledge of medicine?" he asked. "You have done a fine job with me. I should know. I am a physician myself. Are you the local healer?"

Logrus's eyes showed little, though Aiul thought he could see confusion deep within them. "Skill at healing comes from understanding the inner workings of the body. There is more than one reason to know such things."

Aiul shrugged, not really certain what Logrus was getting at, but unwilling to pursue the sinister implication. "I suppose," he said. "Explain to me how I have come here."

Logrus nodded, his brow furrowing in thought for a brief moment. "What do you remember?" he asked.

"Prison. A voice, terrible, horrific. And a dream."

"You spoke to someone in the dream, yes?"

Aiul stared at the table in discomfort. He knew little of the man that sat before him, and what he did know gave him pause. There was a strange air about Logrus, one that Aiul found difficult to examine directly. Like a dim star, it seemed to vanish when he focused upon it, only revealing itself peripherally, at the edges of his thoughts. It was nothing visible or tangible, and yet Aiul had the distinct sense that there was something draped over the man, like a cloak or a shroud, something that smelled of grave dirt and rotting corpses, tasted sour and metallic, and radiated a cold that was felt not by flesh, but by soul. *How am I to share my nightmares with someone who seems to wear them like clothing?*

"Yes," Aiul said at last. "I dreamed of the Dead God."

Logrus nodded, as if he were simply going over established facts. "And you spoke with him, yes? Made a bargain?"

"A bargain?" Aiul allowed himself a bitter laugh at the memory. "No, no bargain. He merely expounded on just how little my life was truly worth. He…" Aiul paused briefly, as his voice began to tremble, and cleared his throat. "He pointed out how total defeat was not necessarily a position of impotence. And I agreed."

Logrus scowled, obviously confused. He placed his elbows squarely on the table and steepled his fingers against his forehead as he considered. "Then you are of the other order," he said slowly, as if he were trying to convince himself of something he did not fully believe.

"All that from a dream, eh?" Aiul sneered. "I am not a member of any 'order'. You're mistaken."

"It was no dream," Logrus said. "It was a vision, a true one. Don't be foolish. How do you imagine you are free from your prison? Why do you think I came for you?"

"I don't know," Aiul answered, sullen. "I was hoping you could tell me."

Logrus nodded. "Elgar wore your flesh and left a path of destruction and flame through the heart of your city when he liberated you. Now you are one of his knights. Like me."

"Preposterous," Aiul declared, though with less conviction than he would have preferred.

"Logic is not your strong suit, it would seem," Logrus said.

Aiul felt anger rising within him at Logrus's barb. He struggled to master himself, but still, his words were coated in acid as he said, "I will not be insulted by you! I am House Amrath! I am well familiar with logic!"

Logrus cocked his head and regarded Aiul with bewildered eyes. "Why would I insult you? What purpose would it serve? I need your cooperation."

As quickly as the anger had come, it passed, and Aiul found himself clearheaded once again. "Of course," he answered. "I'm sorry, I don't feel quite myself."

"It is to be expected," Logrus said. "But this is difficult. I do not know how to proceed. The situation is irregular. I have never heard of a mentor from one order guiding a newcomer of the other."

"I told you, I am not a member of *any* order," Aiul shot back, irritation rising in him once again.

"Not an order of choice. An order of *kind*," Logrus told him. He leaned back in his chair, his brow furrowed in thought. After a moment, he rose to his feet and said, "I must seek guidance."

"You're leaving?" Aiul asked. He found Logrus's presence disconcerting, but the idea of being left alone in a foreign land was even more troublesome.

"Yes," Logrus replied. He lifted his robe from the table and slipped into it.

"What about me?" Aiul asked.

"Stay," Logrus told him.

"I am not a dog to be commanded!" Aiul shouted.

Again, Logrus looked at him with a slightly confused, yet icy stare. "So much energy wasted on unnecessary things," he observed. "You *must* stay here. It will be another day or two before you are fit for travel, and I will be back by then."

Aiul glared at Logrus, but said nothing. How many times had he been on the other end of the conversation, explaining to an obstinate patient that he was not yet mended, only to be ignored. There was little use in being angry about simple truth, and yet, Aiul found, there was great satisfaction in it.

"There is food and drink aplenty," Logrus said as he gathered several things from drawers and dropped them into a bag. "Stay inside. The neighbors are…" He seemed to be searching for the appropriate term, and at last came up with "Troublesome."

"Will they attack me?" Aiul asked, alarmed now. He had not thought to look outside to see what sort of town they were in.

"No," Logrus told him. "They're terrified of us." He opened the door and stepped out. Then, as an afterthought, he peeked his head back inside and added, "But if they *do* bother you, kill some of them. They are stupid, but they are cowards." And then he was gone.

Aiul awoke to an insistent banging on the door. His first instinct was to dismiss it and continue sleeping, but Logrus's warning of troublesome neighbors was still fresh in his mind. It seemed wiser not to ignore such people. Surely, that would only excite them further.

It was dark, and as he made his way, the banging outside growing more intense, he cracked his shin painfully on a low lying table, and again on what he thought might be a crate. He cursed himself for not having had the presence of mind to leave a candle burning, but he had planned on sleeping through the night.

In the kitchen, he armed himself with the most wicked-looking knife he could find, then carefully felt his way toward the front room. He could hear voices now, beneath the banging. Perhaps, he thought, it was better that he had no light. It would certainly warn of his approach, and surprise might be preferable, here. He moved to the window and lifted the curtain just enough to peek out, uncertain of what to expect.

Two figures, dressed in black robes similar to the one Logrus had given him, stood on the wooden porch outside the door . One held his torch high, as the other slammed his fist against the door. At some other time, they might have been comical, but here in the flickering torch light, their features twisted with the telltale signs of inbreeding and malnutrition, their eyes lit with unknown, sinister purpose, there was nothing humorous about them.

"What is it you want?" Aiul shouted.

"We seek the Dark Lord!" one replied.

"He's gone!"

"Liar! The Dead God himself says the Dark Lord is here! Open the door and lead us to him, or you will suffer and die!"

Again, the jagged thing twisted in Aiul's mind, rage surging through his heart and veins like a drug. Never again would *anyone* command him, or threaten him! Ever!

Aiul did not plan what he did, he simply acted. He jerked the door open. Banger and Torch-Holder stood frozen in place, Banger's arm halfway to hammering against Aiul's chest, blinking in awkward shock and confusion. Aiul seized Banger's outstretched arm, snatched him forward, and brought the knife up and across his neck. Banger went to his knees with a gurgling, muffled cry, blood spraying from his wound to cover all three men. Aiul kicked him in the chest and sent him tumbling over the edge of the porch.

"What say you now, dog?" Aiul hissed at Torch, brandishing the blade at him, willing, wanting even, to use it again.

To Aiul's surprise, the remaining man seemed unmoved by his companion's demise. If anything, he seemed more resolute.

"I serve the Dead God," he said. "I do not fear your blade."

"Shall I kill you, too, then? Or will you leave me to my rest?"

"I am sent to fetch you, Lord. Elgar commands it, and I obey."

"Bah!" Aiul sneered and wiped his blade on Torch's robe. "Before, you said you were here to fetch some Dark Lord, and now you're here for me? Can't you even get your story straight?"

Torch nodded toward his companion, who was still busy dying, and said, "You are the Dark Lord, surely. Elgar speaks to us of a tall, white-haired slayer from the city of demon men." He licked his lips, a look of uncertainty briefly crossing his features, then vanishing as he seemed to push aside some nagging doubt. "You are *he*, Lord! There can be no doubt! Is this a test?"

Aiul stared at the blood on his hands, his distress growing as his anger faded. He could not explain his actions, but he knew that he had quite willfully killed a man for nothing more than his tone.

"These hands once healed," he murmured, ignoring Torch's question. "Now I am a murderer."

"The Dead God's works are wondrous to behold," the other man noted, his face beaming with fervor.

"Fool!" Aiul shouted at him. "Villain! Can you not see the evil in this?"

"Aye," Torch whispered, nodding reverently. "It is beautiful, Lord!"

Aiul stood gaping, unable to decide if the man was serious, or if he were mocking him. Either way, it was a disgusting display. He struggled against the urge to kill Torch as well.

"Leave here," Aiul told him, and began to close the door, but Torch stepped forward and grabbed his arm.

"Dark Lord, you *must* come with me!" he pleaded. "The Dead God *commands* it!"

Aiul looked at the man's flat, alien features, considering. He seemed sincere, but it was all so *insane*. Still, he had to concede Logrus and these people's versions of reality fit the facts, whereas his own did not. Perhaps, if nothing else, he would find some answers.

"Fine," he said. "I'll come." *Wait. Did he say 'white hair'?* The thought was appalling! "In my own time. Wait here." He pushed Torch away from the door and slammed it in his face.

He needed a moment to have a look in the mirror before he left.

Aiul followed Torch through the tent city, wary of the throngs of Elgar's minions. He ran his fingers through his now bone-white hair, idly noting it didn't *feel* any different. *I've been branded, marked like cattle, though to what end I have no idea.*

Hundreds of the cultists, perhaps thousands, meandered about, young and old, men and women, all dressed in the same dirty, black robes. Some talked or ate, ignoring the Nihlosian, but most turned and stared at him with sinister elation, their eyes lit with zealous fervor.

"Make way for the Dark Lord!" Torch shouted as he led Aiul through the crowd. Ahead, Aiul could see a lone building rising above the makeshift dwellings, an island of permanence in a sea of transient squalor. The place looked newly built of rough-hewn lumber, triangular and single storied. Various blasphemous sigils, many bordering on the pornographic, were carved into the sides of the place. Foot long metal spikes jutted upward from the corners of the roof, like fangs from a lower jaw. The moon, orange and swollen, hovered above, a single, unblinking eye over the teeth. Smoke curled from an unseen vent in the roof.

Torch led him to the entrance, a heavy wooden door, also covered in sigils, and stopped. "I can go no farther," he said. "Only those chosen by Elgar himself may enter the tabernacle."

Aiul glared at the cultist for a moment, his mind racing, suspicious of a trap. "Fine," he growled at last, and opened the door.

A wave of heat poured from the opening, accompanied by the sound of chanting voices. Soft, flickering candlelight illuminated a short passage that ended in a heavy curtain. Resigned to whatever fate awaited him, Aiul pulled the door closed behind him and moved down the corridor, shoving the curtain aside as he passed.

There were twenty-some-odd cultists in the room, all chanting and mumbling. They rocked back and forth on their knees, muttering their dark songs and offering supplication toward a makeshift throne of skulls in the center of the room. To either side, two bloodstained altars sat, each bearing a gagged, bound, terrified woman. Their eyes locked with his, pleading silently as they struggled in vain against their bonds.

Upon the throne sat a girl of no more than six. Blood oozed from a hideous gash in her throat, a wound that Aiul's practiced eye recognized as quite fatal. And yet the child moved, turning eyes black as midnight upon him. Steam rose from her skin in tiny wisps, creating a ghostly halo about her.

"The scion has come," the girl said, her voice, like her body, that of a small child.

"What is the meaning of this?" Aiul barked.

"*Enlightenment,*" the girl said, her voice no longer her own, but the now all too familiar assault on the senses that characterized Elgar's speech. As the images and sensations ripped through the room, the cultists cried out in terror and pain, but Aiul stood fast, weathering the storm as a grizzled sea captain stands against a gale.

"You have much to answer!" Aiul spat, his hands balling into fists.

The child spoke again, her voice once again sweet and innocent. "There can be no answers until you have shown your loyalty to me. Blood must be shed in my name."

"Damn your barbaric rituals!" Aiul spat. "You will give me answers *now*."

The child shook her head in sadness. "I cannot guide any but my true followers," she said. "You must show yourself to be mine before I can aid you."

"I will not kill for you, fiend!" Aiul said.

The child shook her head again, her black eyes glittering in the torchlight. "You are not yet ready," she declared. "These creatures are here to assist you." She gestured to the cultists and their victims. The voice of the Dead God roared from the impossibly tiny body, "*Show him the way!*"

The five cultists on the left side of the room rose as one, grinning despite Elgar's vocal assault. They moved to the altar closest, and began viciously beating the bound woman with their fists. One fumbled with dirty fingers, finally tearing the gag from her mouth, letting her cries of pain fill the room.

"Stop it!" Aiul shouted. The cultists on the floor continued to chant as if nothing were happening, their song seeming more and more like the beating of a heart. The throne of skulls stared at Aiul with empty, black eyes, as did its occupant. Aiul blinked, and his vision blurred, then focused again, but the image before him had changed. There was now a huge, blackened mace propped against the stacked, grinning skulls. The girl's tiny hands caressed the hilt of the weapon like a favored pet. The head, resting on the dirt floor, was shaped like a mailed fist. Spikes circled the gauntlet, jutting out several inches from the fingers, like nails driven through to keep it clenched forever. It was a brutal weapon, without doubt, as tall as the girl on the throne, and heavier than any Aiul had ever seen.

"Make them stop!" Aiul shouted at the girl, ignoring the sudden presence of the weapon. Perhaps, if he paid no attention to the fact that he seemed to be losing his mind, he could recover from such insanity. Still, it was difficult to ignore. He was beginning to feel dizzy. Blood pounded in his temples, and the entire room seemed hazy, indistinct, slightly veiled by a thin, red mist.

"They will show you the way," the girl said sweetly.

The cultists had begun raping the woman on the altar. They cackled at her misery and her cries.

"Think back," the girl said. "There is a bright place in your mind. Try to remember."

"No!" Aiul shouted. "I will not join in this, monster! Stop it!"

Elgar's roar ripped through the room, a cry of rage that stretched on and on. To Aiul, the Dead God's voice was now little more than a slap, but it was not so for the cultists. They began screaming. Smoke rose from their clothes. Wailing in fear and pain, they tried to beat out the rising flames on their robes. Two drew knives and tried to carve out their ears.

The silence when it was over was marred by three more cultists, who did not stop screaming, and would not, for the remainder of their brief lives.

"*Show him the way*!" Elgar roared again. The Dead God's voice tasted of copper, smelled of lightning, thundered like a hurricane, splattered like drops of blood from a slashing blade. Cultists leapt from their knees, drew blades, and rushed at both of the struggling captives.

Aiul saw the indescribable symbol once more in his mind. It beckoned to him to hate, to destroy, and suddenly, all was clear.

With a mad cry, Aiul rushed forward to the throne and seized the mace. He swung it around in a fluid motion and brought it crashing into the child's head. Her tiny skull flattened and exploded beneath the giant metal fist, scattering fragments of gore over Aiul and across the throne. Yet Aiul was certain that he had seen the child's dead lips turn upward in a satisfied grin even as the weapon had wiped everything away.

The cultists gaped in silent horror as Aiul slowly turned from the ruins of the host body. Blood and gore dripped from his face and hands. His chest heaved with excitement. He hefted the mace as if it were a feather and stared back at them. "You want blood?" he roared. "Take your fill!"

One of the bound women screamed.

And then he was among them, the vicious black mace swinging like a scythe. For a moment, they stood, confused, but panic quickly ensued as Aiul killed one, then another, and another still. They trampled each other as they scrambled for the door, and Aiul waded forward, striking them down from behind as they grappled with one another. Three managed to escape the building. They barred the door behind them, leaving the rest to Aiul's mercy.

Aiul had no mercy to give them.

Some raised their arms in feeble attempts to ward off his blows, while others tried to grapple with him, but he had the strength and stamina of a madman. He swung the enormous mace over and over, splintering bone and splitting flesh, until they all lay splayed on the bloody floor, shattered and still.

Even then, he was not finished, not satisfied. He dashed frantically about the room, smashing the corpses, pounding them over and over until they were nothing but bloody chunks of meat hanging from bones and rags.

Finally, the madness released its grip on him, and slowly, he began to tire, faltering in his swings, staggering as he moved, until at last he fell to his knees amidst the gore, gasping for breath. As the pounding in his temples gradually receded, he slowly became aware of a quiet sobbing, and the intermittent dripping of blood from the ceiling.

Spent as he was, he still struggled to his feet and looked about for the source of the weeping. One of the sacrificial victims still lived, and had somehow, in the chaos, managed to free herself from her bonds. She was huddled against the door, scratching at it with weak fingers. As he approached, she turned her face to him, eyes wide, trembling.

"It's all right," he said to her in as gentle a voice as he could muster, though it still came out as little better than a croak. He dropped the mace to the ground and held up his hands. "I'm a doctor."

The woman stared at him in horror as he knelt before her and considered the several stab wounds she had received. They were superficial, but one on her arm would definitely need stitches. He reached for her, and she began screaming.

"It's all right," he told her. "I can help."

Her screams grew hysterical as he took her wrist. He tried to hold on, but she was frantic, struggling against his grasp. He released her before she did herself further damage.

Aiul knew that he should be more patient, that he should appreciate that the woman was in shock, but it was all too much for him. Proper bedside manner was simply too much to ask at the moment.

"I am not the villain here!" he shouted at her, but his words were wasted. She simply continued her vain attempts to open the door, screaming all the while.

It was useless. He was too tired to help her at the moment. Exhaustion rolled over him in black waves, and his legs were suddenly weak. With a groan, he reached down and retrieved the mace. It made a fine crutch for him, bearing some of his suddenly enormous weight as he staggered to the throne. He collapsed into it, feeling as if he might never rise again. He closed his eyes to the gruesome scene, and waited.

The woman stopped screaming after a while, and Aiul fell into fitful sleep.

Logrus was unprepared for what he found in the black lodge. Not many things were truly unsettling to him, certainly not a few corpses, but the grim tableau before him seemed to whisper of dire events to come.

Aiul, looking as if he had bathed in blood and viscera, sat upon a throne of skulls, his head tilted low, chin on his chest.. His long, thin fingers curled like talons over the hilt of a great mace propped against the throne as if it were a scepter. The weapon's head, shaped to depict Elgar's symbol of war, was likewise crusted with red. The Nihlosian's sunken, haunted eyes rolled upward beneath his furrowed brow, glaring at Logrus through a screen of matted, gore-streaked hair. Dust and ashes, stirred by Logrus's swinging of the curtain, circled Aiul's head, the motes winking and glinting in the light from the door. About the mad king, his subjects lay in silent supplication; their broken bodies needed no explanation.

Logrus raised an eyebrow as a question, but Aiul, he remembered, preferred many words to few. "Are you king of the dead, now?" he asked.

"Of these dead," Aiul mumbled. "You *did* say to kill a few of them."

Logrus nodded. "Why this one?" he asked, pointing at the woman by the door.

"I didn't kill her," Aiul sighed. "They did." He stared at the floor again, shamed. "She wasn't hurt that badly. I could have saved her, but…."

Logrus pushed at the woman's arm with the toe of his boot, exposing a ragged tear in her wrist. "I think you could not have saved this one," he declared. "This was done by teeth. Her own, I would guess."

"You knew," Aiul said. He stared at Logrus, his eyes glinting with undisguised hatred.

"You are of the other order," Logrus said with a shrug. "I do not know your rituals."

"I killed him," Aiul said, his voice stronger now. He pushed himself up and stood on still weak legs. At Logrus's blank look, he added, "Your Dead God is truly dead, now."

Logrus rolled his eyes at the madness of such a statement.

"Look for yourself," Aiul told him, gesturing to the corpse of a tiny girl. It lay where it had fallen, its head an unrecognizable wreck of flesh and bone.

"He wears bodies as you or I wear clothes," Logrus shrugged.

"You're a fool," Aiul told him.

Logrus shrugged again.

"You'll see!" Aiul shouted.

"King of the dead, slayer of gods," Logrus sneered. "If this was a test, I'd say you passed. No ordinary man is so arrogant. Or deluded."

Aiul started toward Logrus, hefting the mace for a mighty swing, but Logrus snatched a candlestick from the wall and hurled it at Aiul with deadly accuracy, catching him squarely in the crotch. Aiul fell to his knees, gasping.

"I am no weakling cultist," Logrus told him. Aiul, clutching at his groin, had no reply. "I think it is necessary to kill you." He reached for one of the cultist's blades and advanced toward Aiul.

"It is not necessary," a voice whispered from the floor. Logrus turned to see the foreign woman's corpse stirring, dead lips twisting as it hissed, "You must have patience with him. He does not understand."

Logrus fell to his knees and lowered his gaze to the floor as the dead woman rose to her feet. Her cold, black eyes seemed to warm a bit as she regarded him.

"I understand well enough!" Aiul said. He rose and glared at Elgar.

"Do you?" Elgar asked, her eyebrows rising in amusement. "Tell me what you have learned, then."

Aiul sputtered, "I see what your servants do, monster! What you would have *me* do! Is that not enough?"

Elgar shook her head patiently. "You have done what I wished, scion," she said. "You were slow to act, but the first lessons are difficult. I am pleased with the final result."

"Are you mad?" Aiul shouted. "I killed your people!"

"Not my people," Elgar replied.

"Then who are these lying here on the ground?" Aiul sneered.

Elgar's black eyes grew cold again as she regarded the fallen cultists, her delicate features twisting into a mask of hate. She spat upon the corpses. Where the spittle fell, it smoked and bubbled, eating into the flesh and cloth.

"*I do not kill for amusement,*" Elgar said, speaking once again in the voice of the Dead God. "*I kill for hatred, for vengeance.*" He raised his hands before his eyes and regarded them, turning them back and forth. "*What reason was there to hate this flesh I now wear?*"

Aiul's eyes fairly bulged as he tried to reconcile the situation. "But you stood by! Your people tortured them and you did nothing!"

"You *did nothing,*" Elgar rumbled. The tabernacle shook and vibrated with his words. "*I am constrained by the order of things. I told you as much, but you did not listen. They are not my people.*"

"They use your name!" Aiul shouted. "They follow you!"

"Jackals follow war," Elgar said. "Maggots revel in the aftermath. Which side do they serve?"

Aiul began to tremble, and his breath seemed to stutter in his chest. Logrus almost felt sorry for the Nihlosian. He seemed less a bad man than simply a poor combination of ignorance and arrogance. *Both, I think, will be reduced in you this day, demon man.*

"So I am a fool," Aiul sighed. "Why did you not explain? If I had understood…."

"*I am constrained by the order of things,*" Elgar said. "*I can only point the way. Faith is the key.*"

Aiul nodded, saying nothing.

"My Lord, I have questions," Logrus said, his voice low and respectful.

"*You wonder about your master,*" Elgar said.

Logrus nodded.

"*I have taken him to me,*" Elgar said. "*And many others. Few but the two of you remain.*"

"Am I to know why?" Logrus asked.

"*I am weak, child,*" Elgar told him. "*I am dying. You know this. I needed the power I lent them to bolster you. You must undertake a dangerous quest, or all is lost.*"

"I will do as you command, Lord," Logrus told him.

"*And you, scion?*" Elgar asked. "*Will you, too, serve me?*"

"I will do what I must to have my vengeance on Nihlos," Aiul hissed. "But I will not do it for your sake. I do not care if you die."

"*It is your vengeance that will aid me,*" Elgar said, his voice once again the woman's. "*But you will need weapons.*" Elgar smiled, as if contemplating a beloved memory. "*Weapons such as can only be found in Torium.*"

Aiul gasped at the name of the forbidden city, and rose to his feet. "Madness! Torium is death! Even Alexander gave it wide berth!"

"Nevertheless, you must go there," Elgar said. "You must claim my blood, and the Book of the Gods. Only then will you be able to crush Nihlos under your boot."

"There must be another way!" Aiul shouted.

"There is no other way," Elgar said. The corpse that he wore dropped to the floor, lifeless.

"We will die there," Aiul muttered to the dead woman.

After a moment, Logrus rose. "We must prepare for our journey."

"We'll need a shovel," Aiul told him.

"Eh?" Logrus asked, confused. "Why?"

"The better to dig our own graves with."

CHAPTER 7
ILAWEH'S WILL

A HMED and his men had made for open sea as a first destination, well beyond the reach of any of the other vessels in Brust, and held position. He had decided it would be a good time to give the men a day of rest, and Sandilianus agreed.

It is good. I need time to think. Ahmed had yet to broach the most difficult subject with his second, the question of where to go and what to do next. Sandilianus had been pretty clear on what he thought of the prophesy months ago, when Brutus had thrown Ahmed an honorably earned beating. Sandilianus would obey, but he did not believe, not in the way Ahmed needed. In the end, the price to turn doom aside might be all of their lives. A man needed to be more than loyal to pay the ultimate price. He had to be unwavering, convinced of the truth. Sandilianus could prove difficult to sway, perhaps impossible unless Ahmed's reasoning and persuasion skills were flawless. *This cannot end as it did with Brutus! I will not fail us again.*

In the meantime, there was much to learn. The sun was already sinking, and only a few hours of daylight remained. Ahmed walked along the starboard side of his new ship, examining each of the captive sailors as he passed, looking for some sign of…what, exactly? Whatever Sandilianus had sensed, the unformed evil that had yet to surface. Sandilianus, on the port side, was doing much the same. *So, he does not know yet, either. At least I have learned that much about him.*

"Have they a leader?" Ahmed called.

Sandilianus crossed the deck to join him. "No signs of one. I suspect he was among the few who leapt overboard before we could secure the decks." Sandilianus's face grew thoughtful, then sly. "Or else he is hiding here, still."

Ahmed raised an eyebrow in appreciation. "Aye. If he were here, and we were so inclined, it might go badly for him. Have the men do a search. There is much we might discover."

Sandilianus thumped a fist against his chest and departed to carry out his orders. Ahmed continued his tour, examining the men and machinery, at last reaching the bow where he had started. He looked back along the deck, trying to take in the whole picture, connect the strands of information that he had gathered. Beside him, one of the captives was squatted on the deck, busy doing something with rope. Ahmed considered asking the man what it was. Perhaps it, too, might somehow be important, but he decided it was merely a distraction.

He knew that the small brown men ran the ship, the same men sold as slaves in Aviar. The ship was a Gruppenwalder vessel. The Gruppenwalders were notorious for their greed. They would sell their own mothers for the right price. Yet there were no Gruppenwalders here. Why would the brown men have such a ship? They could have bought it, but why? Why would they need a vessel capable of crossing the ocean? To trade? But they had nothing.

Ahmed ground his teeth as it all fell into place for him. Of course they had something to trade: their brethren, their children. Fury welled in him, demanding an outlet. Ahmed provided one by kicking the man with the rope solidly in his backside, sending him sprawling.

The roper looked up at him in fear and confusion. "What did I do?" he asked, his accent so thick it was barely intelligible.

Ahmed considered explaining, but what would be the point? It would be far more satisfying to simply give this coward a beating. Perhaps he would sell the lot of them to the slavers once they reached Aviar. It would be just, and Ahmed could use the money.

Sandilianus's shout rang across the deck, interrupting Ahmed's dark musings and turning all heads aft. "Ahmed! We've found something!"

The man Sandilianus marched into Ahmed's cabin was tall, an inch or three over six feet. *But thin. My arm is nearly as big around as his leg.* Blonde hair, blue eyes, high cheekbones, all made Ahmed feel ill. The man regarded him with an air of resignation, and offered no resistance.

"Who is this animal? Their Gruppenwalder contact?"

The prisoner's eyebrows arched in confusion. Sandilianus shook his head in frustration. "He is *Nihlosian*!"

Ahmed had to struggle to keep his jaw from gaping wide. This was the last thing he had expected. He searched for words, at last finding some he was proud of. "You will have trouble making me believe you saw this through the spyglass."

Sandilianus stared back in confusion for a moment, then smiled as he made the connection. "Ah, my 'leadership lesson'. No, this one was no part of that, but I see you have already worked out what I suspected there. These dogs sell their own as slaves."

Ahmed nodded, watching the Nihlosian man's face for clues. "And you?" he asked the man. "What is your part in this?"

The Nihlosian shrugged. "I swab decks." He scratched at his chin with dirty fingers, and offered a roguish smile. "Coil ropes, polish bright work. Oh, and fight. I used to do a lot of that, but it's less as the fools wise up and stop trying me."

Ahmed had just the perfect words come to mind to call the man a liar. The problem was that he did not believe them. "What is your name?"

"Eleran."

Sandilianus cuffed Eleran in the head hard enough to stagger him. "What *house*, dog? We are not as ignorant as you think." Eleran moaned and sank to his knees, sobbing, held up only by Sandilianus's firm grip on his collar.

Ahmed kept his face placid, seeing no reason to admit that he, for one, was indeed that ignorant. "You fold easily for one who claims to fight often."

"I'm better when I'm sober," Eleran mumbled, and Ahmed suddenly realized the man had not been sobbing at all. He was shaking with barely contained laughter! "We've been in port here for a week. I used to have some money, but it's gone." He looked up at Sandilianus and pursed his lips in a kiss. "I don't remember what it was like to be sober. So fuck you." He erupted into a fit of giggles.

Sandilianus released him and let him fall in a heap. "You're hardly my type, dog. And you didn't answer my question. What house?"

Eleran oozed slowly to a face down position on the floor, then, with clear effort, levered himself onto his back. "House? You're an idiot. Why would I be piss drunk and swabbing decks in this shithole if I were a fucking noble?" He pointed a finger at Sandilianus. "I'd just tell one of my slaves to chop off your head. So obviously, *you're* the one that's confused, and you can see now how that's a good thing. I'm sure you're very fond of your head, after all."

Sandilianus raised an eyebrow in appreciation. "Ah. You are that sort of culture. I am afraid I did not have time to absorb it all. I was fairly busy fighting for my life in one way or another."

"Yar, they're bastards. That fucking guy Caelwen—"

"You *know* him?"

Eleran squinted at Sandilianus a moment, then nodded. "In a manner of speaking." He raised himself to a sitting position and scooted backward to lean against the bulkhead. "In that his guys arrested me more times than I can really remember. That fuck Lorinal nearly knocked my brains out more than once."

Ahmed caught Sandilianus's eye and grinned, then turned back to the Nihlosian. "So you are an outlaw, then?"

Eleran shrugged. "Exile is a better word. As in, 'If you come back we'll kill you.' It was nothing formal."

"And what did you do to earn such hatred?"

Eleran chuckled again. "Fought. Stole. Drank. And definitely fucked the wrong woman."

Sandilianus nodded in sympathy. "Women can be quite cruel. I have no truck with them, personally."

Eleran gave Sandilianus a confused look. "I don't think you understand."

Ahmed waved a hand. "We understand well enough. Our ways may differ, but we know women complicate things. I am more concerned about the business of this ship. How long have you been aboard?"

A look of intense concentration came over Eleran's face, as if he were performing complicated math in his head. "Almost two years. And, yes, I know what they're up to. I don't care. I can't afford to."

"How does it work?"

Eleran scratched his head and yawned, bleary eyed. "They have a route they run, a bunch of small towns and villages. They catch people alone or in small groups, and eventually fill up the ship. They meet some other people on an island a long way out and trade people for gold. Then it starts all over."

"And you help them?"

Eleran shook his head vigorously. "I swab decks, set sails, haul ropes, whatever they tell me, but I just do labor. I wouldn't take part in the rest, and they wouldn't trust me to do it even if I would."

Ahmed nodded, satisfied. "I plan on selling these dogs to the slavers myself when we reach Aviar. It would serve them right. But what shall we do with you?"

Eleran shrugged again. "Well, I don't suppose you feel like giving me a lot of money and booze and sending me on my way?" he said with a giggle.

Sandilianus stroked his beard and offered a cruel smile to their prisoner as he waited for Ahmed to continue. *You really are the perfect second in command.*

Ahmed shook his head and waved it aside. "Put him back to work. We will let the prince decide his fate when we reach home."

Sandilianus gave Ahmed a fiery glance that he quickly, almost ruthlessly forced back to a blank expression, then gestured for Eleran to show himself out. The elder soldier watched until he was certain Eleran was well and truly gone, then spun on Ahmed, cold fury in his eyes.

I am out of time. Ilaweh, give me strength and wisdom. The battle is joined, and everything hangs in the balance.

Sandilianus drew in a deep breath, his fists clenched by his sides, his eyes dark with anger. "So you are giving up on the prophesy, going home?" he hissed. "*Now*, after *everything*?"

Aye, it would not do well for this conversation to be overheard. Ahmed said nothing for a moment as he considered his second's unexpected reaction. "Never. You misunderstand me. To be honest, I've been working on how to get you on board without a fight. It's one I'd surely lose."

Sandilianus's anger faded as quickly as it had come, and he sighed in relief. "Good. I was certain I was going to have to beat you into staying!" he said with a laugh. "And even if I was of another mind, I am not that stupid."

"I do not understand."

"Ah, you never heard this story! I forgot, you were back on the ship." Sandilianus smiled wistfully at the memory. "Brutus quarreled with Yazid over such matters, and Yazid decked him with a single punch."

Ahmed nodded, remembering Yazid's discipline. "I do not doubt it. I heard as a child that he once laid out a bull the same way, and I believe that, too. I have been on the receiving end of his blows."

"Oh, I take nothing from Yazid. He was as fine a fistsman as I have known, but as Brutus told the tale, it was the hand of Ilaweh himself that struck him down."

Ahmed felt a sad smile on his lips. "A pity the lesson didn't stay with him." He shook his head at the waste of it all. *Too many dead on account of stubborn pride. But perhaps it was necessary to get us where we are.* He would leave it to Ilaweh to judge such things. He had plenty to occupy him here and now.

He had been expecting a war with Sandilianus, only to find they had been allies all along. *If only all wars could end so cheaply.* "I assumed you would stand against me, too. You sided with Brutus before."

Sandilianus's gaze wavered momentarily toward the floor, an uncomfortable look crossing his face and quickly passing as he recovered eye contact. "I took no side, as I recall. I did my duty and cheered the fight, and kept my mouth shut like a good soldier."

Ahmed felt true surprise at this, along with some anger. "You believed and did not side with me? We might have saved many lives together!"

Sandilianus shrugged. "I doubt it. I knew Brutus well. *Very* well, you understand, yes? We would not have changed his mind, not short of Yazid punching sense into him again. All we could have done was lose his respect." He looked at the floor again. "Perhaps I was weak, even so. Maybe I had carried enough beatings and didn't want another. Maybe I didn't want a man who was my occasional lover to think me a fool. I don't know the truth of it. I don't think much about motivations. I follow orders. All I can say is it didn't seem the right time to speak."

Ahmed, too, hung his head. "Ilaweh as my witness, I had no idea what Brutus was to you. I must have cut out your heart with my words."

Sandilianus waved a hand, dismissing the notion. "I was numb to everything. I had just seen Ilaweh intervene and force us back on course, and the price we paid." Sandilianus paused and looked back up at Ahmed, an almost pensive expression on his face. His next words were nearly a whisper.

"And I had just seen a man rise from the dead. At that moment, I knew it was all true. Everything those sorcerers told me."

Ahmed scoffed at this. "I was unconscious, that's all!"

Sandilianus shook his head in vigorous denial, and folded his arms across his chest. "You were dead as stone, Ahmed. I took your pulse myself. I could lie to the rest of the men, to you even, but not to myself." He hesitated, as if reluctant to speak of something, then charged forward. "And there was a green glow about you. I thought at the time it was sea creature caught in your shirt, and I had no intention of reaching in to be stung by it. But now..." He sighed and gestured towards Ahmed's makeshift necklace, a half-lion's head on a simple leather thong. "I am certain it was that. No reason, just my gut."

Ahmed fingered the talisman, his 'souvenir' as he tried to absorb what Sandilianus was saying. *What is this thing?* It was indeed something to consider, but later. More pressing matters demanded his attention. Slowly, carefully, he asked, "Why speak of this now?"

"When was there time before? I should have trotted this out in front of the men?" He waved his hand as if to bat the notion aside like a fly. "Even you are close to calling me mad for this. If I had lost their faith spouting wild stories, where would either of us be right now?"

Ahmed stared back at Sandilianus in silence, feeling as if the world were slipping out from beneath him. *I died!* It was madness, but what else could he believe? "Dead men do not come back!"

Sandilianus's gaze was unwavering. "At least one *has*. I swear it Ahmed, I swear it before *Ilaweh*. Why else do you think a veteran like me would follow an unblooded boy, guide you and groom you? The same reason Brutus at last began to believe in Yazid."

"Yet he would not see it through."

"No. I think Yazid's death left him feeling a fool, and to have to flee the battle on top of that, it was too much for him. It's why I say we could never have changed his mind. Once he turned away from believing, he would never have gone back again, so Ilaweh called him home and put me in his place." The veteran wore a wry, wistful smile. "Ilaweh knew him well, too, it seems."

Ahmed took a deep breath and let it out slowly, still having trouble digesting Sandilianus's revelation. "We must work out what to do next."

Sandilianus stared at him in horror. "Do you not *know*? Did not Yazid prepare you for this?"

Ahmed shook his head, feeling terribly weary. "Yazid's

writing and books are at the bottom of the sea, and even then, he kept most of it in his own head."

"But surely he taught you?"

Ahmed knew his discomfort must show, but there was no good way around confessing. "I was a poor student. He tried to teach me much, but I often did not listen, even knowing I would get my ears boxed if he caught me daydreaming. I wanted to fight, not sit in a classroom. I thought because I could sometimes feel Ilaweh's will in my heart, it would be enough." He stared at the ground, feeling tears of shame burning in his eyes. "In truth, I never imagined it would be me to bear this duty. I leaned too heavily on Yazid's strength, and now I am on my knees as Talifah smiles. I am not worthy of this task."

Sandilianus moved forward with the speed of a lion and crashed his hand down on the desk, his eyes aflame with fury. "You blaspheme! *You* are the man Ilaweh *chose*! Who is the fool, Ilaweh or you, eh?"

Ahmed ran his forearm furiously across his eyes, full of shame at such weakness. "I am the fool."

"Then stop this whimpering and do his will!"

"I would, if only I *knew* it!"

Sandilianus stepped back, rubbing at his chin in appreciation of the problem. "I always assumed you prelates knew the answers, but perhaps that is unfair. Yazid *seemed* to know, but I suspect in his heart he had as many questions as we do. He put on a bold face to lead. There's another lesson for you, if you will learn it, poor student."

Ahmed smiled at this. "Your lessons are more to my liking. With Yazid, I wanted to fight, not study books. Your lessons seem more practical."

"They are. And here is one more. War is risk. Sometimes we must give orders without full knowledge, and sometimes men die because of it. If we do not gamble on occasion, the enemy will get ahead of us. If we cannot be certain, we must make a choice and pray Ilaweh guides us."

"Aye. We planned a day of rest, so let us finish it. Sometimes answers come in dreams. We will make our decision in the morning, whatever the case."

"*You* will make the decision," Sandilianus corrected. "Rest well, Ahmed." He hammered a fist to his chest and left without another word.

Alone now, Ahmed bowed his head, folded his hands, and began to pray.

Ilaweh, show me the way.

Ahmed woke with a start, still seated at the desk. The lantern had burned out, and it was pitch black inside the cabin. *Something is wrong!* For a moment, he felt his innards chill with seawater, imagining they were once again sinking, but that was not it. The ship was rolling gently. There were no sounds of storm or breakage, no cries of terror.

This was something entirely different.

It was absolutely quiet. *Too* quiet. The night watches tried to be courteous, but there was always some conversation or accident that made noise. Now? Nothing.

Ahmed checked his sword and moved to the door. He hammered the latch and threw the door open hard enough to slam against the outer bulkhead. Silvery moonlight streamed into the dark room through the open hatch as he stepped out onto the main deck.

It was, indeed, bad. The decks were empty, meaning the ship was essentially out of control! Where was the crew?

"Battle stations!" he cried.

That seemed to upset someone. He could hear his own men

scrambling to readiness, but he also heard cries from…overboard?

He turned his head to the port side to see the ship's small boat had been lowered. Damn them! They were fleeing in the middle of the ocean? It was madness!

Ahmed sprinted over to the railing and saw he was right. The thirty or so natives were packed into the small lifeboat, and almost ready to depart. The Nihlosian was nowhere to be seen. The mutineers looked up at Ahmed in shock and fear, then redoubled their efforts to cast off their remaining lines

"Fools!" Ahmed shouted. "We are deep at sea! You will all surely die in that punt!"

One of them, the ringleader Ahmed supposed, shouted back, "It is a better death than sailing straight to the demon realm over the edge of the world!"

"Superstitious wretch! There *is* no edge to the world!"

"So says a black-skinned demon. Better to drown than go back to your home!" The last of the lines came loose, and the boat began to drift away.

For a brief moment, Ahmed considered letting them go to their doom, but he knew it was too cruel a punishment for simply being idiots. Besides, he really needed them. His men could likely run the ship without them, at least for a while, but it would be dangerous with no extra hands. They could limp back to the coast on their own, but without a navigator, they would never be going home. Ahmed thought briefly of Tahir, remembering how much he had hated the halfbreed.

Ahmed looked about, hoping some of his men would be closer, but they were only just now emerging onto the main deck. If the mutineers got the boat even a short distance away, it would be damnably difficult to overpower them. His men were soldiers, not sharks.

His eye fell upon a great hunk of metal lying against the rails.

It was tied to a long rope. An anchor, perhaps? No, too small, and he didn't really need to know exactly what its actual use was in order to give it a new one. He pulled at it, grunting. It was at least a hundred pounds. *Good. That should do.* He hauled the thing onto the top of the rail with a grunt.

"Will you not turn back, fools?" he called down.

They looked up in horror, realizing his plan, but this did nothing to dissuade them. They scrambled for oars and plunged them in the water, cursing and shouting at one another.

Ahmed heaved the chunk of metal over the side. The escapees watched it fall, screaming and scrambling to get out of the way. It hit the bow like a catapult missile, tearing away the entire front of the boat with the thunderous crash of snapping timber.

Ahmed turned back to his approaching men. "Someone help them aboard before they drown. And find me that damned Nihlosian!"

They found him quickly enough, bound and gagged in the aft crew's quarters. Eleran glared about in impotent fury as they laughed at his plight, his eyes making promises for his fists to keep when he was free. Ahmed grinned at this and brought out his blade to cut the bonds. "Hold still, fool, or I'll end up opening an artery."

Eleran groaned, but held still long enough to get a hand free. He tore the gag from his mouth and groped for Ahmed's blade. Ahmed pulled it back, smiling. "A man's sword *means* something. Would you grab at my woman, too, if I had one?"

Eleran's rage faded, and he offered Ahmed a wry smile. "Probably."

Ahmed relented and handed him the blade. "No wonder they didn't include you in their plans."

"Yeah, that and the fact that I'm the 'paleskin'," Eleran said as he began cutting through the rest of his bonds. "Like I said, I do a lot of fighting."

Ahmed scowled at this. It was surely true, and even something he might have done himself. But suddenly, it seemed *wrong*. A beast did not *know* it was a beast. If it had the presence of mind to object to being treated as such, then it would not *be* a beast.

Eleran handed the blade back and massaged aching muscles. "Thanks."

"Did you see what happened to the midwatch?" Ahmed asked.

"Nope. I gotta take a leak, ok? Then I'll help you look for them."

Ahmed nodded, and the two headed up the ladder to the main deck. Ahmed scowled at the mutineers, currently being held at swordpoint by several of his men.

Eleran did his business over the side, looking about as he did so. Too late, Ahmed realized that the entire business about the rail was less biological and more scouting. When Eleran was done, he charged headlong at the mutineers' ringleader, knocked him flat, and rained a truly impressive series of blows on the man.

Ahmed and his men didn't know the exact reason for the fight, but they followed decorum, gathering round in a circle and pounding rhythmically on the deck and rails.

It quickly became apparent that Eleran was not merely boasting when he claimed he did a lot of fighting. It was likewise apparent that the ringleader did very little. Ahmed let it go on for a bit. It was rude to interfere in a contest of fists or steel, but a contest of fists was supposed to be non-lethal.

"Enough!" Ahmed called. Eleran seemed not to hear. Ahmed stepped in and grabbed him from behind. It took three more of the Xanthians to completely restrain Eleran's flailing fists and pin him to the deck. Ahmed put a knee on the Nihlosian's heaving chest and looked down at him with admiration. "We will release you when your blood cools. You are a good fighter."

Sandilianus's head poked from below decks, followed by the rest of his body as he mounted the ladder. "Did I miss it all?"

Ahmed pointed to the ringleader. "This fool needs a medic."

Sandilianus eyed Eleran, who was still gasping and struggling against Ahmed's men. "What did he do to you?"

Eleran took a deep breath and relaxed. "What didn't he do?" His captors, sensing he was in control once again, backed away cautiously, ready to seize him again if this were a ruse. "But lately? He took my stash, for one thing. That shit was worth a fucking month's pay!"

The ringleader spat through bloody lips, "Fuck you, demon man dog."

Sandilianus kicked him in the ribs, drawing a grunt from the man. "You have made enough enemies today. No need to encourage more. Now shall I throw you a beating as well, or will you have my aid?"

The ringleader snorted blood and shrugged. "I got no choice."

Ahmed laughed. "Smart man."

Sandilianus spoke as he examined the ringleaders wounds. "We found them below, Ahmed, piled up in the sail locker, sleeping like babies. We should beat them for being stupid enough to get drugged."

"I may just do that. Meanwhile, I have other problems. I want you and your patient in my quarters as soon as he can walk." He turned to Eleran. "You too, 'demon man dog'." He chuckled. "That's too many words for a good insult."

Eleran shook his head, embarrassed. "Sorry about the trouble."

Ahmed nodded. "Don't be."

Sandilianus shook his head in dismay. "What I can't understand is what you imbeciles hoped to accomplish! You were going to your *deaths*, fool."

He stood leaning against the bulkhead of Ahmed's cabin, arms crossed over his chest. Ahmed sat at a great desk, and Eleran and the ringleader occupied the two chairs facing Ahmed. The ringleader, who had identified himself as Bendaro, hunched his shoulders and scowled at the floor.

"We know how to sail," he muttered.

"Thirty leagues of open ocean? In a fucking *punt*?"

Bendaro shrugged, looking more resigned now. "We knew the risks. We ain't gonna get sailed over the edge of the world! Better to die."

"Idiot!"

Ahmed had accepted the fact that he was dealing with a primitive, superstitious people. Sandilianus was still learning that. Ahmed spoke as if addressing a child. "Bendaro, if what you say is true, then why would Eleran go willingly?"

Bendaro's head jerked up and he stared at Ahmed with wide eyes. "He is a demon like you! Why would he fear your land?"

Eleran chuckled. "If I was a demon, I'd set you on fire or something. You deserve way more than a beating for stealing my stuff."

Bendaro shot him a look of pure poison, then turned back to Ahmed. "If you was *really* a man, and not a demon, you'd have mercy! My people *believe* it's true, even if it ain't. Don't you think we knew the risks?"

Ahmed slammed a fist on the desk. "And what of the slaves you sent there yourself, dog?" he shouted. "Did you fear for them as well? What right have you to speak to me of mercy when you have none?"

Bendaro sat straight up in his seat, shaken and pale. "You know about that, huh?" he asked in a quavering voice.

"Answer the question!"

Bendaro sighed. "At first, it was only prisoners, bad men. But then the captain got greedy." He began to shake as he spoke, pleading with his eyes for understanding. "What could we do? The captain was crazy! He even hired on a demon man to spy on us! If we didn't do like he said, he'd send us to the demons, too!"

Sandilianus rolled his eyes at the tale. "And where is this captain, hmm?"

"Fled! Over the side when you came."

Ahmed considered the man's tale a moment. It could be true. Perhaps they were not evil men. Just very, very stupid. He turned to Eleran. "What say you? Is this true?"

Bendaro shook his head in resignation. "If it's his to say, we're doomed. Either he is a demon and he'll screw us for fun, or he's a man and he'll screw us for revenge."

Eleran kicked at Bendaro's chair. "I may be a lot of things, but I'm no liar. Well, not unless it saves my skin, anyway." He turned to Ahmed. "That's pretty much how it was. The captain told them all that demon shit, threatened them with it pretty regular. All except the part about *me* being a demon." He scowled at Bendaro again. "That, they came up with all on their own."

Ahmed leaned back in his chair and looked down his nose at Bendaro. "Then you should be grateful to me for freeing you from a villain, should you not?"

Bendaro stared at the floor again, his face growing red. "If you ain't a demon, I reckon we should."

"Then let us work together! When our mission is done here, we will want to go home. You can sail this vessel without us. You will take us home, and then the ship will be *yours*. We could even pay you wages once we arrive. It is a simple bargain. Surely it is less wicked than the one you struck with your captain!" *They are not the real villains.*

Bendaro shook his head slowly. "Even if I believe you, the men won't never buy it. They're *afraid*."

Ahmed nodded gravely, saying nothing. He had expected as much. Ilaweh was answering. *I am listening. Show me the way.*

Eleran cleared his throat. "Actually, I might have an idea."

Ahmed looked at him. "Well?"

Eleran looked around nervously. "We could find crew in Nihlos. They sell prisoners all the time there. They would be rowdy, probably, but you guys look like you're on top of that sort of thing. They wouldn't be a bunch of superstitious fools."

And there it is. Ilaweh shows the way.

Sandilianus scowled at this notion. "Did you not just tell us you would be killed on sight in Nihlos? So will we. Who will buy these prisoners?"

Eleran took a deep breath. "They'd have to recognize me for that to matter. I could grow a good beard, maybe color my hair. We could do it. But we'd need money."

Ahmed ran a hand over his head in frustration. "And we have none."

Eleran grinned. "Wrong. We have gold. *Lots* of it."

Ahmed eyed Eleran warily. "So you say? And where is this gold?"

Eleran pointed to the deck beneath Ahmed's chair. "Under those boards, in a safe. I've seen it. I even tried to get at it once or twice, but I never could open the box."

Ahmed leapt to his feet and hurled the chair aside. He stamped a foot against the boards, and they did indeed ring hollow. "Show me."

The Nihlosian walked over to Ahmed and took a knee. He rapped his knuckles against the wood, searching. "It's been a while. Wait...here!" He pulled at a knot in one of the planks. A small trap door, cunningly designed from whole planks so as to be invisible from above, swung open to reveal a heavy metal safe about the size of a footlocker.

Ahmed examined the box and hauled at it experimentally. It wouldn't budge. "Let's get it on deck and get a better look."

Sandilianus stepped over and grabbed hold of the safe on one side, and Eleran did likewise on the other. Ahmed pulled on the top. With a great heave, the three men managed to lift it on to the deck, then sat down on the floor against the bulkhead, panting.

Ahmed spoke first. "It must weigh a ton. How much gold is in there?"

Eleran shrugged. "Uh, lots? I couldn't exactly measure it. I wasn't even supposed to know it was there."

"How do we open it?"

"If I knew that, it wouldn't be here."

Sandilianus chuckled at this. "Aye, true."

Ahmed studied the safe, fiddling with several dials and latches, but he could make no sense of it. "Useless. So we are back where we started."

Bendaro cleared his throat. The three had nearly forgotten him in the excitement. "I got a deal for you."

Ahmed glared at him. "If your deal doesn't include how to get into this safe, you're going to get a second beating this morning!"

Bendaro nodded. "It does. I seen him do it lots of times. I was just too scared to try for it."

"And what is it you want in return?"

"We head back right now, as soon as you open the safe. You can hire men with the gold, and we can *all* go home."

Ahmed considered a moment. "*If* there is gold. Because if there is none, we cannot hire anyone."

Bendaro nodded again. "Here's what you do."

Ahmed followed his instructions, twisting dials, flipping switches, and finally, turning a large bolt. A low, audible click filled the small cabin, and the safe door opened to a collective gasp.

Ahmed blinked in shock. "Ilaweh is great!"

The safe was filled to overflowing with gold coins. Sandilianus snatched one up to bite it and verify the metal, but paused with it halfway to his face. "Ahmed, this is a sword!"

Ahmed saw that it was indeed a coin from his own land, and rifled through the others. Mixed in the safe were Gruppenwald crowns, Laurean shields, Xanthian swords, and a number of vaguely round lumps of gold scarcely worthy of the name 'coin'.

Eleran reached into the pile and held up a coin Ahmed did not recognize. "Nihlosian, too. The captain was a busy man."

Ahmed grinned at him. "Aye. Is it enough for a crew?"

Eleran boggled. "Are you joking? It's enough for a hundred!" He looked back at the heap of gold. "Maybe there's jewels, too!"

Bendaro called out, "So now we can go home, yes?"

Sandilianus looked at Bendaro as if the man were mad. "Do you not see we have found a great treasure here? You might have a share of it, and a ship if you were not a superstitious fool."

Bendaro shook his head. "No. No more work with demons, whatever the pay."

Sandilianus stared aghast at him for a moment, then turned back to Ahmed. "Shall we head back, then?"

Ahmed tore his attention from the box of gold with some difficulty, but there was business to attend. "I am a man of my word," he told Bendaro. "I will take your people home, but we must acquire our new crew first. Fair enough?"

Bendaro spat in his palm and extended his hand to Ahmed. Ahmed shook, sealing the deal. For the first time since Ahmed had known him, the man smiled, showing bloody teeth beneath his swollen lips. Observing Eleran's handiwork, Ahmed thought again that the Nihlosian was a fine fistsman, perhaps a match for most of his own men.

"What course?" Bendaro asked.

"Do you know Nihlos?"

Bendaro's face grew sour at the mention of the name. "A dangerous place, but they have few ships. We can get close."

"Then turn us around. And do not think to play games with me, or our bargain will be broken."

With a grimace of pain, Bendaro rose and left the cabin. Ahmed heard him shouting orders to the crew. The commands he gave were meaningless to Ahmed, but the result followed quickly: the ship began to turn about.

Ahmed felt a rightness in it, that he was at long last going where he was meant to be. *Nihlos, to find the sorcerers, just as Yazid planned.* Beyond that, he still knew little, but he was on his way. After so much uncertainty and strife, that was enough. Surely when the time came, if the sorcerers had no knowledge to add, Ilaweh would guide him as he had done today.

Ahmed turned to Sandilianus and Eleran, who were still gleefully rifling through the gold coins. "Are not ships supposed to have a name?" he asked Sandilianus.

"Aye," said the soldier. "I do not know this one's, but we have every right to rename her. We have captured her well and true."

Eleran grinned at Ahmed. "How about 'Lady Luck'?"

Ahmed shook his head. "No, my friend. We should praise our true benefactor. Our ship will be named 'Ilaweh's Will'."

Sandilianus grunted his appreciation of the name. "So you think you know the path now, eh? What is it?"

Ahmed shrugged and offered a mischievous grin. *I have waited long for this moment.* "I cannot say. But I will tell you why."

Sandilianus laughed. "Damned prelates, always with their mysteries and riddles. Don't want to look a fool when it turns out wrong, eh?"

Ahmed grew somber at this. "If what I am planning goes badly, I doubt I will be in a position to feel much shame." *I have no idea how to fight a sorcerer, should it come to that. They would likely make short work of me.*

He would just have to hope their god or gods were as interested in saving the world as his own.

CHAPTER 8

A BRIEF THAW

WAKING came as something of a shock to Caelwen, chiefly in that he had not expected to do so. He found himself staring at an unfamiliar ceiling, lying in an unfamiliar bed, his head spinning with confusion and dislocation. *Why is everything white? Where am I?*

Memory rushed back as he came fully awake. The encounter with Davron had not gone as well as he had hoped. *Of course, it seems to have ended better than I imagined. Assuming I'm not actually dead.*

He was quickly disabused of that notion as he turned his head slowly to see the stern face of his father, blurry but clear enough to recognize. Polus sat in a large chair next to the bed, reading a book, and had yet to notice Caelwen's awakening.

"This is hardly the afterlife I had expected," Caelwen rasped through dry lips.

Polus looked up quickly and rose, his face brightening, his lips not quite forming a genuine smile. *It's a birth defect, or nerve damage, I swear. His mouth has been frozen like that as long as I've known him.* Polus's eyes told the truth, though. Caelwen knew him well enough to understand his father was practically dancing a jig.

Polus laid a hand on Caelwen's shoulder and gripped it hard enough to hurt. "It's good to see you again. You had me worried for a bit, there." Then, before Caelwen could even respond, Polus stepped back to make room for someone else.

Caelwen was fairly certain his shock was written on his face as Kariana leaned over him, her waif-like face broadening in a grin. Her violet eyes peered down at him from behind her black tresses, twinkling with mischief. *It must be mischief. It certainly wouldn't be tears for* me. "It's good to have you back, Captain," she said.

Caelwen smiled weakly back at her. "Not rid of me yet, Empress."

Kariana giggled at this. "I thought maybe you had this in mind as your escape from me!" She swiped at what, for all the world, appeared to be actual *tears* in her eyes. "But your position is still secure. It seemed prudent to make sure I actually needed a new bodyguard before conducting interviews." She looked at Polus and said, "I'll leave you two to catch up."

When the door had closed behind her, Polus stepped forward and extended a hand to Caelwen. Caelwen took it and grasped it as firmly as he could, but he felt very woozy still. "How long?"

Polus reached for a decanter of water and poured a glass full. "Just the night." He handed the glass to his son, careful to make certain Caelwen had a firm grasp before releasing it. "I hear you died well. Not many men get the chance to know how they will fall. Davron gave you quite a gift."

Caelwen drained the entire glass, then set it on a small table beside the bed. "You've seen him since?"

"Aye. He sent you back slumped over your horse, accompanied by a few of his men, but I had to go to him to get the story. He's dug in and not coming out without a fight."

"I'm surprised to be alive. I thought certain he meant to kill me."

Polus waved a hand, dismissing the thought as foolish. "He dotes on you like you were his own. If you didn't have my chin, I'd wonder about him and your mother." Polus almost smiled. "I've never heard him speak so well of anyone as he did you."

Caelwen laughed out loud at this. "You should have heard what he said about me last night. He was more than a little upset."

"Well, then, he shouldn't have taught you to be insufferable. It serves him right."

They both laughed at this, but Caelwen's humor was brief as he remembered other details. "What of Rithard?"

Polus's expression grew grim. "Unknown. Davron won't speak of it. Personally, I suspect he's dead."

Caelwen nearly shouted his dismay. "How can you not know? Davron should be arrested for this!"

"Mind your tone. I am still your father, even if it was Davron who most recently whipped you for insolence." His mouth was stern, but his eyes still said otherwise. "Whose army do you propose I use to dig him out, if it came to that? Shall we ask him to lend us his men?"

Caelwen snickered despite himself and the seriousness of the situation. "It's unseemly to do nothing."

"And it would be stupid to go off half cocked. Even if we could take him, we'd lose so many men that we couldn't keep order. Davron has all the cards, and more to the point, I'm not even convinced he is in the wrong."

Caelwen sighed and laid his head back on his pillow. He noticed the pain for the first time. His head and jaw throbbed with his pulse, though not as badly as he might have expected. *Ah, they've drugged me, of course. That's why I'm woozy.* He wondered idly who was even running the place, with Aiul gone berserk and Rithard dead or captured. "You suspect he's murdered

Rithard, and you know for a fact he has kidnapped him. How is that 'not in the wrong'?"

Polus chuckled at this. "Here you lie bruised and battered, and you still don't understand what I have tried to teach you your whole life. The law is what men of might and will say, nothing more. Davron has the might and the will. Unless the Meites choose to involve themselves, this is his hand to play."

"And the Meites? What say they?"

Polus was silent for a moment before answering. "There have been...other developments that have distracted them."

Prandil watched as Maranath sighed and pushed back from the examining table, shaking his head in disgust. *He's tired. We're all tired.* Whatever dark power had driven the creature that lay before him, it was departed, and the thing was merely a corpse again, albeit a very well ventilated one. What hadn't been exposed to the air by sword had been finished by scalpel, but they were none the wiser for having done so. *I would have expected to learn a bit more from opening the thing up and having a look.*

"I've no damned idea what I am doing here," Maranath said quietly.

Prandil stabbed his scalpel into the corpse's face and left it there like a planted flag. "None of us expected this. I am uncertain how to proceed."

Ariano, too, heaved a sigh and shook her head in defeat. "Cautiously."

Maranath looked at both of them. "Indeed. Of all the mistakes we could make, underestimating him is the easiest to avoid."

"We have *no* information," Prandil groused. "We can't even begin to predict what he can throw at us. That juggernaut that tore through here was no man."

"No," Ariano agreed. "That was the Dead God himself. I sensed his passing, even in my sleep."

"Perhaps he would be like the Fallen?" Prandil mused.

Maranath scratched at his chin, considering a moment. "I've never heard of the Fallen raising undead. They were first and foremost warriors. They had minor sorcery at best compared to a Meite. Amrath doesn't even mention specifics."

"He mentions brave soldiers fleeing in fear of them!"

Maranath waved a hand to dismissal the notion. "That hardly means they were using sorcery. They were fearsome warriors. Wouldn't you flee from someone who was going to chop off your head with a great hunk of steel?"

Prandil hunched his shoulders and leaned in toward the old sorcerer. "I have read it many times, and I remember being told about it by my father before then. Amrath said the Fallen wore cloaks of fear."

"He said they were 'cloaked in fear'," Maranath nearly shouted. "It's metaphor, you ass!"

Prandil gaped at him a moment. *No one is this ignorant. It must be senility.* "Mei, it says no such thing!" he shouted. "It says 'cloaks of fear', and Amrath meant it literally! I can show you the passage right now!" He began casting about the room for a copy of the book.

Ariano groaned and waved her hands between the two. "This is no time for trivia! We know *enough*!" She glared at the two of them briefly, then intoned, "This is the prophesy of Elgar: one thousand years do the gods grant for the Sleeper to dream."

Prandil nodded, taking up the verse. "One hundred decades does the Eye of the Lion lie sundered."

"Ten centuries does Torium rot and fester." Maranath said, joining in. In unison, they spoke the rest from memory, "Then will the Sleeper awake, the Eye be made whole, and the chancre of Torium burst to spill its corruption upon the world. The scion of Elgar will rise from the blood of Tasinal, the Eye about his neck, in the City of Nothing, and the world shall become as ash. So says the Destroyer."

"We were such arrogant fools," Prandil said softly. "Kariana was never the scion. She was the catalyst."

Ariano jabbed a bony finger at him. "*You* were wrong." She shot Maranath a withering look as well. "The both of you. I've told you since the day he led that raid on her, it was *Aiul*."

"So you did," Maranath conceded. "I suppose I didn't really want to believe it, so I chose not to." He shook his head and cast his gaze to the ground. "How can you even *think* of this?" he whispered. "The boy—"

"*Don't!*" Ariano's voice exploded in the small room like a bomb, complete with a shockwave. Trays full of surgical tools upended, sending scalpels flying like spears. Glass jars full of water, alcohol, and other, less identifiable liquids burst under the assault, scattering their contents about the room.

Prandil staggered backward from the impact, barely reacting in time to dodge the scalpels. A jar that might have been a potent acid burst right next to him. He caught a whiff of the acrid scent only briefly, as it quickly began to eat at his cloak before he could decide the vessel had held merely water. *Not soon enough to save the cloak, though. She's a menace!*

Maranath was unmoved, of course. *He's a pillar of stone.* He was watching Ariano in silence, his face torn between anger and misery, his beard twitching. A scalpel, its blade bent in two from the impact against his forehead, clattered noisily to the floor.

Ariano, chest heaving, returned his stare, her blazing eyes glowing a soft red, as if backlit. Her eyes cycled through the spectrum as she spoke, her voice more controlled, but in multiple, harmonic tones. Colored lights with no apparent source danced on the walls in rhythm with her words. "Don't you dare speak as if I don't appreciate the gravity of the decision, Maranath. Don't you *dare!*" When she was done speaking, she began to hum, or perhaps growl in the back of her throat, and the lights followed suit.

This is explosive! Prandil addressed them softly, wary of making himself a target. "Stop it. Remember what we're here for."

"She intends to kill Aiul, you imbecile!" Maranath growled, his gaze still locked with Ariano's.

"I am not quite the dolt you imagine," Prandil retorted in an acid tone, his caution evaporating in a flash of annoyance. "I worked that out on my own." He raised his hands in a placatory gesture, struggling to regain his calm. "The problem I have right now is whether or not she intends to kill the both of us as well."

Maranath grunted at this. "Good question." He nodded toward Ariano. "Do you?"

"It is my decision to make!" she said, her voice still more song than words. "Not yours!"

"Then make it when you *must*! Don't make it *now*, when there might be another way!"

Ariano continued growling for a moment. The room seemed to hum and vibrate as she considered, the lights growing more chaotic. Then, all at once, everything faded. Ariano herself seemed to shrink a bit, like a deflating balloon. "Fine," she answered, her voice now sullen and tired. "But when that time comes, you will accept the decision I make. Are we clear?"

"Agreed," Maranath said. "The question is, where do we go from here?"

"We have nothing to go on," Prandil noted.

"We might," Ariano said. "There are a number of Elgar cults on Prima. I try to keep track of them, but they are unstable by nature. I know of one nearby."

Prandil waved a hand in dismissal. "What will those fools know? I doubt Elgar consults with them on his plans."

"Perhaps more than you might imagine," Maranath said. "If

we're looking at the fulfillment of a prophesy, he'll likely want minions."

Prandil nodded. "I suppose that's true."

Ariano's wrinkled faced tightened into a cruel smile. "If they know anything, we'll pry it from them."

Alone in her quarters, Kariana sat on her bed, brooding. She had sent for the Meites as soon as she had heard the news from her guards. One of their own had been turned into a murderous zombie, and had come after them. What she had turned over to Maranath was a fairly poor specimen, but at least she would not be blamed for hiding anything from them.

They had asked for privacy, and she had given it to them, in the form of a small examining room where she often received her own medical treatments. She had waited hours before finally concluding that she would only get answers by demanding them. She hadn't meant to eavesdrop. Not that she was above such a thing, it was just that she'd had no chance. They had been screaming at each other loud enough that she might as well have been in the same room.

Just the one thing had been enough to turn her around and resolve to pretend she had never come: "She intends to kill Aiul, you imbecile!" Knowing that bit of information could be fatal, if they were aware of her knowledge.

So she plotted, staring at a lovely, pornographic tapestry she'd had placed over the gaping hole Aiul had left in the wall. She contemplated the exaggerated anatomy of the figures it depicted as she brooded, imagining scenario after scenario, searching for the one that would end with the Meites choking on their own blood. So many possibilities, so many variables! But there had to be a way. There was *always* a way. She was not going to let them kill Aiul, not if she could stop them.

A knock on the door startled her from her fantasy. "Come," she called out.

A guard she didn't recognize opened the door and leaned into the room. He was young, and more than a little nervous. "Empress, a visitor from House Prosin is here for you."

"*Prosin?*" she shouted. "Execute them at once!"

The guard blinked at her a moment. "Execute...ahh?"

"It's a joke," she assured him, and gave him The Smile that melted all men. Well, all men except Caelwen. "I never execute anyone without knowing who they are first." *Except when I've been drugged and tricked.* She waited for some response from the man, but he said nothing, seeming even more bewildered. "Well, who *is* it?"

The guard stammered and finally answered, "I don't know. The slaves just told me it was a visitor from House Prosin. I'm really sorry!"

It was Kariana's turn to be confused. "Um, for what?"

The guard took a knee and bowed, "If I offended you somehow. I didn't know I was supposed to find that out. I didn't even know I was supposed to come up here and tell you about visitors until the slaves told me."

Kariana tittered at this. "That's because it's *their* job, and they're taking advantage of you."

The guard nodded back, the expression on his face one of great enlightenment. *Clearly, we are not one of Caelwen's sharpest tools, are we?*

"Tell the visitor I will attend them shortly." By which she meant 'longly'. House Prosin had no business expecting to be received at all, much less in a timely manner.

An hour seemed about right. She spent the time perfecting her makeup and hair. When at last she sauntered to her reception room, she was feeling quite beautiful. She would dazzle a man, and intimidate a woman.

That view of the world was dashed against the ground at first sight of her visitor. The woman was tall and well curved, ruby lips and raven hair such that men might kill for. Kariana self-consciously folded her arms across her chest, as if to hide herself from the much more amply endowed Prosin woman. *I look like a little boy next to her.* "What business could House Prosin have with me that doesn't involve poison?"

The woman gave a disarming laugh, seemingly honest. *She's Prosin. Everything they do is manipulation. Never forget it!*

"I see you've met some of my house. But, no, I am here for something entirely different." The humor faded from her face as she continued. "My name is Teretha, and you saved my son's life. I am here to offer my gratitude and my service."

Kariana could barely suppress her shock. "I what?"

Teretha laughed again "Rithard, of House Amarath. Had you not sent Caelwen as a witness, I think he might have been found dead along some roadside in the undercity, instead of being taken prisoner."

"Well, that's novel. It's the first time I've had Prosin visitors who weren't threatening me."

Teretha's expression grew somber. "Maralena, yes? I doubt I liked her any better than you did. It would seem some Meites liked her even less. One of them did the both of us a favor, hmm?" She flashed a knowing smile.

Kariana nodded, not trusting this a bit, but not wanting to make another enemy. "I'm listening."

Teretha took a deep breath, preparing her pitch. "Maralena made threats. I make friends. Let's be friends, you and I, hmm?"

"Oh, how lovely! We can make pretend tea and play with our dollies! Oh, and brush each other's hair!"

Teretha smiled gamely at the barb, then answered smoothly, "I was thinking of a different sort of friends. The sort who tell each other secrets, and warn each other of trouble."

Kariana gave a grunt of disdain at this. "I've never had any friends like that. Well, except for the one I stabbed because she was a *Prosin spy*."

Teretha nodded, her expression filled with loathing and disgust. "Again, Maralena's doing, not mine."

"So you say."

"I bring a gift, to show my sincerity. It was Narelki who sent men to attack Lara and started the whole mess. She stood by and let Aiul think it was you."

Kariana shrugged, pleased to see the Prosin woman's disappointment. "Old news. Maralena told me that just to hurt me, to make me feel guilty for stabbing Marissa."

Teretha's expression darkened at this. "I see. Did she also tell you it was my son Rithard who deduced it?"

Kariana stared at her for a moment, considering the implications, hearing Caelwen's words in her memory, *"He has very special talents*!" "No," she answered at last. "No, she most definitely did *not* mention that."

Teretha extended a hand, gravely serious now. "Maralena was a disgrace to our House, and made an enemy of you for no reason but pride and arrogance. I would undo that. We share a common enemy in Narelki. I propose an alliance."

Kariana shrugged again, ignoring Teretha's outstretched hand. "Narelki will get what she deserves, but she's hardly my most pressing problem. The Meites are."

Teretha nodded, even as she lowered her hand with an air of resignation. " I have a plan for that, and it involves Narelki. She *is* my problem. She wants my son dead."

"Well, then, I suppose Davron's holding him prisoner works in your favor, doesn't it?" Kariana tittered. "They don't care much for each other, Davron and Narelki."

Teretha's jaw clenched as she bit back a retort. "I'm negotiating for his release, but it is less than useless if Narelki can still strike at him. Rithard will never be safe as long as she remains a threat."

"So we know what *you* get. What's my benefit?"

Teretha smiled again. This was where she wanted the conversation to go, it seemed. "My plan would deal with the Meites *and* Narelki in one fell stroke. Help me, and you gain the loyalty not only of House Prosin, but Amrath as well."

Kariana raised an eyebrow at this. "How is that possible?"

Teretha raised her eyebrows and rocked forward, grinning. "By acquiring the right friends."

Kariana listened intently as Teretha explained her plan, and smiled at its simplicity. She felt her mistrust slowly replaced by awe at Teretha's cunning and audacity, her simple cutting of an impossible knot. *I could learn so much from her.*

Yet a nagging voice in her head argued it was not enough. She remembered staring up at the statue of Tasinal, blood running down her face, and dreaming the mad dream of dispensing with cunning once and for all, to have the power to simply smash her enemies rather than fence and spar for every advantage. The notion of living by her own rules, and not having to lie and manipulate was a powerful one indeed, but to reach that, she would need to prove herself. This was a stepping stone.

I could be more. If my father hadn't held me back. If I had been trained. "I'll play this game," she said at last. *And win.*

Narelki looked up from her desk in the library as Slat opened the doors. "You have a visitor, Mistress," he told her.

Kariana, seeming even shorter standing next to Slat, gave Narelki a look of grudging surrender.

Narelki nodded to Slat. "You may leave us." She waited until the doors were closed before addressing her uninvited guest. "Did you truly imagine you could *summon* me like a slave?"

Narelki was expecting rage, petulance, or perhaps even feigned long suffering nobility, but she was taken aback by what she saw on Kariana's face: sheer terror.

Kariana's eyes darted back and forth, as if searching for spies. "I felt safer in the palace, and I couldn't trust a messenger. I'll just have to hope Amrath's Library keeps its secrets."

Narelki was tempted to simply eject Kariana and go back to her treatise. *This is such an obvious production.* Still, it wouldn't do not to find out what the child was up to. She was possessed of a certain low cunning that could prove troublesome if not watched carefully. "Nihlos would have fallen long ago if the Library of Amrath were not inviolate. Speak whatever lie you came to tell and begone."

Kariana began to blink quickly, her features trembling as if her brain were being overloaded. *Ah, there. A little more pressure at that crack, I think, will prove telling, or at least amusing.* "It's more than one thing," she stammered.

You are absolutely infuriating with your idiocy. "Then perhaps you ought start with the first, hmm, then proceed on to the others?"

"Okay, okay! I'm just trying to figure out which *is* first." Kariana fidgeted like the child she was for long moments as Narelki's patience unraveled even further, but at last she blurted out, "They're going to kill Aiul!"

Narelki felt a brief chill, the natural reaction to hear one's child is in danger, before she considered the source of the information. She gave Kariana a patronizing look. "Who?"

"The Meites!"

The chill in her gut rose again, briefly. *They are indeed capable of it, but why would they?* She pushed it down again, feeling her lips purse in annoyance. Kariana was a habitual liar and a crude manipulator. This story was likely the hook for something, though precisely what remained to be seen. Still, there was something in her demeanor, her choice of words, that made hearing her out seem worthwhile. Narelki offered Kariana a cold, calculated glare. "Let us say for the moment that you had fooled me with this pathetic attempt at deception. How did you come by this knowledge and continue breathing?"

Slowly, with copious amounts of hand waving and self aggrandizing, Kariana trotted out her obviously rehearsed back story. *There I was, just minding my own business, thinking only pure thoughts, when suddenly yadda yadda. Youth are so arrogant, imagining their plodding, mundane attempts at cleverness are unique or even very effective.* A zombie no one else had seen was convenient, and Kariana's feigned noblesse oblige was sickening, her bravery in going to demand answers from powerful sorcerers absolutely ridiculous.

"I was working up my nerve to go in when they started chanting this poem, and then they started fighting, and Maranath yelled out, 'She intends to kill Aiul, you fool!'" Kariana paused and looked at the floor, embarrassed. "And then I ran away."

The ice in Narelki's belly refused to go down this time. *No! Oh, no, it cannot be that!* She stared intently at Kariana, forming each word carefully, like a sculptor chipping ice from a block. "What were they chanting? What words?"

Fear shone on Kariana's face at Narelki's new tone. "I can't remember!". She sputtered. "Something about a thousand years, and ten centuries, and –."

Narelki could not help herself. She had spent years since her fall, working so hard to master her once raging emotions. She no longer had the luxury of that freedom. Yet the fury could not be contained. Kariana forgotten, Narelki leapt to her feet, seized a vase from her desk, and smashed it against the wall where it exploded in a rain of pottery, water, and flowers. *"Traitors!"*

Kariana slowly backed toward the door, eyes bright with sudden fear, hands up as if to ward off a blow, shouting. "What? What did I say?"

Narelki barely noticed her. With a shriek, she grabbed at the edge of her desk and flipped it over, scattering papers over the floor. "I'll kill you *all*, you back stabbing, treacherous whores!"

It was, Narelki thought, like having a seizure, or the closest experience she had to compare. One felt it coming on, the jaw clenching like a vise, the pressure inside the skull demanding release, and then the feeling that one's head were literally coming apart at the seams. Control fled in a blinding flash as everything was blotted out. Then came the flailing about, smashing things, often enough of great value, as if they were a sacrifice. Control returned slowly, some time later, and one often enough found themselves in a humbling position. She ran her hand over her face as she contemplated the mess. "Brilliant," she muttered to herself. "I'll be lucky to salvage that treatise." *Undignified, but better than feeling helpless.*

She suddenly remembered her guest, and cast a tired glare her way. Kariana stood cringing in the corner, pallid and wide-eyed like a prey animal.

"Wretch," Narelki spat as she struggled to regain her dignity. "Even a fallen Meite terrifies you, I see."

Kariana blinked several times. "What? I don't–"

"It doesn't matter," Narelki snapped. She considered calling for Slat to have the slaves clean the mess, but it was bad enough that Kariana knew of her tantrum. She could not bear the shame of Slat's disapproving, silent stare. He had never whipped her as a child, but that was only because her own father had been quite handy with a switch, and Slat had learned from a master. She put the thought from her mind and bent down to pick up pieces of the vase. "What else did you have to tell me?"

Kariana was trembling now. "You're a Meite?" she asked in a near-whisper. After a moment, she added, "Are you going to kill me?"

Narelki stood and deposited the shards into a waste basket, then turned to address her insolent, mocking, and soon to be ejected guest. But looking at the girl, it seemed less mockery and more genuine ignorance. *We've done you no favors, have we?* Narelki sighed and allowed herself a brief smile. She suddenly felt very old again. "I once was. But no more. And no, I think I'll let you live for now, at least until I've heard the rest of what you've come to say." A million new questions seemed to float in Kariana's shocked stare, but now was not the time. "Your news first. What is the other issue?"

Kariana nodded, eager to comply. "Teretha Prosin wants an alliance with you and me. She says to remind you of the Continuity of Government plans, and you will understand how we can take control of the council."

Narelki heard herself speak, even as she was absorbing the information. "That's patently ridiculous. It hasn't been used in..." She trailed off as she thought more deeply. *Perhaps.* Kariana, still nervous and blinking in confusion, seemed to be trying to understand, and failing. *Mei, I don't remember the details!* She began scanning the bookshelves, looking for a specific volume, the name of which she could not quite remember. *I'll know it when I see it.*

Kariana, of course, lacked the grace to simply silence her prattle while her elders were thinking. "She doesn't know about Aiul and the Meites. But we could stop them if we did this, right? They'll listen to the will of the council?"

Narelki laughed softly, nodding at this even as she continued her search. "And of course I would have to absolve Rithard. That's what this is really about, yes?"

"Isn't it worth it?"

Narelki paused and raised an eyebrow at Kariana, considering, then turned back to the shelf. "It is. I have no real hatred for Rithard. It was Davron's doing." She felt a brief flare of rage at the thought of Davron's arrogance, followed by a small, lustful thought. She had to admit, grudgingly, he was all the more attractive for it. "I can hardly fault the boy for being afraid, and I can't help but admire how well he carried it off. But he should have come to me. I could have protected him." She grimaced at the correction that came to mind, as if swallowing a bitter pill, but felt it would be simply weakness not to speak the plain truth. "*We* could have protected him."

"So you *are* still a Meite?"

Narelki placed a hand where she left off her search, shook her head sadly, and gave Kariana her attention once again. "No. I have nothing left. It's all gone. They coddle me, as if I am a child they need to protect, but my own power fled me long ago. I've had to learn other ways." She ground her teeth momentarily. "Such as this bargain you propose."

"Which I don't even understand, just so we're clear," Kariana said, her tone acid despite her obvious terror. "Nobody ever taught me about this kind of thing. I'm lucky I'm still alive."

Narelki couldn't help but feel some empathy for her. "I suppose you know something of how it feels, hmm? To lose your whole life and find yourself having to learn to swim in deep water." Kariana, for once, was silent, and suddenly seemed to find the floor a subject of great interest. *We did it to her, for our own selfish reasons. She's absolutely right—it's a wonder she's survived.*

Narelki turned back to her search once again, and saw the book she wanted just below her hand. "Ah, here!" she exclaimed as she hauled a large, leather bound book from the shelf. She was somewhat surprised to see not even a mote of dust. *I really must remember to congratulate Slat on this.* Of course, he didn't do the work on his own, but clearly he held his people to a rigorous standard. Even she wouldn't have demanded such perfection, but then, Slat had always been that way.

"Teretha is referring to an ancient law that hasn't been invoked since the days just after Nihlos's founding." She showed Kariana the book briefly before opening it and thumbing through the pages. "You must understand, in the early days, when all of the houses were ruled by Meites, there were often battles, literally, amongst the council members. There was a distinct possibility that a particularly nasty struggle could end up with someone dead or incapacitated." *As you, yourself have suffered from, though no one had the decency to tell you.*

"If the battle were large enough, it might leave the council unable to field a quorum, and prevent them from governing, so Amrath wrote a contingency into the law. The normal quorum is nine, two thirds of the full council plus one more. But should one third of the council members die or become otherwise unable to perform their duties, the quorum changes, but only for confirming new members. It becomes a simple majority of the active members, until there are at least nine again."

Kariana's eyes grew wide as she made the connection. "Sadrina's never been replaced!"

Narelki nodded. "And Davron is in open revolt. While I'm not certain it qualifies in the sense the founders meant it, he's made no friends with this stunt. Most of the councilmembers would see it our way." Narelki considered a moment. "Presumably, Teretha will have her own puppet suddenly fall ill or resign. Now I understand why they put that idiot in charge. He was disposable all along. But we would need one more to reduce quorum to five."

Kariana's expression darkened. "Prandil! I'll seduce him and poison him!"

Narelki barked a harsh, humorless laugh at this. "Mei! You are bold, aren't you? Or are you completely ignorant of the fact that he and I were lovers once?"

Kariana quailed at this. "I'm doing a good job of making sure I don't get out of here alive, huh?"

Narelki laughed again, and dabbed at tears in her eyes. *She's actually quite hilarious, if one thinks of her in the proper mindset.* "I didn't say I objected, child. It's just that you wouldn't be able to carry it off."

"I see the way he looks at me!"

"Oh, you could seduce him well enough. But poison a Meite? Not possible. If he even noticed the attempt, he'd refuse to believe it, and then beat you within an inch of your life, if not beyond."

"That's impossible! No one is immortal!" Kariana said.

"Oh, he's hardly immortal. Meites bleed like anyone else. It's just that you'd need to be considerably more up front about it, and you'd need to do it quickly."

"So you don't care if he dies?"

"If I am to believe what you've told me, he's part of a conspiracy to murder my child."

"'If,'" Kariana sighed. "I told you all I know. You seemed like you believed me when you were wrecking the place."

"You are correct. I find myself fairly convinced, even knowing who you're bargaining with. No one outside the order would know enough to mock up that story you told, including Teretha Prosin."

"So what do I tell her, then?"

"Tell her I'm considering her offer. Until I have a plan to deal with Prandil, it's irrelevant, anyway."

Rithard sat unmoving in a comfortable chair, fingers steepled, contemplating how to escape his cell. Oh, it had the appearance of a nicely appointed room, but it was a cell nonetheless. The door was locked, making him a prisoner, something he intended to rectify.

He remembered Davron hammering a mailed fist into Caelwen's skull, and Caelwen going down to the prodigious blow. They had taken Rithard then, giving him no chance to even find out if his friend had survived. Rithard offered little protest. It was not the time. They were strong, and he was drunk and weak.

But now, sober again, with time to think, and left alone and in reach of any number of things he might turn into weapons, they would soon regret underestimating him. Did they not realize he could make poison gas with the cleaners they so thoughtlessly left unguarded? Perhaps even an explosive?

Rithard chuckled darkly to himself. *Or a powerful acid that will melt the flesh from your skulls. You imbeciles should never have given me a means of cooking.* He took his small grenade from his pocket and cradled it in his hand in anticipation. *They will come soon.*

'Soon' was a relative thing. He had almost lost his enthusiasm at the prospect by the time he at last heard a key rattling in the lock,

Rithard leapt to his feet and took up a position to the side of the door, poised to hurl his vial of acid at the head of whomever entered. As it happened, however, the door opened to reveal the one person who could stay his hand.

Teretha, resplendent in a provocative black silk dress, stepped through the door. Davron entered behind her, literally in tow. She was arm in arm with him.

Teretha looked Rithard, frozen in place, hand held high and ready to strike. Her eyes widened in surprise, then narrowed in suspicion. "What are you about, Rithard?" Davron's hand lowered, hovering at his blade, but he said nothing.

Rithard lowered the vial with a great sigh, and cast his eyes to the ground. He was neither pleased nor surprised to see Davron's hand move away from his sword and around to Teretha's backside. *So, she's taken control here. I should have expected as much.* "It would seem I misunderstood the situation." He gave her a sour look and added, "Of course, I was lacking any number of data points that might have prevented that."

"Don't be petulant, Rithard," she chided. "It's a safe bet that if I didn't have you snatched up, Narelki would have."

"And my friend is dead because of it!"

Davron rolled his eyes at this. "Mei, he's fine, nothing worse than a headache and a sore jaw. We can send for him later if you'd like proof of that."

Rithard raised an eyebrow. "An interesting way to put it. You imply I am your prisoner."

Teretha reached up with delicate hands and turned Rithard's head to face her. "I want you *safe* until this sorts out."

Davron nodded. "The sooner it's done, the sooner I'll get my father's sword back."

Teretha turned to him and laid a hand on his chest. "In good time." She smiled at him and added, "It will be pleasant enough, I assure you."

Davron's face seemed to go to war with itself for a moment, torn between outrage and desire, at last settling for surrender." My father would not approve."

Teretha's eyebrows rose in shock and offense. "Of *me*?"

"Oh, no, my dear. My father was quite fond of women, too, to my good fortune. No, I was thinking of my ignoring the theft of his blade in order to plant my own."

Teretha patted his cheek. "Your father would want you to have an heir, and theft is such a strong word. I've merely borrowed it for while. It's not as if I've asked overmuch for its return." She turned back to Rithard, a calculating smile on her face. "Save one son, and make another. Fighting and fucking have ever been passions that men find difficult to resist."

Rithard shuddered to hear her speak so frankly, and thanked whatever gods might have had a hand in his birth that he was the one man in the world immune to her manipulations. *At least those kind. She has other strings to pull on me, but they are not so strong.* "So I am a *guest*, now?"

Davron waved an arm toward the hallway. "You'll have the run of my grounds, but no farther. I can't protect you if you leave."

"So I am to spend my life as a refugee at House Noril?"

Teretha caressed his cheek, her eyes suddenly deep wells of compassion. *And here are her strings for me.* "No, my love," she said softly, as if he were still her babe in the cradle. Then her eyes grew cold again. "I think you will not have to wait here very long at all."

Rithard knew when she was taunting him. She enjoyed dangling bits of information in front of him, like teasing a cat with string. "You know something. Tell me."

She gave him a cryptic smile. "You'll work it out soon enough. In the meantime, I'll enjoy knowing something you don't. It happens so rarely, it really ought be relished."

CHAPTER 9
VOODOO BOOTS

SHORTLY after midnight, Ilaweh's will anchored fairly close to the spot where Ahmed had last seen Yazid, at the mouth of the river near Nihlos. Ahmed allowed himself a brief moment to grieve for the loss of the only father he had ever known, and another hoping that somewhere, Yazid could see what he had accomplished and was proud, then forced himself to sleep. There was much work to be done.

Early the next morning, he and Sandilianus sat across from one another at the desk in his cabin. From the quarterdeck, the crew struck six bells. The crew would be waking for breakfast, which meant he and Sandilianus needed to come to a decision soon.

Ahmed drummed his fingers on the desk as he thought "It is a tricky issue, to be certain."

Sandilianus nodded in solemn agreement. "I once heard a puzzle about a farmer trying to cross a river with his animals and grain. This feels similar."

"Aye. Eleran is a fine fistsman, but I would not trust him with the gold alone."

Sandilianus, who had spent much time with the Nihlosian of

late, laughed out loud. "He would tell you himself not to trust him with it. It would be too much of a temptation."

"If we go with him, these fools will steal the ship, though."

Sandilianus shrugged. "Obviously, we must split our forces."

"I do not like that notion, either. We are in enemy territory. We must not split up and weaken ourselves even more."

Sandilianus shook his head, frustrated. "We have been over this! You must choose one unpleasant alternative or the other. Stop acting like a boy and be done with it!"

Ahmed glared at Sandilianus, and considered challenging him to fists simply to prove he was not afraid, but he did not relish a beating merely for pride's sake. Some other time, perhaps, but now there was important work to be done.

Ahmed closed his eyes, thinking. The ship was certainly a rarity, but he would never find another warrior to equal the ones he had, not here. Losing the ship would be a setback; losing his men would be disaster.

The ship, then, must be risked. Yet leaving it in the hands of these savages was no 'risk'. It was sacrifice, plain and simple. Was there truly no other way?

Ahmed listened intently for guidance, for the voice of Ilaweh, but heard nothing. It was not entirely unexpected. If Ilaweh intervened at every stubbed toe, there would be no need for men of resourcefulness and courage. Ilaweh cultivated such things in men through adversity and challenges just like this one. Ahmed was on his own.

That very realization shifted stumbling blocks in his mind. He could feel his face warm as a grin spread over it. "Bring me the Nihlosian!"

Some hours later, Ahmed was ready to implement his plan. It was hardly perfect, but it at least tilted the ship back into the 'risk' category. That was enough for him. It had to be.

Sandilianus's voice rang throughout the ship. "All hands before the mast!"

Ahmed took his own place at the fore of the ship, standing at parade rest while the crew gathered. Sandilianus made a run through berthing, searching for stragglers, slapping the backs of their heads.

When they were assembled, Sandilianus took his place at Ahmed's side. "All hands present and accounted for, Captain."

Ahmed nodded. "Very well." He took a moment to look over the fifty-seven men, ranging in color from coal black to tan to (in one, singular case) fish-belly white. It was a motley crew, indeed. Would the locals buy it? They certainly wore that gullible, stupid look on a fairly constant basis of late, so there was that factor on his side.

There was really only one way to find out.

"As you know," he called out, "We are here to hire on a new crew to replace you. This is the bargain I have made, and I will stand by it." He paused for dramatic effect, then pressed on, "We demons are bound by certain rules, and must adhere to the letter of our bargains."

Murmurs rippled through the natives. Ahmed studied the faces of his men carefully, searching for any hint of humor. They were strong warriors, but it could be very difficult not to laugh at such things. He was relieved to see that each and every man's face was a mask of gravity.

"Yes, it is true. We thought to deceive you and take you all to hell, but your man Bendaro saw through us. He forced me into this bargain. You should thank him."

Ahmed paused again, allowing the natives to do just that. They looked at Bendaro with reverence and gratitude, some bowing, some stepping up to shake his hand. Bendaro, for his own part, looked quite uncomfortable. *Damn! Has he changed his mind?*

"But know you this!" Ahmed roared. "Bound by a bargain I may be, but I am a powerful sorcerer, as well as a demon! And if you break our bargain, you will break my bonds, and you will feel my wrath!"

The natives' eyes were wide with fear. Ahmed could see some of them were actually trembling. Good. Time to rub it in.

Eleran spat on the ground and called out, "Bullshit."

Desperate, strangled cries burst from several of the crew. Shouts of, "Idiot!" and "Shut up, fool!" rang out across the deck. Eleran clenched a fist and took a step toward his closest detractor. The man shrunk away.

"Yeah, you know what to be scared of, don't you?" he muttered to the man, then spoke to the crowd at large. "I've told you fools for years! They ain't demons! And he *ain't* no sorcerer, either! I've *seen* sorcerers!"

Ahmed pointed a finger and him and shouted, "Dog! You dare defy me? Suffer!"

Eleran clutched at his chest and screamed, staggering this way and that over the deck. The natives screamed along with him, stumbling over one another, desperate to avoid him as he bumbled about. At last, he collapsed to the deck, writhing and screaming.

The crewmembers were practically gibbering in fear by now. Sandilianus drew his blade and brandished it. "Silence!" The other Xanthians also drew their blades and stepped back from the crowd.

Ahmed gestured to Sandilianus. "I will show these fools I am not to be trifled with! Bring me his boot!"

The crowd parted before Sandilianus as he moved toward Eleran. Eleran had stopped screaming now, and was flopping about the deck like a fish. His lips were flecked with foam, and his eyes rolled in his head, unseeing. Sandilianus grabbed his right boot and began pulling.

"The left boot!" Ahmed shouted.

Sandilianus switched to Eleran's left foot, scowling.

Ahmed called out, "It *must* be the left boot, fool! You do not understand sorcery. Do *you* wish to test me today?"

Sandilianus shook his head, fear on his face. "No, dark master!" He jerked Eleran's left boot from his foot and brought it to Ahmed.

Ahmed twisted his face into a caricature of evil as he cried out, "Behold, dogs, what happens to those who incur my wrath!" He raised the boot high above his head and brought his other hand just beneath it, fingers twisted into a claw.

Fire sprung from his hand and licked at the boot. On the deck, flames sprung up on Eleran as well. Within seconds, he was engulfed by them. Screaming, he leapt to his feet, ran to the ship's railing, and dove overboard.

Ahmed waited a moment for the whole scene to sink in, then cried in his best voice of doom, "Bring me your boots, dogs! The left ones! And know if you betray me, you will suffer the same fate!"

As Ahmed and his men walked down the makeshift gangplank of *Ilaweh's Will*, there was little doubt in his mind that the ship would remain just where he had left it. Sandilianus, just behind him, carried a heavy sack containing thirty-seven boots over his shoulder. The natives watched them go, their faces so pale with fear that they looked more like Eleran's people than their own.

Ahmed bit his tongue to keep from laughing. "Don't look," he gasped. "It only makes it harder!"

Sandilianus nodded. "I know. Too late. I already did."

Eleran met them a mile upriver, looking none the worse for wear. "Did they buy it?"

Sandilianus laughed loudly. "I am almost ashamed at the fear we have put in their souls. Those men will starve to death before they leave."

Eleran beamed. "Neat trick, eh? Did I earn my share of the gold?"

Ahmed clapped him on the shoulder. "Indeed! How *did* you manage that flame, anyway?"

Eleran smiled. "I could tell you. But then I'd have to—"

"Kill me," Ahmed completed, rolling his eyes. "Fine, keep your secrets. Let's get on with this. We have far to go."

CHAPTER 10
PAIN AS A TRUTH SERUM

PRANDIL paused writing for a moment and considered the image in his head. House Veril was a wretched lot of indulgent, insipid fools who practiced the most shallow of arts, performance. They were barely a half rung above thieves and beggars. It wasn't as if their opinion mattered overmuch, so there was no worry about going too far. Still, insult and mockery were art forms in and of themselves, and it wouldn't do to get it half right. The rest of the houses would all be reading this in the morning paper, after all.

He was still considering when Thrun, his personal slave, entered the study, a piece of paper in his hand.

"Ah, just in time," Prandil called. "Are the presses ready for the morning run? I have some fine print here. Tell me, would you prefer outright calling Sadrina Veril a vacuous, flatulent cow? Or something more subtle, say a waste of food and air?"

Thrun leaned against one of the many bookshelves, raised both hands overhead, and stretched. "She's dead, Prandil. Kind of harsh."

"Oh, it's not *kind of*. It's full and intentional. You know what they're doing, don't you?"

"The protest? Yeah, it would be hard not to, with you bitching about it all the time."

Prandil grinned and raised both arms in victory. "That's just the point! I intend to mock them without mercy until they grow up and nominate a house leader." He paused a moment and lowered his hands, noting the paper in Thrun's grasp. "What have you there?"

Thrun started a bit, suddenly remembering why he had come. "Oh! A letter from House Amrath. The slave who delivered it said it was 'very important', so I assumed some juicy news on recent events."

Prandil raised an eyebrow at this. "Well, there are all sorts of leaks we might find useful from there of late, eh?" He made a twirling, hurry-up gesture with his hands. "Go on, let's hear what it says! We *have* taught you to read, yes?"

Thrun gave him a sour look, but opened the envelope and began to read. "Amrath Narelki extends her invitation to Idlic Prandil to join her for dinner at a place to be determined, and would visit House Idlic to discuss said location."

Prandil considered a moment, pulling at his beard, his smile growing. "Well, now, that *is* a pleasant surprise!" He quickly took the letter from Thrun and held it to his nose to sniff it. "Perfumed. So it is, at least ostensibly, a romantic overture." He looked at it again. "Mei, I thought you were just a clod paraphrasing words you didn't understand. This is the actual text, hmm? Who wrote this? A slave?"

"A lawyer, more likely," Thrun opined.

"Certainly not an editor or other literate."

"I hear tell editors can fix your mistakes, but are otherwise unable to communicate via the written word."

Prandil nodded at this wisdom. "That is true. I actually have to remove one hat and put on another before I can perform my duties properly." He looked at the letter again, then folded it and put it in his pocket. He took in a deep breath, relishing it, and let it out, the scent of the perfume still faint in his nose. "So her writing is stilted. She has other qualities that interest me."

"I haven't seen you this excited since they started adding bran to the pancakes."

"Nonsense! I'll have you know I was at least as excited to run the headline of Sadrina's timely demise."

"Well, true, that was a happy day for us all," Thrun chuckled. "Still, I guess there's more between you two than I know about."

"I suppose you *are* a bit lacking in details compared to your father." Prandil suddenly felt wistful. First Narelki stepping out of the past, and then to think of Alric. The man had practically raised him. "I won't apologize for outliving him, but I miss him terribly."

"He told me a lot of stories about you, but not this. I'm guessing there's a good reason."

"I shudder to hear the sort of tales he might have told you of my youth, but this is from a bit later, and nothing complicated. Narelki and I used to be lovers some hundred years ago." Again, Prandil felt a deep, pleasant nostalgia rising in him, remembering things he had thought gone forever. *Ah, it is so lovely to find a hope one counted lost.* "She was the sort of beauty that might freeze a man in place, just contemplating her. And a regular demoncat in bed!" He gave Thrun a conspiratorial wink, then waved as if dismissing a ghost. "It's not surprising you don't remember. What are you, all of fifty and learning to shave?"

Thrun chuckled at this, and poked back, "What's that make you, like a thousand?"

Prandil rose from his desk, feigning shock and placed his hands on his hips in an indignant pose. "One hundred eighty seven and still vigorous enough to thrash a strapping young lad like you!" He flung a pen at Thrun and grinned as the slave caught it mid-air. "And take your women, too. You remember that, boy. Age, treachery, and cold, hard currency trump youth and beauty every time."

Thrun rolled his eyes. "Well of course you can beat me up. You're a Meite!"

Prandil gave him a smug look. "And why aren't you?"

"You're stalling. Misdirecting. Must be some real meat to this one."

"You're like a pit bull, Thrun. Who taught you this tenacity for getting a story, I wonder?"

Thrun looked dubious. "I wonder. Come on, plate the meat. Why'd you quit her?"

Prandil, never the sort of man to try to conceal even the tiniest emotion, suddenly wished he had bothered to learn at least some small talent for it. Clearly, just the look on his face told plenty.

Thrun's eyes widened and he grinned. *"Oh!"* he shouted, slamming a fist into his palm as if he had scored a goal in a ball game. *"She* quit *you!"*

Prandil heaved a great, dramatic sigh. "Indeed she did. I loved her quite completely, and I suppose I still do, after a fashion."

"So even Meites have to deal with rejection now and then."

Prandil grew serious. "It was considerably more than my wounded pride. If it were just that, it would be trivial." He gazed at Thrun for a moment, remembering Alric. The boy had much of his father in him. He was thick and strong, and quite fearless. He was almost the right material to be trained, but the small lack was the difference between the lightning and the lightning bug. To try and fail would be so much worse than to never have tried at all. "How much do you know of our order?"

Thrun cocked his head, thinking. "Besides the fact that you're all crazy? Not much."

"That's quite a bit, actually. More than most understand." Prandil steepled his fingers beneath his chin. "It *is* a sort of madness, a carefully cultivated one. We spend our lives denying reality, deciding what we feel based on what we want." He heaved a great sigh and lowered his hands to his knees as he leaned forward. "What I am trying to say here is that while I remember my heart being broken, my soul utterly crushed, it was just a moment before I *chose* to see it another way, to realize I never cared very much for her at all, to see her as a dalliance I was well rid of."

"Yeah, that's the same advice I got after my first heartbreak."

"You're not fully grasping what I'm saying here. I wasn't merely playing sour grapes. I *believed* it because I chose to. The same way that I can convince myself that physical laws are not real things. I can *fly*, Thrun. *Anyone* can. They just have to stop believing in gravity."

"Just like that," Thrun said, snapping his fingers. "Stopped loving her. It's easier to disbelieve gravity, I think."

"Just like that," Prandil agreed. "A Meite defends his mind as a miser defends his gold. If something hurts us, we lash out. If that won't help, we choose to see it another way, one in which we are the victor, or in which we're merely biding our time, gulling our enemy into a false sense of security. Often enough, we get excited about some other matter and completely forget what troubled us in the first place. It's our way."

Thrun shifted and threw an arm over the bookshelf, seeming uncomfortable, as he absorbed the idea. "So how does it play into this story?"

"She didn't do that," Prandil muttered. "She turned away from me, and then she turned away from everything." Prandil paused, feeling unexpectedly haggard and mean. "And all because of that wretch. I should have murdered him when I had the chance."

"Who?"

"I don't remember his name, if I ever even knew it. He was a commoner she took a a brief fancy to when she and I were split. She got pregnant, then tired of him. He didn't take it well."

Prandil paused a moment. *Perhaps I ought not tell this part, but Elgar take it.* "He forced his way into her home, and then into her bed. Into *her*, if you take my meaning."

"Wow!"

"She was one of us before him, and he stole that from her."

Thrun's eyebrows arched in genuine shock. "She was a Meite? How do you *steal* that?"

Prandil nodded gravely. "Psychological trauma. A deep and personal violation. Something to shake her to her very soul and make her doubt herself."

"The rape? Mei! But that's crazy! She could have torn him to shreds!"

"And now you see the tragedy, eh? She *chose* not to. That always irked me, honestly. She stabbed me more than once, you know, but her plaything, she couldn't bring herself to harm. Not until it was too late." Prandil tapped his pen sharply against his desk several times. "Another Meite would have simply decided to enjoy it, to want it even, or at least look at it as indulging a pathetic creature. We change our minds like we change socks. It's whatever we want today, and yesterday be damned, typically. But she had a weak spot there, I suppose. She couldn't get past it."

"Rape is pretty traumatic, I guess."

Prandil dismissed the thought with a wave of his hand. "It wasn't the rape. I've forced myself on her a time or two, just to prove a point. It was her reaction to it."

Thrun's face went from shocked credulity to sly amusement. "Mei! I thought you were serious. You're just jerking my chain."

"No, not at all. Meite relationships are stormy. I did mention she'd stabbed me on occasion, yes?"

"For raping her?"

Prandil snorted. "No, once for burning the toast, and another time because I was too drunk to service her properly. I don't actually recall what set her off the other times. And those are hardly the worst incidents, but there were damned fine times too, I assure you. The highs far exceed the lows."

"Then why? What made her change?"

Prandil found his gaze wandering to the floor, and forced himself to maintain eye contact. "My best guess is that she couldn't bring herself to hurt him. Being defeated in battle is one thing. If he had actually been strong enough to take what he wanted, she would have respected him. It's our way, you understand." He felt his eyes wandering again, to a shelf filled with ancient texts, and decided to let it stand. "We revere power. We acknowledge no master but ourselves, no morality but our own. But we do not waste. We capitulate to the stronger, usually. When we're stupid enough not to, someone usually ends up dead."

Thrun said nothing for a moment, then shrugged. "I never knew any of this."

"We've been remiss in training, to be frank. There are any number of things I ought to have explained to you, any number of students we ought to have taken and enlightened. But I fear we've grown too selfish." Prandil shook his head in consternation. "I only recently decided to take one on. The boy who comes here, Jareth."

"He's your student? Honestly I thought..." Thrun grinned widely, almost snickering.

Prandil paused in confusion a moment, then sneered at Thrun's subtle jab. "Oh, please. If my tastes ran that way, I'd have pushed you into some closet or another around here and had my way with you long ago. I'm sure you'd have enjoyed it."

Thrun placed a hand on his chest as if he'd been shot with an arrow. "Oh, ouch! I'm not sure if that's a compliment or an insult."

Prandil shot him a smug, patronizing grin. "Well, it's both, don't you think? I thought it was clever, telling you you were attractive while insinuating you were gay. I get paid well for that wit, you know."

"You deserve it, Prandil. You're the best, and everybody knows it. Including you. There, is that what you were fishing for?"

"You've quite the acid tongue yourself these days. It's a terrible habit. Where could you have learned that from, I wonder?"

Thrun shook his head, playing the obedient slave, but still grinning. "I wonder."

"Clever, handsome, and rude. You're the son I never had, Thrun. I think I'll make you my heir."

Thrun's eyebrows rose in genuine shock. "What? You can't do that." He paused a moment, looking at Prandil with suspicion and curiosity. "Can you?"

"Make a slave a full house member? With a word. I'm the *patriarch*. Happens all the time."

"Yeah, but not putting them in charge! It would be scandalous!"

Prandil cackled like a madman and slapped his knee. "Oh, Mei forbid it, then! Which simply inclines me to do it."

Thrun shook his head in disbelief, clearly certain Prandil was pulling his leg. "You will not."

Prandil rose to his feet and inclined his head to look down his nose at Thrun. "Have you learned nothing from this conversation?"

Maranath cringed as Ariano's victim screamed in agony. The small, ugly man, currently pinned to the dirt floor by Ariano's will, seemed unimposing, but he was holding up quite well to the torture. Maranath was hardly squeamish, but his partner was being forced to become more creative with her efforts, and he found it easier not to watch her work. Instead, he busied himself searching through the cultists' meagre personal effects, hoping to discover some shred of information that might make the interrogation moot.

It was, he knew, perhaps a bit too hopeful, but then, so was this entire misadventure, a complete shot in the dark. Apparently the one cell that Ariano knew of was comprised of the most stubborn and stupid cultists on Prima. The fools barely knew their own names, and they were fanatical enough to refuse even that information.

The whole tiny village didn't seem to have a pot to piss in. The buildings barely qualified as shacks, ramshackle, single story huts with dirt floors and a few sleeping mats. The one they occupied seemed special, a gathering hall of some sort, so they had made it their target. It had a fireplace and even a makeshift chimney, though the walls had enough leaks that Maranath had to wonder if the fire actually did much to ward off the cold. *I suppose the roof at least keeps the snow off.*

Maranath pulled a desiccated severed human hand from a rucksack and tossed it to the floor in disgust, cursing under his breath. It was hardly the first body part he had found, and Mei knew what the fools kept them for, or how they were obtained. *Most likely, the usual way, by lopping them off some unfortunate.*

Outside, he could hear more wails, cries of fear rather than pain, presumably from the women and children who had fled his and Ariano's assault. He shook his head in dismay. He had expected to deal harshly with the cultists, of course, but *children*? Why were they even here? *Do they really make a family business of murder and mayhem?*

"You think this is suffering?" the victim gasped, his words slurred but defiant. "When our lord strikes at you, you will *beg* for such tender mercies! I will tell you *nothing*!"

Maranath heard a sharp crack, and the cultist screamed again. Ariano muttered, "I gather such is the general consensus."

She's flagging. And well she should be. Ten corpses, covered in dancing shadows of the torchlight, littered the room. *She's running out of them.*

"He's the last one, you know," Maranath called over his shoulder. "Unless you intend to start on the women and children."

"Don't test me, Maranath!" Ariano hissed.

He spared her victim a sorrowful look. "I can't stop her, you know. If you don't give her what she wants, she'll go there next."

"Just so," Ariano said to her victim.

Maranath turned back to his own business. *She's not foolish enough to think I will tolerate it if it comes to that, but let the fool believe it is true.* He jerked open another bag to find a rotting foot, and hurled the container against a wall in disgust.

"Kill us all!" the cultist cackled. "I long to feel my lord's dark embrace! Let my blood be spilled in Elgar's name, and that of my children, too!"

"Oh, let's not hurry," Ariano told him. "I do so enjoy a visit with a handsome young man like yourself." The cultist screamed again.

Maranath was just about ready to admit defeat when he spied a lump beneath one of the sleeping mats. His intuition sang, and he snatched the mat aside to reveal a small backpack, partially buried, as if someone had tried to hide it in a great hurry.

He worked at the buckles, not wanting to get his hopes up. *It could just as easily be someone's cock and balls as anything useful.* To his surprise, he opened it to reveal not more body parts, but a small book that looked to be a journal of some sort.

As he began to flip through it, the prisoner's struggles turned violent and he roared something unintelligible. Maranath turned to see him, a bloody, half-dead corpse struggling against invisible bonds. His wide, mad eyes stared intently at Maranath as he sputtered. "Elgar! Give me your power to stop these unbelievers!"

Maranath held up the journal to Ariano as the prisoner

screeched in fury. The old woman smiled, then turned back to the cultist. "It seems I may have no further need of you."

The old woman smiled sweetly at the cultist as she tended his broken arm. She was harmless and kind, just the sort that he most enjoyed causing suffering.

"There!" she chirped. "It will heal now. In a few months, it will be good as new!"

"I thank you," the cultist said, licking his lips as he imagined the taste of her blood. She and the old man were weak. He could kill them both, if he wanted. Perhaps he would. Surely, Elgar would reward him with power! That they were of the Demon Men simply added to the satisfaction he would have in flaying them. Yet something stayed his hand. There was a sense of wrongness about this pair.

"Who did this to you?" the old man asked.

"A false prophet," the cultist spat. "He will suffer for his blasphemies. My lord Elgar sent him to his death in Torium!"

The old pair's eyebrows rose in unison, and the cultist immediately regretted his remark. Damn do-gooders! They would probably try to aid the heretic! There was no question, now. They would have to die. Yet he could not put aside the sense that there was more to them than met the eye. Perhaps it would be best if he had help, just to be safe.

"I must return to my people," he said, gesturing toward the camp. He struggled for a moment, trying to think of an appropriate lie. "To get money," he said finally, with a wicked grin. "To repay you for your help."

His smile faded as he looked into stone faces of the crone and her companion. All pretense of kindness was gone from their bottomless, brilliant eyes.

"No, my dear," the old woman said, her voice no longer a warbling twitter, but a commanding, rich, mellifluous tone. "I'm afraid that won't be possible."

He did not hear her voice after that, but he felt it slash into his head like a knife. And then he felt no more.

Maranath stared at the remains of the cultist in disgusted awe. The young fellow's head had simply…*exploded* in a fine, pink mist. It was *gone*. "Mei! Not how I would have handled it, but I won't argue the effectiveness. It would do a damned site on anyone else watching, too. You should have tried that on one of the first lot. We might have gotten here sooner."

Ariano kicked the corpse, then spat on it for good measure. "They would have welcomed a quick death. Though I suppose I could have drawn the process out a bit, thrown in some effects." She shrugged. "Some noblewoman or another is always claiming to have revolutionary techniques, but the truth is simple: the old, brutal methods work best. Everything else is salesmanship and psychology."

Maranath shrugged. "I wouldn't know. I'll leave that to you women."

"Men are so squeamish."

And women are so cruel, you doubly so. Perhaps that's why I love you. "Are we done here?"

"I think so. We got lucky with this one. Surely his 'false prophet' is Aiul, on his way to Torium with a piece of the eye."

"You have some theory on what it means?"

"It's very bad, Maranath. Indescribably so."

Maranath shook his head and grumbled, "Why not go ahead and try to describe it anyway? Humor an old man."

Ariano's eyes were full of fear as she looked back up at him.

"I swear to you, once I have worked it all out, I will tell you everything. But for now it's just pieces, red flags, alarm bells."

And bad memories, no doubt. "Fine. I'll give you a little more rope. But my patience is growing short. If I get the notion you're holding out on me, things will proceed in a very different direction. Am I clear?"

Ariano glared at him, but she said nothing. It was a normal thing by Maranath's reckoning, Ariano simultaneously outraged and smitten with him. *How alike we are, two sides of the same coin.* She was not the sort of woman to want a man she could rule. The only concern Maranath had was to be alert for the odd bit of crockery or surgical equipment she threw at him from time to time. He shrugged, and repeated, "Am I *clear*?"

Ariano, still angry, nodded. "We need to return to Nihlos at once. We'll have Polus send men to capture him."

This, Maranath found surprising. "You don't think we can handle it on our own?"

"I should rather have overwhelming force. I want to take him alive."

"*If* we can. So you see things my way now?"

Ariano's eyes filled with flame, and her voice rose to a shout. "It will be *my* decision, Maranath, and if you try otherwise, we'll test your theory of who is the stronger. Am *I* clear?"

Maranath nodded. "You are."

Ariano gave him one last withering glare, then shot like a bolt into the sky. *Ah, well, she knows her way home.*

As for himself, Maranath preferred things slow. Measure by measure, he reminded himself why gravity did not affect him, and why it should be plain to any fool. As it became an ever more compelling argument, he felt himself lighten until he was barely a feather hovering above the ground. He pushed up with his toes and sailed into the air, and it occurred to him that his toes were much stronger than he had realized. His speed increased as the truth sank in, that his launch must have been quite powerful indeed.

At some point, he would probably choose to believe otherwise on both counts. But he was far too old to let such contradictions bother him.

Polus had found himself quite surprised when his slaves reported Maranath's and Ariano's arrival. His first thought was that, for good or ill, they had at last come around to discuss Davron's rebellion, and he had welcomed them into his sitting room, but of course the welfare of Nihlos hadn't been their concern. They wanted something.

"A hundred men?" he asked Maranath "To capture a single man?"

Maranath nodded gravely. "More, if you can spare them."

"I can't field even that many and maintain order. In case you've forgotten, we have factions in open rebellion."

Ariano hissed at him. "You've *plenty* of men! At least five hundred, perhaps as many as a thousand!"

Polus gripped the arms of his chair tightly as if throttling someone's throat, a small, invisible act of violence instead of the more blatant one that briefly occurred to him. "*Had*. The South-landers killed twenty, then Maralena Prosin killed nearly a hundred more, and *you two* killed at least a hundred beyond *that*. Another two hundred or thereabouts have decided that guard work is no longer a field in which they wish to labor. We've had to fill in with men from the military forces, whose loyalties are not to me."

Ariano shrank back in her seat, momentarily vanquished. Maranath sucked at his teeth a moment, absorbing the hard facts. "We need those men, Polus," he said at last.

Polus shrugged. "And? They are not mine to give. You'll have to discuss it with Davron, and I think you left that situation poorly." He paused, waiting for a response, but the two Meites were remarkably quiet for once. *Like shamed children, contrite for the moment, but soon to be back at mischief, I'll warrant.* "At any rate, why do you need men? Why can't you handle this on your own? I've never known Meites to beg for martial support."

Ariano found her voice and muttered, "We're in uncharted territory. This is the Dead God's doing. We have no idea how many cultists we're dealing with, but at least a hundred. If they have sorcery of their own..."

Polus relaxed his grip on his chair and tapped a finger against it instead, considering. "If it frightens the two of you, I'll take it as a given that it's serious."

"It's every bit the threat to Nihlos that Davron's rebellion is."

Polus slammed his fist against the chair arm. "Mei! Then why do you not apologize to him and get on with what needs doing?"

Maranath looked at him, seeming both amused and indignant at the same time. "For what? Taking his bait? He started this fiasco by kidnapping Aiul."

Polus shook his head slowly. "That's not how he sees it. Nor how I do."

Ariano glared at him through narrowed eyes. "Explain that accusation."

Polus folded his arms over his chest. "I made no accusation. Quite deliberately so, whatever my private thoughts. Davron, on the other hand, has very strong opinions on the matter. I am sure he will be happy to discuss them with you in great detail if you were to pay him a visit. That's really the only way to get what you need here."

Kariana lay on her bed, struggling not to bite her nails. Where was Sadrik? She had sent for him almost an hour ago.

It was another half hour before his knock finally came. He entered, scowling as usual, but his eyes grew wide as he noticed her new tapestry. "Lovely." He contemplated it for a moment, then turned back to business. "What's this emergency?"

Kariana considered throwing something at him, but felt fairly certain her cousin would catch it and throw it back. "What took you so long?" she snapped.

Sadrik looked her up and down with a cool air. "You're worked up. What have you screwed up now?"

Kariana grabbed a decanter of liquor from her nightstand, but caught herself halfway to hurling it at Sadrik's head. She poured herself a drink to make it seem as if she never planned to bash his skull in with the bottle. "Well, now that you mention it..." She knocked the drink back. "Screwed is a mild word. I think we could say I've fucked up so completely even you won't know what to do."

Sadrik's jaw clenched, and his eyebrows knitted in annoyance. "Well, go on! Out with it!"

Kariana looked at the mirrored ceiling, then down at the marble floor. "I lost the Eye."

Sadrik's eyes bugged so profoundly that Kariana thought surely his head must be about to explode, and how would she ever clean up that mess? Well, the question was really how her slaves would clean it, since Sadrik was certainly about to murder her.

"You *what*?" he managed to choke out. "*How*?"

"It was Aiul! He took it when he was...you know, invulnerable and really scary!"

"Mei! Well, then there's no point being angry at you about it, I suppose."

"You'll find a way, I'm sure."

Sadrik shot her a sour look. "It *is* your fault in the end. You should have let him stab you in the throat. It would have saved me quite a bit of trouble."

Kariana pulled the dagger from her blouse and held it out to him, smirking. Sadrik slapped her hand aside. "Killing you now wouldn't solve a thing would it? It would just be one more mess for me to clean up!"

Kariana tittered as she returned the blade to its hiding place. "I know. Isn't it ironic?"

Sadrik stood glaring at her. *Oh, he's boiling. I could swear I smell smoke!* "Tell me what happened," he said. "*Exactly*, do you understand?"

Kariana put the knife and the pose away and grew serious. She told him about Aiul taking the Eye, in as much detail as she could recall.

Sadrik's constant sneer was gone now, replaced by dead seriousness. "Caelwen knows. You and I make three. Who else?"

Kariana didn't really want to have this discussion, but there was no way to avoid it. "The Big Three. Maranath, Ariano, and Prandil."

"You count that as a bad thing, hmm?"

Kariana rolled her eyes. "Hello! They're Meites! They can't be trusted."

Sadrik responded with a grunt. "Is that so?"

Was there just the faintest hint of mockery in his eyes? Kariana thought so, but then, there was usually even more. "Well, would *you* trust them?"

Sadrik laughed out loud. "Absolutely not. So why *did* you tell them before you told me?"

"Caelwen told them while I was unconscious. He didn't even know enough to understand he shouldn't, and they worked it out from what he described. They've had me pretty much on a leash since then."

"You do realize they have just returned?"

"Yes. I hear they are with Polus. That's why I called you here. And you took your sweet time!"

Sadrik shrugged. "I have a life, Kariana. On occasion, I am actually doing something other than waiting for you to call me screaming for help." He slammed his fist against his leg in frustration. "Keep this as secret as you can, do you hear me? And try not to do anything stupid for a few days! Mei, I need time to think!"

"I didn't do anything stupid *this* time except not get stabbed!"

Sadrik cast what was obviously meant to be a terribly severe look at her, but it was spoiled by a slight trembling of his lower lip. "Yes, well, see that you don't make that mistake again," he snickered.

"You are so mean to me!"

"It is my birthright." He flashed her a brief, genuinely kind smile, and turned to leave. He reached to open the door just as someone knocked from the other side.

Sadrik turned back to her. "Which of your toys is this?"

Kariana shrugged. "I wasn't expecting anyone."

Sadrik opened the door. Narelki stood outside, looking, as always, well groomed and in complete control. But there was something about her that made Kariana think there was trouble.

Narelki looked up at Sadrik and gave him a cool nod. Sadrik answered her gesture with a look of mild disdain. Narelki's face grew slightly more stiff than normal, but she said nothing as Sadrik slipped past her and departed.

The look was disturbing, like they had some kind of shared secret. Kariana felt her stomach flop around a bit. Surely Sadrik wouldn't betray her? No, that would be ridiculous. If he *were* her enemy, he would be *much* nicer to her. But perhaps he was fucking the old hag? It was a rather revolting thought, but then, she had been noticing Prandil of late. Perhaps Sadrik had similar thoughts about Narelki? Kariana shuddered and forced the image out of her mind. She focused on how truly annoyed she was with Narelki, which helped immensely. "What are you doing here? You've waited too long, and you've botched everything."

Narelki looked out the door to verify no one was nearby, then closed it. When she turned back to Kariana, her eyes were cold chips of diamond. "Save your imperious tone for the weak. You're a sniveling little girl weeping over being spurned or pouting at her disappointment. I doubt this alliance will last long, unless you grow considerably tougher."

Kariana's hand fluttered over her breast. Narelki saw the gesture and smiled like a cat about to pounce. "Oh, by all means. You'll lose, but it's the trying that counts."

Kariana jerked the dagger from her blouse and pointed it at Narelki like a spear. "Bitch, Prandil isn't here to protect you this time!"

Narelki's eyes widened in amusement and appreciation, and she struck a fighting stance. *Shit, she knows how to fight? They never taught me any poses like that.* Narelki beckoned Kariana forward with a hand gesture. "Let's see what you have little girl. I promise not to kill you. *This* time."

Kariana charged like a bull, aiming the dagger for the older woman's heart. Narelki calmly stepped aside and grabbed Kariana's wrist. She twisted and pulled, using Kariana's own momentum against her, and slammed her face-first into the wall to become, for the moment, one more player in the scene depicted on the tapestry. Kariana felt her body melt, and she slowly collapsed in a heap. The dagger dropped from her fingers clattered to the marble floor.

And I thought Maralena Prosin was a challenge.

Narelki, apparently just noticing the new tapestry, laughed out loud. "Oh, that scene suits you well, dear! Head down and ass in the air!" She grew somber again, and spat, "It's too bad you didn't show this sort of mettle *before* Aiul made his mess, or we'd be family by now. Get up, fool."

Kariana staggered to her feet and wiped blood from her nose. She gave Narelki a nod of surrender. "Well, that didn't go like I had planned."

"It went like *I* planned. Remember that and you'll bleed less."

Kariana sat on her bed and turned her nose up to stanch the steady drip. "Prandil beat me the first time, not you."

Narelki nodded agreement. "A fair point."

"Besides, I do believe I mentioned before how no one ever trained me to rule. You all left me to sink on my own. Don't blame it all on me."

Narelki, still in a combative stance, clenched her fists and actually *growled*. "You are being trained this very moment! Are you submitting or are you buying time, child?"

"Oh, definitely submitting." *On the field of arms, at any rate.* "I have no idea how I am going to get this blood out of my robe!" Kariana took a tissue from her nightstand and lay back on her bed. "So, did you come here specifically to give me a beating, or was there something else?"

"Now that you mention it, yes. Maranath and Ariano have returned."

"Yes. As I said when we started this conversation, you've screwed everything up by waiting too long."

Narelki laughed. "I'm not an idiot like you. I had no intention of moving forward with a doomsday scenario until it was verifiably doomsday. They might not have found him, you know."

"Well, they did. They're with Polus right now looking for some men to capture him."

"And so I am prepared to move forward."

Kariana sat up in her bed. "They're together! It's *suicide*!"

"Suddenly you've lost your nerve?" Narelki shook her head. "And your senses, it seems. You don't really think they will leave things to underlings, do you? They'll be off again soon, and for the moment they're looking to capture him, not kill. Now is the only chance we have."

Kariana lay back on the bed again. "I suppose so. But what if Prandil goes with them?"

"One way or another, he won't."

Davron entered his reception room and prepared himself for the coming battle. He was uncertain as to whether it would be mental or physical, but conflict was inevitable, and the thought of either invigorated him.

The reception area was filled with books for some reason, stacked on shelves around the periphery, though Davron had never really understood why. Reading material for guests was something the slaves managed. Supposedly, visitors appreciated the stuff. Davron paid for the things they told him were necessary, but he had no interest in them beyond being a gracious host.

Rithard lounged on one of the several low, plush couches, reading some dusty tome or another. "Put it away," Davron ordered. "Time to face your destiny, boy. Either you're about to get a reprieve, or we die in a legendary battle."

After a moment of defiance, Rithard closed the book and laid it on the low table in front of him. "Explain."

Davron gestured to the door as Ariano and Maranath entered. *Pathetic. Ragamuffins. No sense of style.* He gave them an imperious look, hand on hilt. "Are you here for parley or glory?"

Ariano's face twisted as if she were about to snarl some curse, but Maranath held up a hand. "Parley," he said.

Davron looked at them a moment, taking their measure. Ariano was clearly at the edge of violence, and Maranath, despite his calm demeanor, was close as well. *Hardly unexpected, but they will restrain themselves in my home.* "A truce, then. Say what you will."

Maranath put bony hands on bony hips. "You made quite a mess of things with that stunt you pulled. We're going to need your help cleaning it up."

Davron snorted at this. "You spend your lives telling the rest of us how inferior we are, and now you come groveling to me? And worse, you claim it is my fault!"

Ariano pointed an accusing finger at Davron and shouted "It most certainly *is* your fault! Are you denying you imprisoned Aiul?"

"Are you denying you killed Sadrina and Maralena?"

"I damned well *did* kill Sadrina," the old sorceress said with pride. "I make no apologies."

Maranath laid a hand on Ariano's shoulder and gently pulled her back. "Neither of us had anything to do with Maralena, however," he said, clearly struggling to keep his voice calm and conciliatory.

Davron was not fooled. *Everyone fears her. The fools have no idea which of them is the real threat.* "It was clearly Meite work."

"Be that as it may, it was neither of ours."

Davron scowled at them. "I didn't say it was *bad* work. But if you'd hold my feet to the fire for taking matters into my own hands, I expect you to present the two from your camp to stand trial with me, or admit I've done nothing you wouldn't do yourselves."

Ariano sneered. "Aiul was hardly worthy of such action."

"Was he not? He conspired with foreigners to attack Nihlos, and you would have set him free."

Maranath slammed his cane against the floor and shouted, "Now see here! I am the one who sentenced him to the pit!"

"You sentenced the Southlander to *death*. Yet you came here and freed him without so much as consulting me! You violated my *home*, Meite!" His grip tightened on his blade. Hopefully, his face was a mask of righteous rage. "House *Noril*, your eldest, truest allies!" He slammed a fist against his chest to emphasize the point. "Warriors and sorcerers have always been united against the politicians, and you *betrayed* us!"

In sudden fury, Davron kicked the low table, sending it flying past Rithard, the book atop it spinning off in a flutter of pages, to land with a thud. Rithard scowled at this, but had the good sense to keep his mouth shut.

Davron stepped toward the old sorcerer, took him by the shoulders, and looked him the eye. *Not so confident anymore, eh, old man? There's a lot of doubt and shame in those eyes. You know* just *what you did.*

"You betrayed *me*, Maranath." The point made, Davron stepped back and clasped his hands behind his back. *A victory, I should think.*

Ariano looked back and forth between them, as if she were trying to decide if there was to be a fight or not. Maranath, ashamed, put a hand on her shoulder and again gently pushed her away from Davron. She allowed it, but she was clearly unhappy with his decision.

Shaking his head in regret, Maranath slowly lowered himself to a knee and bowed his head. "You speak truth. We made a terrible mistake." He cleared his throat before continuing. "No. *I* made a mistake. And worse, I did not see it until you made me look at it."

Of all possible outcomes, this was the one Davron had never considered. To fight Maranath, to pry a concession from him, that would be well, but to have a powerful elder kneel before him and beg pardon? It was all terribly wrong, and worse, it was being witnessed by their juniors. Davron turned to Rithard. "Get out! You did not see this!"

Maranath, despite being on one knee, spoke with authority.

"Let him stay. I am not ashamed. This is no submission to your power. It's a submission to propriety. We gave you genuine offense, Davron. You have the right of it, and I know it. It does me no harm to admit it. It would harm me if I didn't, knowing I am in the wrong." Ariano, standing behind Maranath, nodded at this. *I will never understand these creatures. They are all mad.*

Davron, very uncomfortable with the situation, beckoned Maranath to rise. "Kneel before me no longer, Maranath. The point is made, on both our counts. I would not see you this way."

Maranath rose to his feet again and looked Darvon in the eye. "Very well."

Davron focused on Ariano, trying to judge her mood. "And you?"

For a moment, Davron thought she would fight, even though she had just agreed with Maranath that they shouldn't. The moment passed, and Ariano's face grew pinched. "It is so. We treated you poorly. I apologize."

"I accept your apology. Peace, then?"

Maranath nodded. "Peace."

"Peace", Ariano agreed.

Davron raised his hands in a magnanimous gesture. "Then what would you ask of me, friends?"

"We need fighters," Maranath said. "A lot of them."

An odd request, from powerful sorcerers. "For what purpose?"

"We intend to capture Aiul," Maranath told him. "But we have learned there may be a large group of Elgar cultists with him."

"You have my attention. How many?"

"If Ariano's tracking of them is correct, our best guess is a hundred, perhaps two."

Davron rubbed at his chin, thinking. "Poorly equipped and trained, no doubt, but in numbers, still dangerous. I can provide two hundred men on short notice. More will take time."

Ariano shook her head. "Time is something we lack. We'll take the two hundred and hope it's enough. If not..." She shrugged.

"War is risk," Davron agreed. "I will place my men under Caelwen's command. Don't let your egos cloud your minds into thinking you're military tacticians."

Ariano was clearly displeased. "What sort of fools do you take us for?"

Maranath smiled. "He takes us for Meites, dear. We're rather well known for making impulsive decisions, hmm?" He turned to Davron. "We've some other business to tend before we head out. We'll meet you back here in, say, two hours?"

"Done."

Narelki had not been in Prandil's private quarters for many years, and it troubled her to be here now, for more reasons than she cared to contemplate. Chiefly, it was that she was here to deceive him, but it was more than that. It brought back too many old memories, pieces of the past that both of them had cast aside.

Prandil raised his glass of wine in toast, and said, "To old friends and fond memories. It's been too long."

"It may be longer, still," she murmured. "It should have been you calling out to me. But clearly other things occupy your mind."

"Be reasonable," he purred, stroking her with his words. "I could write you a poem," he offered, grinning.

"That might get you into my bed," she said softly, allowing herself a ghost of a smile. "But it will hardly make all well between us. It seems you've lost your taste for me."

"Oh, no," Prandil assured her with a hungry look. "Not at all."

"It's been years."

"A taste for one thing doesn't preclude delighting in others as well. One can only eat so much at a time." He raised a hand to her cheek and stroked it softly. "Besides, I do believe it was your turn."

He was good. He always had been. Refusing to take the blame for their split, even as he carefully avoided pushing it back on her. Even now, he was a match for her better judgment. She had to forcefully remind herself just what sort of person she was dealing with, what was at stake. It was all too easy to allow him to gull her into acquiescence.

She gave no answer, simply looked past him, studying their reflection in his full-length mirror. His charm was obvious, even in a simple reflection. The confidence in his eyes, the way he stood as if he were the central character in the history of the world, it was enough to make her swoon like a virgin. But then, they all had that bearing, even Maranath. To be a Meite was to view the world as one's plaything, to see oneself as a god. Time bore down on their flesh, but their souls seemed immune to its passing. The light in their eyes never seemed to dull with wisdom and pain. If anything, it grew ever more intense as they sensed their final grains slipping through the neck of the hourglass.

And yet it was a fragile state. For someone standing atop the world, a fall from grace could prove disastrous. Seeing herself beside him, her own years weighing upon her shoulders like stones, her eyes dim and troubled by truths that he and his kind denied, she hated him, even as her heart sang with giddy, childish passion. It was unfair that the universe would reward fools like the Meites, and deny those who saw things as they truly were. *Damn you! Damn you all!*

"I'm not a commoner," she said with a scowl. "I've hardly been celibate, you know. It has nothing to do with other women. Just that you prioritized me out of your life."

Prandil considered this a moment, then nodded. "It is a fair complaint. What shall we do to change that?"

Narelki smiled at him. "Let's start with something simple. I know a place that would make for a fine picnic."

Prandil's face lit up at the notion. "And what shall I bring?"

"Yourself. I'll handle the rest."

"Generous. I presume you'll be expecting something in return, eh?" He gave her a seductive glance.

Narelki played to him. "Talk is crude."

"Indeed it is." He leaned in closer, but Narelki pulled back.

"There is one thing that concerns me, though," she said.

"Oh, and what could that be?"

"Ariano."

Prandil stepped back, his smile gone. "Why bring *her* up? That quite ruins my mood."

"She frightens me, Prandil. She's made threats."

"She makes lots of threats."

"Sadrina Veril? Maralena Prosin?"

Prandil pursed his lips. "Sadrina, yes, and can you really blame her? Maralena, I have no idea. I suspected you, to be honest."

Narelki waved the idea aside as a nuisance. "She's out of control."

Prandil's eyes narrowed. "I should expect better of you. She is stronger, so she chooses."

"Perhaps I still hold out some hope that reason might some day enter into Meite philosophy."

Prandil laughed, not yet understanding how deadly serious she was. "I am shocked, absolutely *shocked*, to hear such heresy from you."

"I'm a failure, remember?" she snapped. It was stupid. She was losing her temper, and that was dangerous. But the old bitterness demanded release. "We lesser creatures are to be indulged, yes?"

Prandil's smile faded to an expression of great sorrow. He stepped forward and embraced her. There was no lust in his touch, simply compassion. "We did not cast you out. You are the victim of your own self doubt."

She was losing her resolve, but for the moment, she didn't care. Here was Prandil, and he was strong, and she was so very, very weak. She buried her face against his chest and sobbed.

He held her for a while, until she was able to master herself once again. Her timing was good. She was just getting herself presentable again when two figures descended from the sky and lit on Prandil's veranda.

Ariano spied them at once, and entered without bothering with the pleasantry of being invited. Maranath followed, looking a bit embarrassed.

Ariano pointed at Prandil. "We need to talk." She cast a glare of loathing at Narelki. "Leave us, weakling. This is not for your ears."

Prandil's face darkened with anger. "This is *my* home! You have no right to dismiss my guests!"

Ariano regarded him with a cool stare, her green eyes flaring with challenge. "I have all the right I shall ever need."

Maranath, even more embarrassed now, laid a hand on Ariano's shoulder. "Power is no excuse for incivility. Haven't we just had to swallow that bitter lesson? We are guests in Prandil's home."

Prandil snorted. "Uninvited guests, I might add."

Ariano shrugged. "Fair enough. If, in my passion, I occasionally step on people's toes, so be it. I apologize to you, Prandil. But not to her."

Prandil shook his head in disgust. "And you continue to insult me by lashing out at my guests."

Narelki put a finger to his lips. "I'll go. We'll work out the details later."

Prandil shouted at the top of his lungs, "You will not treat me as a child in my own home, you wretched crone!"

Ariano raged back, "If you were an adult, you would be more concerned about Elgar than your petty pride!"

Maranath didn't like the way things were going. Grousing and minor insults were fairly constant amongst Meites, but this was getting truly hostile. "Enough! Ariano, it is time for you to explain yourself."

Ariano looked hurt at the rebuke, but nodded. "Not in front of Prandil."

Maranath's eyes grew wide. "We *agreed* on this! Why did we even come here if you're...bah, this is just an excuse to avoid coming clean with me!"

"It is *not*," Ariano said. "It's just that I remembered some events that he shouldn't be privy to."

Prandil was incensed. "Mei! What is wrong with you? Can you do nothing without taking a stab at me?"

"It's your own arrogance that makes you think you're important enough to be the issue, here!" Ariano shot back.

"I think it's all a fraud. First it was not for Narelki's ears. Now it's not for mine?"

Ariano hunched her shoulders. "Two different things, pup!"

"So you say, but you've been deceiving me all along."

Ariano was at volcanic levels at this point, her voice rising to a shriek. "I *can't* tell you, fool! I swore it! I can't tell *anyone*."

"Anyone except Maranath, eh?"

Ariano lowered her volume, her voice a multi-harmonic growl that communicated well just how far Prandil had pushed her. "*Including* Maranath. It's just that his being able to best me will at least be an excuse. You know, pup? Waste not, bend a knee to superiors? You don't meet that bar!"

Prandil, too, grew quiet and stern. "You're very smug in your superiority. Shall we put it to the test?"

Maranath stamped his foot, and the building shook with a tremor strong enough to rattle the glass in the windows. "That is enough, Prandil! Unless you would put me to the same test! How do you think you will fare, eh?" He turned to Ariano. "And from you, too. Since when do you do as you're told?"

Ariano snorted, her nostrils flaring. "It depends on the teller, doesn't it? The one who told me is capable of crushing the lot of us like bugs, so I do as he says."

Prandil's eyes grew wide in shock and disbelief as he first mouthed the name, then spoke it. "Tasinal? He lives?"

Ariano nodded, looking much aggrieved. "He certainly still did when Lothrian and I made our little raid on Torium."

Prandil raised his hands to the sides of his head as if he were physically restraining it from exploding. "You did *what*? How many secrets do you have, you wicked witch?" Ariano, for once, was not inclined to meet his gaze. He turned to Maranath and asked, "Did you know about this?"

Maranath nodded. "But not about any encounter with Tasinal."

Ariano's chagrin was short lived. "It's not as if he came to honor me! He just felt the threat would be more clear if he delivered it in person."

Prandil's anger seemed quenched by the thought. He began to laugh softly, almost in sympathy for her. "That must have been quite awkward."

Ariano scowled at him, then looked at the floor. "Lothrian didn't survive the mess we made, and Tasinal cleaned it up. Did you really think Tasinalt had Lothrian put to death?" She shook her head in regret, her eyes haunted with the memories. "As if he had the power."

Prandil waved aside the notion. "Of course not. It was obviously a cover up, but I had no idea of what." The bitterness began to creep back into his voice as he groused, "I was clearly not valued enough to be trusted with the truth."

Maranath laughed softly. "A couple of your elders had already demonstrated they couldn't be trusted."

Ariano pursed her lips, obviously not pleased to be on display. "Exactly. I'm not the one who made the decision to keep you or anyone else in the dark. I'm the one who *provoked* it. No need to hate me for it."

Prandil frowned, but he seemed to at least understand the situation. "Go on, then. I'll just stay here and play mushroom."

Ariano sneered at him and spat, "No, you'll be diddling the weakling, no doubt."

Prandil's eyes blazed with reignited fury. "Better than diddling *you*, you wretched crone! Assuming your crotch hasn't closed up from lack of use!" Prandil's face suddenly went bright red and he turned to the elder sorcerer and stammered briefly. "I apologize for that. But she started it."

Maranath laughed out loud. "As irritable as she is, I should think everything must be functioning just fine."

Ariano, trembling with fury, seemed unable to find any words. She glared at one, then the other, then looked up at the ceiling. Prandil groaned as the boards above his head bent and buckled outward, then exploded in a hail of flinders and debris, leaving a gaping hole to the sky. Ariano shot up and out of it.

Maranath looked at Prandil and shrugged. "I always thought you had a way with women. Couldn't tell from that display, though."

"You should put yours on a leash!"

Maranath gave him a scowl of disapproval. "She's very upset by all of this. Something happened all those years back, something she never spoke of, but it haunts her. She is convinced this all ties together, but she won't explain why." He looked up at the hole Ariano had left and sighed. "Your prodding just makes it worse."

"I suppose. Then what do you recommend?"

"Besides shutting up? Not much."

"Then why did you even come here?"

Maranath shrugged. "Just to tell you we're off again. The two of you have a way of complicating very simple things."

CHAPTER 11
THE HUNTER'S TALE

AIUL rode slump shouldered and head down, as if he had died in the saddle, swaying as the great, black horse beneath him walked ever eastward. He wore his robe's hood over his face in a vain attempt to hide the steady flow of tears, but he felt certain that Logrus saw, and was secretly laughing at him.

They had been traveling for three days, through snow covered plains and sparse woodlands, a wall of silence between them. Logrus, Aiul knew, had little to say, and Aiul, for his part, had no desire to share his thoughts with a stoic killer. Yet silence left him with little to do but think, to remember horrors and pains that the action of late had pushed from his mind. He was falling into a black spiral of depression from which there seemed no escape.

The gaping, putrefying wound in his soul, born of Lara being torn from him as she was, was always present, a constant sword through his gut. His hatred for Kariana, for all of Nihlos, was not merely an emotion, but a way of life. And yet he had weathered these torments for months. They had not dulled, but at least the outlines of their scars were mapped. Men have the capacity to adjust their expectations of life, to adapt to a known horror, and

Aiul had done just that, lowering them to just what was necessary to survive. The old Aiul, the doctor, the husband, the lover, had slipped away in the prison, died screaming, welcoming with open arms the cold embrace of oblivion, leaving in its place a new Aiul, who lived only for revenge and had no need for anything else. Enough time had passed that he had become familiar with his new self.

His actions of late were another matter. Aiul closed his eyes, remembering slashing Banger's throat in casual contempt. But it was the sheer euphoria that had come over him during his killing spree amongst the cultists, the complete satisfaction he had felt in the act, that stung him most. He had lived so long as a healer, and now, without really understanding why, he was a murderer with a growing list of victims. That they deserved it was little comfort. He did not mourn them. He mourned himself.

Logrus rode beside him astride a twin of Aiul's mount, seemingly unaware that he even had a traveling companion until he shattered the illusion by speaking. "Why do you cry?" he asked, his words jarring Aiul after so much silence.

Aiul glared at him, then returned to staring at nothing. "You say not a word to me for days," he growled. "My shame amuses you when nothing else penetrates."

"No," Logrus answered, without a hint of guilt. "I am curious. It seems strange to me."

"Mei!" Aiul spat. "You treat me like baggage, and now you would hear my secrets, as if I were a friend?"

Logrus shrugged, confusion on his face.

"Are you really such a fool?" Aiul wondered. "You expect me to believe you see nothing uncivil in responding to every attempt at conversation with grunts and gestures?"

"I had nothing to say," Logrus told him.

"No doubt," Aiul said. He huddled deeper into his robe,

longing for warmth, envying Logrus's casual indifference to the weather. "Better to be thought a fool then speak and prove it."

Something akin to rage crossed Logrus's features and passed in an instant. He turned his gaze back to the road and took a deep breath. "You know nothing of me."

"Nor could I," Aiul shot back.

Logrus rode on in silence, retreating back into his self-imposed isolation. As the hours passed, however, Aiul noticed with grim satisfaction that Logrus's normal air of arrogant indifference seemed more like Aiul's own brooding.

Just before dark, Logrus stopped to make camp, selecting a small copse of needled trees where the snow was thin on the ground. They tied their horses, and Logrus busied himself with preparations for the night. Aiul resolved to give him no assistance until it was asked for. His spiteful game did not go unnoticed, but Logrus refused to play, eventually setting up the entire camp alone.

Aiul took a seat by the fire and rummaged through his pack for something to eat, studiously ignoring Logrus. It was, in the end, something that kept his mind from wandering to darker places.

Logrus took a seat on the ground across from Aiul, his face shimmering in the rising heat of the flames, angry. It took him several minutes to speak, and when he did, it was with some difficulty. "I could kill you in an instant, with whatever I could lay my hands on," he said. "Should I despise you for your weakness?"

"It's hardly the same," Aiul groused. "Combat is a skill that is years in the learning. I have only the most basic training."

"It is just the same with me and talking," said Logrus.

"That's ridiculous. You'd have to have lived you life in isolation!"

"Not my whole life," Logrus said. "Just most of it."

Aiul was stunned. He could think of nothing to say. After

several moments of silence, Logrus waved a dismissive hand and rose to leave.

"Because I hate what I have become," Aiul said quickly, answering Logrus's earlier question. "I cry for what I have lost. Which is pretty much everything I valued."

Logrus stared at him a moment, then sat again, nodding. He dug through his own pack and found some bread, took a bite of it, and chewed while he considered his response. "What were you, before?"

Aiul stared at the ground, unwelcome memories tearing at him, summoned by Logrus's question. He had hoped to hold back his demons a bit longer, but now that they were upon him, perhaps speaking of them would sap their strength. He fingered the strange amber talisman he wore about his neck, surprised that it was warm despite the near freezing temperature. "Just a man," he sighed. "A man who healed, not killed."

Logrus listened intently, but without any sign of emotion, as Aiul told him of recent history. At times, Aiul paused for long minutes, sobbing, choking, unable to shape his words, and Logrus waited in patient silence as Aiul mastered himself. The story poured from him like water from a collapsing dam: a slow trickle of his fragile, naive life; more forceful outpourings of the ill-fated assault, his impressions of the Southlanders, the fury of the Meites; the thunderous crash of rage, horror, and despair as his life shattered before his eyes; and the trickling away of his will to live within Davron's prison.

"This Nihlos is, as I have always heard, a city of evil," Logrus said. He held one of his curved blades at eye level, staring at it a moment, letting the firelight glint from it. "There is no good enemy in your tale, no one person to strike down and have revenge upon."

Aiul wiped his sleeve over his eyes for what seemed the thousandth time. His skin felt raw from the contact. As fresh tears welled in his eyes, he looked at Logrus, grim, serious, sincere, and could not help laughing, even through his tears. He grew somber again before responding. "It is all Nihlos who will pay. I would kill them all, if I could."

"Truly?" Logrus asked, his eyes widening in shock. "Your hate is that great?"

"Greater. I just don't have the words to describe it."

"But surely there are those who are innocent in the city," Logrus said.

Aiul stared into the flames of their campfire, the jagged thing in his mind stabbing viciously at what few vestiges of his humanity remained. "No," he whispered. "They must all die for what they did to my Lara. Those who acted, and those who allowed them to act. All of them."

"I cannot condemn your hate," Logrus told him. "Righteous hate is good, and Elgar is pleased by it. But I do not understand it. What you propose seems…" He paused, searching for words. "Unnecessary."

"What do I care about *necessary*?" Aiul growled. "Nihlos is an organism. If a man kills with his right hand, do you spare his left as innocent?" Aiul rose and stalked about the fire, shaking his fist at the heavens, and shouted, "I would kill the *world* if I had the power!"

"I believe you," Logrus told him.

A long silence passed between them, and then Logrus went into his pack and began searching. "I have something for you," he said, producing a large bottle full of clear, amber liquid. He handed it to Aiul.

"What is it?" Aiul asked, opening the bottle. He sniffed it, recognizing the potent smell of alcohol.

"Strong," Logrus said with the ghost of a smile.

Aiul nodded and turned up the bottle, grimacing as he swallowed a mouthful. Logrus had told the truth. It was potent, indeed. He passed the bottle back to Logrus, and once again fingered the charm about his neck. "Is this for healing?" he asked.

Logrus shrugged and took a long drink from the bottle.

"I thought you must have given it to me while I was feverish," Aiul said. "Do you know where it came from?"

"You had it when I found you," Logrus told him as he passed the bottle. "Here, this will be easier," he said. A look of mischief crossed his face as he produced another, identical bottle of liquor.

"Then I should sit back down," Aiul said with a laugh. He tossed another log onto the fire, and made himself comfortable on the ground before it.

"One more question, and then I will tell you my tale," Logrus said.

Aiul nodded, waiting. Logrus seemed to be having trouble phrasing his question, opening his mouth to speak, then stopping several times, before he finally spoke. "What is it like to love a woman?" he asked, his eyes brimming with curiosity.

Aiul cocked his head in confusion. He stammered briefly, trying to avoid insulting Logrus. The man had just begun to speak openly. It would be a shame to send him back into silence with an ill-considered comment. He seemed too old to be a virgin. His people were considerably shorter-lived than humans, something on the order of two or three times. Aiul did a quick conversion in his head.

"I would guess you are around thirty five," he said. "Am I mistaken? Perhaps you are younger?" Even that seemed hopelessly late. In Nihlos, sex was something of a pastime among those mature enough to practice it, but too young to conceive. Aiul himself had spent most of the years from thirty to sixty in rank, inconsequential debauchery, before he had taken up his study of medicine. Kariana had been a constant source of amusement during that period. He felt slightly ill at the thought and forced it out of his mind.

"Thirty-three," Logrus answered. "Why?"

Aiul squirmed, unable to find his usual clinical detachment about matters medicinal. "Well, it's just that it seems, ah, well, unusual for a man to arrive at such an age and know nothing of women."

"You misunderstand me," Logrus told him. "I have known women, in the way you speak. But I have never loved them."

Aiul's eyebrows rose in surprise, and his lips twitched in wry amusement, not quite believing Logrus's claim. "Not even in mad youth?"

Logrus shrugged. "My youth was spent doing other things. Necessary things. It is much like talking."

"I see," said Aiul, trying to imagine what sort of scarred upbringing Logrus must have had. He thought for a moment, trying to find words to describe something that seemed hopelessly impossible to convey except from experience. "It is a kind of madness," he said. "A yearning, a joy, a poison, all at once, at least at first." Logrus stared at him with uncomprehending eyes. He decided to try a different tack. "Has there ever been anything in your life that you felt you could not live without?"

Logrus's eyes brightened. This, clearly, he understood. "Oh, indeed," he said. "I could not live if I did not do what was necessary. There would be no point to me."

Aiul paused, uncertain if he wanted to link love with whatever dark passion drove Logrus. As near as Aiul could tell, 'doing what was necessary' was a euphemism that Logrus used to justify an urge for mayhem. Still, if such were his only passion, it was the only connection possible. "That is what loving a woman is like," Aiul said. "It is not desire, or excitement, though those are part of it. It is when you find someone and realize that you cannot walk away, any more than you could walk away from yourself."

"Like I feel for Elgar?"

"Something like that, I think."

Logrus stared at Aiul in unabashed horror. "And that is what it was like for you?"

Aiul nodded slowly, pained at the thought.

"Then I understand your hate, now," Logrus said, with an empathy that Aiul would have guessed impossible in his companion.

Aiul sipped sparingly from his bottle, already feeling the effects of the liquor. He gestured at Logrus. "Now, your tale," he said.

Logrus nodded, a look of sadness on his face. He took a long drink from the bottle and began. "I never knew my father. He left, or he died. My mother told me both, at different times. It doesn't matter.

"We were poor. My mother entertained men for money, so we could eat. One of them was a soldier. He came often." Logrus paused, looking wistful as he relived old memories. He pulled his blade again, and began cleaning his fingernails with it. "I think maybe he loved my mother. Maybe he loved me, too. He taught me things. How to hunt. How to kill."

"What sort of beasts did you hunt?" Aiul asked.

"Deer, mostly. Sometimes wolves, or bear. And once a man."

"A man? How old were you?"

"Seven."

"Mei!"

"That is unusual?" Logrus asked.

"Indeed," Aiul assured him.

Logrus nodded, absorbing the information. "Perhaps he was like me," Logrus theorized. "He knew little but his own trade, I think."

"But why did he kill the man?"

"He was angry with him," Logrus said. "It was another man who came to see my mother. I think he may have hurt her, or stole from her." He shrugged. "I was very young. I just remember that he told me it was necessary. He said that as her son, it was my duty."

"And this man raised you," Aiul guessed.

"No," said Logrus. "He went away when I was nine. To war. He never came back. I missed him. But that did not change things.

"I was thirteen when my mother died."

He had made her tea and toast. Usually, she awoke earlier and did the same for him, so it had seemed a kind gesture.

With eyes still a bit clouded from sleep, Logrus did not understand at first, why she was so cold, so stiff. He shook her, panic growing within him, and drew back the thin quilt. It was then that he saw the dark bruises around her throat, and understood.

The dishes in his hand fell, taking hours to reach the floor, as his scream echoed from the drafty timbers of the tiny cottage.

Time, it seemed, had lost its meaning. He had no idea how much had passed as he sat in the splintered wicker chair by her bed, holding her cold hand. Only the urgency in his bladder served to mark the passing of time. He ate and drank, he relieved himself, he returned to her side, over and over, until there was nothing left to eat or drink. Then he had no reason to move at all.

A part of him understood that he needed to go out, to find food, or at least water, but the fear in him was overpowering. What else would change if he allowed his attention to waver, his guardianship to lapse? It was unthinkable.

The world grew smaller and smaller for him, keeping time with the shrinking of his own body and soul. His lips cracked. His throat became a desert. Yet he remained at vigil, as if his mother might return to her body if it was kept safe.

There came a point where he knew he would not survive, that

he was too weak to change his mind and seek sustenance, even if he chose to do so. The knowledge came as a relief. The vigil was too hard, his fear too overpowering. Death would be a welcome lifting of his burden.

It was then, in the darkness surrounded by the stench of his mother's rotting corpse, that he first heard the voice.

It was like none he had ever heard, a comforting, warm, fatherly voice. It seemed to stroke his cheek with compassion, and drive away the fear in his heart.

"How long will you suffer here, child?" it asked.

Logrus waited in the darkness, unable to respond. His throat refused to form any words. The fear soon returned, but somehow, it seemed weaker, his hunger and thirst more noticeable.

Time passed unmarked for him. He no longer had the means to measure it, though he knew that he had been in and out of consciousness. He longed to hear the voice again. He became convinced that it was a herald of his death, his release from suffering, and he hoped fervently for its return.

"Blood calls for blood," the voice said at last, the same voice, but different in form. It was not warm, now, but cold, the scream of winter wind, the clatter of hailstones on a roof, the bite of water so icy that it can kill in seconds.

Logrus struggled to reply, but his body would not cooperate. Despair welled within him as he struggled with his last reserves of energy to answer, to ask the voice for help, but he was simply too weak. At last, he felt the darkness close in as his body slipped towards death.

He had not thought the dead would dream.

He was in a tiny room without windows or even a door. The walls were smooth, dull metal that turned the slightest sound into a symphony of echoes. The light was dim, without a source, as if the walls themselves emitted some tiny luminescence. Fear gnawed at his gut, vague, undefined, fear of nothing in particular, of everything in general. The world was simply too much for him, and thus, he preferred the box. How he had come there was, to him, a meaningless question. He had always been there, and he had no desire to leave, no need to understand. Cold comfort was the best he could hope for.

After an eternity, or perhaps only a few moments, he was startled by an alien sound, a click, followed by grating metal. There was scarcely time for him to contemplate it before a door sized section of the blank wall opened, flooding the room with searing white light.

Logrus turned his head away, the pain in his eyes so intense that he was momentarily blinded. Metal rang on metal as someone, or something, entered the room. The grinding sound came again, and another click.

Fear welled in Logrus's chest, strangling him, but with it came hope. Perhaps this was the end. That was the only comfort he could imagine. He closed his eyes and prayed for a blow, but none came. The newcomer remained silent, the stillness broken only by the sound of Logrus's panicked breath and an intermittent dripping sound.

"End me," he begged.

"I am not come for that." It was the voice again! Yet, in the dream, he could not remember where he had heard it before. He only knew that it was an anchor in a world that seemed to be drifting away from him.

"Speak again," he pleaded.

"What would you hear, child?"

"Anything," Logrus sobbed. "It makes the fear go away."

"Look upon me."

Logrus shook his head in denial.

"Look upon me, child!" The voice was changed, now, a hammer striking against an anvil, a command that brooked no defiance.

Logrus opened his eyes, and raised his head slowly, his lips quivering with fear and other, less identifiable emotions. The hole in the wall was gone, and with it the blinding light. A figure stood before him, a tall man, powerfully built, in battered armor. Cold, black eyes stared at him from a familiar face. Logrus struggled to remember where he had seen the sharp features before, and with a shock, realized that they were his own. They were older, with lines that did not yet exist on his own smooth face, and with a pointed beard that he could not yet grow, but there was no denying that he was staring up at himself.

Logrus could not understand, but neither could he tear his gaze from the figure before him.

"It is not your time, child," the figure said. "You understand this, now, do you not?"

Logrus buried his face in his hands, unable to bear the undeniable truth the man spoke. "How can I go on?" he croaked. "I am afraid!"

"It is necessary," said the elder Logrus.

"Who are you to say so?" Logrus asked, angry now despite his terror.

The man stared at him, his black eyes seeming to bore into Logrus's very soul. "I have many names," he answered. "Destroyer. Violator. Monster. Hater… Elgar."

Logrus shuddered at the words. Yet, again, he knew, without understanding why, that they were true. "I know the name," he gasped. "What do you want of me?"

"There are few who can understand," Elgar said. He knelt beside Logrus and touched a hand to his cheek. Logrus gasped at the warmth, the compassion that flowed through him, driving out the crippling fear in his heart. "Those precious few, I am permitted to aid. Those who are cheated." Logrus saw, in his mind, his mother's cold, agonized corpse, stilled forever by a callous hand. "Abused." He saw, as if he were there, her murderer choking the life from her, heard her strangled cries as she struggled against the inevitable. "Abandoned." His vision was of a half boy, half man, lying in his own filth beside a rotting corpse, too dehydrated even to shed tears.

Elgar grasped at something, and Logrus felt a wrenching sensation deep within his chest. As Elgar drew his hand away, he seemed to draw something out of the boy. A wispy, shimmering, barely visible streamer hung from his hand. It was like a living creature, nearly liquid, with tentacles like an octopus. It struggled vainly in Elgar's grasp, becoming more visible, turning a putrescent, mottled yellow and red. Logrus stared at it with loathing. There was a malevolence about the thing that Logrus had no words to describe. He hated it, wanted to destroy it, but, with a shock, he realized he did not fear it.

He did not fear anything at all.

Elgar shook the viscous, slimy thing once, and it changed form, oozing into a flat, diaphanous sheet. He shook it again, and it changed substance, becoming a simple black cloak.

"I take the fear from your heart, and forge armor for you," Elgar said. He stepped forward and draped the cloak over Logrus's shoulders. To his surprise, Logrus found the garment warm and comforting.

"Is there a price?" Logrus asked.

"A small one," Elgar said. "What you do in my name, I would have you record." Logrus felt a sudden weight in the pocket of the cloak. He reached in and withdrew a small book. The cover was red leather, embossed in black with a mailed fist shot through with spikes. He flipped through the pages, but they were all blank.

Logrus looked at Elgar, confused. "What am I to do in your name?"

Elgar smiled, and raised his hand to Logrus's cheek again. "What is necessary," said the Dead God. "You will know. I swear a pact to you this day. Your flesh will not fail you while you do my work. *Our* work. You will not know defeat."

"So be it," Logrus replied.

Elgar smiled, and waved his hand. The walls of the room shimmered, and vanished. Blinding light shot through Logrus as if he stood in the heart of the sun itself. He felt his flesh melt from his bones, the agony beyond anything he had ever known.

And yet he endured.

Logrus woke with a start. Time was once again flowing normally. The small cottage reeked of rot and filth, and his stomach was howling with hunger. Moonlight streamed through the cracks in the walls.

He struggled to his feet, staggering with weakness. Something slipped from his lap and thumped on the floor. With supreme effort, he bent to retrieve the book he had seen in his dreams, marveling that it could be here. The dream had, at least in some way, been real. He lit a candle and looked about for the cloak, but it was nowhere in sight. He shrugged. Perhaps the cloak was just part of the dream.

Whatever the case, he was clear minded now. He knew precisely what he needed to do. With a wistful smile, he looked on his mother one last time, seeing her not as she was, but how she had been. He laid the burning candle to her bedclothes and left.

As he staggered away from the burning cottage, he paused briefly, staring back at the conflagration. He would have liked to stay, to watch until it was truly done, but hunger and thirst gnawed at him with terrible urgency, stronger even than the fear that had ruled him before. He had to find food and water immediately.

There was a stream nearby where he usually fetched water. He drank until he felt he would burst, and it still seemed too little, but the thirst faded to a dull throbbing in the back of his mind. Now he had to find food.

He set off down the worn, rutted road to town. He had no money, and knew no one. How he would eat there was a mystery, but it was the only place to go. The three miles seemed more like three months, but Logrus was determined. Had Elgar not promised that his flesh would not fail? He endured the pain and hunger, because there was no alternative. At least there was moonlight, so that he did not stumble from blindness as well as weakness.

The town was a tiny hamlet of no more than two hundred citizens. Its few wooden buildings huddled about the road like vagabonds at a campfire, their aging walls barely shelter against the wind. A small cemetery lay outside the town limits, the final destination for most of the townspeople, who lived and died all within a few miles of where they started.

Logrus felt a change within him as he neared the graves, an urgency that dulled his hunger. Images crowded into his mind unbidden: gray visions of peaceful death in sleep; of disease wracked, final throes; of precipitous falls that ended in darkness. Each of these, while jarring, gave him little pause.

But one was different. Through a red haze, he saw the pair, a girl his age and an older man. She was gasping for breath as he held a pillow over her face, the muscles in his arms corded in effort. More images tore through his mind like lightning strikes: the girl being raped by the man, over and over, through many years; brutal beatings and dire threats of consequences if she spoke; a whispered conversation with another woman. Logrus closed his eyes, staggered at the train of horrific images, praying that they would end. He felt himself drawn into the cemetery, at last settling before a particular grave. The ground and tombstone glowed red, pulsing in time with his heartbeat.

Logrus pulled the book from his pocket and opened it. A black stylus, depending from a silver chain, fell from the pages and hung in the air, waiting, as pained, whispering voices filled his ears with names. Logrus took the stylus and wrote:

"It is necessary that Jerado Arvina die for his crimes."

Aiul, fairly drunk, nearly fell over as he gaped in shock at Logrus's tale. "Mei!" he slurred. "Did you kill him?"

Logrus nodded. "Ate his food, too," he said with a slight smile.

Aiul chuckled, then grew somber. "Did you hunt down the man who killed your mother?"

"I tried," Logrus told him. "But he had fled town the night before." Logrus sighed as he contemplated what was clearly a long-standing source of frustration. "I have tracked him off and on over the years, but there is always something that comes up."

"Elgar?" Aiul asked. "He blocks you? To keep you in his service?"

Logrus shook his head. "There are... so many," he sighed. "They can't act for themselves. So I must. My vengeance seems less important. I take theirs while I can. Mine will come when there is more time."

"A dark avenger," Aiul marveled. "Elgar is much maligned."

Logrus's eyes narrowed as he regarded Aiul. "Perhaps," he said. He reached into his pocket, produced a book, and tossed it to Aiul. "I am tired," he said. "The rest of the story is there." Logrus flattened himself on the ground and closed his eyes.

"Good night to you, too," Aiul muttered as he turned the book over in his hands. It was just as Logrus had described, but it seemed too small to hold the rest of Logrus's story. He flipped through the pages in growing amazement as he realized that there were far more in the book than he would have guessed. It seemed to grow more pages as he neared the end, and absorb earlier pages, never changing size.

As Logrus began to snore, Aiul read with growing fascination and horror. The pages detailed twenty years worth of bloodshed, written in Logrus's spiky, clipped penmanship. The writing was stilted, matter of fact, and dry, but for all that, it was meticulous. Aiul was transfixed by his companion's attention to detail, his relentless pursuit of his quarry. None were ordinary criminals. They were all *fiends* that even pirates and bandits would strike down: child killers, torturers, cannibals, *beasts* unworthy of being called human.

For every entry declaring that it was necessary for some monster to die, a series of them followed detailing the hunt, sometimes covering *years* of dogged pursuit. And for every entry, there was a final description of how the villain had met his end at Logrus's hand. Apparently, they had all died in screaming horror. They seemed to see Logrus as something from a nightmare. Logrus had dutifully recorded their last words. Aiul was uncertain, but it appeared that each final entry was written not in ink, but in blood. He counted over a hundred deaths before he closed the book with a shudder, unable to continue.

Drunk as he was, sleep was a long time coming, and when it did, he was plagued by dreams where Logrus, Kariana, and Southlanders struggled against one another as Nihlos burned.

CHAPTER 12
CYANIDE AND CHEAP THEATRICS

SADRIK had rarely visited Maklin Yorn, and certainly never out of fondness. The young sorcerer could have listed fifty or so unpleasant things about Maklin without breaking a sweat, not the least of which was that he had a peculiar smell. Nevertheless, that and his other myriad eccentricities would have to be borne.

One of Maklin's slaves answered Sadrik's insistent knock. He was a large man, broad of shoulder, and bald. He was not quite as tall as Sadrik, but he looked up at him with a scowl that said such things did not matter. "It's very late," the slave observed.

"So it is," Sadrik replied, finding the man's tone irksome "Be that as it may, inform your master that Sadrik of House Tasinal must speak with him at once."

The slave made no move to do anything other than bar Sadrik's entry. "The master needs his rest. He is old."

"I assure you, he will continue to be old for quite some time. Must I grow so as well before you fetch him?"

The slave's eyes narrowed, and he reached to grab a handful of Sadrik's shirt. "You don't understand— " He cut himself short with a squeal of pain, and withdrew his hand quickly. Smoke and the scent of singed hair wafted through the air.

"No, my friend. I think *you're* the one who doesn't understand, hmm?"

The slave offered a series of nods in quick succession, considerably less belligerent. "I do now. You're one of the master's special friends. You're usually older, though."

"I suppose I'm something of a prodigy, at that."

"I'll fetch him at once."

Shortly, Sadrik found himself ushered into what seemed best described as a mad scientist's laboratory. Books and beakers, mortars and pestles, wrenches, and a thousand other random items were scattered about various shelves and tables in an almost but not completely random manner. There *was* an order to it, but that order was visible only to Maklin.

That individual sat at a desk in the heart of the chaotic mess, eating a sandwich and glaring at his unwelcome guest. "Sadrik! I should have expected it would be you roughing up my people!"

"Oh, please. I barely singed him."

Maklin picked a hair from his sandwich and examined it, apparently decided it belonged to him, and ran a hand through the tangle of white hair covering his head, trying, unsuccessfully, to corral it. He took another bite of the sandwich and muttered around the mouthful, "Jonas is a good boy. He brought me this!" He waved the sandwich at Sadrik in accusation.

"It's not quite the remarkable feat you make it out to be," Sadrik groused. "You know, some of us actually manage our own affairs instead of having slaves do everything for us."

Maklin waved the notion aside. "Some of you are idiots."

"Hmm, well, then I suppose I can't possibly have anything of worth to tell you. I'll be on my way then."

"Oh, you needn't be such a baby about it! Fine, fine, what was it, then?"

Sadrik waited a moment, smirking, enjoying the old man's growing impatience. "Oh, nothing too important. Just that my cousin mentioned, in passing you understand, that the piece of the Eye of the Lion she keeps is missing."

Maklin sucked in a bite of sandwich with his gasp and began choking. From a dark corner of the room, a young woman shrieked, ran across to the old sorcerer, and began pounding him on the back, knocking over several flasks and beakers in the process. Maklin, wide eyed, took the beating for a few moments before hacking up the offending matter. He breathed a sigh of relief, then promptly resumed a demeanor more befitting the end of the world.

"Mei! Impossible," he wheezed. The young slave looked on worriedly.

For some reason, Sadrik found the whole affair extremely annoying. "Do you really have slaves standing by in the event you might choke on a sandwich?"

Maklin looked at Sadrik in confusion for a moment, then shook his head. "Me? No, they do it themselves."

The slave looked at the old man with something akin to worship in her eyes. "The master tends to forget himself. We keep him safe."

Maklin frowned at this, but tolerated it. "Yes, yes, that's fine, Mara." He scowled at Sadrik. "They want me to produce an heir, you know. As if I have the time!"

Mara, busy checking Maklin for any signs of injury, commented softly, "I'd be glad to help you with that, master."

Maklin had had enough. He shook himself free from Mara and slapped at the air around him, making it difficult for her to approach without being hit. After a few moments of deft attempts to smooth his hair she stepped back and gave him a stern look, hands on her hips in exasperation.

"Now see here, Mara," Maklin told her. "I appreciate your care, but this is private business. Out you go!"

Sadrik gazed in wonder as the slave, pouting, slipped quietly out of the lab. "I'm not exactly certain who is the slave here."

"Nor am I! Now, what is this idiocy you come here spouting? It's absolutely impossible. No one can even access it without keys from House Tasinal, House Amrath, *and* House Yorn. She couldn't even know it was missing!"

"Apparently, there *are* ways to access it, assuming one is capable of punching through several inches of steel with a bare hand."

Maklin was growing angry now. "Several inches of steel protected against sorcery! What game are you trying to play, boy? Get me to open it and have a go at stealing it? Prodigy or no, I will squash you like a bug if you test me, make no mistake"

"It was not a Meite, and, no, I am not testing you, old man. It was, apparently, *Elgar* who took it."

Maklin's jaw fell open, and he very nearly toppled from his stool. "What?" he gasped, eyes wide in shock.

Sadrik started to respond with something acid, but the realization struck him that Maklin was truly *dumbfounded*. "They didn't tell you, either."

"Who didn't tell me what?"

"Maranath, Ariano, and Prandil. They've had my cousin under very close observation since Aiul's escape."

"And what does that have to do with Elgar?"

"Everyone is convinced that it *was* Elgar."

Maklin leapt to his feet. To Sadrik's discomfort, any number of items about the room began to move and gather together into vaguely humanoid forms: twenty books floated together and struck a threatening pose behind the old sorcerer; fifty or so beakers arranged themselves into a semblance of a spider and scuttled menacingly toward Sadrik. A flock of knives rose from a workbench and circled in the air overhead, blades flashing deadly and sharp.

Maklin was no longer a silly old man. He asked Sadrik, in a very calm voice: "How long have you known about this?"

Sadrik took a deep breath and let it out slowly as he raised his hands in surrender. This could prove disastrous. The elders were not merely powerful, but quite volatile as well. It was certainly possible he could beat the old man, but no one would have given any odds in that direction. Truth was far and away the better option. It wasn't as if he had come here to deceive anyone.

"I've known about the Elgar connection for weeks, ever since Aiul escaped. I thought it was common knowledge. As for the Eye, I only know because Kariana told me this very night, and I came straight to you."

Maklin's gaze held Sadrik's for several long, very tense moments. At last, apparently satisfied, Maklin gave him a nod, and the deadly constructs retreated back to their tables and shelves. "We must go to the vault at once."

Maklin wasted no time with talking. Instead, he simply grabbed Sadrik by the collar and shot toward the ceiling. Sadrik looked up in dismay, cringing at an impact with the metal ceiling which never came. Cunningly disguised doors opened as they approached, and the pair shot into the night sky.

Sadrik shivered, partly from the cold, and partly from real fear, as Maklin swept them high above Nihlos. He had the sense that all that stood between him and a drop to the roofs a hundred feet or more beneath his feet was the thin cloth of his shirt, though in fact it wasn't under any pressure at all. It *felt* as if he, too, were simply flying, but he was all too aware of Maklin's hand grasping his garment. *If he were to let go, would I fall? Or is that just his way of showing me the leash?*

Even so, it was truly a marvelous, wonderful thing, an experience beyond anything he had ever known. Nihlos lay spread below him, small and toy-like. It was the proper position for a sorcerer to view the city, but so far, Sadrik had yet to master flight. It was damnably difficult, even being a gifted student of an art that involved convincing himself of contradictory notions. It was easy to believe objects were on fire, that temperatures were malleable, and many other variants. But Sadrik had never been able to accept that if he walked off a ledge, he would not plummet to the ground. He had no idea how the elders managed it.

Maklin said nothing during the trip. Sadrik couldn't discern the exact cause for his silence. Perhaps flight required focus? Or maybe he was simply so furious about the Eye and the associated chicanery that he had no words. Did it really matter? In either case, pursuing it at the moment could very well end in a precipitous drop. Sadrik decided to keep quiet.

Maklin set them down in a dark, discrete alley near the palace grounds. Sadrik noted with relief that the old man hadn't completely abandoned decorum. It would have been awkward if he had dropped them right on the palace doorstep, what with sorcery being illegal. Not that Maklin would have had a real problem dealing with anyone foolish enough to try arresting him, or many regrets about what he did to them, for that matter, but Nihlos was already running low on guardsmen. It was rumored to be a dead end job.

As they came the palace stairs, the guards at the doorway seemed to debate whether or not to challenge them. The guards had no idea they were sorcerers, of course, but certainly Maklin was well known as a Patriarch, and had an aura of seriousness about him that gave them pause. The sergeant in charge opened his mouth, closed it, opened it again, and Maklin simply walked past him, Sadrik at his heels.

The elders were not people to be trifled with.

Kariana lay curled like a cat on her bed, eyes sleepy and drooping. Caelwen stood at the foot of the bed, blathering on about some thing or another. Did it matter? She had the important part: he was leaving the city to capture Aiul, and during his absence, she would likely be assassinated if she stepped out of her quarters for even an instant. She couldn't help but titter at his feigned concern.

Caelwen gave her a suspicious look. "Have you heard a word I've said?"

Kariana's eyes widened as she struggled to feign attention. "Oh, yes, of course."

"What's so amusing about it, then?"

Kariana wiped the smile off her face and assumed a pose of rapt attention. "I hear nothing but your voice, Captain."

"Don't call me that."

"Is it not your title?" she mocked.

"You make it sound like…" He trailed off, jaw bulging, as she smiled at him in smug satisfaction. "Fine. As you will."

"You were saying?"

Caelwen rolled his shoulders a bit, his face still lined with annoyance, preparing to speak when the door to the room burst open as if it had been kicked. Maklin Yorn, looking as if his tangled, white hair was on fire, stood in the door frame. Sadrik leered over his shoulder like a buzzard waiting for a lion to finish with its kill.

"Kariana Tasinal!" the old sorcerer shouted. "What have you done?"

Caelwen and Kariana, both momentarily stunned by the interruption, blinked at the two sorcerers in confusion. Sadrik was doing something with his hands. *Oh, really, is he actually trying to communicate that this isn't his fault?* Kariana waved a hand of dismissal at him, a subtle betrayal, but one that Maklin recognized. Kariana could barely suppress jumping up and down with glee as the old sorcerer turned quickly and caught Sadrik mid-denial. Maklin scowled at Sadrik for a moment before turning his glare back to Kariana. "Well?"

Caelwen recovered first. He cast Kariana a baleful glance. "What could it be this time?"

Maklin gave Caelwen a suspicious glare. "She's hardly the only one in the shit house!"

Caelwen raised an eyebrow in surprise. "Are you insinuating I've done something, old man? Why not come out and say it outright?" *Oh, bravo! Perhaps there will be a fight!*

Maklin chuckled at this. "Fine, boy, I will. You've failed miserably and let some miscreant abscond with a piece of the Eye of the Lion!"

Caelwen's eyebrow stayed in its raised position. "What, pray tell, is an 'Eye of the Lion'?"

"Never you mind that! What's important is that the two of you have lost it, and I am here to get it back!"

Caelwen's face grew dark as he made the connection. "I'd like to have seen you do better!"

Maklin poked a finger into Caelwen's chest. "Oh, I will, sonny. Watch and see."

Kariana watched them both for a moment, hoping for more, but it seemed played out. No fight, not for the moment. She shot Sadrik a sour look. "I thought I could trust you!"

Sadrik shrugged in response and put on his 'I am terribly wise' face. "You can, cousin. This was the proper course of action. He's just more excited about it than I expected."

Maklin scowled and stepped to Kariana's bed. "Let's see the vault. Then we'll talk." He stood, glaring down at Kariana while she smiled back at him. "Do you prefer to move yourself, or do you want me to move you?"

Kariana giggled as she slipped from the bed wearing nothing but her nightclothes. What would the old man do?

As it turned out, he waved a hand and the entire bed vaulted on edge and slammed into the wall, smashing her lovely collection of intoxicants. *Mei! Some of those were older than I am!* Kariana felt tears welling. "Really?" she shouted. "That was unnecessary!"

Maklin looked her up and down, and not in the way she preferred. It was as if he were searching for someone worth talking to, looking for brain rather than boobs, and finding none. It was distinctly uncomfortable and insulting. "I'll decide what's necessary," he muttered, and turned back to the wall.

Maklin reached toward the tapestry, then recoiled at the scene. "People actually do these sorts of things?"

Caelwen grunted. "*Some* people."

Maklin looked as if he were about to be ill. "How revolting." He reached for the tapestry again but paused. Was the old man squeamish about sex?

"It's no wonder you don't have an heir," Kariana spat.

Maklin turned back to her, annoyed. "Now see here—" he began, then, with a look of surprise, asked, "Do you smell smoke?"

Kariana not only smelled it, but could see the source. Her beautiful tapestry was burning! She let out a wail as Caelwen rushed forward to beat at the flames.

Sadrik gave Kariana a reproachful look. "These Meites are powerful creatures, cousin. You would do well not to anger them."

Maklin snickered at Sadrik, then shrugged and turned back to the wall. "Quite right."

Caelwen had managed to stop the flames from spreading, but the tapestry was a total loss. Kariana bit her lip in frustration, and resolved to say as little as possible. Maklin obviously enjoyed destroying her favorite things, so it would be best not to give him any more excuses.

Maklin brushed the charred ruins of the tapestry aside to reveal the gaping hole in the plaster. He turned back to Kariana in shock. "You just left it here?"

"It's not as if I could lift it!" she shouted back in a shrill voice. Her promise to be quiet had lasted all of ten seconds, if that. *Oh, well, it's hardly the first time.*

Maklin chuckled softly and elbowed Sadrik. "Oh, she's feisty!" He turned back to Kariana, the humor gone from his face as if it had never existed. "Tell me how this happened. Leave nothing out. And be aware I have not yet decided if you actually survived this encounter."

Caelwen grunted. "You're late to the party, old man. Your friends already grilled us at length, though we're none the wiser ourselves about what we're mixed up in."

Maklin glared at him. "You assume much, boy! *Friends* is the wrong word." A chair rose from where the flying bed had toppled it, righted itself, and took up a position behind Caelwen. "Sit."

Caelwen made no move to do so. "My master has taught me much about will, too."

Maklin laughed out loud at this. "Oh, doubtless. But how many years do you think I have on you, eh? It gets harder to swing a sword as you age. Not so with my craft." He accented the point with a jerking motion, and the chair slammed into the back of Caelwen's legs. Caelwen fell to the seat with a huff. "'Old man' might be an insult for your type, but for me, it's a compliment." He turned to Kariana and grinned. "Do I really need to do this twice?"

Kariana shook her head vigorously and sat down on the floor. *Maybe I should clamp a hand over my mouth, just in case.*

Maklin nodded to himself, pleased. "Now. Let's hear it. And leave nothing out!"

For the third time, Kariana told the story in exacting detail while the old sorcerer grunted and muttered to himself. Caelwen refused to speak unless spoken to, proving once and for all that he was, in fact, smarter than her. When it was done, Maklin turned to Sadrik, worry etched on his face. "Why didn't they tell me?"

Sadrik rolled his eyes. "Oh, I don't know. Maybe it has something to do with you being completely uninterested in anything but your sketchbook and your laboratory? How are people supposed to know what's important to you if you never *speak* to them?"

Maklin stamped his foot. "Insolent upstart! It's hardly *that* bad!"

Kariana had a brief, terrified moment where she caught herself nodding in agreement with Sadrik. Fortunately, Sadrik himself seemed to have become increasingly stupid in the last few moments, and was currently the target of the Meite's attention. Kariana tried to communicate with Sadrik via telepathy. *Shut up, you idiot! He's going to kill you!*

If Sadrik received her message, he gave no sign of heeding it. "Oh, I should say so! Why, if half the continent were to split off and fall into the ocean, you'd care not a whit as long as you were on the dry half."

To Kariana's surprise, Maklin actually began to laugh at this. "Well, you have to admit, it would get rid of a lot of idiots."

Sadrik raised an eyebrow in appreciation of this point. "That it would."

Maklin grew crabby again, as if he had suddenly remembered he was annoyed with Sadrik. "Besides, who are you to talk? At least I apply my sorcery to practical things. What do you do with yours other than assassinating people and acting mysterious, hmm?"

Sadrik's eyebrows seemed about to leap off the top of his head. "Listen here, you! How is assassination not a practical matter?"

Kariana looked across at Caelwen to see him wearing a dumbfounded look that almost certainly was the mirror of her own. "Mei! Sadrik! *You're* a Meite?" she cried.

Sadrik and Maklin turned back from their conversation, both looking a little unfocused and sheepish. Maklin coughed and looked sideways at Sadrik. "It's always polite to speak when spoken to, you know."

Sadrik shot him a withering glare. "Oh, let's not pretend I was the one who let the cat out of the bag."

Maklin waved a hand in dismissal. "So they know. What are they going to do about it, hmm?"

Kariana shouted again, "Sadrik!"

"You had no need to know, cousin," Sadrik replied. "And I'm hardly the only one with secrets around here. You kept this thing with the Eye under wraps far too long! By now, Ariano and Maranath may damned well be assembling the thing!"

Maklin waved a hand at her. "Just so!"

Caelwen groaned, the look of surprise on his face intense enough to make Kariana wonder if he had been stung by a bee. "Mei! Did you kill Maralena Prosin?"

Maklin pointed a gnarled finger at Sadrik, one eye closed, his face twisted in mock fury, then burst into laughter. "Look how *indignant* he is!"

Sadrik folded his arms and turned a stony stare toward Caelwen. "As a matter of fact, I did."

Kariana felt as if her head were being crushed in a vise. "You said it was *friends*!"

Maklin was choking with laughter. Sadrik grinned and clapped him on the back. "There, you see? If you ever want to kill him, you need only make him laugh until he keels over. As for *friends*, I find I get on quite well with myself."

Kariana suddenly realized there was more to this tale than she preferred to come out. "Don't you say it!"

Sadrik boggled at her. "You just *did*, fool!"

Maklin, now red faced, cackled in glee. "Mei!" he gasped. "It's like that tapestry! Who's fucking who, and who'll end up pregnant? Shall I tell her about that too?"

Sadrik answered with stony silence, and Maklin's laughter ebbed, then subsided. The old man cleared his throat and turned back to Kariana and Caelwen, somber now. "I suppose I needn't mention this should stay between us?"

Caelwen rose to his feet. "I shall have to inform my father."

Maklin made a scrunched face and mouthed Caelwen's words in mockery. "I'll tell him myself, boy. You'll be with me. It's where we're going next. If Maranath and Ariano have gone rogue, I'll want Polus and Davron behind us all the way. But this cannot leave the circle of elders. It's too explosive. Am I understood?"

Caelwen nodded. "We'll let my father be the judge of it, then."

"Agreed." Maklin looked at Sadrik. "We need to think about how to handle Prandil."

Kariana, suddenly excited, blurted out "Oh, I don't think he'll be any problem," and immediately regretted it.

Sadrik looked at her, suspicious. "And what makes you think that?"

Kariana tried to look meek and compliant. "Just a feeling," she squeaked.

Maklin sighed. "Does it really matter? We'd best just leave him out of it. He might be with them, and then we'd have a mess." He gestured to Caelwen and Sadrik. "You two, come with me." He started toward the door, Caelwen and Sadrik in tow.

Caelwen called over his shoulder as they departed, "Try not to do anything stupid until I get back, will you?"

Kariana snatched a broken bottle from the floor and hurled it at him. She missed by a good three feet, and the missile shattered against a wall.

She heard Maklin chuckle. "Feisty, indeed."

Prandil breathed in the night air. It was crisp and cool, enough to make a couple prefer to be close without being miserable, a perfect evening for a moonlight picnic. Narelki had chosen the spot well, the remains of an old brewery that had burned a year before and had yet to be rebuilt. The roof was open to the air, and the floor had long since rotted out, but the cobblestone walls still stood. It was in a secluded enough area that passersby were unlikely, but if one were to happen along, he'd not notice them unless they were too loud.

It had been some time since Prandil had entertained the foolish notions running through his head. He had long ago decided that love was a fool's errand. Once, eons past, some version of him had believed in such fantastic delusions as soul mates and true love, but that was someone else, a man who had died, not this one.

And yet here he was, a century later, looking across at the one woman he had ever imagined his equal, his soul mate. She had come back to him after all this time, and the rush of old feelings, old beliefs cast aside, made his chest feel as if it would burst trying to contain them all.

Mei, this is the true purpose of life, is it not? To dream, to fight, to love. To heal.

It was a thought he dared not speak. It was like wishing for the dead to return to life. There was no known case of anyone recovering from a fall. It was simply impossible to rethread a soul once its tapestry came unraveled. The irony of being a Meite was knowing this truth, and still having the arrogance to believe he could change it, that he could do what no one else could, defeat the invincible.

I can bring her back.

He was missing so much of what she was saying, sipping at

his glass of wine, doubtlessly very expensive, tasting nothing. He was lost, looking into her eyes. They were clear again, where they had been clouded. Was it the moonlight? No, it was *real*. She *was* still in there, passion blazing away.

"… my son!" she finished.

Now I've done it. She's caught me with my pants down, almost literally. "I'm sorry, my love. I was lost in your beauty. I'm afraid I missed what you were saying."

Narelki's normally placid face grew pinched, and Prandil marveled at this, too. Everything about her was truly amazing, even her anger at his distraction. *My ice princess, come back for my fire at long last.*

"I'm sorry, Prandil," she said, her voice barely a whisper.

"Don't be. It was both of us. We—"

He saw the flash of her hand just before the impact. He was slow, so very, very slow. *It can't be true.* But it was. The heavy bottle of wine smashed into his temple, and his head filled with light, pain and the sound of shattering glass.

She seems to have taken my distraction considerably harder than I would have expected.

Moments later, he felt a blade penetrate deep into his back, cold, steel violation, surely every bit as traumatic as any rape. He screamed in horror, in agony, in pure rage at having been so artfully gulled, so indescribably stupid.

"Elgar take you, traitor!" she roared at him. The blade bit deep into him again, and the knowledge in his mind bit deeper still. *Mei, she didn't bring me here for a romantic dinner. She brought me here to murder me.*

The realization of that truth was almost enough to make him lie down and accept it. He was already on his knees, his face in the dirt, humiliated and blind. The roaring in his head was almost too loud to hear her cursing him as she wound up for another strike. It was difficult to remember who he was even fighting.

One hundred eighty seven and still vigorous enough to thrash a strapping young lad like you! He heard his own words to Thrun echo in his mind, and felt a surge of strength. The pain drew back a bit, enough for him to find a handhold on the world. *I've been a blind fool, but I'll not die today. Not if I can help it.*

He swept his hand backward, brushing at a gnat. He felt the impact, knew at once it was too much, too hard, even as he heard the crunch of bone and felt his target fold like a rag doll and take to the air.

What have I done?

For long, maddening moments, he was not permitted to know. The world resisted him, refused to conform to his will. He remained on his knees, keening in agony, guilt, and fear, yet she did not speak, nor did she strike. What other conclusion was there to draw?

Mei! What have I done?

His vision slowly returned, because it had to, even if his eyes were full of blood and glass. His internal organs, pierced or not, continued to function because he *needed* them to, if for no other reason than to live long enough to know the gravity of his crime, the depths of his ignorance and shame.

Perhaps, when he was certain, he would keel over dead. But for now, he had to know.

He rose slowly to his feet, his blood-soaked tunic cold and clinging to his skin. He winced at the rapidly fading pain, dashed blood and glass from his vision, and faced what he already knew he would see.

Narelki lay in a broken heap against one of the cobblestone walls, a smear of blood marking where she had impacted and then slowly sank down the wall, a marionette with her strings suddenly and permanently cut.

The face he had only moments before been dreaming of was now streaked with blood and gore, but her eyes were still open, still dimly aware. *Perhaps there's still hope.* But no, he could hear the labored, rattling sound of her breathing, see the flattened, bloody mass of the back of her head. *No hope, then. Not unless she can help herself.*

He knelt before her and bowed his head, unable to find any words. His vision was going again, this time from tears he could not hold back, even though he knew he should try to put on a brave face.

For long moments, she simply breathed in ragged, wet gasps, but finally she managed to speak. "I didn't hesitate that time, did I, you bastard?" she choked out, blood bubbling at the edges of her lips.

"No, my love," Prandil sighed. "Not for an instant." He put a hand to her face, and she took it in her own.

"Going now," she sighed, clutching at his hand. "Very soon… I can feel it… I can't see… anything." She paused a moment to catch her breath, then sighed, "Stay with me."

"I will," he said softly. "But wouldn't it be so much better if *you* stayed with *me*?"

"I'll wait for you, if there's anything beyond," she said. "It won't be so long." She gave a weak chuckle. "He'll kill you all when you go against him. And then the world. I care so much less what will happen, knowing I won't be here."

"Stay and watch the fight, then! Whatever the outcome, it will be *glorious*! Perhaps we'll see Ariano get hers, at least!"

"I would so like to have seen that," she said, then coughed again and winced. "I've been afraid for so long, Prandil," she whispered, smiling. "Now, finally, I'm not anymore." She closed her eyes and murmured, "I feel like... me again." The breath of her last words ran out of her and her eyes closed. She did not take another.

"Goodbye, Narelki," Prandil whispered.

Slat watched the sky of Nihlos lighten over the walking bridges and spires, turning slowly from mottled orange to yellow to near white, his old bones aching from his vigil. It was time to follow his orders.

"If I am not back by sunup, go to my desk. You'll find your instructions there." Narelki had told him nothing beyond that, but she had given him a genuine smile, just for a moment, before she turned and departed. She had been, for the first time in ages, beautiful again. The bitterness she had worn like a cloak for so long was gone, her clouded eyes full of life and vigor like they had been when she was a child. He had wanted too much to believe it was a good thing, though he had known better.

She would have come to me, if she had returned at all. Still, it fell to him to make certain. It was just possible that she had been too tired, or too busy with her own thoughts. *Perhaps she forgot. They forget, when they're excited.*

He knew he was lying to himself, even as he rose and shuffled quietly to her room, not wanting to wake anyone else in the house. He could not deal with the questions. He could barely hold himself together. The hours ticking by had taken their toll on him, as each passing second made it less likely he would ever see her again.

She never told him what was on her mind, neither last night nor ever. He had always been able to work it out from her manner, though, and last night had been no different. *She was going to a battle. That was why she shone so brightly.*

Her room was empty, as he had known it would be. Every-thing was in place, her silk sheets tucked with crisp corners, her cosmetics and personal items all arranged neatly on her vanity, next to her sparkling clean washbowl. *She never planned on coming back. She put everything as she wanted it.*

Slat made his way downstairs, looking in various rooms as he passed, but it was pointless. There was only one other place she might be.

He stood before the great doors of the library, suddenly filled with the belief that she would be here, *must* be here. He had worried all night for nothing. He would find her in her chair, cold, arrogant, busy writing, or perhaps pouring over one of the many books of The Law. He was so convinced of it that he sighed with relief as he opened the doors.

His face fell as he saw her empty chair, the hearth cold and dead. He spied the packet on her desk, just as she had told him, and felt the full weight of his years settle once again on his shoulders.

Three generations I have raised in this House, and each has come to a terrible end. He had been barely twenty when he had been assigned to Lothrian as his personal slave. He had bathed and cleaned the boy dutifully, done his best to guide him, but somewhere things had gone wrong. They never told Slat what had really happened to his first charge, but the old slave had not been fooled by the official lie. Tasinalt had not the power to slay Lothrian. No one did, as far as Slat knew. Lothrian had been a titan, the undisputed master of his order.

Narelki had kept Slat on in the position of authority Lothrian had given him. She had never known a time when House Amrath was not run by Slat, and that was how she wanted things to remain. He had tended her son as he had tended her and her father before, whipped the boy when it was needed, and watched him grow into a fine young man, a strong, willful heir who would lead House Amrath well.

And then he, too, fell, and now his mother followed.

Was it my failure? Perhaps. But surely the Meite madness bore the greater responsibility. It had destroyed Lothrian and his daughter. And try as she might to shield Aiul, forbidding he ever be instructed in sorcery, it seemed his fate had found him still.

He glared at the statue of Amrath, feeling helpless and alone. *I cannot bear this any longer. You ask too much of me. I cannot raise and nurture your children just to watch them all die like this.*

"No more, do you hear me?" he shouted at the stone likeness of the Great Father. If Amrath, wherever his spirit might be, heard or cared, he gave no indication.

"Fine," Slat muttered. "This one last duty then. But after this, I am done." He snatched the letter from Narelki's desk and gently opened the seal. Tears welled in his eyes to see her handwriting and to know it was the last he would hear from her.

"After this, I'm done."

CHAPTER 13

CAPTURED

DESPITE the snow covering the road and the thin woods around him, Aiul found the clip clop of the horses hooves combined with the noon sun shining down on him made him drowsy. He startled awake when Logrus broke another hours-long silence. "We ride to our doom, you claim."

Aiul shook his head to clear the sleep fog and tried to focus on the other man. "If rumors are to be believed," he said. "Forget I said it, it was foolish."

"This Torium is an evil place?"

Aiul glared at Logrus, willing him to find another topic, but his travel mate was determined. Aiul gave in with a sigh. "My grandfather said that no one who goes there ever returns."

"Why not?"

"I don't know. That's all he told me."

Logrus eyed Aiul with suspicion. "I think you must know more," he said. "Why else would you have resisted it so?" Aiul shrugged, playing Logrus's game, but Logrus was not so easily dismissed. He stared at Aiul with feverish intensity, hungering, now, for more. "Tell me."

"It's silly. Childish fears, that's all."

"Liar!" Logrus exclaimed, but his grin belied any real anger.

"No, it's truth," Aiul said. "My grandfather used to terrify me with tales of that place."

"Tell!"

Aiul frowned, not wanting to admit that he was, to this day, still frightened by his grandfather's stories. Still, he had to offer Logrus something, if he wanted any peace at all. The man was certainly not going to pick up any social cues to let it go. "Fine," Aiul said, in more severe a tone than he had intended. "There are... *things* there."

"What sort of things?"

"I don't know, damn you!" Aiul snapped. "Things that eat strong warriors and powerful sorcerers as easily as they eat little boys, so I was told. *Things*."

"So someone *has* been there and returned!" Logrus said in triumph. "No one could know what was there, otherwise."

"Listen to me," Aiul tried to explain. "I was a child. My grandfather used to tell me the most dreadful tales."

Logrus waved a hand in derision. "Men do not fear children's tales," he said. "I saw your face! You were pale!" He paused, struggling for words once again. "*More* pale than usual. And Elgar did not deny it. I speak little. That doesn't make me a fool."

Aiul stared at the back of his horse's head, sullen.

"I must know what you know!" Logrus pressed. "We may have to fight. I must be prepared!"

Aiul looked at Logrus and saw that he was quite sincere. "You're right, of course," he said. "It's just that I don't know what's true and what's fantasy. It feels foolish to tell campfire tales about the place. What's the point of frightening ourselves?"

"I fear nothing. And you already know your tale. Speak."

"Fine," Aiul said in as cheery and upbeat a voice as he could muster. "Grandfather claimed Torium is inhabited by horrific monsters that torture and eat anyone who enters. Yes, even warriors, and even sorcerers. It's been around since before Nihlos was founded. It was the only city to survive Alexander's War, as far as I know, so it's at least a thousand years old, but probably a *lot* older."

"We will not be eaten," Logrus promised. "We cannot fail, so that will not happen." His face grew grim as he added, "But we could be tortured."

"I admire your confidence," Aiul sneered. "And since I have suffered essentially all that it is possible to suffer in one lifetime, I have no need to fear torture, either. Huzzah!"

Logrus's fist rose more quickly than Aiul's eye could follow, and cuffed him in the ear. Aiul yelped and raised a hand to strike back, but Logrus's innocent expression checked him mid swing.

"You do not appear immune," Logrus declared.

Aiul rubbed his ear in silence. He was uncertain whether Logrus was stupid enough to take his sarcasm literally, or smart enough to counter it with a dose of his own. It hardly mattered. Either way got him punched. "I'll keep that in mind," he mumbled.

Satisfied, Logrus fell silent again, and remained so until the sun began to set and he called a halt to their trip for the day. Aiul was less than enthused about the location. Until now, most of their journey had been through thick evergreens, which had made for plenty of sheltered spots to set up and stay out of the snow, but there were no such havens here.

They talked little as they set up camp. Aiul was tired, and Logrus, unless prodded, would go days without speaking. Some other night, Aiul might have pressed him anyway. Mei knew the man needed the practice, but the snow continued to fall, and Aiul was certain he was in for a difficult night. Drink and conversation were fine in their place, but tonight he needed rest, and the abominable white misery falling from the sky was going to make that a challenge. He bid Logrus a good night and did his best to get comfortable.

Aiul had seen snow as a child, on brief excursions beyond the limits of Nihlos, but he had never been forced to *endure* it. Before, it had been a novelty, a toy, but now, a week into the journey, he viewed it as a relentless assault. No matter what he did, it snuck into the nooks and crannies of his clothes, seeping, melting, leaving him wet and cold. Logrus slept peacefully near the remains of their dinner fire. Aiul wondered if his companion was better at sealing his garments, or if he was simply oblivious to the hardship.

With a snarl, Aiul huddled deeper into his bedroll and pulled his blanket over his head, longing for warmth. He blew softly on stinging fingers as he waited for sleep, wishing he could find a unique curse to match each hateful flake as it drifted down to cover him.

He awoke with a start. He was numb with cold, but he could still feel the hand gripping his shoulder. He started to speak, to ask why Logrus was bothering him, then caught himself. Logrus was not a 'touchy' sort of person. Something was wrong.

Quietly, he lowered his blanket. The night was pitch black, save for a dull glow from the nearly-spent coals of the fire. Logrus was crouched beside him, his curved blades in hand, head whipping back and forth as he tracked some unseen target.

Aiul pushed back the thought that Logrus was trying to murder him, well aware that if such were his companion's intent, the deed would have already been done.

Logrus burst from his crouch and surged forward like a pouncing tiger, as figures loomed from the darkness. A cry of pain tore through the snow covered woods, and wet, warm droplets spattered on Aiul's exposed face.

Aiul struggled in the dark, panicked, desperately trying to locate his mace, as grunts, thuds, and ever more screams battered his ears.

He was inches from retrieving his weapon when a brilliant light tore through the darkness, blinding him. Something hard and heavy crashed into the back of his head, sending even jagged red streaks across his vision. Snow packed into his mouth and nostrils as he fell face first to the ground, agony flickering in his head like lightning behind clouds.

"Don't kill them!" he heard, as consciousness began to slip away. "Mei! They'll have our guts for bowstrings!"

Hands seized him, and ropes bound his limbs, as he slipped into blackness.

CHAPTER 14
THE HUNTERS CONVERGE

AHMED tensed as another of the strange, screeching cries rang through the woods. He searched the mostly bare tree limbs above, but whatever the thing was, it was well hidden, and surely it had best remain so. It seemed to have no regular pattern, shrieking randomly, a grating sound that set his heart pounding. If the beast showed itself, he would put a javelin through it just for the nuisance it was making of itself.

They were making progress, better than he had expected. The winter temperature, while unpleasant, was still helpful, freezing otherwise muddy ground and thinning plant growth that would have required hacking through to pass.

That acknowledged, and Ilaweh be thanked for it, the constant cold did little for morale. They were ill clothed for winter, though their armor helped greatly. For the first time in his life, Ahmed was actually pleased at how warm armor could make a man.

Even so, he could feel the cold sapping away at his vitality, stiffening his muscles, sinking into his bones. He thought back to a time not so long ago when he had promised himself that someday he would see snow, and shook his head at the irony. Surely, he had seen enough of it now, and surely he would see much more before he was done here. One should truly be careful what he wished for.

His men took the weather stoically, and he could do no less. It was likely they were more experienced than he with such things. Erikar was rumored to have similar weather at times, and surely these men had endured much during the fighting. Even so, it would look ill for a leader to seem weak to his men. Ahmed tried to show his discomfort as little as possible.

For this reason among many, he was actually pleased to encounter a hostile force. This threat, at least, they could fight.

A large group of men, at least thirty, stood directly in their path, weapons drawn, highwaymen without a highway. They were dressed in little more than rags, a dirty, irregular lot, some natives, others who might pass for Gruppenwalders or Laureans if they were bathed. Ahmed found himself strangely unsurprised at this. Save for Nihlos, this was a land of bastards and half measures.

Sandilianus called out "Arms!" The men reacted quickly, shields and swords readied in fluid motion without breaking stride.

Eleran spat on the ground. "Elgies."

Ahmed turned to the Nihlosian. "'Elgies'?"

Eleran nodded, his face full of loathing. "Cultists. Freaks. They kill people and think they'll get special powers from Elgar."

Ahmed nodded gravely, remembering his encounter with similar men in Brust. Yet this did not feel the same. These were villains, true, but they were minor evils at best, common. They lacked the malignant wrongness he had felt from the others. Ahmed would have preferred to know more of them, but it would be bad form to halt and discuss the matter. It would make them look hesitant and embolden the enemy. "Kill them, then?" he asked. That would have to be enough.

Eleran answered with a single, quick nod, and then they were upon the hostiles. Sandilianus marched the men within ten feet of the Elgies and called a halt.

The 'enemy' hardly merited the honor of such a word. An enemy was someone you fought, not slaughtered. These idiots stood stoop shouldered, hesitant, some crazy eyed, trying their best to look fierce, but Ahmed was unmoved. He saw not a single fighter of worth amongst them.

One of the Elgies, presumably their leader, stepped forward. He reminded Ahmed of a weasel; his beady eyes darted between Ahmed and Eleran as he approached, rubbing his hands together. He opened his mouth to speak, but Ahmed interrupted him. "Dog! Why should we not slaughter the lot of you?"

Weasel stopped short and blinked. That was obviously not in the script. "Give us your money and we will let *you* live."

Ahmed couldn't help himself. He burst into laughter, and the rest of his party joined him. Ahmed struggled to master himself as Weasel grew more incensed.

The flesh below Weasel's left eye began to pulse with a nervous tic, making him look as if he were winking. "Laugh all you want, but we outnumber you, and we have archers in the trees."

Ahmed raised an eyebrow at this, and turned to Sandilianus. The elder soldier pursed his lips in disdain and shook his head, his meaning clear: a lie.

Ahmed looked once again at the pathetic gang before him. Some were young. Too young. He would give them a chance. "In ten seconds, all who stand before us die."

A number of the Elgies looked back and forth, shaken. Weasel's entire face seemed to twitch now, but he was committed. "You will be the ones to die! Surrender!"

Sandilianus called out in his high-pitched command tone, "Javelins!"

Ahmed allowed himself a grim smile, listening to the sound of the men at the rear switch weapons. This was ridiculous. "Five seconds."

Two of the younger Elgies wavered, knees shaking, then turned and bolted. Six more, emboldened by their example, followed.

Ahmed reached zero in his mind, stretching the time for any others with sense to flee. He gave them another few seconds, and three more men chose life. The rest, he judged, would stand.

"Cut them down!" he called.

It was not a fight. It was, as he knew it would be, a slaughter. The Elgies rushed forward, impacted harmlessly against the Xanthian shield wall, and were promptly skewered by javelins and short swords. In less time than he had given them to flee, they lost nine men.

Fools they may have been, but even a fool knows when his comrade has been spitted like a pig and is lying screaming on the ground. The twelve survivors, Weasel among them, turned and bolted.

Sandilianus called out, "Archers!"

Ahmed held up a hand to stop the slaughter. "Let them go. Except for the leader. I want him alive."

The aftermath of the battle was as distasteful as it was necessary. A few of the enemy were still alive, though none would survive more than a few days, their last moments filled with agony. Ahmed took it upon himself to give them mercy. It was pointless to ask what a coward wanted, so he did not give them a choice, any more than he would a dog. It was for the best.

Ahmed waited on a great, gnarled root at the edge of the river, sharpening his newly cleaned blade and watching Sandilianus and Bashir drag Weasel toward him. Weasel was considerably less belligerent with an arrow in his thigh. He squawked at the two Xanthians as his heels bounced against the hard ground, craning his head around to see where he was being taken. Ahmed smiled, knowing full well it must appear to Weasel as if he were being taken to an execution. Ahmed saw no reason to disabuse him of that notion.

They dropped Weasel before Ahmed with a thud. The Elgie groaned in pain and rolled on to his good side, then his belly, and coughed furiously.

Ahmed poked Weasel in the back of his neck with the point of his sword. The wounded man flinched, but would not meet Ahmed's gaze. Ahmed let out an exaggerated sigh. "So, you are a coward as well as a fool."

Weasel stared at the ground, both eyes already darkening with bruises, a thin, bloody line of saliva trailing from his swollen lips. "Aye. So it seems."

"My Nihlosian friend tells me you are murdering scum, cultists who do not deserve the mercy of a sword. He urges I use fire instead. What say you?"

Weasel grunted and, to Ahmed's surprise, raised his gaze up to meet his captor's. "I reckon he mostly has the right of it. Murdering scum, maybe. But we ain't cultists. Not no more."

Ahmed snorted at this. "Gave it up, eh?"

Weasel shook his head. "Everybody went to some gathering, claimed Elgar summoned 'em. It was pretty much a one way trip as I figured." He laughed, a cruel sound, and spat more blood in the dirt. "Turned out, some of us were there more for the murdering scum part, and screw the religion."

"So you became bandits?"

Weasel grunted. "That was the plan. It didn't work out so good, like you see."

Ahmed nodded and raised his sword overhead. "Are you prepared to die?"

"Nope." Weasel's eyes narrowed as his lips formed an ironic, resolved smile. "Reckon me being ready don't matter much, though."

"No. It doesn't." Ahmed brought the sword down in a flash, his blade passing little more than a hairsbreadth from Weasel's neck. Weasel shuddered a moment, slowly realizing he was still alive. Moments later, he heaved up the contents of his stomach.

Ahmed waited until Weasel had regained control of himself, then spoke. "The next time we meet will be the last."

Weasel struggled to his feet and wiped his mouth with the back of his sleeve. He looked Ahmed in the eye, his face pale like a corpse, except for the bright sincerity in his eyes. "This was the last."

Two days passed without incident. Ahmed assumed they were at least halfway to Nihlos by now, though no one was really certain. Sandilianus was the only one who had made the trip before. They should have had a detailed map, but their notes had been taken by the Nihlosians when their scouting party was captured. Sandilianus's dead reckoning was all they had.

Sandilianus scowled as he gazed through the spyglass. "You are too merciful, Ahmed. The fools stalk us."

Ahmed shook his head, amused. "Paranoid."

"I am no such thing! I *saw* a man."

"And how do you know it was these Elgies?"

Sandilianus's mouth thinned to a hard line. "Aye. I am assuming. For all we know, it could have been Nihlosians."

"It might have been farmers, or goat herders, or teenagers slipping off for a fuck. Did you see weapons?"

"No. But it means little. We should be alert."

Ahmed looked at Sandilianus and grinned. "Are we not?"

They saw more fleeting figures as the terrain changed from thick woods along a steep riverbank to flatter land dominated by scrub. Their field and distance of vision increased significantly, and Sandilianus relaxed a bit, but the respite was brief. A few more miles, and he tensed again and pointed to the horizon. "Look there. Smoke. A lot of it."

Ahmed nodded. It was difficult to miss. "What of it? A town?"

"Too many plumes. That is a large camp. Mark my words."

Ahmed looked at the smoke, considering Sandilianus's pronouncement. He could not see the distinction, but he trusted his second's experience. "Call a halt. We will need to investigate."

Sandilianus turned and shouted orders, and the men stopped where they were, some looking about curiously, confused at the delay. Sandilianus turned back to Ahmed. "It is likely the Elgie dogs. The one you call Weasel mentioned a gathering."

Ahmed watched the plumes in the distance a moment longer, considering his response. "It is possible," he said. But it feels something else." He mused a moment more, then turned to Sandilianus. "Ready some scouts."

They camped cold, no fires, and waited until dark to dispatch their men. Sandilianus led a group of three, leaving Ahmed to brood and pray. Ilaweh, as usual, did not answer. His will would be done whether Ahmed liked it or even understood it. *This is how Ilaweh teaches patience.*

It was four hours past dark when the scouting party returned. Ahmed took one look at Sandilianus and knew the situation was explosive. He forced himself to ask no questions until his second gave his report.

He did not wait long. Sandilianus gestured with a roll of his head, and the two stepped away from the others to speak in private.

Sandilianus offered him a wry smile. "You were right. It is not Elgies. It is a Nihlosian camp. We estimate two hundred men."

Ahmed raised an eyebrow. "That is no mere patrol. It would not seem to fit their pattern. Eleran says they keep to their city for the most part."

"Aye. There is something going on alright. I am half a mind to attack them and avenge Yazid."

Ahmed frowned. "We are under orders to return with intelligence, not fuck around and get ourselves killed for vengeance." *And it would absolutely put an end to any hope of cooperating with the sorcerers.*

Sandilianus nodded. "It's was just angry talk. There is more reason than that to hold. They are not the only ones moving out here. We found the Elgies, too."

Ahmed could not conceal his surprise. "What? What are they doing?"

"Hiding. Waiting. Our best guess is that they plan to attack the Nihlosians in their sleep."

Ahmed clenched his jaw a moment, absorbing the information. "How many?"

"Three hundred or close to it. They are idiots, but they have weapons. With numbers and surprise, they stand a good chance of slaughtering the Nihlosians."

Ahmed felt a deep revulsion. "In their sleep. Without declaration of war. It is inhuman."

"I told you before, boy, you are naive. It is all *too* human, in my experience."

Ahmed glowered at his second, insulted, but knowing Sandilianus had spoken nothing but truth. *Ilaweh is kind to have given me such a wise and strong guide. I am ungrateful and proud.* "What do you recommend, then?"

Sandilianus's eyes widened in mirth. "Me? I don't make policy. I follow orders. Give some. You need the practice."

It was Ahmed's turn to chuckle. "So it is my choice? Then I say we intervene."

"And who is our enemy?"

He is testing me. Making me answer the questions I ought to have already asked myself. Ahmed gave him a solemn, quick nod, and answered with confidence, "We are at war with the Nihlosians, but it is an honorable war for the most part. We can hardly condemn them for being confused. They did the right thing in the end. But the Elgies..." He spat on the ground in disdain. "They are evil men, murderers who attack like cowards, unannounced. It is the duty of all Ilaweh's followers to destroy evil."

A broad grin spread over Sandilianus's face. "Bold. The twenty of us against three hundred? You want to make sure we all die well, eh?"

Ahmed scowled at him, annoyed at the mockery, and stammered a bit as he answered. "The Nihlosians will be fighting them as well." *Ilaweh preserve me, if I lose the sense to even speak, how can I lead?* His reasoning was sound, and he knew it. He took a deep breath and found his normal voice again. "The Elgies won't come at us as a mass. They will straggle in and we will cut them down like the dogs they are."

Sandilianus gave him a cool stare, considering. "The Nihlosians may attack us anyway, even if we are aiding them. They fear us greatly."

"As well they should," Ahmed answered, his words strong, his confidence rising again. "If they turn on us, we will likely die. But I do not fear death in the service of Ilaweh. This is the *right* thing to do."

"And the prince? If we die here, our mission fails."

"Philip serves Ilaweh just as we do. He will understand, if not in this life, then when he sees us again."

Sandilianus stood for several moments, mulling Ahmed's words and stroking his chin. *Damn you! You needn't draw it out so!* Finally his expression changed to a grim smile, and hammered a fist against his chest. "Then it is a good day to die." He clapped a hand on Ahmed's shoulder and squeezed. "You did well. You've learned much."

"Is it what you would do?"

Sandilianus chuckled and shook his head. "If we survive, I will tell you how I would have handled things."

Ahmed tried to give the elder soldier a sour look, but it was spoiled by his grin. "Old men and riddles."

"Incentive to keep me alive," Sandilianus answered. "An important consideration in this business."

Now that the decision had been made, Ahmed felt the weight of leadership settle firmly on his shoulders once again, but it seemed to fit him better this time. *Good. Perhaps I have some small chance of finishing Yazid's work after all.* "Pass the word. To arms, and quickly. We will crush these dogs or die in the attempt." He paused for a moment, knowing his next command would not be liked. "And tell the Nihlosian to stand down."

Sandilianus regarded him with confusion and some anger. "Ahmed! He has proved himself well enough to fight with us! Why would you insult him so?"

"So he has, and I mean no insult. But things are already precarious. He said himself, his people are not fond of him. If they see him with us, it may make it even harder to get them to see reason. We cannot risk it."

Sandilianus ground his teeth and nodded. "I will tell him."

CHAPTER 15

HAIRBALL

LOGRUS awoke to darkness, the scent of blood and smoke heavy in the air. He was in a tent, lying face down in the dirt, tied hand and foot. Aiul, likewise bound and bloody, lay motionless on the dirt floor beside him, perhaps dead.

Logrus waited where he woke, silent and unmoving, listening and taking stock. He heard voices outside the tent, arguing, from the tone. Flickering shadows announced that a fire burned nearby, in front of the entrance.

He tested his bonds and found them only marginally secure. There was a little play in the rope that he could make use of, given time and privacy. Fortunately, this was exactly what he had. The fools had guards outside, but none actually observing him. He allowed himself a small, wry smile, knowing exactly why that would be. What had he been, this time, in their eyes? It was doubtful that they even agreed upon it, save that it was a monster.

The tent flap hung open slightly, just enough to allow him to peek out. It was a small window on the outside world, but enough to show immediate threats. Six guards sat around a fire outside, two on a bench directly in front of the tent flap. They were playing some sort of game and drinking, not terribly concerned about their captives. All were armed, but one had apparently taken Aiul's mace as a trophy. He held it across his lap like a child, apparently quite proud of his find.

It will be trivial to kill you all.

He worked at the binding ropes, stretching them as much as he could, then twisted his left arm and pulled until he dislocated his shoulder. It was less painful than it had been in the past, but it was enough to make him bite his tongue to stay quiet. *Putting it back will be worse.* He wriggled his hands beneath his backside and around his feet, clenching his jaw at the pain of overstretched muscles, then used his teeth to untie the knots.

Once free, all that remained was to reset the shoulder. It was a difficult process to do alone, and doubly so in that it needed to be silent. A tree would have been lovely for that, but there was none within the tent, and the poles were fragile. Logrus settled for lying on his side and pressing the shoulder against the ground. He put as much of his body weight against it as possible, and prayed to Elgar it was enough. For a moment, he feared it wasn't, but at last he was rewarded by a satisfying pop and a jolt of nauseating agony. He bore it in silence. It was hardly the first pain he had endured, and it would certainly not be the last.

He clamped a hand over Aiul's mouth to stifle any unexpected cry, then shook him gently. Aiul gave a slight moan, at last rousing and looking at Logrus with cloudy, confused eyes. Logrus held his hand in place until Aiul was fully conscious, then released him, raising a finger to his lips.

"Are you injured?" Logrus whispered as he removed his companion's bonds. When his hands were free, Aiul probed his various aches and pains a few moments, testing for damage beyond bruising, then shook his head.

"I don't think so," he whispered back.

"You can fight, then?"

Aiul's eyes grew distant, his face pinched. He turned his head away and stared at the dirt floor, a bad sign. He was wavering. Logrus punched him in the arm, a hard blow, and glared at him, pushing with his eyes.

Aiul rubbed at the pain and gave him an evil look. "No. No more fighting."

Logrus sighed. This was unexpected, but not unbelievable. The knights of flame were at times moody children. "Idiot. We *must* fight. There is no choice."

Aiul shook his head, still refusing to meet Logrus's gaze. "It's gone too far. I can put a stop to it right now."

"Fool! We will die here!"

Aiul at last faced him, and Logrus saw there were tears welling in his eyes. "I am a healer, not a killer! Yet look at what I have become!"

Logrus stared at Aiul. What did Elgar see in this weak, flinching buffoon? "Do you not know our captors? They are *your* people! The ones who killed your wife!"

Aiul swallowed hard. "Yes. And all I need to do to prevent any more killing is to walk outside and bend a knee."

Logrus ground his teeth in cold anger. This was not mere moodiness. This was a betrayal of Aiul's own goals. "You would bow to the woman who murdered your wife? I should kill you for such treachery!"

Aiul looked, if anything, even more resolute. "Did you not hear what I said? There need not *be* any more killing!"

"You make fine excuses, but here is another explanation, a simpler one: cowardice! You told me what it was to love a woman. And now you betray her memory to save your own skin!"

Something dark and malignant flashed in Aiul's eyes, and Logrus smiled in his own mind. *There it is.*

Aiul hunched his shoulders and leaned toward Logrus. "I would trade my own life for hers if I could!"

Logrus sneered at this. "Words. You've said before your life means nothing to you, so what is the sacrifice in that?"

Aiul sat for long moments, stunned, his mouth working but forming no words. When he finally did speak, his voice was more a croak than a whisper, harsh and dangerously loud for their circumstances. "Shut up!"

Logrus fancied he could see a faint gleam of red in Aiul's eyes, a glowing ember needing only to be blown to burst back into flame. "If you will not kill for her, then I say your love was a lie!"

Logrus could see it clearly in Aiul's eyes as the jagged thing surged forth with the strength and savagery of a hurricane. He could almost hear the thunder, see the flash of lightning as the storm overtook Aiul.

"You want me to kill for her?" Aiul roared, not caring if his captors heard. "I'll start with *you!*"

Aiul surged forward, but Logrus was both ready for the attack and significantly faster. He dodged Aiul's charge with ease, leaving the lanky Nihlosian to careen headlong through the tent flap and trip over the occupied bench. Aiul, guards, and bench hit the ground in a flailing heap as the remaining four men gaped in shock.

Logrus rushed to the entrance. Aiul lay face down in the dirt, cursing in pain and rage alongside an untended, dying fire. A boiling coffee pot, balanced precariously on a grate above the coals, steamed and dribbled around its lid. The fire hissed and sputtered fitfully at the unwelcome drops of moisture. Two guards were likewise entangled with one another and the bench, trying to regain their senses and their feet.

The other four guards leapt from their seats, scrambling for their weapons and shouting for help. The one with Aiul's mace took a bead on the back of Aiul's head and raised his weapon high.

Logrus tore a heavy pole from the tent as he stepped out, and hurled it like a javelin, sparing Aiul's life by scant seconds. The pole caught the attacker full in the mouth, sending him to the ground in a spray of blood and shattered teeth. Aiul's mace fell with him, landed with a leaden thud, and rolled within easy reach of its owner. Logrus wondered bemusedly if such was Elgar's work, or blind luck.

Does it really matter?

Logrus lunged at a guard on the other side of the fire, one still reaching for his sword, and tackled him, sending them both spilling over the bench and to the ground. The soldier screamed and began flailing with bare fists. Logrus drove his fingers to the second knuckle into the man's eye sockets, noting absently that the man's scream of agony was slightly different than one of fear. Why had he never noticed that before? He had no time to contemplate it overmuch.

He ducked another guard's wild, panicked swing, feeling the weapon part his hair as it passed overhead, and lunged back toward the fire. He snatched up the boiling coffee pot and dashed its contents into his attacker's face, then spun to deal with the next as his victim fell to the ground, screeching and clawing at his eyes in agony.

Aiul, on his feet now and still insane with rage, snatched up his mace and swung it with both hands at Logrus's head. The nearest of the two remaining soldiers blocked Aiul's blow out of reflex. This was followed by a pause as the other combatants gaped at him while he cursed himself for a fool. The battle resumed a second later as Aiul, now inside the man's guard, swung the mace backhanded and stove in the side of his helmet.

Logrus leapt on the back of yet another guard and hammered the coffee pot against the man's head. As the two went down in a crash, he saw, peripherally, the remaining guards fleeing, and Aiul chasing after them.

In some ways, it was good, he reflected as he bashed the coffee pot against the guard's now-cracked skull. He didn't relish being hit from behind by a supposed ally. By the time he saw Aiul again, he would likely have forgotten any quarrel he had with Logrus. The Knights of Flame were like that.

Logrus pushed the bloody corpse aside and sat alone for the moment, catching his breath.

How many will we have to fight?

Ahmed watched the camp from a nearby hill through Sandilianus's spyglass. Men were fighting in the camp now, but why? And why so few?

He passed the glass to Sandilianus. The elder soldier grunted and shrugged. "Odd. I don't like it." He passed the glass back to Ahmed.

"Nor I."

A runner came pounding up and skidded to a halt before them, waiting breathlessly for recognition. Damn, what was his name? Ahmed was embarrassed that he could not remember. A generic would have to do. "Report, soldier."

"The Elgies are moving. They began their advance not thirty seconds ago. They have split their force and are approaching the camp from east and north."

Sandilianus raised an eyebrow at this. "Whatever is going on down there, it's spurred them to action."

Ahmed nodded and raised the spyglass again, confirming both the Elgie advance and the fact that the fighting below now was something of an entirely different nature. The first of the Elgie forces were even now reaching the periphery of the camp. Fire sparked in the darkness as they struck torches. He could see their faces, made even uglier in the flickering torchlight.

They were going to use fire. Not even the mercy of a quick blade. He passed the glass back to Sandilianus. "It's time. Get a good look."

Sandilianus considered the situation in the distance. "We strike from the east as well, hit that section in the rear. They will be caught between us and the Nihlosians. We'll break them easily, and deal with the rest once we join forces."

If we join forces. "Recall the scouts. We must move at once."

Sadrik sat bolt upright, highly perturbed at having been awakened from a lovely dream. Maklin, on the other side of the tent, let out a single, trumpeting snore, then rolled over. Other than that, silence. *What woke me, then?* He rose to his feet quietly, listening.

He heard the snap of a twig outside, near the tent opening. Orange light bloomed as a torch flared. Shadows danced across the inside of the tent, making it seem as if there were dozens of people outside. But that was impossible. *Unless...*

Sadrik charged the tent flap and snatched it aside. A dirty, ragged man grinned at him in awkward surprise, the gaps in his smile more numerous than the teeth. His torch was inches from the tent, and any number of others like him were running through the camp, setting tents ablaze.

"You little shit!" Sadrik shouted. Flame from the torch poured down the gap-toothed man's arm like water, spilling over him in a fountain of orange, yellow, and blue as he wailed in horror and jumped up and down.

Maklin made a sound somewhere between a chuckle and a cough, and followed it with a disgusting hawking of phlegm. Sadrik didn't know which was worse, the screaming human torch or the human bagpipes.

The flaming man dropped to the dirt and tried to put out the flames by rolling, but Sadrik was in no mood for benevolence. The flames rolled over every inch of his body. The air filled with the scent of cooked meat as the man leapt to his feet and ran in circles, his cries just one voice amongst a sea of screams. He stumbled into another tent, setting it ablaze, and staggered out of view behind it, still screaming.

Maklin hacked again and stood. He stretched and gave a huge yawn. "Flashy but stupid."

Sadrik glared over his shoulder at the old man. "What's to stop me from setting you on fire, too?"

Maklin struck a contemplative pose, rubbing at his chin as if deep in thought. "The fact that our mission is important, and it would likely fail if I had to kill you and confront Maranath and Ariano alone?" He flashed Sadrik a wicked grin.

Sadrik smiled back. "Fair enough. Let's sort this out."

Caelwen staggered as his helmet turned most of a blow meant to bash his head in. Out of reflex, he struck back with his sword and was rewarded with a scream of pain. He couldn't see the result, even if his helmet hadn't twisted and blocked his vision. It took several seconds for his sight to clear of jagged, black lines. He jerked his head to the side, righting his helmet, and thanked whatever gods were watching that his opponents were too stupid and cowardly to even recognize his lapse, much less capitalize on it.

Somewhere, in the corner of his perception, he heard what distinctly sounded like a guttural call for javelins. *Impossible. Mei, what would they do if they knew I was hearing voices?*

Five thin, dirty bandits surrounded him, dancing and probing at him with rusty blades, cackling like madmen. His lone ally, a young, inexperienced officer from House Veril, stood trembling beside him, less than useless. *Politics and blood be damned!*

Caelwen would have given his left testicle to have Lorinal at his back instead of this green fool. Lorinal was stupid and uneducated, but the man could fight.

Caelwen's breath was ragged and loud in his helmet. This was insane! Where had these people come from? Not that it mattered. They were going to be the end of him, it seemed. As they closed their circle tighter, Caelwen clenched his jaw. He would take as many with him as he could.

He heard the voice again, distinctly now, from behind: "Javelins away!"

Caelwen sighed in dismay. He would have preferred to go as he had lived, clear headed, instead of collapsing into self-delusion. He had heard tales of men who, in their last moments, lived entire lives of fantasy in which they were saved. He had never imagined he would be one for that. It was a bitter thought.

When the man in front of him suddenly sprouted a very convincing javelin in the middle of his forehead, Caelwen was uncertain to be relieved or frightened. His confusion ramped as the rest of his opponents brandished thin, unhealthy appendages from their bodies.

What is going on?

He came back to his senses as he heard his young ally shriek like a woman, "Southlanders!"

This could not be a fantasy! Why would he hear terror in the man's voice if this were some soothing reaction to impending death?

The enemies in front of him were dead. Caelwen spun on his heel just in time to see his underling rush headlong toward a shield wall of at least a dozen Southlanders. Caelwen cried out, "Solinas! Stand down, you idiot!"

It was far too late. The young fool would be butchered. These men were hardened killers, and their blood was up. Their shields and short, brutal blades were streaked with gore. Try as he might,

Caelwen could not help but feel his guts churn with guilt, knowing it was his fault. He should never have allowed politics to influence his rosters.

Solinas slammed into the foreign soldiers, his swings wild and harmless. Caelwen forced himself to watch. It was his duty to suffer that, his punishment for failing. And yet, the butchery he expected never came. The Southlanders slammed Solinas to the ground with their shields and pummeled him into submission, some cursing him as a fool, others praising his bravery even as they pounded him into unconsciousness.

This done, they turned to Caelwen, raising shields and weapons again. Helmets blocked their features, but dark, savage eyes regarded him carefully, watching for his reaction. One stepped forward and lowered his sword and shield.

"Ilaweh is great!" the man called out in a voice Caelwen found, to his shock, that he recognized. *But from where?*

As if he heard the question in Caelwen's mind, the South-lander snapped loose his chinstrap and jerked his helmet off by its horsehair crest. Sandilianus, the one Southlander he knew by name, offered him a fierce, joyful grin. "We have unfinished business, you and I!"

Caelwen, despite his ringing head, found he was still capable of chuckling at the irony. "So we do." He bowed deeply to the Southlander. "Can we hold our business until we put an end to these scum?"

Sandilianus jammed his helmet back on his head. "That we can, Caelwen Luvox." He stepped to his side and opened a hole in their ranks. "Have you a shield, demon man dog?" He and his men laughed loudly at this, as if it were the height of humor.

Caelwen flashed a vicious grin of his own. "I'll find one."

Ahmed had no idea how it had occurred. He had begun this battle with his brothers, but something had happened. War was chaos. What else could be said? There had been a fight, one of many, and he had found himself on the other side of a writhing, screaming mass of enemies. Since then, he had been on his own, trying to peer through the smoke and chaos to locate his men, and fending off enemy stragglers as needed.

It was more than stragglers, now. They had taken notice of him, a lone, easy target, and came in twos, then threes. He put them down in small groups, but they seemed to have unlimited numbers.

The group harassing him seemed to grow despite his best efforts to reduce it. He had killed several, or at least so he assumed. Who had time to verify that a downed enemy was dead? Once a dog fell, he had no time to care what became of it. He moved on to the next. He blocked, slashed, occasionally fled, the only concern in his mind the urgent need to stay alive.

He had hoped to find something to put his back against, but there was precious little in the way of cover. The scrub land where the Nihlosians had made camp was damnably clear. He had fought well, but there were simply too many, and he was too tired.

There were six circling him, and for the moment, it seemed none of the others had taken notice. If he could get clear of this bunch, he might have a fighting chance of survival, but he was exhausted. He needed a few moments, just long enough to catch his breath, and he wasn't going to get them. It might as well have been six hundred as six.

He swung about him as best he could, holding them at bay for the moment. They were fools and cowards, and the slightest thrust toward any sent them back-peddling in fear. If he were less mortal, he might have held them at bay forever, or at least until support could arrive.

Now, though, his arms were tired, sagging. His sword was

heavy in his hand, his arms wailing in exhaustion. His shield had grown in weight tenfold, and he slowed with each blow he blocked. If these dogs had any courage, he would already be dead.

It suddenly irked him. Why did they not wolf-pack him and end this dance? He was not afraid to die. He was *anxious* to meet Ilaweh, and anger rose in him that these fools lacked the prowess to beat a tired warrior of moderate skill. He spat toward them, cursing them, daring them. "Cowards! Dogs! Kill me! Ilaweh awaits!"

How grand it would be to stand before Ilaweh, knowing he had fought well and true to the last. Could a warrior ask for anything more? And yet these wretches hesitated. He could not simply throw down his weapon and welcome them with open arms. Why did they not *come*?

An Elgie slashed at him, halfhearted, and Ahmed parried the blow, despite his desire to see an end of things. "You will earn this, cowards!"

From off to his side, he heard a commotion, and smiled. More of them. This, then, was the end.

But it was not more Elgies. Four Nihlosian soldiers, running and screaming as if pursued by demons, plowed into his final scene, ruining everything! Ahmed, resolved to die, found himself shocked into near paralysis by this new and unexpected development.

The Nihlosians, still screaming, hacked at the Elgies with mad abandon. For a moment, Ahmed thought they must be truly fearless warriors, but he quickly realized that this was not a battle for supremacy, merely passage. The Nihlosians hewed at the Elgies as they would trees or vines in their path, using their swords more like machetes than weapons, all the while screaming not from fury, but stark, raving terror. Their lips were flecked with spittle, their faces pale and stretched even for their own kind. Wide, bulging eyes stared at him, past him, without seeing.

As the cultists parted before them, confused and in disarray, the Nihlosians surged forward. They swung at Ahmed as well, the force of their blows like hammers. He was barely able to raise his shield in time, and his bones wailed at the shock. His knees gave way, and he fell to the ground. Rather than finish him, the Nihlosians simply stepped over him as if he were a log, still hacking at the cultists with mad abandon, maniacal woodsmen felling trees

Ahmed covered himself as best he could with his shield and held on for dear life. If he was to meet Ilaweh, he would do so with pride, but now living seemed the more admirable goal. Feet stomped about him, bashed his shield, his face. Screams and blood filled the air.

Now came yet another, neither Nihlosian nor Elgie. He bore a blade in each hand, and swung with the speed of a demon. More blood flew, more screams erupted, and corpses fell like cord wood.

It was only a few seconds, and more fled than died, but it was a massacre nonetheless. The silence following was as ominous as the sounds of battle preceding it.

Ahmed coughed and raised his shield. Four corpses lay on the ground, all bleeding from multiple wounds. Two were Nihlosian, the other two Elgies. Amidst the carnage, the man with two blades knelt, breathing hard, clearly near collapse.

They eyed each other as Ahmed staggered to his feet. The newcomer made no hostile move, but stiffened slightly, wary. Ahmed leaned against his shield and simply observed the man, trying to divine his intent. He would be tall if he stood, a powerfully built man, pale of skin, but at least his hair was black. A curious, pale nimbus surrounded him, hazy and indistinct. Ahmed blinked, blaming the smoke, but the aura remained.

Ahmed reached out a hand and stepped forward, cautious. The stranger nodded and took the outstretched hand, and Ahmed gave him a pull to help him up. As he did so, the man's sleeve slid down his arm a bit, and Ahmed gasped in shock. The tattoos on his arm were unmistakable. Crows, and a mailed, clenched fist with spikes driven through: the marks of Elgar!

Had his head been clearer, his reflexes less worn, Ahmed might have reacted on impulse and attacked. But something more than exhaustion stayed his hand and begged him to withhold judgment. He locked eyes with the man, calling upon his talents. *Who are you?*

There was not a trace of evil in him. His were hard eyes, yes, eyes that had seen much battle, but they were innocent nonetheless.

Ahmed stood dumbfounded for a moment, memories of his lessons as a youth echoing in his head: Yazid explaining how he had a special gift, a talent for judging men, for knowing the smell, the taste, the feel of evil. And yet it failed him now, of all times?

No. There were other lessons to which Ahmed had given only half an ear and had both boxed for sloth. All he could remember now was one salient point: the followers of Elgar had not *always* been villains.

Some had been great heroes in the old days.

Ahmed held a firm grip on the man's hand, staring into the warm, hazel eyes, searching, but nothing changed. *This is a good man.* Ahmed shook his head in amazement at the contradiction. "You saved my life," he said, his voice more of a croak than speech. He coughed again at the dust.

The stranger shrugged, his pointed beard quivering as he offered a hesitant, crooked smile. "So it seems. Should I have?"

Ahmed grinned back at him. "Don't you know?"

The man withdrew his hand and gave a slow, contemplative nod. "You are a good man. But you are not of the orders I know." He paused, curiosity brimming in his eyes, marveling. "You are new." He took a step back and scanned the battlefield, searching for something, then glanced back at Ahmed. "I must save myself, too, friend. And one other." He turned to leave.

"Wait! My name is Ahmed Justinius."

The stranger smiled and nodded. "Logrus." He offered a slight bow, then turned and faded into the smoke and chaos.

Ahmed stood long moments, bemused and wondering. Had anyone attacked him, they would have found him a very easy target, but as Yazid had often said, Ilaweh sometimes watched over fools.

Ahmed was roused from his musings by the sound of a familiar voice. Sandilianus, in his command tone, shouted over the noise, "'Ware right flank!"

Ahmed ran toward his brothers.

Maranath pulled his tent flap aside and gazed out on the battle. While he couldn't say for certain why a pack of Elgies was running about setting things on fire, he certainly had several ideas. "Do you suppose they are here to rescue Aiul, or just to have their vengeance on you?"

Ariano shot him a withering glare, then stepped past him to take her own stock of the situation. "You're not actually concerned, are you? About *them*?"

Maranath was about to respond when a familiar voice called, "If you're concerned about anyone, old friend, you should be concerned about *us*."

Maranath turned, shocked, toward Maklin Yorn. Sadrik Tasinal hovered over the elder's shoulder, looking rather smug. Their presence was no accident, and it couldn't be a good thing.

Maranath gave them a nod of welcome. "What brings you two here?"

Maklin regarded him with a cool gaze for a moment before replying. "We might ask you the same!"

Ariano stiffened. "We are pursuing Aiul to stop him from meddling in Torium!"

Maklin raised an eyebrow. "Torium, eh?" His expression was as triumphant as it was accusatory. "A clever lie!"

Maranath was shocked at Maklin's tone. "Now see here, Maklin! Just what are you accusing us of?"

Maklin opened his mouth to speak just as a group of Elgies spilled out of a larger tent behind him. They seemed to be both fighting and fleeing at the same time. Was there someone in the middle of that herd of cats? Maranath couldn't tell.

Ariano jumped upward a few inches and settled immediately back to the ground. She let out a howl of fury, reached to the ground for a stone, and hurled it at Sadrik, barely missing him. "Stop it, you little shit! You interfere with me at your peril!"

Sadrik looked back at her, eyes wide, shaking his head in denial. "Not me, grandmother."

Ariano's voice took on the strange, harmonic tone once again as she replied, "I am no relation to you, boy!"

Maranath laid a calming hand on her shoulder. He couldn't let this get out of hand, not now of all times. "I feel it, too. It's not them. It's something else, something very strong."

It was like a weight pulling, dragging him down, hardening the world. He turned slowly, trying to get a sense of direction. The other three followed his lead, and all four found themselves facing the pitched battle going on amongst the Elgies.

Maklin spoke for everyone: "Mei!"

Aiul shook his head, struggling to clear his thoughts. Killing Logrus was still very much on his mind, but Logrus was not convenient. He would kill him later, perhaps, if he were not too tired. For now, there were other, more pressing matters to attend.

Aiul brought the fist-shaped mace down on the head of yet another Elgie, bashing the skull into a shapeless, bloody pulp. More Elgies swarmed around him, in fives and tens as they were able to gather and attack, but their numbers were meaningless against the juggernaut. He hurled the heavy mace about him as if it were a bamboo stick, cutting a swath through them as they approached. He had reach on them, and his speed and stamina was inhuman. None could get close enough to scratch him without being cut down.

Oh, this is the gift Elgar promised! His soul sang with the knowledge. *Unlimited vengeance!*

Ariano cried out, "Great Tasinal and Amrath! Look!" She slapped the back of Maklin's head and pointed at Aiul. "Look at what he's wearing!" Maklin turned on her, hand raised to strike her back, and froze, the anger on his face fading to shock as he saw what she was pointing at. He slowly lowered his arm and gaped in astonishment.

Maranath was certain he already knew what Ariano was excited about, but his gaze was drawn to it, even so. The small amber sphere dangled from Aiul's neck by a simple thong, swaying back and forth. To Maranath's surprise, it was glowing, lighting Aiul's face from beneath, casting shadows that made him appear demonic.

I didn't know it did that.

"His hair," Ariano murmured. "Why is his hair *white*?"

Maranath merely shook his head. *Not a clue.*

Sadrik leaned toward Maklin and tapped his shoulder

cautiously, wary of being caught in the crossfire between him and Ariano. "Is that the Eye of the Lion?"

Maklin shot Sadrik a brief look of annoyance before turning back to Aiul in fascination. "No, you idiot, that's a cheese sandwich."

Maranath couldn't help but chuckle at this. Maklin was an old friend, with emphasis on the 'old' part. They had all grown more cantankerous as they aged, but Maklin had *started* that way. "It's a *piece* of the Eye," he told Sadrik "The one from Nihlos. Can you feel it?"

Sadrik nodded, looking slightly ill. "Like a boot on my neck."

Maklin turned back to face them, his jaw set. "You won't have it, you know! You'll have to go through us!"

Maranath was, for a Meite, slow to genuine anger. The sharp words, the grandiose pronouncements, the shouts and insults and bickering, such things were mundane, part and parcel to the craft. It was rare that he found himself provoked to more than wry, cynical amusement, rarer still when he found himself motivated to abandon barbs for genuine threats.

Now, though, he was truly angry. Suddenly, things were clear. His old friend suspected him of treachery, and had come here to capture him. Such arrogance, and at such a critical moment! It was infuriating!

"That is enough!" he roared. The earth beneath their feet trembled as Maranath clenched his fists, pinning Maklin with his gaze.

Maklin glared back at him, unshaken. "I don't *want* to fight you, Maranath. And not because I'm afraid of you. You're like a brother to me!"

"A brother you condemn without trial, without even allowing him to speak?"

Maklin shook his head in vehement denial. "Oh, that's hardly the case! You had *ample* opportunity to speak! Or did you forget where I lived?"

Maranath's anger faded as quickly as it had come upon him. He felt a grin spread across his face. "The last time I remember you paying *me* a visit was—"

Maklin's eyes bulged. "You shut up about that! It was a long time ago!"

Sadrik raised an eyebrow in curiosity. "Oh, no, do tell. I have the distinct sense there is a woman involved."

Maranath laughed aloud. "A long time indeed. It must be fifty years!"

Maklin shook his finger and stammered, "Now don't you think to change the subject with blackmail, Maranath!"

Ariano punched Maranath in the arm and gestured at Aiul, who was even now vanishing into the mob of combatants and smoke. "You senile fools are wasting time! He's getting away!"

Maranath raised a hand to her, begging patience, but continued talking to Maklin. "In fifty years, you couldn't visit me once, and you're bent out of shape that I am up to something without consulting you?"

"Up to skullduggery!"

Maranath shook his head, feeling his muscles relax. "No, old friend. I swear before Mei, it is not so. Will you trust me long enough to sort this mess? I promise you, you'll know everything as soon as there is time."

Maklin scowled back at him, working his jaw as he considered.

Ariano howled in dismay, "I can't see him anymore!"

Maklin stamped a foot on the ground in annoyance. "Fine! But as soon as this mess is cleared, you're going to tell me everything, and if I don't like it, we'll have some sorting of our own to do!"

Maranath accepted Maklin's temporary surrender with a relieved sigh. "Good enough."

Logrus blinked and wiped tears from his eyes. The smoke was thick here, and yet here was where he had to be. Aiul was nearby. He could feel it.

It was hard to tell one man from another, one *thing* from another, even. Figures darted back and forth in the haze, appearing, disappearing. Logrus almost struck a killing blow at what turned out to be a tree.

When at last he found Aiul, it was by nearly tripping over him. Aiul was hunched down in a crouch and staring at the empty ground beneath him, mace across his knees, breathing in ragged gasps. He was alone in the smoke and chaos. It would seem he had won his battle, for the time being at least.

Logrus settled beside him and crouched as well. "You've taught these fools a lesson, eh?"

Aiul snorted, but said nothing. Perhaps he was wounded? Logrus took a closer look. All seemed well, but who could say for certain? They were both covered in blood.

Logrus waited with him a while. It would be good if Aiul would be silent more often. Company was better than Logrus had expected, but the talk grew tiresome at times. "We must go," he said at last. "Time is short."

Aiul shrugged. "Go, then."

"And you."

Aiul let his weapon drop to the ground. "No. I think I'll just sit here for a while. It's nice here."

Logrus half grunted, half chuckled. "Smoke, chaos, and carnage. Nice? You will die here."

Aiul looked up, his blood-streaked face oddly serene. "That's the notion."

"We have work. Die later, when it is done."

Aiul voiced a grim chuckle. "Death is the end. All gone, like it never was. Why should I care about our 'mission'? Why should I care about anything?"

"Do we truly argue the meaning of life on a battlefield?"

"Yes!" Aiul stood, eyes blazing, his face almost glowing with inner madness. "Where better? Life, death, struggle, surrender, it's all here. Make sense of it for me, holy man!"

This was ridiculous. Clearly, Elgar had sent these fools to allow them to escape. Delaying with philosophical debate was ludicrous, and yet this was how Knights of Flame behaved: as children.

Children are predictable and easily led. "You want my thoughts?"

Aiul opened his arms wide, his smile dripping sarcasm. "Oh, I await your wisdom, Great Teacher!"

Logrus leapt to his feet and hammered a fist into Aiul's sneering, waggling mouth. Aiul staggered and fell over on his ass.

Logrus turned on his heel and ran as fast as his legs would carry him.

Aiul would follow.

Ahmed stabbed at an Elgie with his right hand even as he reflexively blocked a blow aimed at the man to his left. His comrade turned cold blue eyes toward him and gave a quick nod of thanks, then turned back to his own nasty business. Ahmed couldn't help but note the pale, angular face of his ally, the short bit of yellow hair protruding from his helmet. Nor could he help what he felt about it, the distinct sensation that he was fighting side by side with beasts.

He ground his teeth in frustration. It was wrong, this feeling. It was an evil thing. His head knew it, and so did his heart, but his gut disagreed. Which to follow? A man might easily be torn in two from such struggles. How could such a thing even be? How could he know so clearly that his thoughts were wrong, and yet still think them?

Yazid seemed to speak to him from the grave. *There is evil in you, as there is in all men. Why are you surprised?*

It was a sobering notion, an unpleasant one that nagged at him as he fought. And yet, perhaps it was a good thing after all. He could *see* evil. Was it such an odd thing that he could recognize it in himself as well, even an evil so common and banal? How many men must go through life blind to their own sins?

One thing was certain: he must fight this evil with as much dedication as he would any other. He could not slay himself, but he could certainly see that he did no harm. And perhaps someday, he could find a way to purge himself of it.

Things were not going as he had hoped. There were many Elgies, too many by far. There were scarcely twenty Nihlosians still standing, and three of his own had fallen. The Elgies, by design or fortune, had managed to flank them, and Sandilianus had called their forces into a tight, fighting circle. They were pressed from all sides, and the fighting was more difficult now. The cultists seemed less frightened now, less stupid. Perhaps that was simply because the worst of them had already been killed.

What was left, then, was a few less than forty men against a hundred. As good as Ahmed knew his fighters to be, it looked grim. They were soldiers, not gods. For the second time since the sun had risen, Ahmed resolved himself to his death. It seemed to be a regular thing for him of late. Eventually, he was bound to be right. Yet it was also the second time that day that he was proved wrong on that matter.

He felt the ground tremble beneath his feet and tried to work out what it could be. Surely these fools had no artillery? Even as he puzzled over this, he saw in the distance a massive, ancient oak stagger, then slowly keel over into the midst of the throng of enemies. It burst into flames before it hit the ground, and came hurtling horizontally through their ranks like some great flaming scythe, smashing dozens of them before settling barely twenty paces from his own position. Flaming Elgies ran in every direction, some on foot, others flying from the blow.

The tree had cleared a wide path through their attackers. Ahmed struggled not to gape at what he saw there now. Four figures, three men and a woman, three old and one young, strode purposefully toward him through the chaos. Short, squat creatures no more than three feet tall surrounded their party, things that looked for all the world to be composed of rocks and pebbles dancing in the air, playing at the shapes of men. The rock soldiers heaved about them as the party advanced, using the very stones that composed them as weapons to smash Elgies aside who came too close.

As the Elgies began to regroup, the old woman let out a piercing wail, her voice unearthly and strong, full of depth and harmonies that made the dirt beneath their feet dance in agitation. Elgies close to her clamped their hands over their ears, silently screaming as blood burst from their eyes, noses, and ears.

Ilaweh is great! These are sorcerers!

For the life of him, Ahmed was unable to decide if this was a good or a bad thing.

Maranath realized the ground beneath another tree was terribly wet and muddied. It must have rained cats and dogs here, and recently. It was amazing, really, that the thing still stood at all. In fact, even as he observed the precariousness of the situation, the tree keeled over, crashing down amidst the throngs of idiots to a chorus of shrieks.

It was more difficult to simply believe, though. The world

seemed harder, reality more solid than the usual tapestry of lies. On a good day, 'real' was whatever he desired. He could twist the weave as he liked, limited only by his creative interpretation, the momentary choice of how he preferred to see things. But today? Today, it was stiff and unwieldy, resisting his will. Such was, to be certain, at least partly the influence of the Eye, but Maranath had the nagging suspicion that there was something else at work.

Not all those of great will applied it in the same way a Meite would. Some were insufferably provincial in their thinking, doggedly clinging to tradition, to rules that need not apply. What a terrible waste, to throw in with all of the useless fools of the world, the sheep and followers not strong enough of soul to recognize the world was their plaything.

A pox upon them all!

He could see them ahead, now, cowering behind steel. What was the point? While he had his doubts about some of the Nihlosians, surely the Southlanders all had the spirit to do more. It was always so with true warriors.

Why, Mei, is everyone a simpleton?

He shook his head in consternation, frustrated that he knew the answer, and yet had chosen to be part of the problem. People had to be taught, and he and his order had been woefully neglectful of that. Sadrik was fortunate. His young cousin? Oh, that was a tragedy, indeed.

It was a subject to be dealt with later. He had never bothered with students, but it was high time he started.

You should have trained Aiul, and Elgar take Narelki's objections.

Ariano pulled at his sleeve, breaking him from his guilty ruminations. He turned toward her and was shocked by her expression. She was deathly pale, her eyes wide in what could only be described as fear.

"What?" he shouted over the noise. "What is it?"

Ariano pointed a gnarled finger ahead, her hand trembling. Maranath followed her gaze to the Southlander who stood twenty yards ahead, staring back at them with wide eyes.

It's him. He's the source of the extra resistance. He had no idea how he knew. The information was simply in his mind, and he knew it to be true. But why would that upset Ariano so?

As Maranath drew closer, he took stock of the Southlander, noting the way the man stood, the sense he projected of himself. The young man was powerfully built, though a bit more lithe than his brethren, perhaps yet to come into his full stature. His eyes seemed older though, and his face, surrounded by dreadlocks, was firm and full of conviction. *Strong, this one. Strong as any Meite. He will be the leader.*

Maranath led his group toward the Southlanders, paying little heed to the occasional Elgie who rushed toward them. The fools inevitably burst into flames before getting too close, that or were chopped to bits by Maklin's golems. Sadrik was indeed powerful, more than he knew, and he truly enjoyed battle. Now if no one coddled him overmuch, or conversely, killed him for being too cocky, he'd be one of the more powerful of their order some day.

Thus preoccupied, Maranath didn't recognize what Ariano was trying to point out until he was nigh on top of the Southlander. When it did penetrate his consciousness, it was all he could do not to cry out in shock.

Another piece of the Eye hung about the man's neck.

Ahmed watched the quartet approach with a wary eye. They seemed frail, but it was illusion. He could feel their power radiating from them like heat. He tried to get a sense of them, to know the depths of their evil, but it was like trying to read a language he did not know.

Chaos. Gray. White noise.

That made no sense. He focused on the eldest man, clearly their leader, struggling to take measure of him. *Who are you, old man?*

But he was no one, or rather, everyone, so many conflicting notions that it was impossible to sort out. Ahmed shuddered. He had only felt such things once before, when he and Yazid had visited a house for the sick. Ahmed had not understood at the time that the men were sick not of body but of mind.

They had felt like this. Jumbled, contradictory thoughts, fractured world views, senseless arrangements of values and impulses. *Gray.* How could it be that all of these sorcerers were madmen, though?

They were almost upon him now. The leader's eyes widened in surprise that was quickly, almost ruthlessly suppressed, but not in time to hide it. The old man knew something! He must sense Ahmed probing him. He might even interpret it as an attack, and who could blame him?

Ahmed shouted, "Are you friend or foe, sorcerer?"

The sorcerer waved his hand, sending another fallen tree spinning through the ranks of swarming Elgies. "Which does it seem to you, Southlander?"

"Both."

The old man's eyes twinkled with amusement. "We should talk, then. But there are so many distractions." Another Elgie ran past, screaming, and the old sorcerer nodded in his direction. "Difficult to parley with flaming idiots running about."

Ahmed gave him a curt nod and shouted across the lines to his second. "Sandilianus, this front is secure! End these Elgie dogs!"

With their flank protected by the sorcerers, the beleaguered defenders became lions amongst hyenas. Sandilianus shouted the battle orders, and the fighting circle flattened and reshaped itself into a spearhead that he hurled at the enemy with devastating results. In short order, the only Elgies not dead or dying were in panicked flight.

Ahmed kept a wary eye on the newcomers, all the same. The fact that they had briefly shared similar goals was most certainly not proof of their friendly intent. It was a good sign, then, to hear the leader of the sorcerers himself call for an end to the fight.

"Hold!" he called out to one and all. "We would parley!"

Ahmed nodded and gestured to his own men. With a collective sigh, both camps of combatants lowered weapons, shields, and themselves to the ground. Sandilianus took up a position at parade rest behind Ahmed, and tall, muscular Nihlosian man did the same behind the old sorcerer.

The ancient fellow regarded him with a bemused look, his eyes twinkling with mischief. "Was it fortune that brought you our way, or providence?"

Ahmed inclined his head in disdain. "We are here by the grace of Ilaweh. We are at war with your people, but we could not let these dogs murder you in your sleep."

The old sorcerer held out a hand. Ahmed considered a moment, wary of a trap, then clasped it with his own and shook firmly. The man's grip was surprisingly strong.

"I am Maranath of House Aswan," he declared. "My companions: Ariano of House Talus, Maklin of House Yorn, and young Sadrik of House Tasinal."

Ahmed nodded to each in turn. "I am Prelate Ahmed Justinius." He gestured over his shoulder with his head. "My second, Centurion Sandilianus al Rashid."

Maranath nodded at them both. "We've met."

Ahmed raised an eyebrow in surprise and turned to Sandilianus for confirmation. Sandilianus answered with a single nod.

"They are the very ones I spoke of. And the man behind him is Caelwen."

The old sorcerer winked. "And perhaps we need not be at war, eh?"

Ahmed shook his head. "Who are you to even say such a thing?"

"One quarter of the ruling council of Nihlos."

Sadrik cleared his throat and spoke quickly, as if he were rushing to complete his words before someone silenced him. "Unofficially, we'd be a third. My cousin, the *Empress*, is very partial to my advice."

Ariano looked up at the younger man and scowled. "Pity you only bothered putting a leash on her *after* she started a war!"

Maranath shot them both icy looks over his shoulder, and they fell silent. He smiled apologetically at Ahmed. "You must forgive us. We are a passionate sect."

Ahmed shrugged. He saw nothing out of place. "I am hardly some dainty courtier. I am an advocate of solving disagreements with fists."

The old sorcerer chuckled softly as Sandilianus leaned toward Ahmed, his voice low so as not to carry beyond their immediate circle of conversation. "He speaks truth. It was this very man who sentenced me to death, and he and this woman released me." He looked at them again, searching. "Where is the other? The dark-haired man?"

Ariano rolled her eyes. "He means Prandil."

Maranath placed a calming hand against her back as he spoke to Sandilianus. "Prandil is another Council member in our camp. He's within Nihlos, keeping a watchful eye on our young demoncat empress."

Sandilianus's eyes grew wide. "The one who tried to kill you all?"

"The very same."

"I am amazed you did not put her to death!"

Maklin hacked and spat on the ground. "That's what I told them, but no one listens to me. I might as well be a mushroom."

The young sorcerer giggled at this, but quickly fell silent at a glare from the elder.

Caelwen took the brief pause in conversation to add, "My father is also a council member. I am certain he will trust my word on the matter."

Sandilianus muttered, "I have heard that tale before."

Caelwen bowed his head, chagrined. "So you have, to my shame. Neither I nor my father had a hand in what happened to your people. But I had a duty to stand by my empress once the die was cast."

"Aye, there is honor in that."

Caelwen looked Sandilianus in the eye. "Things are different now. There will be no repeat of Tasinalta's evil. I swear it to you."

Sandilianus held Caelwen's gaze a moment, then gave him a grudging nod. "I believe you. I have seen nothing to make me doubt your honor. Only your sense in pledging it."

Maranath waited a moment until he was certain the exchange was complete, then continued, "And there is another in our camp, as well, Narelki. Seven votes on the Council of Twelve. That's who I am. You may as well call me Nihlos."

Ahmed studied the old man a moment, searching, grasping, but there was nothing but fog, gray mist. It *seemed* the old man was being truthful, but who could say? And if he were not? Did it matter? "Let us say we were no longer at war. What then?"

The old man gave him a faint smile. "Well, I should say the first order of business would be to stop killing each other."

Ahmed laughed. "Truly, I can see you know the intricacies of war. Then what?"

"We go about our business and trouble one another no more."

The old man made it sound so simple, but it meant letting

Yazid's murderer escape justice. Ahmed did not even know the villain's name. But there had been enough fighting. Yazid had died well, and Ilaweh's will had been done. What was the vengeance of one man, to stand against such things?

"We come to hire crew for our ship," he said. "Our man Eleran of no house, one of your people, says it is possible to buy the freedom of prisoners."

Maranath raised an eyebrow in surprise. Caelwen gave a wry chuckle and replied, "It is possible to purchase prisoners. What you do with them after is your own affair." His face grew stern as he continued. "But I warn you, Southlander, do not enter Nihlos. Until the council actually meets again to call off any hostilities, I am duty bound to arrest you if you do."

Ahmed and the sorcerers rolled their eyes almost in unison, and Ahmed allowed himself a smile. These sorcerers, it seemed, had as little patience with such things as he. It was a good thing to know. "And what of Eleran?"

Maranath again showed some reaction at mention of the name. Caelwen nodded and said, "I know him. A troublemaker and a drunk, but hardly a public enemy. As I heard it, he was told he would live far longer outside Nihlos, but I know of no formal charges beyond drunk and disorderly."

"He said he fucked the wrong woman," Sandilianus said with a grin.

Caelwen pursed his lips and nodded bemusedly. "That should be plural, I think. Where is he? I still owe him a thing or two."

Sandilianus cracked his knuckles and offered a wicked grin. "You owe *me* something, Caelwen Luvox."

The sorcerers shared a brief glance back and forth, and Maranath spoke for them. "I find myself forced to agree. You gave him quite a handling in court."

Caelwen shrugged, unmoved. "I did my duty, and the Southlander and I have already spoken of this. We agreed to put that business aside until things are sorted out."

Sandilianus nodded. "It is so."

Maklin punched Sadrik in the arm. "It seems sorted enough to me."

Caelwen shook his head, disappointment clear on his face. "Would that it were. I should like very much to accept the challenge, but I am on duty. I won't shirk it for personal matters."

Sadrik grunted in disbelief as he rubbed at his arm. "A convenient thing, that."

Caelwen shot him a withering glare. "What would you know about duty, Meite? I've kept your idiot cousin alive even though I despise her. Is that not proof enough for you?"

Sadrik considered a moment. "When you put it that way, I suppose it is."

Maranath gave Caelwen a piercing look, as if probing him. "Do you want to fight, Caelwen?"

"Of course I do!"

"Then I relieve you and assume your post. I have that authority."

Caelwen stared at Maranath, a look of astonishment and gratitude on his face. "Thank you, sir!" He snapped a salute. "I stand relieved!"

Maranath turned to Ahmed, pleading with his eyes. "Must it be lethal?"

Ahmed was shocked at the notion. "It will *not*! They will go fists, or I will not stand for it. I cannot afford to lose Sandilianus, and I will not see him kill an honorable man when there is a choice."

Maranath regarded him for a moment with a quizzical smile. "We are much alike. We, too, despise waste. Do you have rules for your fist battles?"

Ahmed nodded. "Some, but few. We form a circle. They fight

within. No eye gouges or other attempts to maim. Fists and honor. The first man to cry off is the loser. You and I shall judge."

Sadrik cocked his head and asked, "Is there a prize?"

Ahmed shot him a contemptuous look. "*Victory* is the prize."

Sadrik gave him a slight bow and spread his arms. "I like you, Southlander. You are a kindred spirit."

Maklin cleared his throat and raised a hand like a child in a classroom, though he didn't bother to wait for recognition. "And wagers?"

Ahmed considered the old sorcerer a moment, then grinned. "There is no rule against such."

Maklin rubbed his hands together and cackled. "Then what will you bet me, Southlander?"

Ahmed shook his head and smiled back. "I am no fool. I will bet you that we will see a good fight."

A good fight it was. The two combatants stripped off their armor and shirts and took their places. The fighting men, Xanthian and Nihlosian, gathered in a circle around them and shouted cheers to both combatants, pounding their shields as the two warriors scrambled in the grass and dirt. Ahmed stood with Maranath, watching carefully for foul play, but both men were as scrupulous as they were skilled.

Ahmed found himself truly fascinated as the battle raged. First one, then the other pressed his advantage. Sandilianus managed to slam Caelwen to the ground and rained blows on his head and chest. It seemed as if Caelwen were finished, but with a burst of strength and speed, he grabbed the Xanthian's shins and lifted, sending him tumbling to the ground.

The two rolled about, fists flying ever more slowly. Before long, both warriors were covered in blood and dirt, exhausted. They struggled for advantage, trading it back and forth, but neither held it for long. Soon enough, the blows became ponderous, one man slowly crawling to the other, raising a fist like an anvil, crashing it down, then falling aside in pain from a knee in the gut or an elbow to the head.

Maranath looked at Ahmed, asking with his eyes if this were excessive, or whether they should let it continue. Ahmed nodded agreement. "Enough!" he shouted.

It took a moment for his message to sink in. Caelwen and Sandilianus continued to flail at one another until Ahmed cried out again, "Stand down! It is over!"

Maranath walked slowly to the circle. The men parted to allow him passage. The old sorcerer bent with painstaking effort, and grasped both men's arms. They looked up at him with confused, punch drunk eyes as he raised both arms and called out, "Victory!"

Maklin snorted. "Both victorious means both lost, you know."

Ariano elbowed him in the ribs. "Shut up, you old fool."

As the crowd cheered and several men from Nihlosian camp began to administer first aid to the two combatants, Ahmed caught the sorcerer Maranath's eye and gestured slightly with his head as he moved away from the group: *Let's have a word.*

The old man seemed to have no problem understanding the gesture. He disengaged himself seamlessly from the crowd and seemingly without intending to, found himself walking alongside Ahmed.

Ahmed wasted no time with pleasantries. It seemed his companion would only find such things a waste of time, and time was precious at the moment. "Sandilianus tells me you know of Carsogenicus and the prophesy."

"Aye," the old man answered. "You call yourself 'prelate'. I presume you're the second of the man our demoncat empress murdered."

"I am."

Maranath was silent a moment, then heaved a great sigh and said, "You'll want revenge for that, I'll wager."

"Later, perhaps." *I don't even know what kind of revenge I would have on a woman.* With a man it would be easy: fists or steel, depending on how strong one's hate was. With a woman? Ahmed had known perhaps ten in his entire life, and certainly never felt compelled by honor to seek vengeance on them. He had no experience in such matters. *I suppose I will ask Sandilianus when I get the chance.* "Time is short. You know why I am here."

"Indeed."

"Much knowledge was lost with Yazid. I am stumbling along almost blind. Tell me you know more."

"We do. In fact, I think we've damn near worked everything out. But this is not the place to speak of it. Your men can ride horses, yes?"

"They can."

"Good. Nihlos is a day's ride from here. If you set out at dawn, you'll reach Nihlos near dark. We have horses to spare, and I'll have Caelwen join you as a guide. We'll come to your camp tomorrow night and put our heads together on how to deal with this prophesy, agreed?"

"That will be acceptable." Ahmed almost left it at that, but there was one more thing, a poisonous, vitriolic acid that had been gnawing at his guts for the better part of a year, now, and growing ever stronger. "Do you know Torium?"

Maranath stopped in his tracks and whipped his head sideways, his brilliant blue eyes smoldering with emotion. "We do. It figures strongly into what's going on."

"More than you think," Ahmed sighed.

"And what do you mean by that?"

"This all ends there, for good or ill. It's like water draining from a tub, a vortex of evil drawing us all down. Make no mistake: it is our destination, but I do not know if we survive."

Maranth's eyes widened. "You have visions, yes? Can you read auras?"

"Aye. But not yours. You all appear gray, like madmen."

The old sorcerer chuckled at this. "I think you see ours just fine."

Ahmed could not tell if the sorcerer was joking or speaking truth. Either way, it told him nothing, and time was short. "We might sleep a few hours still tonight if we start soon. Let's talk to your man about those horses, and then rest."

Aiul had no idea how far he had run, only that Logrus was just out of reach. He was not winded, but that told him nothing. It seemed he was not even subject to such a thing anymore. All he had to measure the time was his own sense of frustration, which had become a loud voice screaming in his ear.

Perhaps, were he a different man, Logrus would have called back taunts or insults, and been caught for his efforts, but no. Logrus simply ran, doggedly, without distraction, and held his own. That, perhaps more than anything, irked Aiul beyond reason. It seemed unfair that Logrus, being superior at so many things, should even be near Aiul's equal in a skill Aiul had actually trained to perform.

It soon became apparent, though, that Logrus was not quite Aiul's equal. The manhunter was indeed fast, but Aiul was gaining, inch by slow, agonizing inch. Aiul grinned with anticipation at how he would make Logrus pay for his transgressions. A distant part of his mind realized that it no longer remembered exactly what those transgressions were, but that was hardly important.

Logrus's cloak fluttered before Aiul in the icy wind, tantalizing him, but Aiul paid it no mind. It would likely tear off, perhaps even trip Aiul in the process. No, he had only one goal: Logrus's calves. That was the key to taking a man down with certainty. He judged the distance as it closed, then, when the moment was right, leapt and clasped his arms about his quarry's legs. Both men crashed to the ground in a spray of snow.

"Now you pay!" Aiul roared.

Logrus answered with a boot to Aiul's face. "I have no money."

Aiul felt as if his brain might burst at this. Logrus was a fool, a dullard, a literalist, an odious churl! *This* was why he needed to be beaten severely!

Aiul let out a wild, mad cry and surged forward, crawling like a crab, then swinging for Logrus's head. "Die! Just die!"

It was simply another, maddening nettle that Logrus should actually answer this, but answer he did. "No."

Aiul felt his mind tear away, like layers of an onion, as rage overtook him, a pure, unreasoning thing, white hot and warming in the cold. He no longer really understood what his arms and legs were doing, the odd pumping and hammering motions they made. He felt as if he were in the midst of an orgasm, limbs flailing, salty taste in his mouth, sweat on his skin. Light exploded within his mind, multicolored, bright, beautiful in its perfect hatred.

Such moments pass, as they always do, fading to a brief flash in the mind, followed by the drag of weariness, the urge to lie just a moment and contemplate. Aiul saw his arm rise for another blow, and then it seemed whatever demon that possessed him simply fled, leaving him once again in control of his own body. With a groan, he rolled to the side and collapsed.

He looked at his companion, his enemy, with weary eyes, and was shocked to see not a mark on his face. How could that be? The snow was riddled with droplets of red, spray from repeated blows, both his own and Logrus's. They had fought like animals. It was impossible that Logrus was unharmed!

Aiul lay gasping a moment, trying to find his breath. At last, he muttered, "Impossible."

Logrus, despite being unmarked, was likewise winded. "Possible."

"Idiot!"

Logrus chuckled. "Elgar does not approve." He paused again for breath, then continued. "He undoes our work."

Aiul glared across the snow, slowly accepting the truth of it. He would not be permitted to kill Logrus. He could no longer remember why it was even important that he do so, though it definitely was. He felt his face twist into a scowl of frustration as he lay back on the snow, his breath steaming out of him in rapid gasps, clouding the air above him. "Fuck you."

Logrus grunted. "Me? Or Elgar?"

"Both."

Logrus nodded to the sky, contemplating this for a moment, as if choosing his words very carefully. "Fuck you, too," he pronounced at last.

Aiul chuckled. Perhaps there was some humanity to Logrus after all.

CHAPTER 16
CONFESSIONS AND CONSEQUENCES

MARANATH rubbed at his temples, knowing what came next would be neither quiet nor particularly pleasant, but there was no avoiding it. For the moment, at least, things were peaceful. That would change as soon as they landed.

He looked down, watching their shadows stretching and warping over the moonlit, snow-covered trees below, searching for a clearing that would lend itself to a private conversation. *Hah! A fight, that's what we'll be having, not a conversation.*

He had at least managed to convince Maklin that the 'conversation' was best held several miles from the camp. "They need their rest, and this isn't going to get hashed out without shouting."

Maklin had responded, "That's on the rest of you! I'm perfectly capable of having a calm, rational discussion." The synchronized eye-rolling that followed had set him giggling, though, and he had abandoned the pose, grabbed the back of Sadrik's shirt, and shot off into the star-filled night sky. Maranath and Ariano had followed.

Maranath felt a bit regretful at not having spoken further with the Southlander leader. *I should have told him.* He was not quite sure in his own mind why he had not spoken to the Southlander about the piece of the Eye the young man wore about his neck, but in part, it was just too damned big a thing to discuss while taking a leak by the roadside. There would be plenty of time tomorrow evening to go into the full story and answer all of the questions.

He was significantly less conflicted about not telling the other Meites. It would just be one more thing to fight over, and they had plenty of that. When it came right down to it, Maranath had yet to decide if he would include them in the meeting. Ariano's obstinacy and secrets were beginning to genuinely annoy him, and Maklin's petulant accusations were likewise grating. In truth, there was no sense in making solid plans until this was resolved. He wasn't entirely certain everyone would survive. It wouldn't be the first time Meites had ended up dead from an argument. *Young Sadrik knows that all too well.*

Maranath glanced to his left at Sadrik and chuckled at the poorly concealed terror on the boy's face. *You can burn and kill just fine, but you're not a* real *Meite until you have the arrogance to leap from a tower and deny the ground itself.*

Ariano shouted, "There!" and gestured toward a clearing below as she dropped like a stone. He saw the dirt fly from her impact just before he heard it, and shook his head in amusement. She would be forever young at heart, still terribly amused both by her own power and the thrill of demonstrating it to others.

I'm not so old as that, either, am I? And the boy could use all the examples he could get, not to mention it's amusing to terrorize him.

Maranath did more than remember gravity. He remembered a force far stronger, one that sent him hurtling from the sky like a falling star, the world flashing past him in a blur. The impact would surely have smashed him into paste if he were a normal human, but he was not, and never had been. His flesh was made of sterner stuff, a unique material for which he had no name, save the one he had been given at birth.

Maranath was just climbing out of an impressive crater, cackling with Ariano, when Maklin impacted the ground like a comet with Sadrik's scream for a tail. Dirt and stones flew in every direction.

"Oh, shut up you big baby," Maklin groused once the dust settled. "I could have just dropped you, you know, and let you manage on your own." He grinned at Maranath and mimed releasing something from his grip. "Think fast!"

Sadrik, ashen and shaken, glared at Maklin as Ariano and Maranath chuckled.

He's had enough, though, and we have places to be. "Alright, Maklin, you were practically jumping out of your wrinkled old skin back there. No need drawing things out."

Maklin's humor faded quickly. He cleared his throat, a serious expression on his face. "Obviously, the appearance of a second piece has complicated matters. We're dealing with something very serious."

Ariano, too, was no longer laughing. *Fun and games over, time for sarcasm and insult, thank you, come again!* She glowered at Maklin now, her lips curling into a sneer. "Welcome to last week, you stupid codger! Last month, even! It's *your* fault Aiul escaped!"

Maklin, obviously offended at being attacked from an unexpected direction, turned and shot her an indignant look. "*My* fault? How in Mei's name do you get to that lunacy?"

"We had things under control!"

Maklin waved his arms in the air and looked about as if he were the only sane man alive. "You didn't bother telling me a thing, knowing I'm supposed to be the one looking after it! If my showing up ruined your plans, it's because you were idiots to begin with!"

Ariano opened her mouth to speak, but Maranath waved a hand and said, "It's true. We made a mistake. We were, I suppose, rather caught up in the excitement. We're hardly the first Meites to behave so."

It took Maklin a moment to shift his mood, but at last he smiled ruefully. "Aye."

Sadrik said, a sour look on his face, "This is all my cousin's fault. We shouldn't go at each other about it. I can think of much more satisfying reasons to kill the lot of you, after all."

"Just so!" Maklin shouted. "I told you we should have put her to death months ago, and no one listened to me!" He paused a moment as if replaying Sadrik's words in his mind, then shot the younger man a dirty look. "Just the first part, I mean, not the rest about killing us. Fat chance, junior."

Ariano cast a scornful look at Sadrik. "I seem to recall having a similar discussion with you."

"About me killing you all?" Sadrik tittered.

"I am *not* amused by such talk. I'm talking about your idiot cousin, the one only slightly stupider than you."

Sadrik's left eyebrow rose high on his face. "*You* three voted to return her to power. She hardly needed to be killed to declaw her."

Maranath pointed a gnarled finger at Sadrik, not so much in accusation as to prod at him for sport. "And who would take the throne, then?"

Sadrik blanched and began fidgeting, his recent abuse seemingly forgotten at this new topic. "Well, who would take the throne either way?" he stammered, looking at each of them in turn.

Ariano spat on the ground in disgust. "Theron, if you hadn't killed him."

Sadrik's pallor vanished, his cheeks flushing bright pink. "You know full well I never meant to kill him! Why else help cover it up!"

Ariano gave him a disinterested shrug. "It seemed a shame to lose two Meites instead of one. The both of you were fools to go at it as you did. It was wasteful."

Sadrik nodded, sullen. "I am well aware of that. Why do you feel the need to rub my face in it?"

Maranath chuckled softly. "Practice and repetition, young one." He gave Sadrik a wink. "And for amusement, of course. We old coots like preening."

Ariano gave Maranath a sour look. "You wouldn't know it from your dress."

Maranath picked at his brown robe and considered taking up the barb, but thought the better of it. *It's a distraction, and I've had quite enough of those.* "We need to make a decision here. What is our goal? To stop Aiul at whatever dark business he's up to, or to secure the Eye?"

Maklin stared at Maranath in disbelief. "To secure the Eye, of course!"

Ariano wrinkled her nose. "It's more complicated than you think."

"Why not uncomplicate it?" Sadrik asked with a smirk.

"Quite so," Maranath replied. "Ariano, my dear, I love you, but you've been holding out on us too long. We can't make a good decision without all the pieces before us."

Maklin eyed her with clear suspicion. "Yes, do tell."

Ariano rolled her shoulders, suddenly reticent and seeming very uncomfortable. "I haven't put it all together yet, but I'll tell you this: the Torians meddled in dark sorcery, darker than anything you can imagine. Secrets men were never meant to know, much less apply. The Eye reappearing, Aiul, Southlanders, Elgar's return, madmen running around setting fires, it's all connected. Aiul is key here! The Eye is meaningless if we put a stop to whatever dark purpose Elgar has for it."

Maranath scowled at her. "And what *is* that purpose?"

"I don't know!" she shouted. "But I am very close to it. I don't have all the pieces. I need more time! Will you not trust me just a bit longer?"

Maklin folded his arms across his chest and declared, "I will not. You're lying, or at the very least holding out on us."

Maranath shook his head tiredly, ignoring the pleading look Ariano gave him. "You leave me little choice. Either you don't know, or you won't tell. In either case it is the same." He turned to Maklin. "We need to consult with Cruentus."

Ariano jumped with alarm, eyes wide in what looked for all the world like genuine fear. "What? That's madness! We can't afford the delay!"

Maklin is right. She's hiding something, and unless I miss my guess, Cruentus knows something about it.

Maklin nodded his agreement as he said, "The dragon is the only one who actually witnessed things. If there are any answers, he will have them."

"Or Tasinal," Maranath noted. He stared pointedly at Ariano, who was looking ever more miserable and trapped.

She shook her head, defeated. "I told you, I don't know how to find him. He found me."

Sadrik's eyes grew wide as he suddenly understood their meaning. "He *lives*? How?"

Maranath had no desire to go down this path, but saw no way out. "He does, though the semantics could be argued. It's unseemly."

Sadrik slapped both hands against the sides of his head as if his brain were about to escape the confines of his skull. "It's *impossible*!"

"Apparently not," Ariano sighed.

"But *how*?"

Maranath felt his temper rising. This was no time to play twenty questions. "By deciding otherwise, just like flying or setting things on fire."

Sadrik stammered unintelligibly for a moment, trying to absorb the implications, as Maklin aped him in mockery. At last, he said, "Did he look— Well, I mean, was he—"

Ariano rolled her eyes. "He was thin and a bit pale, but he was no corpse. He damned well propositioned me, even as he took me to the woodshed."

Maranath stared at her a moment in shock, struggling not to laugh. "You never told me that! Did you take him up on it?"

Ariano looked at the ground, her cheeks burning. "Submit to the stronger, we always say."

Maranath and Maklin burst into peals of laughter as Sadrik looked on in shock and horror, and Ariano's face turned a brighter shade of red.

At last, Maranath wiped tears of mirth from his eyes and said, as seriously as he could manage, "I suppose that settles that question, but he's of no concern to us at the moment. Are we resolved?"

Ariano, near tears now, continued to stare at her feet. "It seems you are."

"You keep too many secrets. If you would tell us the whole tale, perhaps we would choose otherwise."

Ariano dug at the dirt with the toe of her shoe. "There are too many gaps. You would still want to go, and Cruentus will demand the tale from me anyway. I might as well tell it only once."

Maranath waited a moment, to see if things were really settled or if they were just pausing for breath, but it seemed over. Ariano was muted, Sadrik in a state of shock, and Maklin was twirling his hands in "hurry up" gestures. "Alright then, let's go. I intend to sleep in my own bed tonight."

Sandilianus struck flint to steel as he bent over the makings of a fire and breakfast. Sparks flew, and a tiny wisp of smoke curled from his kindling. He blew softly, and flame sprouted. "They are strange people," he opined. "But there is honor in them, after all."

Ahmed and his men had managed perhaps three hours of sleep, less than he would have preferred, but better than none certainly. Good food would help the lack of sleep, as would the coffee the Nihlosians had brought. Ahmed placed his open palms near the flame, savoring the warmth of the burgeoning fire. "Aye. Perhaps we truly are no longer at war with them."

Sandilianus shrugged. "That is for The Prince to decide."

"Do not be naive."

The veteran frowned at him, obviously offended. "A strong word from a boy who has seen little of the world."

"Even so, it is the right word. You apply it to me often enough, eh? We are Philip's eyes and ears. It is for us to decide. It always has been."

Sandilianus prodded at the fire, his expression thoughtful. "It is for you to decide, then. I fight wars. I do not know about beginning them, ending them. Or avoiding them."

"Nor do I."

Sandilianus registered surprise at this, and beneath that emotion, a bit of anger. "Ilaweh is with you."

Ahmed waved the thought aside. "Ilaweh is with all men."

Sandilianus shook his head in amusement, and offered Ahmed a look that was now familiar, one that said a lesson was in the making. "Ilaweh speaks to you in ways he does not speak to others, Ahmed. You have vision the rest of us do not share. We can but defer to that vision."

Ahmed rose and stared at the flames. "Do you truly want to know my vision? It has not changed since you first knew I bore this gift, since I pointed to that pit of evil on the map. We are not here to destroy Nihlos, or rescue slaves, or even gather information for the prince. We are here to put an end to Torium, and Yazid would not listen." He kicked at a stone, sending it off into the snow. "If I had been stronger, if I had fought him, he would still be alive today. But I was weak, and acted like a boy, and he went to his doom. I am a coward."

"Ah, no, I will not hear of that. You may be young and foolish, but you are no coward."

"Then why did I not fight Yazid, when I knew he was wrong?"

"It was not Yazid that made you flinch. It was the will of Ilaweh himself you chose not to defy."

Ahmed looked at him in confusion. "Eh?"

Sandilianus cocked his head and looked at Ahmed with bewildered eyes. When he spoke, it was as if he were trying to communicate with a child. "Ilaweh called Yazid to him as a reward, and to leave you with no crutch to lean on. It is the same as with Brutus and me. Yazid died well, so that you would have no choice but become the man Ilaweh wanted you to be, the man in this place, now, with me."

Ahmed laughed sadly. "You still call me boy, though."

"Aye, it is my way." Sandilianus laid a hand on Ahmed's shoulder and looked him in the eye. "But would a boy have given the order to attack those dogs back there, knowing the risks? No, only a man of exceptional courage would have done that."

"Or a madman."

Sandilianus shook his head. "Truly, Ahmed, I think I would have let the foreigners die. It was not practical. But saving them was *righteous*, and Ilaweh walked with us because of that. You saw that. I did not. I *could* not. Not until you explained it to me."

Ahmed stared intently at Sandilianus, considering. "Then are you with me, brother? Will you follow me into that pit and put whatever lies there to the sword?"

Sandilanus nodded without hesitation. "Aye, or at least die well by your side, and so will our men. But how could we destroy such a place?"

"I spoke to the sorcerers' leader. We are to palaver tonight, after we make camp outside Nihlos. He claims to know much."

"Does he know of this Torium?"

"He says so, and I believe him. It's the best we have."

Sandilianus banged his fist against his chest. "Ilaweh is great. It will be enough."

"Ilaweh is great," Ahmed answered with a confident grin. But privately, he was anything but certain about how things would play out. Perhaps there was no hope to avoid doom, and never had been.

I think we have a chance. It was the best they could hope for. It would have to be enough.

I do not belong here. That single thought resonated in Rithard's mind like a scalpel scraping along bone as he looked in awe at the great desk, the fireplace, the shelves of books in the Library of Amrath. Slat, unassuming, stood quietly at the door, allowing Rithard to take it all in. Theretha, at Rithard's side, was positively beaming, much to his chagrin.

The funeral had been a spectacular affair, which was another way of saying everyone had wasted a tremendous amount of time, money, and energy disposing of the corpse of someone few had even known as more than a name. Of those that did, many had loathed her. *It would have been far more dignified had we sent her on privately, just a few of us from Amrath.*

Prandil said she had leapt from the top of a wall at the old brewery, convinced she had recovered her Meite powers. It was a pathetic lie, made all the more pathetic by the fact that her heir was also her coroner. There hadn't even been a need to open her up. One look at the blood spatter showed she had been flung at the wall with killing force, the sort only a Meite might muster with his bare hands. Only a fool could examine the scene and not know Prandil had killed her.

The problem was that everyone *was* a fool, most Meites included. Rithard was alone with the knowledge. It would do no good to expose the lie. It was what everyone wanted to believe, and self deception was a high art in Nihlos. No one, least of all the ignorant, would appreciate his contradicting the official story. Meites killing each other was of less concern than commoners slitting one another's throats, as long as they kept it to themselves. Even Caelwen would simply say there was no proof, whatever his own thoughts.

I might sleep better if I could bring myself to think the same thing. But he had, unlike Meites, never been good at lying to himself. *I am as guilty as Prandil.*

Teretha, as if reading his thoughts, caressed his cheek and whispered in his ear, "You will bring this house back to glory, Rithard."

"I will bury it's dead, Mother. But breathe life back into it? I'm not the man for that task, however fortunate you've been in your machinations." He glared pointedly at her. "

Teretha's eyes narrowed in anger. "I was protecting *you*. I *never* intended this! I sought her as an ally, not en enemy."

"Is that so?" Rithard asked, his tone saying he didn't believe it for even a moment.

Teretha drew back her hand as if to slap him, then seemed to reconsider. "Even you couldn't have predicted that chain of events."

Rithard gazed warily at her a moment before submitting and

turning back to look at the shelves of books again. "No. It's unfair of me to accuse you. But my own guilt is not so easily set aside."

The old slave, Slat, cleared his throat. "If I may say so, sir, her choosing you was no accident. But I can only speak of that to you."

Teretha gave Slat a sour look, but nodded and departed the room.

Rithard nodded respectfully to Slat. "You've taught me any number of lessons with a switch. What would you teach me with words now?"

"First, she had already renounced her vengeance on you. I heard her say it in this very room, that she held no grudge for you trying to keep yourself alive. She just wished you had sought her protection."

"And second?"

Slat reached beneath his robe and produced a sealed letter and a small leather packet. "I believe you will find some of the answers you seek within, young Master."

Rithard took the letter and packet from him. "What's this, then?"

"Instructions, from Mistress Narelki," he said, indicating the letter. "Not for my eyes."

Rithard held out the leather packet. "And this?"

The old slave seemed pained, as if even looking at the packet caused him some harm. "My first thought is to say it is cursed. As for what lies within, I can't say for certain, but I know there are secrets there, passed down from Amrath himself. Things no one in Nihlos knows, things that could start wars, ruin lives."

"Such things generally are," Rithard observed as he toyed with the catch on the package. "Cursed, I mean."

"Heirlooms?"

Rithard grunted at this. "Secrets. Fortunately, I have some

experience working with them. Perhaps I can avoid the grim fate others have met."

Slat nodded, the ghost of a smile on his lips "Perhaps. I will leave you to peruse it, young master." He bowed stiffly, his joints popping, and stepped out of the library.

Rithard waited until the huge doors were closed again, then took his two new bits of evidence to the great desk and pondered them a moment. He looked about and found, to his pleasure, several small glass tumblers. He drew a small bottle from his coat and poured three fingers into it. *Medicinal? No, not this time. Just for pleasure.* He adjusted the lantern on the desk, broke the seal on the letter, and began to read.

> *Rithard,*
>
> *Forgive me.*
>
> *Forgive me for not recognizing you as family when I should have. Forgive me for being so blinded by my own needs that I did not see yours. Most of all, forgive me for placing a burden on your shoulders that you are ill equipped and untrained to bear. You have shown me you have genius and resilience, courage and cunning. You have shown me you can and will serve this house in capacities beyond your comfort zone. You will need those qualities now. The Great Father calls you to step in and fill the breach.*
>
> *I will not explain myself to you beyond noting that I acted as I chose. Take no vengeance. This was my will, and it is my right to command you on this.*
>
> *As for the rest, I will not deign to advise you overmuch. Trust Slat for guidance, and remember that he is wise and old. He has served us beyond what we ought to have asked of him, and when you can make your way without him, I urge you to retire him with dignity. Let him live out his last years in comfort. He will never tell you how tired he is, or how much he aches, both in his*

body and his soul. He has suffered much in our service. As a physician, I trust you will see this more clearly than even I did, and serve him as he has served us.

It is a heavy burden I place upon you. I know this all too well. Nihlos has ever looked upon House Amrath as arbiters, speakers of truth or at least not of lies. Do not embarrass us. As to how to accomplish that, I can offer no counsel, or even a good example. I can only hope I have chosen well.

Slat will have given you The Papers. That is the only name I know for it. It contains the private thoughts and knowledge of every House leader since Amrath. We have, all of us, recorded truths we chose not to reveal to others, but that we wanted our heirs to possess. Amrath's are, of course, the greatest, and when you learn them, you will know much about Nihlos that you did not before. You will understand more clearly why I emphasize the notion that your position is a great responsibility.

I urge you to take note of one truth in particular that I myself recorded. It has to do with the true nature of Theron Tasinal's death and the subsequent cover up. Many of the secrets in this packet should never see the light of day, but this truth, I think, may be an exception.

That decision, though, I leave to you. As for me, I must fight my own battle and die well. Know that I was the aggressor, that I intended to kill, and if you are reading this, I failed. I am wrong in what I intend. I know it all too well. I plot cold-blooded ambush and murder of someone who least suspects it, because I see no other way. I fight, for all the wrong reasons, against someone trying to do the right thing, because in the end I cannot accept the truth: my son has become a monster, and much of the blame for it falls at my own feet. I must do something, even if it is the wrong thing. It is preferable to simply accepting the dictates of fate.

The decisions you make from now on will carry the same

weight. Choose wisely, or if not, at least choose willfully. The Great Father would have had it no other way.

Rithard folded the letter and placed it back in the envelope, his vision blurring with tears he didn't fully understand. *Such pride and quiet passion. I will do my best to be a worthy successor.*

He took another drink and considered The Papers. *Such powerful information. And what connections will I be able to make that she only dreamed of?*

With a shrug, he undid the clasp.

CHAPTER 17
WALKING DEAD

AIUL woke to bright sunlight and even brighter pain. Every part of his body ached in some way or another, but his side was the worst. He supposed, briefly, that this had something to do with the impact of Logrus's boot that even now was swinging toward him for another blow. The impact was hardly pleasant, but less than Aiul expected, considering the events of the previous night.

"Get up!" Logrus shouted. "We finish this!"

"Leave me alone," Aiul groaned.

"Bah! Get *up*! I am ready to kill you now!"

"Too late," Aiul mumbled. "I died sometime in the night."

Logrus chuckled, and moved back to the fire. "Good. Now I will make you into a zombie and have you carry my pack."

Aiul sat up over the course of several curses, and waited for his head to clear. "Any coffee?"

Logrus shrugged, not bothering to look up from his cooking. "No pot."

Aiul blinked at this a moment, trying to decide if Logrus had made a joke on purpose, or if it was a completely straight line. "I suppose we should try to take better care of the next one we find, eh?"

Logrus gestured to a pan of boiling water and shook his head sadly. "You have no sense of humor. There will be coffee soon."

Aiul had every intention of arguing this point, but the notion fled his mind as Logrus emptied the contents of another pan onto a plate and handed it to him. Aiul marveled at the fare: fluffy eggs, toast, and plump sausages like the ones he had loved since childhood. He stared at Logrus in sheer wonder. "Mei! Where did you get these?"

A sly, mischievous grin crept over Logrus's face as he added more sausages to the pan for himself. "Last night, in the fighting, I found a supply tent. Your people travel well! I could not resist. I filled a sack and hid it in the bushes. I retrieved it while you slept late like a princess."

"So you paused to rob them, then went back to killing everyone in sight, eh?"

"I only kill when necessary," Logrus said with a scowl. "*You* were the berserker. You tried to kill *me* more than once. I can't count how many of the fools you slew."

Aiul paused, a sausage raised halfway to his mouth, vague memories bouncing in his head. "I can barely remember it. It's all mixed up in my head."

Logrus laughed, a single, sharp bark. "Lucky!"

Aiul eyed his half-eaten sausage a moment. "Why?"

Logrus cracked eggs into the pan and shrugged. "It must be nice to forget."

Aiul grunted in agreement. "It must indeed."

They ate in silence. When he was finished, Aiul asked, "You spoke of zombies. A joke? That would make, what, the third in a month? A new record for you, I think."

Logrus, still chewing, eyed him suspiciously for a moment, then shook his head and swallowed. "Dead serious."

"And now a fourth!"

Logrus's face was somber, the picture of honesty. "I speak truth. I can raise the dead when necessary, but I would never do such to you."

"Impossible."

Logrus looked almost hurt. "*Possible*. For Elgar."

Aiul stared at Logrus, searching for signs of trickery, but found none. As a physician, he had no choice but to see this process for himself. There could well be something to learn. "Show me."

Logrus stuffed his last sausage into his mouth and rose. He kicked dirt over the remains of the fire and gestured for Aiul to follow.

It was not a long trek, though the snow made it more difficult. Within a half hour, they reached the site of the battle. It seemed different in the light, though the corpses lying about left no doubt that they were in the correct location.

"Nothing left," Aiul said. "And we're on foot in the snow. Not a good situation."

"I have a plan for this," Logrus told him. "Come. We must find one capable of speaking."

"Then we'll need one with at least one lung, a throat, and an intact mouth, I suppose."

"Few enough of those. You were busy."

"Shut up!"

It was a bit ghoulish, rolling the corpses over and checking them, but it was hardly unfamiliar work to Aiul. What was distressing to see was how many had severe blunt head trauma from a blunt instrument.

Logrus noticed this too. "See? You have a style to your fighting. This is your work, certainly."

"Do we really need to talk about it? It disturbs me!"

Logrus shrugged and rolled another corpse over, then beamed with satisfaction. "This one will do."

Aiul looked at the dead man. He had been stabbed cleanly in the heart, and surely had at least one lung intact. "Your work?" he asked.

Logrus shrugged again. "I was not the only man with a blade. It could be me. Perhaps your people, perhaps the foreigners."

"The what?"

"Never mind."

Was Logrus hiding something? Aiul grabbed his shoulder and spun him around. "No, not 'never mind'. What foreigners?"

Logrus eyed him for a moment, seeming to mull over his answer. "You are all foreigners to me," he said at last. "Do you wish to see me raise a zombie or not?"

Despite being fairly certain Logrus knew more than he was saying, Aiul decided to let it pass. "If you can."

"*Elgar* can," Logrus corrected. "Pay attention." He knelt beside the corpse, and raised his hand, fingers splayed over its chest. "It is difficult. You must reach out to Elgar."

"How?"

"Remember when he came to you. How it felt."

"A strange way to work magic," Aiul said doubtfully.

Logrus turned back to Aiul, annoyance on his face. "*I* do not work magic," he snapped. "*Elgar* works miracles through my faith."

"I know nothing of either," Aiul said, moving closer for a better look. "Just science. It's strange even to think about. I still only half believe you can do this."

"You will see. Look."

Logrus took a deep breath and held it. As Aiul watched, sadness flickered over his companion's normally placid face. Aiul remembered the tale Logrus had told him of his mother, and knew these must be the images in Logrus's mind. It was, then, a costly and difficult thing for him to do, indeed.

Logrus lowered his hand to touch the corpse's chest. "Rise, flesh, and remember," he murmured.

Aiul gasped as the corpse twitched, then rose with a mechanical jerkiness and stood slack jawed, wobbling on unsteady feet. Cold, sunken eyes turned to look at Logrus, a mixture of fear and awe glinting from beneath the glaze of death. A low moan issued from its pale blue lips.

"Be silent, and speak only when spoken to," Logrus commanded the zombie.

Aiul shook his head in amazement. "Mei!"

Logrus shot him another angry look. "*Elgar!*"

"It's an oath, not a credit you know."

Logrus shrugged. "If it will quiet you, I will agree."

Aiul rolled his eyes but said nothing. Logrus watched him a moment, wary of a trick or joke, then turned back to the zombie.

"Flesh, heed me. Your group had horses?"

The zombie looked at him, seeming confused and uncertain of its capabilities. At last, its jaw opened, and it hissed, "Yes. Some."

Logrus nodded. "Show us. We are in need of them."

The trek through the snow was fairly long and unpleasant, made all the more so by the zombie's slow, staggering gait, but well worth the effort.

"Mei," Aiul gasped, scarcely able to believe his eyes. The zombie had led them to a small, sheltered copse. Four horses were tethered there, along with several bundles of gear.

Logrus stepped forward to examine the packs. "Food. Water. Everything we need."

Aiul nodded, surprised at how he felt. "This was Elgar's doing. He sent them with this."

Logrus nodded. "And to help us escape. It is the only way the fools *can* serve. They do not understand, but they are, on occasion, useful. As now." He gestured to the zombie. "But now his use is at an end. We must return him to his rest."

"Eh? Kill him?"

"Destroy it, yes. It cannot be killed. It is already dead."

Aiul felt staggered to hear Logrus speak so frankly, and in front of the creature to boot! "Why would you give a man his life back, and then take it again?"

Logrus shook his head in vehement denial. "No. You do not understand. It is cruel to them. This is not *life*. It is suffering. It will always be cold. It will never know warmth, or comfort, or the satisfaction of a meal, the smell of the breeze. It is *dead*. I have seen this many times. They all seek destruction in the end."

Aiul considered the zombie. It stared at the ground, still swaying slightly. There was not a trace of joy about it. Surely, it looked about as miserable as possible.

"I would hear it from the creature itself," Aiul said at last.

Logrus nodded. "Flesh, you may speak, if you would."

The zombie did not bother to look at them. It croaked a single word. "Cold."

Aiul asked, "Would you rest, then? As Logrus says?"

To Aiul's surprise, the zombie turned to face him. "Elgar is pleased?"

Aiul cast an uncertain look at Logrus. Logrus shrugged, gestured at the horses, and nodded.

"Yes," Aiul told the zombie. "Elgar is pleased."

"Rest, then," the zombie rasped. "Cold. Tired. Cold."

Logrus commanded it, "Go and gather firewood."

As the zombie shambled off in pursuit of wood, Logrus began loading the packs onto the extra horses. "You understand, now? It is cruel to ask them to remember, but sometimes necessary. If you tell them to forget, then they are mindless and do not suffer."

Aiul scoffed. "Why tell me?"

Logrus tightened a belt around the horse. "You can do this thing, too."

"Bah."

"No, truly. It is a gift Elgar gives to all of his knights."

Raise the dead? What madness was that? And yet, how could he not explore such a thing? It was a wonderful power, an incredible testament that death itself might be cured. If he could learn this first step, perhaps, with study, he could go further, perfect the process to truly restore life. He would be the physician who conquered death.

"I would try this!" he exclaimed, excited now that he had embraced the idea.

Logrus hauled another pack onto the horse. "Let us finish with the one. Then we will raise as many as we can. We will need them in this Torium, if it is as you say. Come and help me with this while we wait."

Before long, the zombie had piled up a considerable stack of wood, enough for a great fire. *A bonfire.*

Logrus gathered some kindling and soon had a blaze. The warmth was pure pleasure on Aiul's skin. Logrus, too, smiled as he heaped wood atop the flames.

Only the zombie was unmoved. "Cold," it muttered.

Logrus held up a hand. "I know. Just a bit more." He added the rest of the wood and waited for it to catch, then beckoned to the zombie. "Come. Be warm."

The zombie said not another word, but strode immediately into the flames. Aiul winced to watch such a thing, a man walking into a fire. *But it is not a man. It is something altogether different.* It stood in the flames, unmoving, but Aiul was almost certain that, as the flesh melted from its bones, the creature was smiling. Then, even the bones were aflame, and shortly after, it was nothing but ashes.

Logrus nodded toward Aiul. "Now for the others."

Aiul pointed to the fire. "If this gets out of control, we'll bake ourselves as like as not in a forest fire."

Logrus shrugged and began digging at the snow, heaving hands full into the fire. Aiul joined him, and in short order, the fire was out.

"Come," Logrus said, moving quickly toward the corpse-strewn battle field.

Aiul followed, huddling deeper into his cloak. The wind seemed all the more chill now that the fire was gone. "What will we do? How do we go about it?"

"We find some bodies that are in good shape, and raise a few. Then we can command them to find others."

"What constitutes 'good shape'?"

"Few broken bones."

Aiul nodded. It made sense. "What about eyes?"

Logrus stopped in place and turned to Aiul, a strange look upon his face. "I had never considered that. But I have seen even headless zombies do work." He began walking again, shaking his head. "I do not know how they do it."

It was, Aiul thought, a rather preposterous sort of conversation. "I don't really know how I feel about this. I've always heard necromancy is evil work."

"It *is* evil work if you tell them to remember, or if you murder men for their bodies."

"Even so, it's disrespectful to the dead."

Logrus shot him a bemused look over his shoulder. "The dead are dead. Respect is only meaningful to the living."

"I should think you might feel different if it was someone you knew. What if your mother were used so?"

Logrus laughed out loud at this. "My mother was used long before she died. She understood necessity. At any rate, she is not the flesh. Her spirit is gone wherever spirits go. Elgar does not say. But the flesh? It is nothing. It is like a snake's shed skin."

"Then how can you command them to remember?"

Logrus shrugged again, his face showing annoyance, now. Obviously, the conversation was going on overlong for his tastes. He answered in an exasperated tone, "I do not know these things, Aiul. Perhaps it calls the spirit back. If so, it is even *more* cruel. I only do it when necessary, and I release them as soon as possible. You should do likewise."

Aiul decided it would be a kindness to give Logrus a rest, and walked on without asking any more questions. In some ways, simply moving made the time pass more quickly. Perhaps Logrus had some good ideas after all.

Aiul realized they were back on the battlefield when he tripped over a corpse buried in the snow.

Logrus looked back at him. "What condition is it in?"

Aiul did a quick survey of the body. "Another stabbing, it seems. The limbs are intact."

"Good. We will start with that one. I do not relish rooting through this snow any more than we must." He slogged back through the drift to join Aiul. "You will try, yes?"

Aiul nodded, suddenly feeling a bit squeamish. *Mei, as if you've never handled a corpse before!* "Yes. What must I do?"

"Do as I did." Logrus held out his hand, fingers splayed, to demonstrate. "Then, in your mind, go to Elgar. Connect to him, let him flow through you. Once you do this, you can command the flesh to rise."

Aiul scooped snow from the ground, enough so that he had a place to kneel over the corpse. He held out his hand over its chest, looking to Logrus. Logrus nodded. *So far so good.*

"Now," Logrus said. "Reach out to Elgar."

"I don't know how."

"Close your eyes. Think back to when you first felt Elgar's touch. That is where you two connect. You must feel those feelings, relive them."

Aiul closed his eyes and let his mind drift to the dream of Elgar, the sound of the voice in his cell. What had he felt then? Agony, misery, despair, and hopelessness. Were those things the path? It seemed wrong.

He tried anyway. It was no difficult task to feel miserable. All he had to do was lower the barriers he had built of late. The pain would come, and come it did. He watched Kariana stabbing Lara over and over in his mind, let it build in him until it was a tidal wave of grief, then opened his eyes. "Rise," he whispered.

Logrus shot him a glare. "And forget!"

Aiul nodded and wiped at a tear with his free hand. "Rise and forget."

He waited long anxious moments, but the corpse remained motionless. "Something is wrong."

Logrus scratched at his beard as he considered. "You have not touched Elgar, I think. Did you feel the connection?"

Aiul grunted. "How should I know?"

"You would know. There would be no doubt."

Aiul heaved a sigh of frustration and sat back on his heels. "Perhaps you're simply mistaken, and I don't have the ability."

Logrus shook his head. "No. I do not think so. Tell me, what did you think of when you tried to reach Elgar?"

"What you told me, the things I felt when he first came to me. Grief, despair, defeat."

Logrus looked at him with an odd gaze. "That cannot be correct. Those things are not of Elgar."

"I can only go by what you told me."

"No. I think you are wrong." Logrus stared at Aiul for long moments, then said, "Will you trust me? I think I know the answer."

Aiul felt uncertain. Such a request seemed to foreshadow a nasty surprise. "I suppose," he said.

Logrus leapt toward him and hammered a fist into his face. Aiul, caught off guard, fell over backward, howling in pain.

Logrus followed up with a savage kick to Aiul's ribs that felt as if it came within inches of breaking bone.

"Dog!" Logrus cried. "Get up and fight!"

Aiul heaved himself over onto hands and knees and scrambled away, frantic. "You're mad!"

"Mad, am I?" Logrus roared. "I will kill you for that insult!" He slammed his boot into Aiul's backside, knocking Aiul face first into the snow.

Aiul could see his vision narrowing, growing red. He rolled over on to his back and tried to rise, but Logrus stopped him with a boot to the chest. As Aiul cried out again, Logrus ground his foot into Aiul's throat.

"Why are you doing this?" Aiul choked out, struggling for air. Bright flashes, like lightning, burst behind his eyes.

Logrus stared down at him and laughed, a cruel, hacking sound. "Why? Because your suffering pleases me! Because I am cruel and wicked! What other reason do I need?"

Aiul struggled to raise Logrus's boot, but he was pinned, and in a difficult position to get much leverage. "You're killing me!" he gasped.

"Yes! Die!"

More lightning. Red, pulsing like blood. And then a flash, the jagged thing burning into his vision like molten lava. Strength poured into him, hot, furious, irresistible. With a roar of fury, he seized the boot at his neck and hurled Logrus aside.

"Now!" Logrus cried. "Try it now!"

Aiul heard the words, far away through a crimson fog. What was he doing? Killing Logrus, of course. But there had been something else, hadn't there, something important? He cast about, looking for a weapon to bash his enemy with, when his eye seized upon the corpse.

Oh. That.

His hand rose of its own accord, high overhead, fingers dangling like a puppeteer's. He would kill Logrus later. This was something he needed to do immediately!

"Rise!" he shouted, his voice resonating with power and fury. "Rise and serve me!"

"And forget!" Logrus cried.

"Yes, yes, forget!"

For a moment, it seemed nothing would happen again. Then, the corpse twitched, and began to move its limbs. It rose slowly and stood, bobbing like a drunken sailor.

Aiul's rage at Logrus fled from his mind as he marveled at the thing standing before him. "Mei!" he whispered as he examined it, trying to understand the forces in play. It was plainly impossible, and yet still true.

He heard a soft moan. It took him a moment to realize it was coming not from the zombie, but from Logrus. Aiul turned from the zombie to see his companion still lying on the ground, mouth agape, eyes staring wildly, his face so pale it barely stood out against the snow.

"Great Elgar! Never before have I seen this!"

Aiul continued to stare at Logrus, uncomprehending. Logrus raised a shaking hand and pointed past Aiul, and Aiul spun, expecting… what? Something so horrific that even Logrus was unable to shrug it off?

Aiul gaped at what he saw. All over the snowy field, zombies stood wavering. Some were relatively whole, while others with shattered or missing limbs were barely able to stand at all.

"Can these things fight?" he asked after several moments.

Logrus was on his feet now, his shock passed. "A little. Hard to destroy, though, except with fire. It balances out."

"Then maybe we have a chance."

Logrus nodded. "Elgar is with us. Have faith."

. . .

In Torium there was a hierarchy, established long before, through events and rites that were all but forgotten, even by the Torians themselves. In truth, they had no wish to remember, and for the Torians, a wish was reason enough to make something true. Still, it had been so long that, even were it otherwise, they might still have forgotten.

There was no word for their kind. They were not men, though, at some point, they might have been. That, too, they had forgotten, for similar reasons. They simply *were*. They justified their own existence. They did not extend the same justification to others.

In the center of the ancient, decayed city, a hideous, deformed mockery of a man, a *thing*, crouched, humming to itself in near darkness above a black, viscous pool. It dipped a long, razor-edged claw into the liquid and brought it to its swollen, purple lips. Its tongue, blackened by eons of such indulgence, slithered over rows of jagged, stained teeth, lapping at the oily substance. The thing smiled, exposing a maw big enough to engulf a man's head, and had on numerous occasions. It was pleased, as always, with the nectar of a god.

Another thing entered, smaller, subservient, and knelt, trembling, before its master.

"Why do you disturb me?" the master asked, its voice a lower-toned version of fingernails on slate.

"Forgive me, master," the servant answered ritually. "Enemies come. Servants of Elgar."

"Yes," the master hissed, drawing out the 's' like a snake, and ending with a malevolent chuckle. "The Dead God comes to reclaim that which we took."

"Do we let them pass?"

"Pass?" the master asked, as if it found the concept both

bizarre and amusing. It dipped its claw into the pool again and licked the black fluid as it considered.

"Rend them," it said at last. "Make them into art. The Dead god must not send playthings to reclaim his property. He must come himself, and reward us."

"Will he not be angered if we rend his servants?"

"We are better servants," the master declared. "Let him be angered. Will he not, in the end, love us more for our audacity?"

"Perhaps he will rend *us*," said the servant.

"Perhaps," the master acknowledged, dipping its claw again. "But it will draw him here. I wrote his book. I have learned many things. If he will not accept us…" He trailed off in a hiss .

"Yes," the servant hissed back, eager to demonstrate its approval. It touched its head to the floor, rose, and left.

Black liquid dripped from the thing's claw to the stone floor. Where it fell, it bubbled and hissed as it ate away at the rock. The thing licked at the claw again, and smiled.

It would be good to have new art.

EPILOGUE
DIY

KARIANA stood outside Prandil's private quarters, ear pressed to the door. She heard nothing, so it was difficult to tell if he was asleep or awake.

She fingered the brass door knob, still feeling a bit uncertain. This was a very Plan A, Plan B situation, and she really had no idea how it would go. She thought of Narelki's shattered body, a woman who had terrified her, and considered backing out, but she was committed.

Things had begun to unravel in her mind very quickly after Narelki's unexpected death. Well, to be entirely honest, things had never been entirely raveled to begin with. The plan had been fairly rough after the 'do whatever Narelki and Teretha tell me' part, something along the lines of 'and then we will be in charge and the Meites will have to listen'. After that, there wasn't really any plan at all beyond improvising as she was now.

She turned the knob and opened the door quietly.

Prandil was obviously very fond of books. Flickering candle-light played over hundreds of volumes in great shelves that lined the walls from marble-tiled floor to arched, beamed ceiling.

And one more, held in front of Prandil's face. He lounged in

"

his bed, propped up on pillows in a sitting position, regarding her with a bewildered look.

"How did you get in here?" he asked, his annoyance growing as he considered the situation.

Kariana offered him a catty, sexy grin that she thought was something near ninety percent genuine. "I lied to your slaves and told them we had plans. They didn't seem to find spiriting a young, pretty woman up to your private quarters as anything unusual."

Prandil raised an eyebrow at this, then folded his book and placed it on his polished mahogany nightstand. "So that's the shape of things, is it?"

Kariana gave no answer but her grin.

"Oh, by all means. And do lock the door behind, won't you?"

Kariana did so, then sauntered across the room and took at seat at the foot of his bed. She said nothing, simply waited, taking in the aroma of the place. The smell of oiled wood and leather was strong, tinged just slightly by an undertone of tobacco. It was much like Prandil himself, older but not ancient, powerful and vigorous still.

Prandil looked her up and down, nodding with approval. "I would have come to you, eventually, you know."

"Does it bother you? The role reversal?"

"Not at all. I find it rather refreshing."

"You're very certain of yourself."

Prandil chuckled softly. "My dear, you have no idea. You've shown quite a bit of mettle of late, but not nearly enough flesh for my tastes."

Kariana stretched her arms high and yawned, giving him a nice view of her breasts. "You might have joined one of my orgies."

Prandil laughed out loud at this. "Do I look like a juvenile to you? I am a man of taste and discretion. You should try it sometime. It might suit you."

Kariana stuck out her tongue at him, pleased that the gesture could be taken any of several ways. "Maybe you're too reserved. Are you sure you're ready for my brash, classless youth?"

Prandil rolled his eyes. "I've had more women in my life than you've had men, I'll wager. Women are like wine: age adds things, even as it takes others away. Perhaps if you'd experience with men of actual ability instead of boy toys, you'd appreciate that."

"I could have one of them right now, and instead I'm here. What does that tell you?"

"That perhaps you are smarter than you seem."

Kariana leaned forward and crawled to the head of the bed. She propped her head up with an arm as she locked eyes with Prandil. "It's nice to be given some credit now and then."

Prandil eyed her with lust. "I think I should prefer to withhold true judgment on the meal until after dessert."

It was, she had to admit, a very fine dessert indeed. Prandil had skills that her wretched little toys couldn't even dream of. When it was finished, he lit his pipe and smoked, looking up at the ceiling, and she lay there in the afterglow, looking at his regal profile, feeling as if she had, at long last, found a truth, a home, a path.

The words came out before she had even fully considered them, but then again, she was improvising. This was right. "Will you teach me?"

Prandil turned to her, confusion on his face. "Teach you? I doubt it. I'm fairly impressed with your skills, actually. Much more than I expected."

Kariana felt herself blush with his praise. "That's not what I meant."

Prandil waited a moment for her to continue, then prodded.

"What did you mean?"

Suddenly, she felt shy, embarrassed even. And yet she had to plow forward. People have to ask for what they want, after all, or they never get it. "Teach me to be a Meite."

Prandil's eyes grew wide with surprise, which was to be expected. But his peals of laughter came as a painful surprise. He went on for several moments, completely overcome. At last, he wiped tears from his eyes with the edge of the bed sheet and said, "Oh, my dear, you *are* ambitious, aren't you? So here's the bill for the evening's entertainment?" He took a pull at his pipe and blew out the smoke, his smile fading. He regarded her with cold, cruel eyes. "Seriously, you? Preposterous."

Kariana felt the warm glow around her fall away, replaced by a chill wind of anger and humiliation. "Why not me?" she asked, her voice husky with rage.

"Oh, please, don't tear up about it."

The fool thought she was about to cry? Was he truly that oblivious? Of course he was. It was all a sham, his perception. He had no insight at all. He was simply strong enough of personality to persuade people that his ideas were correct.

She asked him again, punctuating each word with a pause. "Why... not... me?"

Prandil's face grew dark now. "You would hear truth? Why not you? Mei! Because you're weak, pathetic, and foolish. You've come here with the notion of replacing a woman you could never match, and it *offends* me! What ever made you think being a good fuck qualified you to be a Meite?"

Kariana ground her teeth, trying to show as little emotion as possible as she reached for her clothes on the floor. She felt Sadrik's knife brush against her fingers as she retrieved her blouse, and she took it into her hand almost by instinct.

Mei! Why did Prandil react so? She had started with little skill, surely, but she had learned quickly. She had defeated

Maralena and even backed Davron down, powerful enemies. She had *earned* his respect!

She let the blouse fall to the floor again, then turned back to Prandil, slipping the dagger beneath her pillow as she did. He had retrieved his book and was again reading from it. She looked him in the eye, holding his gaze without flinching. "So I'm just not good enough to be one of you?"

Prandil sighed and laid the open book on his chest. "You needn't take it personally." He raised the book again and gave her a pointed look. "I do have things to do, you know."

Kariana blinked at him in shock. "Now you dismiss me like a common whore?"

Prandil folded the book and gave her a look of annoyance. "There's nothing common about you. That's a compliment, you know." He opened his book again and began reading. "But, yes, you are dismissed."

Plan B it is, then.

Kariana could feel her muscles twitching. She was, she realized, literally trembling with rage. "Well, I suppose I should regard it as a lesson. I'm learning all the time, you know."

Prandil turned again from his book and sighed. "Oh? And what, pray tell, have you learned from events of late?" he asked in a sarcastic tone.

Kariana moved with the speed of a lioness. Her arm shot from beneath the pillow, the dagger glinting in the candlelight. Prandil's eyes flew open in shock, but there was no time for him to react. She buried the blade to the hilt in his left eye socket.

Prandil's body convulsed briefly, then lay still.

"I learned that if you want someone dead, you should do it yourself."

Find out what happens next.
Grab the next book War God's Will now!

FROM THE PUBLISHER

Thank you for reading *Mad God's Muse,* book two in The Sins of the Fathers.

We hope you enjoyed it as much as we enjoyed bringing it to you. We just wanted to take a moment to encourage you to review the book on Amazon and Goodreads. Every review helps further the author's reach and, ultimately, helps them continue writing fantastic books for us all to enjoy.

If you liked this book, check out the rest of our catalogue at www.aethonbooks.com. To sign up to receive a FREE collection from some of our best authors (including one from Matthew P. Gilbert) as well updates regarding all new releases, visit www.aethonbooks.com/sign-up

SPECIAL THANKS TO:

ADAWIA E. ASAD	EDDIE HALLAHAN	KYLE OATHOUT
JENNY AVERY	JOSH HAYES	LILY OMIDI
BARDE PRESS	PAT HAYES	TROY OSGOOD
CALUM BEAULIEU	BILL HENDERSON	GEOFF PARKER
BEN	JEFF HOFFMAN	NICHOLAS (BUZ) PENNEY
BECKY BEWERSDORF	GODFREY HUEN	JASON PENNOCK
BHAM	JOAN QUERALTÓ IBÁÑEZ	THOMAS PETSCHAUER
TANNER BLOTTER	JONATHAN JOHNSON	JENNIFER PRIESTER
ALFRED JOSEPH BOHNE IV	MARCEL DE JONG	RHEL
CHAD BOWDEN	KABRINA	JODY ROBERTS
ERREL BRAUDE	PETRI KANERVA	JOHN BEAR ROSS
DAMIEN BROUSSARD	ROBERT KARALASH	DONNA SANDERS
CATHERINE BULLINER	VIKTOR KASPERSSON	FABIAN SARAVIA
JUSTIN BURGESS	TESLAN KIERINHAWK	TERRY SCHOTT
MATT BURNS	ALEXANDER KIMBALL	SCOTT
BERNIE CINKOSKE	JIM KOSMICKI	ALLEN SIMMONS
MARTIN COOK	FRANKLIN KUZENSKI	KEVIN MICHAEL STEPHENS
ALISTAIR DILWORTH	MEENAZ LODHI	MICHAEL J. SULLIVAN
JAN DRAKE	DAVID MACFARLANE	PAUL SUMMERHAYES
BRET DULEY	JAMIE MCFARLANE	JOHN TREADWELL
RAY DUNN	HENRY MARIN	CHRISTOPHER J. VALIN
ROB EDWARDS	CRAIG MARTELLE	PHILIP VAN ITALLIE
RICHARD EYRES	THOMAS MARTIN	JAAP VAN POELGEEST
MARK FERNANDEZ	ALAN D. MCDONALD	FRANCK VAQUIER
CHARLES T FINCHER	JAMES MCGLINCHEY	VORTEX
SYLVIA FOIL	MICHAEL MCMURRAY	DAVID WALTERS JR
GAZELLE OF CAERBANNOG	CHRISTIAN MEYER	MIKE A. WEBER
DAVID GEARY	SEBASTIAN MÜLLER	PAMELA WICKERT
MICHEAL GREEN	MARK NEWMAN	JON WOODALL
BRIAN GRIFFIN	JULIAN NORTH	BRUCE YOUNG

9 781949 890389